The Office girls

A Novel

ALSO BY SYLVESTER STEPHENS
Our Time Has Come

The Office girls

A Novel

Sylvester Stephens

STREBOR BOOKS

NEW YORK LONDON TORONTO SYDNEY

Strebor Books
P.O. Box 6505
Largo, MD 20792
http://www.streborbooks.com

ISBN-13 978-1-59309-129-3
ISBN-10   1-59309-129-X
LCCN 2007940441

First Strebor Books trade paperback edition January 2008

Cover design: www.mariondesigns.com

10 9 8 7 6 5 4 3 2 1

Manufactured in the United States of America

For information regarding special discounts for bulk purchases, please contact Simon & Schuster Special Sales at 1-800-456-6798 or business@simonandschuster.com *dedication*

This book is dedicated to the memory of my beloved brother,
J. Dallas Stephens, and my wonderful children,
Bria, Isaiah, Simone and Alex.

The Office Girls is based on true events and actual people. However, the names have been changed to protect the privacy of the individuals involved…

chapter 1

I knew the day I was born with an umbilical cord wrapped tightly around my throat, my mother crying, and the doctor screaming the words, "unless it's necessary, don't look at the face," my life was going to be nothing but pure hell.

I was born the eldest of two boys in Buena Vista, Michigan. My parents were very religious and very strict. They preached two subjects constantly, heaven and hell. If you listened to what they said, you were bound for heaven, but if not, you were on a fast track to hell. Needless to say, I was very obedient. Well, as far they knew anyway. My younger brother, Johnny, on the other hand, wasn't afraid to go to hell. He brought hell with him.

Yes, I was the golden boy in my parents' eyes. So why was my life such a mess, you ask? Well, it's easy to fool Mom and Dad. The world, however, is not so easily bamboozled!

My childhood was one of confusion and misunderstanding. I was always confused why people misunderstood me. I was very bright for my age; I understood situations that were beyond my years. I had superior book sense without having to read books. Intellectual inclination, I think it's called.

I was a social misfit. I didn't fit in with the intellectual kids, and I certainly didn't fit in with the cool kids. I did, however, manage to indulge myself in mischievous behavior to hang out with the bad kids. But I always had limitations on just how much trouble in which I would dabble, and soon, I wouldn't fit in with them, either. Consequently, I spent a lot of time alone.

Loneliness is said to feed the prowess of the imagination. After spending so much time with myself, I started to create my own friends. I'm not talking about the imaginary friends you have when you're five or six years old. I was married and divorced twice before I let my imaginary friend, Bernice, return back to the world of the subliminal. Yes, I had an imaginary best friend, and no, I was not insane. I knew she was only imaginary, insane people don't recognize that!

As a youth I was extremely shy to approach girls. I created Bernice to be my confidante and advisor to the female species. She wore long ponytails and dressed like a tomboy. She wasn't very feminine, but then she wasn't overly masculine, either. She was the type of girl I certainly wouldn't be attracted to in real life. I liked prissy, very feminine girls. But despite her outwardly appearance, I still kind of had a crush on Bernice. Whenever I was around Bernice, I always had a sense of familiarity.

I felt comfortable discussing personal issues with her that I could never discuss with anyone else. As I grew older the comfort remained, and so did Bernice. Bernice always talked about karma, and doing unto others as you would have them do unto you, so to speak. She was very kind, and helped me stay on the right side of the tracks.

Some of Bernice's advice I held under scrutiny. She convinced me to marry my first wife. Bad idea! That didn't turn out well at all. Then she convinced me to marry my second wife, which turned out even worse. After my second divorce, I told her to kiss my ass and get the hell out of my life. And just like that, she was gone.

I met my first wife, Tonita, in high school. We didn't start to date until after we both wound up unknowingly at the same college. We broke up, off and on, until we graduated. We ended up living in the same city and started to date seriously. After shacking up for a while we decided to get married. We both had our doubts, but we had been through so much for so long we figured, what could possibly break us up? We'd been through infidelity, poverty, distance, and managed to survive it all. But to answer that question of what could possibly break us up? Marriage!

Within one year of our marriage we had packed our bags and called it quits. We did, however, manage a beautiful little girl, Brimone, who captured my heart. Once the anger and pain of our divorce subsided, we found that we were still great friends. She remarried, and I got along with her husband quite well.

I met my second wife, Cecelia, shortly after my divorce from my first wife was final. We were passionately in love, but once the passion ran out, so did everything else. We never took the time to become friends while we were together, so now we are strangers who were once in love. Once again, out of my disastrous marriage, I managed a beautiful girl, Alexiah.

It is said that an artist does not know his best work until his heart has known suffering. I can confess that I truly know my best work, and know it well, because suffer my heart has done.

In high school I decided that I wanted to become a lawyer. One of my high school teachers instructed me to choose English and political science as majors—political science to prepare me for law, and English to prepare me on how to articulate the law to others. I took his advice and did simply that.

During my undergraduate studies I was an excellent student, never once dropping below a 4.0 grade-point average in my four years of academia. Physically, my once small, fragile frame had exploded into a strapping muscular young man. A once tenor voice had become deep bass. Though I was not recruited, I tried out for football, and made the team easily as a walk-on. During my senior year, I was an All-American and later drafted by the New England Patriots in the second round.

I played professional football for two years, seeing a little playing time in my sophomoric season. I couldn't, or didn't want to, commit to the brutal time-consuming practices. I simply wanted to show up and play on Sundays. That didn't go over well with my team. So I walked away from professional football and never once looked back. Well, maybe once.

As my sports career dwindled, my romantic career accelerated at a high velocity. Women were plentiful. I was rich! Young! And handsome! I stood six feet, two inches tall with dark-brown smooth skin, a nice clean faded haircut with dark shiny eyebrows and absolutely no facial hair. I had a size forty-eight-inch chest, with a thirty-two-inch waistline. It was once stated that if we ever had a problem landing a 747 plane at the airport, my shoulders were always an option. I spoke poetically and artistically when conversing with women, creating an element of mystery and charm. I guess most people would call this being a bit ostentatious, but I dispute that claim. In my case, it is merely an observation of one's self.

After I completed my undergraduate degree and my short stint in the National Football League, I studied law at Harvard University in Cambridge, Massachusetts. The one major benefit of playing professional football was not the money, but the opportunity to get into Harvard's prestigious law school. After two attempts, I passed the bar and moved to Atlanta, Georgia.

As fate would have it, my career would not be law, but writing profession-ally. I submitted my manuscripts to more publishers than I care to mention, and was rejected by each and every one of them. Somehow my manuscript fell into the hands of an independent publisher who had ties to a major distributor, and he decided to publish my work. I was offered a three-book deal with a pretty generous advance on my sales. I accepted, and I master-fully wrote creative, socially oriented books: books that all Americans should have appreciated, particularly African-Americans.

My books depicted America in her biased political and social structure of race and class. Unfortunately, for my career and me, the books barely made it out of the printer's bindery before they were being shipped right back. I wrote three books in three years, and barely sold enough to cover the cost of the ink. Thank God for that generous non-refundable advance!

In my opinion, I had written some of the most gripping conscientious writings in modern era. The public didn't respond favorably to politically fictional books that didn't scandalize a political figure, so my literary career went down the tube quickly.

I started to write entertainment news after that. I wrote articles for a local newspaper using the pseudonym, Cyrus. The articles led to my own daily column and I made a pretty good living.

One day I ran across an article that read, "Black Women: The New Civil Rights Movement!" I read the article and couldn't believe my eyes. The arti-cle told how black men have been left behind in the movement of political, economic, and social progression due to laziness and ignorance. It stated that black women no longer needed black men to raise a family. The article explained that women in corporate America could be just as competitive and productive as men, without the stress and agitation brought upon by men.

It gave the staggering statistics of black men in jail in comparison to those in college. Those jailed twice outnumbered those in college. And she added that those black men who were successful enough to make it up the ranks in corporate America often became much like their white male predecessors; too competitive, too arrogant, and too greedy. I was furious. When it came to black men, it seemed that we're damned if we do, and we're damned if we don't. I thought to myself, *am I the only person angry by this bullshit?*

I contacted the lady who wrote the article, a Mrs. Jaline Dandy, and found that her column was her moonlighting job. She was actually a manager of the claims department at a major corporation called Upskon. To my surprise, she was a white woman who was born and raised in Oregon. Oregon? What the hell? Are there any black people in Oregon? Her closest contact to a black man was probably watching professional sports on television, so where was she getting her research?

It turns out her research was not based on interviews from black men, but black women only. The perception of black men could be very one-sided if the black man himself was not a part of the research.

I tried to get her to rewrite the article to paint a fair perception of all black men and not those who had only been the perpetrators of scorned black women. We shared our differences of opinions, but she wouldn't change a word. I figured if she wouldn't rewrite the article, I would write an article in defense of black men. That's exactly what I did. I blasted the columnist for exploiting the plight of black men. However, by no means did I intend to insult black women in the process. And once again, that's exactly what I did.

I received more emails and telephone calls in one day than I had ever received in my entire literary career. But it wasn't only black women responding. Women of all races began to email me, calling me such names as misogynist, sexist, chauvinist, and even racist. Black women called me racist! Luckily, they never found out my true name was Michael B. Forrester, and not Cyrus. If they had, I would have had to change my name and move to another country to escape their wrath.

After so many complaints for my politically incorrect article, I was fired.

My boss, a woman of course, called me into her office and kindly explained to me how I had gone wrong with my article. Then she kindly showed me to the door. I worked from my home, so I had no desk to clean out. I left the newspaper in a raging huff. I was pissed off and I blamed every woman on the planet earth for me being fired.

My anger sparked me to expose women for all of their glory. I was angry because I knew that my comments were not chauvinistic and sexist, and certainly didn't warrant termination. I was simply stating that gender does not determine the behavior of corporate CEOs and managers. Power and greed is to blame. I also explained that race does not determine the number of black men in jail to black men in college, poverty does.

This is how my column read:

"Given the struggling conditions of poverty, any man, any woman of any race will take whatever measures necessary to survive. Never say what you will or will not do, if your child needs food for its belly, or shoes for its feet. For those who never have the luxury of living with a bank account to support their bills, crime as it may, may not be construed as a crime, but more of an opportunity. Perhaps if we increase their opportunity to survive like human beings, we will decrease the probability of them resulting to survive like animals with the dog-eat-dog mentality. Which brings me to my point; African-American men are stigmatized as being lazy and ignorant because of the existing conditions of the African-American community. But if you've ever lived in poverty you know the major reason for crime is not laziness, nor ignorance, its hopelessness. I was raised with my parents living from check to check. It wasn't easy for me to stay focused with school and getting my education, but I did. But there were also those days when I wanted new sneakers like everyone else, Or I wanted my own car, or something as simple as just wanting to go to a fast-food restaurant and order a burger. But I couldn't because I didn't have a dime to my name. And after paying all of the family bills, neither did my parents. On those days I felt that it was unfair that I could not afford to buy me a burger when others were living in big houses with money to burn. On those days, I wanted to get money, however and wherever I could. On those days, I felt that if life was going to be unfair to me, I didn't have to be fair to anyone else. On those days, I lost so many friends to jail or the grave because they felt the same sense of hopelessness. Looking back on

those days, I too, had the mind of a criminal. I just didn't act upon my impulse. And no, it wasn't wisdom that prevented me from crime; it was fear, the fear of captivity. The same captivity those who live in poverty try to escape every day.

"And some may say that if I stayed focused and became an educated man and not a criminal, my friends could have withstood the strife of poverty, as did I. But to each man's back, a cross he bears. Some men's backs are tired, but their will is strong, so they journey on. Some men's backs are sore, but their will is strong, so they journey on. And some men, when their will is broken, so too are their backs. And once your back is broken, you don't give a damn about a cross.

"This is not to excuse the behavior of those men who are behind bars who have caused pain or injury to anyone, be it physically, or psychologically. My hypothesis is this: if violence and crime were biological traits of the black man, why is it that white men who are not in poverty, commit many more crimes than black men who are not in poverty? This is a fact that is never mentioned in our articles.

"African-American men no longer have a voice of defense; we are an easy target to judge. Our society, our laws, our government, nor our black women have the compassion or courage to defend us anymore. And when we try to defend ourselves, we are viewed as self-pitying crybabies who complain too much. Anything black men have to say in defense of ourselves these days is considered whining, even when there is a young man lying on the street with his skull bashed in from the club of a white police officer's baton!

"Society's biggest triumph over the black man is when it offered black women their own civil rights movement in conjunction with white women and they accepted the deal wholeheartedly. Their pride and their commitment are to womanhood, and no longer to their race.

"This goes out to black women only: in your usurpation of the household, your rapacious attack upon the character of black men, need I remind you of your history? Do you realize black men have died for you? So that you could have everything that you have now! So that you can vote! So that you can afford to be independent! So that you can own your own house! Your own car! White men didn't do this for you! White women didn't do this for you! Black men did! Black men did this for you! It was OUR blood! The black man's blood!

"And you have the unmitigated gall to turn your back on us now when we need

7

you most because society has offered you a contract without us! I am proud to be a man, but more importantly, I am proud to be a BLACK man. And if a white man were to ask me to join forces with him against my black woman under any circumstances, I would tell him to kiss my black ass!

"My last words are to Ms. Jaline Dandy: are you perpetuating this literary genocide of black men to boost the ratings of your article? You need to be ashamed of yourself, and your poor, ignorant, misguided readers should be even more ashamed of themselves for supporting your diatribe."

❖❖❖

It was the last few lines that drew the ire of most of the female mob. But I stand behind every word!

After my insensitive and cruel termination I set out to prove that in corporate America, women would behave in the same manner as men if given the same circumstances. I would resurrect my literary career by writing a tell-all book about the corporate battle of women's sensitivity versus men's logic, that in the grand scheme of things, women's sensitivity and men's logic don't mean shit! Money and power produce the same result with any gender or any race; greed, selfishness, and cruelty.

But before I could do that, I had to find a job that would allow me the research. I needed a female guinea pig that worked in corporate America. I tried to call on Bernice, but I guess she was still pissed with me for telling her to get lost. No matter how desperate my plea, she refused to materialize.

I bought a Sunday newspaper and half-heartedly browsed through the classified ads, mostly to prove to myself that I was at least making an attempt to get started with the book. I looked back and forth, and back and forth. As luck would have it, I saw an advertisement for a position in an office setting. The ad took up half of the page as if God didn't want me to miss it. It read, *"Upskon Hiring! Claims Dept. Please fax resume to Jaline Dandy."*

I fell on my knees and shouted, "Thank you, Lord!" I wanted sweet revenge and God seemed to be telling me that vengeance is on the way! I typed up a fake resume and faxed it over immediately. I wanted it to be the first thing this Jaline picked up from the fax machine on Monday morning. After I faxed it, I patiently waited for the confirmation. When it finally came through, I put the newspaper down and turned on the television. I had earned a day of relaxation after all that, and I treated myself to an afternoon of ESPN. I told myself that it was a long shot that they would even respond to my resume so I prepared myself for the disappointment.

Two days later I received a call from Upskon asking me to come in for an interview. I jumped up and down like a big kid in a candy store. I called them back and confirmed the interview's day and time. I will never forget my interview. That day started the beginning of my new life, my new life with the office girls of Upskon.

❖❖❖

Jaline Dandy didn't look anything like I imagined. I imagined her being an old white woman with white hair, with wrinkles around her mouth. Perhaps with a Southern dialect, even though I knew she was from the Northwest. But instead, she was a young-looking, middle-aged woman, moderately attractive, and very articulate.

"Good afternoon, Mr. Forrester. I'm Ms. Dandy."

"Good afternoon, Ms. Dandy."

"Any trouble finding us?"

"No problem at all."

"Well, you're a Harvard man, huh?"

"Yes, yes, I am."

"Why would a Harvard man want to work in a small claims department?"

"Harvard men have to eat, too," I said jokingly.

"I like that attitude."

"Thanks."

"Well, Mr. Forrester, your resume is quite impressive. And, the position is available. But I must say that with your credentials you are well overqualified. But as you say, you have to eat, too."

"I sure do."

"Can you start on Monday?"

"No problem."

"Okay, we'll see you Monday."

"That's it? I got the job?"

"If you want it, you do."

"Sure I do. Thanks, Ms. Dandy."

"Welcome aboard," Jaline said, shaking my hand.

"Thank you, Ms. Dandy."

"Stop with the Ms. Dandy, call me, Jaline."

"If you say so, Jaline."

"All right, our business here is done," Jaline said, standing and walking around to the front of her desk. "Tazzy, your supervisor, will meet you on Monday and show you around. That's it. Guess I'll see you on Monday."

"First thing."

I walked out of Jaline's office, and as I scanned the office with my man radar, all I could see was desk after desk of women. I knew immediately that in order for me to fulfill my mission, I would have to deny the dream of every red-blooded, straight American male. And that is to be the only man on an island of women. This may not have been an island intrinsically, but it was the next best thing.

❖❖❖

I showed up for work on Monday bright and early as promised. I didn't have a badge so I had to wait until Tazzy showed up. It didn't take long before she came strolling up to the door with her arms full of bags. We greeted each other very cordially, and I took the bags out of her arms.

Tazzy was a petite young lady, who looked as if she was straight out of high school. She was slightly short of five feet tall and a hundred pounds soaking wet. She had beautiful smooth caramel skin. Her hair was short, but cut very neatly. She showed me to my desk and informed me that a lady named Cynthia would be training me. She then showed me to the break room and told me to relax until Cynthia came to get me. One by one the office girls started to arrive for work.

"Hey, how are you doing?"

"I'm fine, how are you?" I responded.

"I'm fine. My name is Virginia. It's a pleasure to meet you."

"It's a pleasure to meet you, too."

"And your name is?"

"Oh, excuse my manners. My name is Michael Forrester," I said, standing to shake her hand.

She shook my hand with the grace of an angel and the elegance of a queen. There was something insouciant about this lady. She was middle-aged, maybe late fifties to early sixties. Her hair was white, but her face looked young. She showed no signs of wrinkles on her face. She reminded me of a jazz singer named Nancy Wilson. As she left the break room I couldn't help but stare.

Susan, the assistant supervisor, a white lady, came in the break room next and fixed a cup of coffee. Susan had blonde hair, blue eyes, and a thin, tight body. She was about five feet five inches tall, with a high-pitched, squeaky voice that bordered on the verge of annoyance.

"Hey, are you the new guy?"

I was tempted to say, *"What does it look like, fool?"* But instead I courteously replied, "Yes, I'm the new guy."

"My name is Susan, and I'm the assistant supervisor here in the office. If there's anything you need, just let me know."

"Thanks."

"Not a problem," Susan said, walking out of the break room.

I sat twiddling my thumbs for a while when Darsha, Valerie, Lisa and Alicia walked in. They were in full gossip mode. When they saw me sitting at the table they stopped talking and looked at me.

"Do you work here?" Lisa asked.

"Yes. Today is my first day."

"I'm Alicia. Hi."

"Hi, Alicia," I spoke.

Alicia was a very attractive light-skinned woman with a perfect thirty-six-twenty-four-thirty-six frame. Maybe even better! She had long golden hair that was pinned up. Her eyes were big and light brown, very welcoming. She was definitely in the wrong business. There was some modeling agency missing a star! It was all I could do to keep from asking her to marry me on the spot. For the life of me, I could not figure out her nationality. Black, Hispanic, biracial, I couldn't pin it down.

"Hi, my name is Valerie."

"Hi, Valerie, I'm Michael."

Valerie was quite tall with long legs, a nice round butt, slim waist and nice pert breasts. Her hair was about shoulder-length and curled underneath. She had a nice dark-brown complexion. She was quite attractive. She was dressed in a man's suit, which looked very neat on her and business-like. She probably had men lining up to date her.

"Hey, what's up? I'm Darsha."

"Hey, Darsha, I'm Michael."

Darsha was about twenty-two or twenty-three years old. Judging by her attire I could tell she was an active member of the hip-hop culture. That made me wonder what kind of business would hire such a young, inexperienced person. I would find out later that she was very mature and responsible for her age, probably more than I. She was fair-skinned, slim with slender hips, strange-looking eyes, and humorous.

"Hi, I'm last, but definitely not least. I'm Lisa. How are you?"

Lisa was what we black people call high-yellow, light-skinned, with short hair, broad shoulders, and broad hips. She was gentle and soft-spoken.

"I'm fine, Lisa. I'm Michael Forrester."

"Who's training you?" Lisa asked.

"I think Tazzy said it was someone named Cynthia."

"Okay, good to meet you," Lisa said. "Later, Michael."

"Uh, later," I said.

They cleared the break room and then Wanda and Pam walked in.

"Hey, man, you the new dude?" Wanda said, without even looking at me.

Wanda was tough-looking, with a tough voice. She had big bulging eyes, a deep voice, and a presence, which demanded respect, or she'd kick your ass. She was about five feet six inches tall, a little husky, with a delightfully friendly smile.

"Yes, I'm the new dude."

"I'm Wanda. And that's Pam," Wanda said, pointing at Pam.

"Wanda, I don't need you to introduce me," Pam said. "I'm Pam, how are you?"

Pam was an attractive woman with an athletic build, dark-brown, smooth skin. Nice muscular legs. A protruding round buttock that extended from her body at least twelve inches. Her hair was cut perfectly to match the sculpture of her face.

"I'm just fine. Good to meet you."

Pam and Wanda walked out together. I played with the salt and pepper shakers until Cynthia finally came to get me.

"Michael?" Cynthia asked, as she peeked her head through the door.

Cynthia was short, about five feet three inches tall. She was pretty, but in a homely type of way. She wore a long skirt that had to be handed down by her grandmother's grandmother. It revealed no form of human shape within its wrapping. She wore big glasses that she looked over, instead of through. But despite her outward appearance, she was warm and inviting. Upon our first introduction I had a feeling that I knew her from somewhere, but I couldn't quite place her.

"Yup, that's me."

"Let's go, man. You got a date with a computer."

I stood up and followed Cynthia back to my desk, passing everyone else in the office along the way. As I got closer to my desk, I saw Alicia's beautiful face. Her desk faced directly in front of mine. I smiled at the thought of having her picture-perfect view from the time I came in the door, until I clocked out to go home. Maybe my life of recent mishaps was taking a turn for the better. Once again, I reminded myself that no matter how attracted I became to any of the women in the office, I would maintain my objective and keep the project of researching first and foremost. As I sat down, I noticed there was also a vacant desk on my right. I found out later that my neighbor was out sick.

Before Cynthia and I could get started on our training session, Tazzy called a meeting and we all gathered in the center of the office.

"Good morning, everybody," Tazzy spoke.

"Good morning," the office girls spoke in unison.

"Is Tina here yet?" Tazzy said, looking around for her.

"Not yet," voices scattered.

"Well, it's going to be a quick meeting. I'll get the small things out of the way. Can everyone please stay away from the thermostat? I've been noticing the temperature is much lower than where I set it. Secondly, when you go into the bathroom, please, please clean up after yourselves. I cannot stress that enough, especially when Mother Nature is calling. No one wants to walk into a bathroom and be greeted with someone else's tampon or what have you. So please, clean up after yourselves, okay? Now, back to business, we really have to stay focused and stay on task. We have to get our volume of claims down. So please, if you must talk, keep it to a minimum and try not to disturb your neighbor. That's it. Any questions?"

"Can you speak up? I can barely hear you," Pam said.

"You need to quit, Pam. You know you can hear that girl," Valerie said, whispering so that Tazzy couldn't hear.

"I said please keep talking to a minimum. Clean up behind yourself. Stay away from the thermostat. And let's try to work on getting our claims down. Did you get it that time, Pam?" Tazzy said, raising her voice.

"Some of it," Pam mumbled, rolling her eyes.

"I'm sure your neighbor will let you in on whatever you missed."

The girls in the office were beginning to disperse when Tazzy stopped them. "Oh, I almost forgot. I'd like to welcome our newest employee, Michael Forrester," Tazzy said, pointing at me. "Please do your best to make Michael feel as comfortable as possible. Have a nice day, people!"

I waved to the girls to acknowledge Tazzy's announcement, then we went back to our desks. Cynthia and I sat down together at my desk to begin my training. As she started to speak, that irrepressible familiar feeling resurfaced.

"Excuse me, Cynthia," I said. "Do I know you from somewhere?"

"I don't think so," Cynthia said with a smile.

"You seem so familiar to me. What's your full name?"

"Cynthia B. Childs."

"What does the 'B' stand for?"

"It stands for 'B' as in B-quiet."

"Are you ashamed of your name?"

"I'm not ashamed. I just don't know want anybody to know what it is." Cynthia laughed. "It is coun-tree."

"You look so familiar to me."

"Everybody tells me I have that kind of face."

"Yeah, maybe that's it!"

❖❖❖

Cynthia trained me for that first week and I kept my conversations confined to her ears only. On Wednesday she gave me a list of telephone numbers of the women in the office. Strangely, the list consisted of both work and personal contact numbers. She told me both numbers were listed because during the winter hours they would call each other to make sure each of them made it to their cars safely. Although Upskon was a huge building that employed over five hundred people, the security was a joke. It was common knowledge that security seemed to show up after someone was robbed, stabbed or raped. All of these crimes had happened in Upskon's parking lot.

chapter 2

O ver the weekend I did what I did every other weekend: picked up my daughters, went to the movies, and, or rented movies. I had not had a consistent social life since my second marriage. I found my children to be therapeutic. They looked to me for so much. Their need for me kept me hanging on to my sanity.

My oldest daughter from my first marriage was thirteen. And my youngest daughter from my second marriage was five. Their mothers made no attempt to make sure they kept in contact so I made arrangements to have them both on the same weekends and major holidays to assure they would bond as sisters. They got along like most sisters, fighting one moment, and hugging the next.

This weekend was going as any other. Alexiah had fallen asleep on the way to my house, probably still worn out from playtime at school. Brimone, on the other hand, decided to make the evening a little more exciting.

"Daddy," Brimone shouted. "Come here!"

I leaped from the sunken hole in my couch, created by the countless hours of watching ESPN in one spot, and ran upstairs to the bathroom.

"Are you okay, Brimone?"

"Daddy, promise me you won't get upset."

"What's the matter, baby?" I said, walking in front of Brimone.

"Look!" Brimone said, raising tissue from her backside.

"What's that, baby?" I said, backing up.

"I started my period, Daddy!"

I stood back, and slowly inched my face closer until I realized what was on the tissue.

"Oh, shit!" I shouted, tripping backward.

Brimone laughed and shook her head.

"I'll be right back, okay?"

"Okay, Daddy."

"Don't move, baby! Please don't move! Okay?"

"I won't!"

I ran into my bedroom and leaped over my bed to get to the telephone. I called Brimone's mother but I could only reach her voicemail. I left a panicked message and then called Alexiah's mother. She too, was unavailable. I tried desperately to conjure up Bernice for support but she would not appear. I remembered that I had some of the office girls' telephone numbers and I called the first name on the list.

"Hello."

"Hello, Cynthia?" I asked, breathing heavily.

"Yes, this is Cynthia."

"Cynthia, I hate to disturb you, but I have a problem and I need to speak with someone. Got a minute?"

"Sure, what's up?"

"Well, well," I stuttered, trying to tell her my dilemma without making a fool of myself. "Well, Cynthia, I have a thirteen-year-old daughter, and she's with me for the weekend, and I think she just started her menstrual cycle."

"She what?" Cynthia said, laughing under her breath.

"I think she started her period and I don't know what to do!"

"First, calm down, Michael, I can stop by the store and pick up some pads if you like?"

"Would you, please?"

"Where do you live?"

"I live on Sycamore Street. Go north on Genessee until you get to Sycamore, and then make a left. I'm the second house on the right, 1439 Sycamore."

"Okay, I'll be there in a few."

"Okay, thanks again, Cynthia." I tried to compose myself.

"No problem. Go check on that baby and make sure she's all right."

"Okay, Cynthia."

"Okay, bye."

"Bye!"

After I hung up the telephone I ran back into the bathroom and my daughter handed me a couple of sheets of tissue. They were stained in blood and that was the last thing I remember until I heard Cynthia ring my doorbell.

"Michael!" Cynthia said, slowly opening the door. "Michael! Where are you?"

"Uh, right here," I mumbled, standing at the top of the stairs.

"Michael, are you all right?" Cynthia asked, walking up the stairs.

"Yeah, I'm fine."

"I rang your doorbell like a hundred times, man. Thank God, the door was open. And why do you have your door unlocked anyway?" Cynthia said, looking around. "You can tell this is a good neighborhood, you can't even leave your window unlocked in my neighborhood."

"Huh?"

"Michael, snap out of it!" Cynthia said jokingly, snapping her fingers in front of my face. "Where's your daughter?"

"In there," I responded, pointing inside of the bathroom.

"Relax, Michael, I'll take it from here."

"Hey, I'm going in with you. I don't want my baby to think that I can't handle it."

"All that girl is thinking about right now is, what is going on with her body."

"I need to go talk to her."

"You're too nervous, man. You don't need to go in the trenches."

"Oh, okay. I'm out here if you need me."

"Michael," Cynthia said, standing in front of the bathroom door, "you may want to introduce us, though. She may be a little shy, or maybe even a little scared, having a strange woman walk into the bathroom with her unannounced."

"Good idea, Cynthia."

I calmly introduced Cynthia to Brimone and explained to her that Cynthia was there to help. I stood outside, and every now and then, I would ask the girls how things were going. They would affirm that everything was going well and I would resume my pacing.

Eventually they submerged from the bathroom. I kissed Brimone on the cheek and carried her to her bed. Of course she could have walked without any difficulty, but I felt compelled to do it. She placed her head on my chest and closed her eyes. Instead of laying her down, I sat in a chair and rocked her until she fell asleep. I guess that was my way of holding on to my baby. Literally!

Cynthia sat patiently on the bed and we talked quietly as I rocked my teenage daughter like an infant. After I laid Brimone on the bed, Cynthia and I walked downstairs. Since we had resolved the crisis, neither one of us knew how to continue the dialogue.

"Well, Cynthia, I think I can take it from here."

"I guess I better be getting back home then."

While we were saying our good-byes, Brimone woke up and walked down the stairs.

"Thank you, Ms. Cynthia," she said, rubbing her sleepy eyes.

"No problem, sweetie."

"Wait a minute," I said. "What are you about to do, Cynthia?"

"Go home and watch a movie."

"Are you going home to a family?"

"Nope, just me."

"Is it too late for you to watch a movie with us?"

"That sounds nice. You sure your girls won't mind me taking some of their time with Daddy?"

"I'm positive. They're happy whenever we have company."

"Okay then, I'll stay."

"Good."

"Good."

While we were walking to the den, Cynthia scanned my home.

"You have a beautiful home, Michael. I don't live that far from here, but my neighborhood doesn't look anything like this," Cynthia said, walking around my house. "May I?"

"*Mi casa es su casa,*" I replied.

My house was huge—a mini-mansion, some would call it. Most people think I purchased it by either hitting the lottery, or hitting a drug cartel member over the head and taking his loot. I did, however, buy the house for a steal from my editor before she and her family moved to Florida. And although my stay in the National Football League was an extremely brief stay, the job paid well, and I invested well. I think it's safe to say I won't have to worry about finances for a long time.

My house has three levels with antique furniture in most of the rooms, decorated by my ex-wives in Queen Anne and Queen Victoria colonial style. I have seven bedrooms, six baths, three fireplaces, two living rooms, a huge dining room, den, study, and a spacious eat-in kitchen with plenty of windows to allow plenty of sunlight. And lastly, is my glorious place of refuge, the basement. I remodeled and decorated the basement, the only room in the house that I'd had a hand in creating. It has a theater room with nice comfortable leather chairs for viewing. It also has a sitting area with a love seat and recliner. And on every wall is memorabilia from the University of Michigan football team. Some may call it a shrine, but for those who are Michigan fans, it's a way of life.

"Man, this is a freaking castle!" Cynthia said in admiration.

"It's not all that," I said modestly.

Cynthia was excited as I showed her upstairs. Afterward, we went back down to the den to watch movies. Cynthia stayed until after midnight and we enjoyed ourselves. Although we got along well, it was clearly understood that there were no sparks between us. But I was happy to have made a friend. I wasn't sure how I, and my newfound friend, would react to each other on Monday. This was a little strange because I'd never had my work life intrude upon my personal life and vice versa. As fate would have it, I wouldn't have to wait until Monday to find out.

Cynthia called the next day to check on Brimone. After they spoke, it was decided that she would come over to watch another movie with us on Saturday.

The girls were taking a bath when Cynthia arrived so she sat in my den and watched the remaining fourth quarter of the University of Michigan game. Having been a lifelong Michigan Wolverine fan, I warned Cynthia that I might not be much of a conversationalist until the game was over.

"Cynthia, I don't mean to be rude, but this is the Michigan-Notre Dame game. My conversation will be limited. I hope you understand."

"No problem. I love football! Go Irish!"

"Go who?"

"You heard me. Go Irish!"

"That's blasphemy in my house, woman!"

"You're cheering for Michigan, I assume?"

"You have to ask? Go Blue!"

"Did you play ball at Michigan?"

"No."

"Then why are you cheering for them?"

"Because I was born and raised in Michigan, woman!" I said, sitting straight up, as the Notre Dame player was running down the sideline.

"TOUCHDOWN NOTRE DAME!!!!" the television announcer screamed.

"You see what you've done, Cynthia?"

"What did I do?" Cynthia clapped her hands. "GO IRISH!"

"You know what, Cynthia," I said, gently taking her by the arm. "I think Brimone really wants to talk to you about that little girl stuff. So maybe you need to go to her room. Thanks, kiddo!"

"Okay. I'll go upstairs but Michigan is still going to lose."

"All right, all right," I said, escorting her to the staircase.

Michigan won the game and Cynthia and I became good friends.

❖❖❖

The following week, Wanda, Pam, Lisa and I were sitting in the break room for lunch and a conversation sprang up on the radio about men being intimidated by successful women. I sat and listened as they ranted their opinions.

"That's the problem with men nowadays. Every time a woman makes more money than them, they can't take it!" Wanda shouted.

"I know," Pam agreed. "It's hard for me to get a date because I have my own car, my own house, and my own money. Men don't know how to deal with a woman like me."

As I tried to ignore them, I thought to myself, *perhaps men don't want to deal with a woman like you, not because you have a car, a house, or your own money. Maybe, just maybe, it's because you have a rotten-ass attitude that a man can't stand to be around.*

"I don't think all men are intimidated by successful women," Lisa interrupted.

"I ain't never met a man who could handle a woman makin' more money than him!" Wanda snapped. "Never!"

"They start feeling insecure and become possessive," Pam said.

Ms. Virginia walked into the break room and listened to the other office girls as they blasted away.

"If black men wasn't so dam' lazy, we wouldn't have that problem!" Wanda shouted.

"Excuse me, ladies," Ms. Virginia interrupted, "don't you see that gentleman sitting over there?"

"Yeah, I see him," Wanda said. "And?"

"Let's try to respect the fact that we now have a man in the office," Ms. Virginia said.

"Why? He ain't complaining," Wanda responded.

"Wanda, even if he's not, how would you feel if you were in an office full of white people and they were speaking badly about black people?"

"I'd go the hell off!"

"Just because Michael is not going off, it doesn't mean that he shouldn't be respected."

"Okay, Ms. Virginia." Wanda rolled her eyes.

"We didn't embarrass you, did we, Michael?" Lisa asked.

"No," I said, clearing my throat, surprised someone finally acknowledged that I was in the room.

"Well, I know how to settle this," Wanda said, rolling her eyes again. "Mike, do you think men are intimidated by women who make more than they do?"

"Absolutely not," I said, with a half-grin.

"Absolutely not?" Wanda yelled. "You crazy, man!"

"Wanda, you asked the man a question and he answered it. Don't start going off," Lisa said.

"I ain't goin' off! Shit!" Wanda said, defending herself.

"I'm curious, what is your opinion on the subject, Michael?" Ms. Virginia asked.

"I don't think it's a matter of women intimidating men," I replied. "I think gender has nothing to do with it. I think that even if you have two people with equal incomes in a relationship and one of those persons begin to make more money, the dynamics of the relationship are going to shift to the person who makes the most money as being the most dominant. The person who brings in the most money is usually going to be the person who makes the most decisions with his or her money, thus, causing the other person to feel inferior."

"Um, well said, Michael," Ms. Virginia said, sarcastically clapping her hands to Wanda.

"Let's get more specific. If a woman made more money than you, would it intimidate you, Michael?" Pam asked.

"Absolutely not. Now, if more money brings more attitude, maybe that would create a problem. But I think intimidation is an overused word that doesn't apply to most male-female relationships when it comes to finances."

"That's your opinion. I think men are intimidated," Wanda said, rolling her eyes.

"That figures," I said sarcastically.

"What you mean by that?"

"I meant nothing, Wanda."

"See, you're intimidated by me speaking my mind right now!"

"Intimidated?" I asked, annoyed by her comment. "Intimidate means to make afraid, or to feel threatened. There is nothing you can say or do to frighten me. As a matter of fact, I find you to be obstreperous and this conversation garrulous bellicosity, senseless office rhetoric with no foundation of logic or reasoning. And had I not been asked, I would never have commented on a topic with no intent of ratiocination."

I got up and walked out of the break room. But before I left I bade the ladies a warm adieu. I was given warm smiles from everyone, except from Wanda, of course. I'll never know what was actually said after I left, but I have a feeling it wasn't good.

"What the hell that niggah just say to me?" Wanda said.

"I don't know, Wanda, but I think he insulted you." Ms. Virginia laughed.

"Me too," Lisa added, laughing with Ms. Virginia.

"See, here we go. All that it takes is for one man to come in here and break up our team," Wanda said. "Don't y'all see what he's doing? Divide and conquer, y'all! Divide and conquer!"

"Girl, you a mess!" Ms. Virginia said.

"A mess?" Wanda asked, staring at the office girls slowly, "or a prophet? This dude is the devil, I tell you!"

"A hot mess!" Lisa said, as the office girls piled out of the break room.

❖❖❖

Later that week I finally met Tina, my desk neighbor. The office buzzed over her coming back to work on a Friday after being out sick for two weeks. And when she did arrive, she was late. From that act alone, I knew she was going to be fun. But before she made her grand entrance, she called to see if the coast was clear.

"Good morning, thank you for calling Upskon, Wanda speaking…Girl, where you at…Yeah, Tazzy know you ain't here…I ain't clocking you in, girl, you crazy…Just hurry up…Hurry up…Okay, bye…Okay, bye…OKAY, BYE!" Wanda said, slamming the telephone on the receiver. "Dam'! I said bye three times!"

"Was that Tina?" Ms. Virginia asked.

"Who else?" Wanda said.

"That girl is going to mess around and get fired," Alicia said.

"Let's hope not." Ms. Virginia sighed.

Tina dashed into the office practically out of breath.

"Wanda, does Tazzy know I'm not here?"

"I told you on the phone she knew!"

"Maaaan! Shoot! Tazzy gon' fire me!"

"You better get yourself together, Tina," Ms. Virginia said.

"Well, I'm working on it, Ms. Virginia."

"Good! How are things at home?"

"He's still acting crazy! That's why I'm late. I told him I was leaving, and he had a fit. The fool knows I'm on my way to work, and he's still accusing me of cheating. I thought he was going to kill me the way he was yelling and screaming."

"Well, you're here now," Ms. Virginia said.

"I told you not to mess with that fool in the first place!"

"What are you talking about, Wanda? You're the one who introduced us."

"Then after y'all started kickin' it, I told you that fool was crazy and leave him the hell alone!"

"Wanda, we had three kids by the time you told me that."

"Hell," Wanda said, "better late than never."

"If it was me, I would have been gone a long time ago," Pam said.

"You need to leave that man, Tina!" Alicia said.

"That's why I don't mess around with jealous fools," Pam added.

"Yeah, Tina, you better walk out before they have to drag you out!" Wanda said.

"Listen to all of you. There's no telling what's going on in Tina's home, and you shouldn't be encouraging her to leave when there could be serious consequences."

"Forgive me, Ms. Virginia, but I don't give a damn what the consequences are! If you think that man gon' hurt you, Tina, get the hell out as soon as you can!" Wanda snapped.

"I'm tryin', y'all."

"Darling, make sure that when you leave, you are in a safe environment because leaving could only be the beginning of his rage, and not the end."

"Tina, read my lips," Wanda said, slowly enunciating each word. "*Get-the-hell-out!* See, I'm from Chicago, I wouldn't be puttin' up with that shit!"

"Tina, don't listen to that mess!" Ms. Virginia said. "These women don't know what you may be going through at home."

"What makes you think you know, but we don't?" Pam asked.

"Have you ever had a man beat you so badly you couldn't open your eyes for three days?" Ms. Virginia said.

"Have you?" Pam asked sarcastically.

"Yes, I have," Ms. Virginia said, as Pam stopped typing. "And that's why I'm talking to Tina now, because I don't want her to end up in my shoes, running for her life. My husband followed me from relative to relative, friend to friend. He didn't care who it was, if they were in the way of getting to me. He would hurt them, too. I was endangering their lives, so I left. Then he followed me from shelter to shelter, and finally, from city to city. There was no escaping. The police wouldn't help because they said there was nothing they could do until he did something to me. I kept moving until I thought he had given up. I hadn't heard from him in years, but one day after I thought I would never see him again, he showed up at my church here in Atlanta. I was so shocked I didn't know what to do. He asked me to come with him. I didn't want to make a scene at church, so I did. My mistake! He took me to a secluded area of a park, and he beat me, and beat me, and beat me. A young lady, who happened to be jogging by, heard my screams and came to my rescue. Unfortunately, before help could arrive, she was stabbed several times. My husband ran off. And I haven't heard from him since."

"What happened to the jogger?" Tina asked.

"She survived. Her physical scars healed, but I'm sure she will always have some emotional scars."

"Ms. Virginia, I would have never thought a classy woman like you would have to go through something like that," Wanda said sadly.

"Classiness doesn't mean a thing when a maniac is trying to kill you."

"But still, you a strong woman, Ms. Virginia."

"Strength has nothing to do with it, either, Wanda."

"I don't mean no disrespect, but the hell it don't, Ms. Virginia."

"No dear. I did what I had to do to survive and that's it. And although some of you may try to hide it, every woman in this office, once she leaves, has something waiting for her outside of these office doors that may bring tears to her eyes. And every woman in this office should cry those tears, then stand up and face her pain. Regardless if that pain is work! Regardless if it's family! Heartache! Or in my case, death. Amen?"

"Amen!" Tina said, clapping her hands.

"Dammit, Ms. Virginia! I swear you gon' make me cry up in here! You a strong-ass black woman!"

"Thank you, but once again, it's not a matter of strength, Wanda, it's a matter of survival. And I have managed to survive."

❖❖❖

Over the next couple of months Tina and I became very close friends. We laughed and joked every day. I started to spend more time with her, than Cynthia, at work. No matter what she was going through at home, she always made my day happier. I had also become closer to the other women in the office, but Cynthia and Tina were my closest friends.

"Today is my birthday, Mike," Tina said. "Me and the girls from the office are going out tonight. You comin'?"

"To a club? Uh, no, I don't think so."

"Why not?"

"It's going to be all of you women, right?"

"Yeah. And?"

"And some of the women here may not want me to go."

"Hold on, let me find out." Tina yelled across the office, "Do y'all mind if Mikey here goes out with us tonight?"

Everyone responded with approval.

"See, Mike, the girls don't mind."

"I don't know. Where is this place?" I asked.

"Downtown," Tina said.

"I don't know anything about downtown."

"You need to get yo' ass out of Gwinnett County sometime, niggah," Wanda said.

"I go to Hairston's sometime."

"Hairston's is an old folks' club!" Darsha shouted.

"Maybe I'm old then. I don't think I'll be able to make it."

Alicia looked over her desk and said, "That's too bad, I thought I was going to get a dance, Michael."

I quickly turned to Tina and said, "Okay, I'm there."

While we were talking, Tazzy, Susan and Jaline, walked up to our desks. They were coming to check on my progress. Tazzy pretty much kept to herself unless there was an issue with something or somebody. So long as you were doing your job, she wouldn't bother you at all. Susan, the assistant supervisor, usually handed out memos and had much more contact with the girls on the floor. Jaline, my nemesis, was hardly in the office. She traveled most of the time and I had only seen her in passing my first couple of months on the job.

"How's our new employee?" Jaline asked, as they stopped at my desk. "Are the ladies treating you nicely, Michael?"

"Yes, I've been treated very well."

"I'll be here all next week, so let me know if you're having trouble with anything."

"Thanks, Jaline."

"No problem, Michael."

Tazzy and Susan waved good-bye as they followed Jaline back to her office.

"I don't remember none of us gettin' no attention like that when we started working here," Wanda said. "It's some damn jungle fever goin' on up in here!"

"On the real, I ain't get no welcome like that, neither." Darsha laughed along with Wanda.

"That's because y'all are not a black stallion!" Tina joked.

As dark as I am, I was obviously blushing over the attention I was getting.

"Hey, Mike, you need to give us a strip show tonight at the club," Valerie shouted over to me.

"Yeah, baby! Shake it like a salt shaker!" Wanda screamed.

"Y'all leave my buddy alone!" Cynthia said, as she stood at my desk. "You coming tonight or what? I know this is not the weekend you have your girls. So you might as well come hang out. If I have to go, everybody's going!"

"Oh, he's coming, Cynt. Now that *Ms. Alicia* is coming," Tina said. "What kind of car you got, Mike?"

"A Navigator, why?"

"Do you drink?"

"Uh, no I don't."

"Hey, y'all, Mike just volunteered to pick some of us up in his Navigator," Tina yelled.

"Tina! Tina, wait a minute," I said urgently.

"Thanks for picking us up Mike, I'm looking forward to seeing you out of your office clothes," Alicia said.

"No problem," I said.

❖❖❖

It was planned for me to pick up Alicia, Cynthia, Tina, and Pam. Wanda would pick up Lisa, Valerie, and Darsha.

But before I would pick up anyone I had to wash my truck and go through a closet of out-of-style clothes that I had not worn in two years. I somehow managed to accomplish all of my tasks on time, and I was on my way. Ironically, the person closest to me was Alicia, so I would get some alone time with her before the rest of the crew joined us.

I picked up Alicia first as scheduled, but the conversation was all small talk. Next were Cynthia, Pam, and Tina in that order. When I pulled up to Tina's house she was standing outside on the curb. She gestured for me to pull down the street before she climbed in. I didn't ask any questions and neither did anyone else. I assumed this was normal behavior.

On our way to the nightclub, we talked to Wanda's group on our cell phones the entire way. They arrived before we did and waited for us at the door. Once we were in, all hell broke loose. They started dancing with themselves and shouting as if Abraham Lincoln had just set them free.

"Man, I ain't been out in so long, I don't know what to do!" Tina shouted.

"Let's go dance, girl," Valerie shouted back.

They headed for the dance floor with Darsha, Lisa, and Alicia right behind them. They huddled in a group and the party was on.

"Oh my God!" I said out loud.

"What's wrong, man?" Wanda laughed. "This is how the girls from the office get down when we together. We have fun! We don't give a damn who around, or what they think!"

As Wanda and I were talking, a man walked up and asked Pam to dance. Pam took the man's hand and they were dancing before they reached the dance floor. Another man came over and asked Cynthia to dance but she told him she wasn't ready. The next man that came up asked me to dance and I almost fell out of my chair.

"Excuse me?" I asked.

"Would you like to dance?" he asked.

"Bro," I said, trying to remain calm, "I don't know what would make you come over and ask me that, but, *'Hell no!'* I'm not like that."

"I just assumed. You're the only man with a group of women. I assumed that you were, well, you know…"

"Well, I'm not!" I said, waving the man off. "I only dance with women, bro. Everything I do, I do with women!"

Cynthia and Wanda started to pat each other and laugh. But Wanda's laughter stopped when he approached her.

"Well, do you wanna dance?" he asked Wanda.

"Niggah, are you out of your damn mind?" Wanda yelled. "You gon' come over here and ask a man to dance before you ask me? I'll bust a cap in yo' ass, niggah! Don't try to play me like that, you freakin' faggot!"

"Wanda," I said, trying to calm her down. "It's not that big a deal."

"I'm 'bout to blow this fool head off, Mike!"

"Forgive us, man," I said. "You might want to get on out of here."

"Man, that bitch is crazy!" the man shouted.

"I got yo' bitch, BITCH!" Wanda screamed.

The man walked away while Wanda yelled threats at him. Cynthia tried to excuse us from the situation by asking me to dance.

"Wanda is trippin'!" Cynthia asked, "Do you wanna dance, Mike?"

Before I could answer, Alicia walked over and grabbed me by the hand and led me to the dance floor.

"Ooh! I love that song!" Alicia said. "Come on, Michael, let's dance."

It was a slow song, and I thought I was in a dream. This beautiful woman was coming on to me in front of the world, offering her self to me and all I had to do was accept the precious gift. In the middle of the song I pulled her close to me and pressed my body against hers so that she could feel that I was excited. I knew that if she backed up, she wasn't interested in my bump-and-grind tango. But as I pressed against her, she pressed against me with even more intensity. We aligned ourselves with each other and slowly ground our bodies together. It was so intense I thought I was going to have to put on a condom right there on the dance floor. The next song was fast but I couldn't go back to our table in my delicate condition, so as she was walking off the dance floor, I pulled her back to me.

We danced a couple more songs, and then sat down. Immediately, Cynthia pulled me to the floor and we danced a few songs. Eventually, I danced with every one of the girls. I must admit I had the time of my life.

By the end of the night, with the exception of Cynthia, all of the girls were a bit tipsy. I dropped them off in the opposite order in which I picked them up. Cynthia was next to last, which would leave Alicia and me. As Cynthia was getting out, she said, "Y'all be good, okay?"

After we pulled off, Alicia quickly started a conversation.

"I think Cynthia likes you."

"Cynthia doesn't like me. Cynthia is my friend, and only a friend."

"I'm telling you, I know women and Cynthia likes you, Michael."

"Cynthia doesn't like me, Alicia. We're cool as hell, though. We hang, watch sports, but that's it. She doesn't have any romantic feelings for me."

"She's awfully protective of you to only be your friend."

"That's what friends do. Friends protect each other."

"Cynthia is a little overprotective, though, don't you think?"

"Like I said, I think she's just being a friend."

"Michael, you've only known her a few months, how close can you be?"

"Anyway!" I said, changing the subject. "What's your story?"

"I don't have a story."

"Come on now, everybody has a story. What's yours?"

"I'm telling you, I don't have a story."

"Let me help you out. I know you're not married, so do you have a boyfriend?"

"To be truthful, I don't know what I have." Alicia turned her head away.

"What does that mean?" I said, pulling into Alicia's driveway and cutting the car off.

"Nothing."

"Come on, Alicia. What does that mean?"

"I'm in a relationship but it's a long distance relationship."

"So is marriage on the horizon?"

"I don't know what's in the future for us."

I could tell that getting information out of her was going to be like pulling teeth so I decided to back off. I was more interested in talking about how she felt about me anyway.

"So was I out of line by dancing with you the way I did tonight?"

"You did nothing I didn't let you do," Alicia said, stepping out of the car and closing the door. "Besides, it was only a dance."

She waved, and I watched her until she was safely in her house.

chapter 3

The next morning I got up and did my morning workout to maintain as much of my youth as possible. Although I no longer had the chiseled body of my youth, I still had a strong, hard body held together by vitamins and a daily workout. I never lifted weights. Push-ups and sit-ups were always my choice of muscle building. And a morning jog on my treadmill kept my cardiovascular up to speed. It turned out to be a convenient substitute for a nearly forty-year-old man who hates going to the gym. My once neatly cut fade had turned into a smooth-shaven neat bald head; once again, a convenience for a nearly forty-year-old man who hates to go to barbershops. I had no signs of wrinkles so I could fool myself into thinking that middle age was still a few years away. After my workout I took a shower, then planted myself on the couch for a while.

Since I was waiting for the games on TV, I decided to begin writing my novel, my book of feline exploitation, my book that would make me a best-selling author. I went to my computer and I typed the title, *The Office Girls*. Before I could write the first line, the phone rang and it was Cynthia reminding me that we had a full day of football games ahead of us. After we hung up I stared at my computer for a while. But I didn't feel like writing, I felt like watching football, so I cut my computer off and headed back to the couch.

By that time Cynthia was on her way over. She picked up some snacks and we settled in for our games. We never cheered for the same teams. I was a Big Ten Conference man, and she was an SEC—or Southeastern Conference—woman. It didn't mix. Cynthia knew her football and I couldn't afford to slack with my knowledge of the game. She was like being with one of the guys. We argued about sports for most of the day until Cynthia started to ask questions about Alicia.

"So," Cynthia said, pausing before asking her question, "how long did you two hang out last night?"

"Who?"

"You know who, Mr. Owl," Cynthia said, taking the remote out of my hand and turning the sound down. "You and Alicia."

"I dropped her off and I came home and passed out on my couch. Why are you being so nosy?" I said, snatching the remote out of her hand.

"I'm not being nosy. I'm trying to look out for you."

"I don't need you to look out for me, Cynt."

"Okay, but every time a man comes around, Alicia tries to see just how far she can go with him. You won't believe how some men make fools of themselves."

"Alicia and I are only friends, so that doesn't apply to me."

"Boy, please! Everybody in that office talks about the big crush you have on Alicia."

"For real?" I asked surprisingly.

"For real!" Cynthia joked back.

"Everybody thinks I have a crush on Alicia?" I asked again to be certain.

"Everybody!" Cynthia said. "Why is that so hard to believe?"

"I don't know what could make them think that."

"Could it be that every time she comes around you get all goo-goo-eyed?"

"Who? Not me."

"Yes, you do, man. I wasn't going to say anything but while you two were dancing, they were making bets on how quickly Alicia would have you strung out. She's a big tease for our entertainment. Just to show how big of a jerk a man can make of himself over a piece of booty."

"Hey, that's messed up," I said with humiliation.

"You didn't hear us singing 'Another One Bites the Dust'?"

"Yeah, but I didn't know you were singing that crap about me!"

"Stop pouting, boy. I told you so you can stop making a fool of yourself."

"Does Alicia even have a boyfriend?"

"God yes! A model! Fine as hell!"

"I didn't ask you all that, Cynt."

"Think about it, Mike," Cynthia said. "Alicia got that fine man, what would she want with your baldheaded butt?"

"That's not funny, Cynt."

"Stop whining. So what? She played you. Get over it."

"You know what? Just for that, I'm going to get that chick."

"You ain't gettin' nothin' but yo feelin's hurt, buddy!"

"Watch," I said, sitting up, "we're going to see who's going to be biting the dust."

"Alicia don't want you, Mike," Cynthia said jokingly.

"Okay, we'll see."

"Care to make a little wager?"

"I'm a gentleman. I don't bet on affairs of the heart. But it will give me great pleasure to beat you office girls at your own game."

"Shut it up." Cynthia laughed sarcastically. "Men have been doing it for years."

"And while you're having so much fun over there kissing up to Alicia, she told me last night that you have a crush on me."

"What?" Cynthia said, turning her ear toward me to hear clearer. "She said what?"

"Put the claws back in. You cats need to stick together."

"I know you're lying, Mike."

"I'm sorry, my sister, but that's exactly what she said."

"I can't believe she said that. She probably thinks you and I are fooling around and she was trying to get some information because she doesn't want anybody in her territory. I can't believe she said that."

"Stop whining." I laughed. "Let's get back to the game. I'll let you know when I've touched the untouchable Alicia."

"I'm not thinking about you and Alicia," Cynthia said, turning her back to me and folding her arms. "Man, turn the game back up and be quiet."

"Don't get mad at me, Cynt."

"Shut up. And are you in love with this guy or what?"

Cynthia pointed to the posters on my wall of a former University of Michigan player.

"Who?"

"This guy you have plastered all over the place, who is that?"

"That's Johnny. My favorite Michigan Wolverine of all time. I'll introduce you to him one day."

"Don't act like you know that dude, Mike."

"Oh, you don't think I know the guy?"

"Please, Mike."

"All right, don't believe me."

We continued to go back and forth about the games and about Alicia for the rest of the afternoon. Cynthia left around eight that night. Alicia called around eight fifteen and asked if I wanted to go to a coffee shop. I was under the suspicion that Cynthia may have called her and put her up to it. But it still didn't stop me from agreeing to go.

We met at a coffee house in our neighborhood and had a pleasant conversation. Toward the end, I started to ask direct questions because if this was a set-up I was going to let them know that I was on to the game.

"Let me ask you a question, Alicia?"

"Go ahead."

"Why did you ask me out?"

"Why shouldn't I?"

"You have to have like a million men chasing you, so why me?"

"Should I be flattered by that question?"

"I don't know," I said, hunching my shoulders. "I'm trying to figure out why you would be interested in a guy like me. I'm just an average guy."

"And I'm just an average girl."

"Alicia, there's nothing average about you. Look at you. You're gorgeous!"

"That's because you're looking at my shell and not at my soul."

"Maybe you're right. But if you want me to know what's going on in your soul, you'll have to tell me because I can't read your mind."

"Are you sure you want to hear this?"

"I can't think of anything else I'd rather hear right now."

"Okay," Alicia said, sitting back, "here it is…"

Alicia's Story

I was born and raised in Cincinnati, Ohio. I have two sisters and one brother. They're all back in Cincinnati. After I graduated from high school I left to attend college down here in Atlanta. I modeled while I was in college but that was only for kicks. After I graduated from Spelman College, I worked at a few jobs until I finally got a real job here at Upskon. My first few days at Upskon were no fun. It seems every woman in the office had it in for me. They all assumed I was this stuck-up prissy thing who thought the sun rose and fell on her. But our supervisor at the time was Ms. Virginia and she helped me to adjust. She was so sweet. I can honestly say that she was one of my first real friends at Upskon.

At the time it was only five other people in the office. It was Pam, Tina, Lisa, Valerie, and another guy named Charles. He quit shortly after I started. The rest of us became close friends in and outside of the workplace.

Like most people who first move to Atlanta, I went to every club I could find. But after a while, I stopped the club scene and tried to become a part of the middle-class structure. I never married or had children, and I remained single…until I met Julian, that is.

One night, one of my girlfriends and I were eating dinner in Buckhead, when the most gorgeous man I had ever seen walked by. I had never initiated conversation with a man before, but I had to meet this man. He was gorgeous! Jet-black wavy hair, unblemished caramel skin, light-brown eyes and a beautiful smile. I kept staring at him until I finally got his attention. I smiled and he smiled back but that was it. My friend told me to stop being so subtle, and let him know that I was interested in him. I gestured for him to come to me and he got up and started to walk toward me. I was extremely nervous but my girlfriend kept encouraging me to talk to him. When he stopped in front of me, I didn't know what to say.

"Yes," Julian said.

"Um, I just wanted to know your name," I said nervously.

"My name is Julian, what's yours?"

"My name is Alicia."

"Is there something you wanted?"

"I just wanted to say hello."

"Okay, hello." Julian stood and waited for me to say something else.

After an uncomfortable length of silence, he said, "Well, it was a pleasure to meet you."

He started to walk away and as bad as I wanted to call him back to me, I couldn't. He sat back at his table but then returned a few minutes later.

"Here is my business card. You are a very beautiful woman and you may do very well in modeling. Call me if you're interested."

"Thanks," I said, not informing him that I had already done the modeling thing.

I had planned on calling him but it wasn't for any modeling. We eventually started to date and moved in with each other within months. Julian's modeling career took off and now he travels all over the world leaving me here alone. Being with Julian has made me a lonely person with a lonely life.

❖❖❖

As I sat in the coffee shop listening to Alicia's story I didn't see that cockatrice Cynthia had described. However, I do believe that Alicia portrayed that image to them to hide the vulnerable, lonely person who sat before me.

We remained in the coffee shop for a short while longer before we decided to leave. The autumn evening had turn unseasonably cool since we'd walked in from the warm sun of the day. Alicia automatically clung to me as the breeze blew in her face. She grabbed my arm and turned her face into my chest to hide from the wind. I kept her covered until we reached my car. When we were almost to her house she looked over at me and stared.

"What's the matter?" I said, looking back and forth at Alicia and the road.

"I've really enjoyed myself today and I don't want it to end."

"I don't want it to end, either."

"I don't want to go home, Michael," Alicia said, rubbing my hand. "I want to go home with you."

I slammed on my brakes in the middle of the street. I tried quickly to regain my composure and not lose any cool points.

"Excuse me?" I asked in a deep voice.

"I don't want to be alone tonight, Michael," Alicia said. "I want to be with you, if you want to be with me."

"I…I would love to be with you tonight, Alicia," I said nervously.

I made a U-turn in the middle of the street and went back to my house. I told her to make herself comfortable while I took a shower.

"Hey, do you eat pizza?" I shouted to Alicia.

"Of course I eat pizza. My name is even Italian, A-li-ci-a."

"Okay, Mona Lisa," I said jokingly, "one hot pizza coming up."

I ordered the pizza and jumped in the shower. When I got out I dressed in my ESPN attire, T-shirt, and boxers, and then headed to the den to relax with Alicia. We sat in my recliner, with her sitting on my lap, and watched television.

"This is nice," Alicia whispered in my ear.

"Yes, it is, isn't it?"

When Alicia sat directly on my lap, my penis began to rise with no control of my own. It was as if I were a thirteen-year-old boy looking at a *Playboy* magazine. I tried to defuse the situation by thinking of the time my dog Ringo was run over by a garbage truck. That didn't work so I started thinking of verses from the Bible. Alicia positioned herself to the side and slowly relaxed on top of it. And by "it," you know what I mean.

She faced away from me, then straddled my left leg, with her legs on either side, then rested back. She turned her upper torso halfway and rested her head on my chest. Even with her maneuvering, I still wasn't sure if she wanted to make love to me.

I asked myself, *why am I so nervous if she's so comfortable?* I put my arms around her waist and she moved her hips against my hands. With some calculating maneuvering, our faces ended up inches away from each other. She closed her eyes and then I closed mine. I could feel her breath getting closer to my face.

She slowly opened her mouth and slipped her tongue into mine. Our mouths were wide open as we tasted each other's tongues. Our heads turned from side to side as we kissed passionately. I felt Alicia's hand slip into my underwear and grip me tightly. I opened her shirt and pulled out one of her breasts. I removed my tongue from her mouth and twirled it around her nipple. She began to breathe heavily as I engulfed as much of her breast into my mouth as I could. As I sucked both of her breasts back and forth, she started to moan loudly and tighten her grip around my penis. I stood up and told her I'd be right back.

I went into my bedroom and got one of the condoms I thought I would never have the opportunity to use. I put it on while there so I wouldn't have to take the time to do so in the heat of the moment. I rushed back into the den to find Alicia sitting in my recliner stark naked. I stood her up, dropped my underwear, and sat in the chair. Alicia faced me and put her legs on either side of me. She slowly lowered herself on top of me. At the first point of penetration, she made a long agonizing moan, then clenched my neck with her nails.

"Please, go slow, baby." Alicia sighed.

"Okay, baby, okay, I'll go slow."

"Oh shit, baby, it feels so good," Alicia said, lowering herself on top of me.

"You like that, baby," I whispered into her ear.

"Yeah, baby! Yeah, baby! Give it to me like that, baby!" Alicia sighed.

Alicia lifted my head and wildly stuck her tongue in my mouth. We kissed harder and harder as I raised my hips higher and higher to go deeper inside. Alicia started to scream at the top of her lungs. She was so loud I worried the neighbors would hear.

I picked her up, still inside of her, and carried her over to the couch. I laid her down and placed her legs over my shoulders. Her screams became louder with every inch that I slipped inside of her. Her fingernails ripped at my back as I began to stroke her faster and faster.

"Oh baby, I'm coming! I'm coming, baby!" She shouted and furiously jerked her hips until her orgasm subsided.

But I was only beginning. I turned her on her stomach and lay on top of her. I lifted her up and she backed herself into me until the head of my penis was touching her entrance. We twisted and turned until I forged my way in. I turned her head to the side and slipped my tongue into her mouth. I reached beneath her and cupped her breasts in my hands and slowly began to slide in and out. She was so moist I no longer had a problem fitting inside of her. As her screams became louder, I could feel a massive orgasm approaching. I started to pinpoint each stroke so that I could hit the same spot every time. She responded by almost standing on all fours to receive me.

As hard and as fast as I was giving it to her, she was giving it right back to me, thrust for thrust. My orgasm came out of nowhere and I collapsed on top of her still stroking to enjoy every moment. I tried to contain the groans inside of my mouth, but they erupted with deep moans that lasted for minutes. The louder I moaned the more Alicia pushed herself backward into me.

Alicia reached backward and grabbed me by my hips and pulled me deeper into her. It was like an out-of-body experience. I could see myself thrashing around like a fish out of water but there was nothing I could do to stop. When I was completely spent, I lay on top on her. We were both so out of breath it took a couple of minutes for us to speak.

"It's taking that pizza a long time, isn't it?" Alicia asked.

"It sure is. It's been well over an hour."

"Have we been going at it that long?"

"Yup." I stood up to get towels.

"We should get that one for free then," Alicia suggested, with a smile on her face.

"Yeah, we should. Let me call them to see what's taking so long."

I called the pizza place and they told me their driver had been to my house but no one answered the door or the telephone. I told them that I had been in the house the whole time, which was true, and I never heard anything, which was also true. They told me they would be back out within thirty minutes. And no, we didn't get it free but we did get fifty percent off. What a way to earn a discount.

Alicia and I spent the remainder of the night in my den with the television off. We sat and talked until the sun came up. Of course we had a couple of more rounds of pleasure-filled cardiovascular activities, each time better than the last.

We slept until almost noon and then I got up and fixed a late breakfast.

Alicia took a shower and walked around in a pair of my boxers and a T-shirt. She looked so naturally beautiful wearing my too-big clothes with no makeup on her pretty face.

"If you would have asked me on Friday if this weekend had a chance of turning out this way, I would have told you never in a million years," she said.

"A million years? The odds were that far off?"

"For me they were."

"Were you attracted to me before yesterday, Alicia?"

"Yeah, silly."

"You did a pretty good job of hiding it from me."

"I wasn't trying to hide it. I just didn't think it was necessary to act on it."

"So, I guess the question now is, where do we go from here?"

"I don't know, Michael. Right now, my heart is going in several different directions."

"Is one of those directions coming toward me?"

"I'm here with you, aren't I?"

"Yeah, but where will you be tomorrow?"

Alicia didn't answer, she simply walked over and kissed me on the cheek. I took that to be a kiss of comfort, not affirmation. We lounged around for the rest of the afternoon, careful not to mention the expectations of our relationship. Alicia stayed until late evening. I drove her home and we departed with a long, slow, passionate kiss.

"See you tomorrow, Michael."

"Yup, nine to five."

"Bye-Bye!"

"Bye."

Driving away I didn't know what to think. I didn't know if this was the beginning of something beautiful, or the end of something unbelievable. Later that night, I jumped on my computer and entered the events of my time spent with Alicia in my manuscript—one down, and many, many more to go.

❖❖❖

The next day, the ladies gathered in the break room to talk about the events of Friday night. Even Tina made it to work on time to join in. Everybody was there but Alicia. I went to my desk and every ten seconds I looked at the door to see if she was walking through it. It seemed like forever but finally she showed up. And when she did, she was a sight to behold.

"Good morning, Michael," Alicia spoke.

"Hey, Alicia, what's up?"

"Nothing much," Alicia said with a smile, "what did you do this weekend?"

Her question caught me off guard and I stuttered, "What do you mean?"

"I mean, what did you do this weekend?"

"You know Mike probably stayed in bed the rest of the weekend trying to recover from Friday night, Alicia," Tina joked.

"Michael, were you in bed all weekend?" Alicia asked.

"You can say that," I answered without even looking up.

I stood up and went to the bathroom. On my way back I stopped in the break room to fix a cup of coffee. When I returned, Ms. Virginia was sitting at my desk waiting for me.

"Hey, Michael, did you get my message?" she asked.

"What message?"

"I sent you an email inviting you to my house for Thanksgiving."

"Oh! That email, I'm sorry I haven't read it yet. But yeah, sure I'll come."

"Look forward to having you, Michael."

Ms. Virginia walked off and went to the next desk to confirm her visitors.

"So, are you going to be my date, Michael?" Alicia asked, whispering so no one could overhear.

"Sure."

"What time should I be ready?"

"I don't know, what time is best for you?"

"I think she said she wanted us there by six, so I'll be ready by five-thirty."

"It's a date."

"I want some dessert afterward, Michael."

"Consider it done."

"Ummmm!"

As Thanksgiving approached, Alicia and I saw each other every other weekend. Whenever we were together we would always spend the night at my house. But on Saturdays, it would be after Cynthia and I spent our football afternoons.

By Thanksgiving, Alicia was ready to make our little office romance public. She convinced me that our relationship was our business and she didn't care if the people at work gossiped about us, or not.

We were excited about going to Ms. Virginia's together as a couple and we discussed it frequently. On Thanksgiving Day, she called and told me something had come up but she would be there later. I was disappointed but it was no big deal.

I arrived at Ms. Virginia's house fashionably late, after all of the small talk, and before dinner was served. Still, I arrived before Alicia. Everyone else was already there: Lisa, Darsha, Pam, Valerie, and Val's female friend. Susan, Tazzy, and her husband were there as well. Susan was alone, her husband was in New York on business. They were all seated at the table when I arrived. I took my place next to Pam. There were two open seats at the end of the extremely long table. Cynthia, Wanda, Jaline, and Tina were not expected because they were home with their families.

I looked across the table at Val and her friend. Val had her arm wrapped around her friend as if they were lovers.

I whispered to Pam, "What the hell is up with that?"

"You didn't know, Mike?" Pam asked.

"Know what? Val can't be gay, she's too damn fine!"

"Yeah, boy, Val pull more women than you."

"That's not saying much for her game, though, Pam."

The doorbell rang and Ms. Virginia went to answer. I heard Alicia's voice and I wanted to get up and run to one of the empty chairs so that I could sit beside her, but it was too late. It would be too obvious. Alicia turned the corner to the dining room and spoke to all of us at once.

"Hey, everybody! Happy Thanksgiving!"

I couldn't understand a single word she was saying because my eyes were affixed on her hand—clasped inside the hand of another man. As the man turned the corner, I could hear the breathing pause of the women in the room.

"Damn!" Pam said under her breath. "That's a fine-ass niggah right there!"

"Beautiful, just beautiful," Lisa said on my other side.

I couldn't believe what I was seeing and hearing. Alicia and I had spent the last month together making love like wild rabbits and when this Prince look-a-like walks back into her life she drops me like a bad habit. She took her boyfriend around the table so that everyone could speak to him. When she got to me, I could barely keep my head up straight. I felt like my heart was being ripped right out.

"Julian, this is Michael. He works with us at the office."

I was thinking to myself, *'work with you'? Woman, I'm knocking a hole in your back every freaking weekend!*

"Good to meet you, Michael," Julian said with a counterfeit French accent, "how do you do it?"

"Do what?" I asked nauseously.

"How do you keep your hands off all the women?"

I thought to myself again, *how could I keep my hands off your neck, girly boy?*

"You must either be a gay, or you have the strongest resistance to temptation that I've ever seen," Julian said, and then looked at everyone else and laughed.

Enough was enough, so I countered with, "No, I'm not *a gay*. Ask Alicia."

"What do you mean by that?" He looked at Alicia.

I stared at Alicia and she pulled Julian away and they sat in their seats. Dinner was practically over for me at that moment. I totally lost my appetite.

I played with my food until Pam said she was ready to leave. However, Lisa was her ride and she wasn't ready to go at that time. I offered to take her home just to get out of that uncomfortable situation with Alicia.

On the way home, I played some old school music and Pam knew every single song.

"Damn, Mike, I didn't know you even had it in you," she joked.

"Don't act like you don't know, Pam," I joked in return.

"Where you from, Mike, Massatushiss?"

"That's Massa-CHU-setts, and no, I'm from Michigan."

"You from Detroit?"

"No, I'm not from Detroit."

"Where you from in Michigan?"

"I'm from a place called Buena Vista."

"I bet it ain't no black folks up that way, huh?"

"I'll have you know there's nothing but black people in Buena Vista or BV, as we call it."

"Can y'all dance? You don't look like you can dance."

"Hell yeah, we can dance. You ever heard of the dance called the Snake? Or the Sconi?" I said excitely.

"I've heard of the Snake, but I haven't heard of no damn Sconi!"

"All of that came out of Detroit!"

"But you ain't from Detroit, Mike!" Pam laughed. "Why you tryin' to steal their props?"

"Hey, I'm from Michigan, though!"

"So what! You ain't from Detroit!"

"And I don't want to be from Detroit!"

"You think you got some music," Pam said, "wait till you see what I got up in my house."

"What you got up in your house, Pam?" I said, sarcastically mocking her.

"I'll show you. Can you come in and check it out?"

"Is it all right?"

"What you mean?"

"Don't you have children?"

"I don't have children. I have one child, a son."

"Is he at home?"

"No. He's visiting my parents in North Carolina for Thanksgiving."

"So I guess it's all right."

"Yeah, it's all right."

I parked the car and we joked all of the way into the house. Pam turned on her stereo and asked me to put in an old school CD. She handed me several remotes and went to change clothes. There were four remote controls in total and I couldn't control any of them. This technology from hell had so many gadgets, I thought I was in a radio station. Instead of turning on the CD player, somehow, I managed to cut everything off. I tried to manually cut it back on by pushing several power buttons but it still wouldn't play.

In the midst of my bumbling desperation Pam returned wearing a pair of baggy shorts and a cropped T-shirt, revealing a perfectly flat stomach. I knew that she noticed me staring but I couldn't help myself. I could tell from Pam's office clothes she had a nice figure, but my God, I had no idea she was built like that.

I always had imagined Pam as being a smart-mouthed, rough-edged woman. But here she was, smelling fresh, and looking so damn good! She and I were around the same age so she had to be either thirty-seven or thirty-eight. But her body didn't look a day over twenty-one and I'm not exaggerating one iota.

"Mike, what have you done to my stereo, man?"

"I don't know what's wrong with this thing."

"You broke it, that's what's wrong with it!"

"How do you cut it on?" I said, still fumbling with the buttons.

"Mike, you see this button that says 'power'? All you have to do is push it, like this." And just like that the stereo came back on.

"I pushed all kind of power buttons, Pam."

"Which power button did you push?"

"This one," I said, pointing to another power button.

"Mike, that's the damn VCR power button. That has nothing to do with the stereo."

Pam asked me if I wanted something to drink and I asked for a glass of juice. When she returned, we both sat on the floor and talked about the good old days when music was music.

"You know what, Mike? You're a cool brother."

"Hey, you're surprising the hell out of me too, Pam. I didn't think we could ever have a conversation when we saw eye to eye."

"There's a lot more to me than what I show at work."

"I can see that." I tapped her on the leg.

"You better cut that out, Mike. It's been a while for me, man."

"I don't believe that shit, Pam."

"I'm serious! I'm not your type, anyway."

"My type? What's my type?"

"Alicia." Pam smiled.

"Alicia? Why would you say that?" I thought about the conspiracy theory conversation with Cynthia.

"I am too natural of a woman for you. You look like you're attracted to those light-skinned model types…like Alicia."

"No, that's not true. What about me? Are you attracted to me?"

"You're okay, Mike."

"I'm 'okay'? Am I not urban enough for you?"

"'Urban'?"

"Ghetto then, Pam. Am I not ghetto enough for you?

"I know what urban means, niggah! It's not that you're not 'ghetto' enough. You're just too nice!"

"That should be a good thing."

"Nice is good. But too nice is boring."

"How am I 'boring'? You don't really know me if you think I'm boring."

"Well, prove me wrong, Mike. What exciting things do you do?"

"I do a lot of things."

"Like what?"

I sat there and couldn't think of one solitary exciting thing I'd done in recent months. Except for my fling with Alicia but I couldn't tell her that.

"None of your business, Pam."

"That's what I thought!"

I quickly changed the subject. "Why are you so abrasive at work but so easygoing outside of work?"

"It's because I hate that job."

"I would have thought you all loved your jobs the way you get along."

"Well, I ain't gon' lie, I do like my job. But me and management have issues."

"Who do you have issues with?"

"All of 'em. Did you know Ms. Virginia used to be supervisor up there?"

"Yeah, I heard something like that."

"Anyway, she was like my mentor, but then…"

Pam's Story

I was born in Jacksonville, Alabama but raised in Raleigh, North Carolina. I was raised in foster homes. My father was a good-for-nothing that left me when I was four. He would occasionally return to visit, but he'd never stay for long. My mother died giving me life and my father never let me forget it. He hated me and I hated him. Eventually I was adopted by a family that moved to North Carolina and I stayed with them until I graduated high school. I consider them to be my family.

I went to North Carolina State University on a track scholarship until I injured my knee. I was even an Olympic hopeful but after my injury my life changed drastically. I had to drop out of school because I couldn't afford to finish. I was depressed. The only bright spot in my life at the time was my boyfriend.

We were together the entire time I was in college. After I dropped out I still hung out on campus with him in his dorm. My boyfriend was a pretty good basketball player. So good he was drafted for the pros. We were supposed to get married but on the day he signed his contract, he told me we were too young to get married and it may interfere with his pro career. Of course I was crushed. Especially since the day before, I'd told him I was pregnant.

He was never a star but he played in the league for eight years. My son adores him and worships the ground he walks on. He takes good care of his son and although it was difficult at first, we get along for the most part. He also paid for me to finish getting my degree at N.C. State, so he wasn't all bad. But those are all the pleasant things I have to say about the man.

Eventually, I got tired of North Carolina and I wanted to simply move somewhere. Anywhere, it didn't matter. I had a friend from college who had moved down here to Atlanta and she asked me to move here with her. I never really had to work before. My son's father always took care of us financially. But I wanted to be independent and make my own money.

Once I settled in to Atlanta it didn't take long before I was working at Upskon.

When I started working there it was totally different from how it is now. Ms. Virginia was supervisor. And I think the only other person there was Tina. Lisa and Valerie came and then I think Alicia came next. We all got along well. Then the office started to grow and we hired more people. Wanda, Darsha and all of them came later on.

I was cool until Ms. Virginia quit being supervisor for personal reasons. Anyway, she had an opportunity to hire the next supervisor and because I had been there so long and we were so cool, I knew I was a shoo-in. But when they announced the position, it sure as hell wasn't me. It was Tazzy, who really had no experience and was fresh out of college. I felt that Ms. Virginia betrayed me and stabbed me in the back. That pissed me off and I've really had a shitty attitude ever since. Before they hired Tazzy, I really admired and wanted to be like Ms. Virginia. She and I, we try to be cordial to each other, but it's hard. It's harder for me than her, though, I'll admit that. But as far as the office girls, I'm not one of 'em. I may hang out with them as a group, but to me they're all counterfeit. I'll hang out with Wanda, and that's it.

"I need to quit trippin', don't I, Mike?"

"Yeah, because that doesn't sound like Ms. Virginia, Pam."

"Everybody says that. Maybe I'm just bitter."

"Sounds like it to me."

Pam hit me in the stomach, and sat on top of me.

"What you say?"

"All right now, I used to be a state champion wrestler. Now get off of me."

"Make me get off."

I grabbed Pam and turned her on her back. We wrestled for a while until I had her arms pinned above her head and my legs nestled between hers to stop her from moving. She tried to tussle her way out of it but to no avail.

"Now that you got me under your control, what you gon' do, Mike?"

I lowered my face down to hers and we started to kiss. She started to make moaning sounds that seemed to come from deep inside of her chest. Though she had a deep voice, her moans were very high-pitched. Child-like even, as if she were on the verge of crying. That noise drove me wild, but I remained calm and tenderly kissed her.

She opened up her legs and I lay between her tight muscular thighs. We ground on each other for a while until I was about to burst through my pants.

"I want to make love to you," I told her.

"You do?" she asked, with a slight smile.

"Yeah, baby," I moaned.

"Then do what you gotta do."

I kissed Pam up and down her neck. The more I kissed, the tighter she squeezed me with her thighs. I pulled her shorts down her legs and off of her feet. Then I unzipped my pants and wiggled out of them.

"Wait a minute, Mike."

I heard Pam say, "wait a minute," but then again she could have been saying, "we in the minute." I don't know what the hell that means but it sounds better than "wait a minute"!

"Mike! Get up! Get off me!" Pam shouted.

I rolled off. "What's wrong?"

"Nothing, I have to go get something."

Pam jumped and scampered into her bedroom. She made so much noise opening and slamming drawers it sounded as if she were ransacking the place. She finished what she was doing and dashed back into the living room.

"Okay, here, put this on."

Pam handed me a bunch of condoms.

"One of these bad boys will fit you."

"What the hell?" I said, holding the condoms in my hand. "I can tell you're not new at this."

"Please, just had my annual physical, I loaded up, in case!"

We continued to talk as I scrambled through the condoms to find my size. We talked as I slid one on.

"Would you have kept going if I hadn't stopped you?"

"Pam, to tell you the truth, as horny as I am there's no telling what I would have done. Now stop interviewing me and let me do what I 'gotta do.'"

I laid Pam on her back, and opened her thighs. I lay between her legs and on my first attempt to enter inside of her, she grimaced in pain and put her hands between us to resist my entry. I moved her hands out of the way and slowly entered her. Once we found the same rhythm I put her hands above her head and looked her straight in the eyes.

I would go in as far as I could, and then pull out until only the tip remained. Then I pushed back in again. I gave one slow deep thrust, and then pulled out again. Pam reached behind me and grabbed me by my ass. I started to move me at inward, downward, and then upward motion. I could feel her juices sticking, rolling down her thighs and sticking to mine.

We didn't do a lot of talking during our lovemaking session. There was no need to talk, our bodies were communicating well enough.

Pam opened up her thighs wider and lifted herself off the floor to get leverage. I put my hands beneath her ass to lift her even higher. She then wrapped her feet around my lower back area and let her head drop backward in midair. I held her in the air with one hand and braced myself on the floor with the other. It was amazing to see her buck her hips without touching the floor. It was as if she were defying gravity. She let out an ear-screeching squeal and her body shook as if she were having an epileptic fit.

"OH GOD BABY, I'M COMIN'!" Pam shouted. "OH GOD, I'M COMIN'!"

"That's right, come for me, baby!"

"I never thought it would feel this good, baby!" Pam said, breathing heavily.

She shut her eyes tight and tears were rolling down the side of her face toward her ears. Her violent reaction triggered my orgasm and we fell to the floor. Neither one of us stopped bucking. We were both having powerful orgasms simultaneously. I bent her body in half trying to release all of my juices. I let out a low-pitched, long deep groan that ended with loud explosive moans. Pam was finished with her orgasm while I was smack in the middle of mine so she tried to help me through it.

"OH MY GOD! You feel so good, baby!" I shouted.

"That's it, give it to me, baby! Give it to me, baby!" Pam yelled.

Believe me, I was trying to give her everything I had just like she asked.

"WHOO! WHOO!" I screamed, as the last drops shot out like liquid bullets.

"You, okay?" Pam asked.

"Yeah," I mumbled, breathing heavily, "I'm fine."

"You sound like the Incredible Hulk!"

"Ha-ha, very funny, Pam." I rolled over onto the floor, totally exhausted.

"I take it you enjoyed yourself," Pam asked.

"Indubitably."

"What the hell does that mean, Mike?"

"That means no doubt. No doubt, whatsoever."

"This feels so strange," Pam said, massaging my chest and arms.

"It doesn't feel strange to me. It feels natural," I said, caressing Pam's ass.

"I don't know, maybe it's because we work together."

"So where do we go from here?"

"We'll have to wait and see, Mike."

"Pam, can I ask you a question?"

"Sure, go ahead."

"When we were making love, you were crying at one point. I know I have a cracklike substance in my pants, but it can't be that good."

"You're right, it's good, but it ain't that damn good," Pam said jokingly. "I don't know, Mike, even though we haven't known each other that long I feel so comfortable with you. A comfort that I know I shouldn't have for a man I just met a few months ago."

"Were those tears of joy, or tears of sorrow?"

"Both."

"Both?"

"Yeah, the joy of sharing myself with someone and sorrow of knowing that person is not mine."

"Damn, I don't know what to say, Pam."

"Then don't say anything. Just lay here and shut up."

"I can do that."

I held Pam in my arms, and she fell fast asleep. While Pam slept, I wondered. I wondered how this would affect our relationship. I wondered what kind of expectations Pam would have now. Do I go through the same situation with her that I went through with Alicia?

I slept for a few hours, then I got up and went home. We pecked each other when I left but nothing like the passionate kiss Alicia and I had shared the morning after the first time we were together.

chapter 4

The next day was Friday, and we didn't have to work. I spent the majority of the day working on the office girls book. My words were crisp and clear about Pam because she was fresh in my mind. And despite my deep feelings for Alicia, my time with Pam seemed much more meaningful. I will confess that those words could be from a scorned man talking, but that's my story and I'm sticking to it.

My eyes began to hurt from staring at the computer but I was into my writing too much to stop at that point. As I was writing about my fling with Pam, it gave a sweet boost to my ego for the embarrassment Alicia had caused me. Contrarily, I also felt a sense of guilt. I felt as if I was committing an act of perfidy for exposing our relationship. But still, I couldn't let my emotions compromise the big picture. Two down, and the rest to go.

❖❖❖

Cynthia didn't come over that Saturday for our weekly football games because she was still visiting her family. I talked to my daughters on Sunday and we looked forward to our upcoming weekend. Late Sunday evening the telephone rang and it was Cynthia.

"Hey, bald man, what you doing?"

"Nothing, what are you doing, Old Mother Hubbard?"

"Nothing, miss me this weekend?"

"Nope."

"How was the Thanksgiving dinner?"

"It went all right."

"Guess what?"

"What?"

"I met this guy yesterday."

I don't know why it bothered me when Cynthia told me that, but it did.

"You met a guy?" I asked.

"Yeah, I met a guy. Imagine that."

"What kind of guy?"

"Just a guy! What do you mean, 'what kind of guy'?"

"I mean, what does he do? What is he like?"

"He's a chiropractor."

"Where did you meet him?"

"I met him at the art museum."

"What were you doing at the art museum?"

"Looking at art, silly."

"That figures, you nerd."

"Hey! I gotta go, that's him on the other line."

"Hold on?"

Click!

"Damn, Cynt, you didn't have to hang the phone up in my face," I mumbled into the telephone.

Over the last few months Cynthia had been like one of the boys, and just like that she went out and started dating. It didn't seem fair.

I had a hard time sleeping that night. Monday would be very interesting. I would have to sit in front of Alicia, who had dumped me by bringing her boyfriend on our date. Then I would have to talk to Pam, who'd made love to me like we had been in love forever. And I would have to hear my buddy talk about meeting some knucklehead chiropractor who probably didn't know his ass from a hole in the ground. By the time I finally fell asleep, it was time to get up and go to work. I was so wired up, I felt no residual exhaustion.

❖❖❖

I was one of the first to arrive at work. Like clockwork they all began to file in, and I didn't have to wait long before Alicia arrived. I had made up my mind that I wasn't going to pay her any attention. But when she walked in wearing a mini-skirt with open-toed shoes, I was done.

"Good morning, Michael."

"Good morning, Alicia."

"Can I please talk to you about Thanksgiving?" she asked.

"No explanation needed."

"I didn't know he was coming to town until he showed up at my house, Michael."

"Whatever, Alicia."

I stood up to go to the break room and Alicia tried to grab my arm. I snatched away and kept walking.

"Michael," Alicia said softly but sternly so that no one else could hear. "Michael, listen to me, please."

I ignored her. As I was walking in the break room, Pam was walking out.

"Hey, Mike," Pam spoke, with a sneaky grin.

"What's funny?"

"Oh, nothing."

Pam turned around and followed me back into the break room. When I turned around, she grabbed me by my shirt and kissed me slowly, all tongue, I might add.

"Thanks," Pam said.

"What for?"

"For that late Thanksgiving dinner."

"Believe me, the pleasure was all mine."

"Will you call me the next time you want to listen to old school CDs?" Pam asked.

"Indubitably."

I pushed her gently against the vending machine that was at the far end of the break room. That way, if someone came in, we would have time to react before they saw us. I started to kiss Pam savagely. I opened her legs with my legs, and lifted her skirt. I stuck my hands in her underwear and began to fondle her. She was already soaking wet, so I slipped my finger inside. She started to grind on my finger, and we started to kiss harder. Within seconds, her body became limp, and she started moaning loudly. I covered her mouth to keep the rest of the office from hearing her screams. She held on to me to keep from sliding to the floor.

"Oh my, God," Pam said, "oh shit, I needed that."

I helped her stand up and she fixed her clothes. When she was leaving we started to kiss again, but the door came open, and we jumped away from each other. It was Alicia and she was looking directly at me.

"Can I talk to you please, Michael?"

"Is it urgent?"

"Yes, it's very urgent."

"Well, I need to get back to my desk, anyway. Talk to you later, Mike," Pam said.

"See ya later, Pam," I said.

Pam waved as she was walking out of the door. Once Alicia turned her head, Pam secretly blew me a kiss.

"What was that all about?"

"What?"

"When did you and Pam become so buddy-buddy?"

"We were just in the break room at the same time, that's all."

"Michael, look I'm sorry about Thanksgiving. I didn't know he was coming to town."

"You could have told me you were bringing him, Alicia!"

"How? How could I have told you he was coming?"

"With your mouth!" I said angrily.

"Stop raising your voice at me, Michael."

"I'm not raising my voice."

"I'm sorry, Michael, how can I make it up to you?"

"You wanna know how you can make it up to me?"

"Yeah, baby, I'll do anything."

"Kiss my ass!" I said. Then I walked out without turning back to look at her. I went into the bathroom to wash my hands. As I was going in, Pam was coming out.

"Michael!" Pam said jokingly, nodding her head in greeting.

"Pamela!" I said back, then returned her nod in greeting.

Alicia stayed in the break room for a while. When she returned to her desk, she didn't look at me. I guess I had gotten my message across. I pretended I didn't see her as well.

Suddenly I felt the cold well-digger's hands of Cynthia covering my eyes.

"What's up, man?" Cynthia asked.

"What's up, Cynt?"

"I had a ball this weekend."

I knew it was only a matter of seconds before she began to rave about her new boyfriend.

"I can't wait for you to meet Stewart, Mike. You two are going to get along so well."

"Why do you say that?"

"Because you're just alike."

"I don't think so, Cynt."

"How do you know, you haven't even met him?"

"Believe me, I know."

"He's coming to visit me this weekend."

"Is he staying with you?"

"Of course, where else is he going to stay?"

"I don't think that's a good idea, Cynt."

"Why not? He's a nice guy."

"But you just met the guy."

"So what?"

"So you should be more careful."

"What's wrong with him staying with me?"

"Nothing."

"No. Tell me, Michael. What's wrong with him staying with me?"

"I didn't think you were like that."

"Like what?"

"Forget it, Cynt."

"No, let's not forget it," Cynthia said, "like what?"

"Okay," I said, "like meet a guy one week and sleep with him the next."

"Okay, so now I'm a whore?"

"I didn't call you a whore, Cynt."

"That's okay, Michael! Thanks for nothing!" she said as she stormed off.

"Cynt! Cynt!" I tried to stop her but she ignored me. I knew she was pissed. She only called me "Michael" when she was pissed.

"Are you in love with her, Michael?" Alicia asked.

"In love with who, Alicia?"

"Are you in love with Cynthia?"

"Aw, damn! Now what are you talking about?"

"I heard you, Michael. Why were you so against her having a man visit? It's none of your business who she sees and what she does."

"See, that's where you're wrong. It is my business. It's my business because she's my friend and I care about her."

"I believe you're in love with her."

"A woman like you can never understand a man and a woman just being friends."

"What do you mean by that?"

"You think you're so beautiful that a man can never love you for being you. You're never going to be happy and you're never going to be satisfied because you can't see past your own beauty to see your own soul."

"You black bastard!"

"Black, I am. Bastard, I am not. Unlike that mutt of a boyfriend you had on your arm Thursday night."

"At least he loves me."

"Woman, please, he only sees you every six months; the other six months, he's sleeping with real models."

"So are you calling me a fool, Michael?"

"You said it, I didn't."

I could see the tears begin to form in her eyes and I wanted the arguing to

cease. I also realized the times we'd spent together were much more important for Alicia, than me. To me, she was the fantasy I had always dreamed of
fulfilling, a beautiful sexy woman making love to me. To her, I was the man
she had always dreamed of marrying, a man who loved her for her soul, and
not her beauty. I had just destroyed what made our relationship special. My
lack of understanding of who she was made me every other man to her.

"Alicia, I'm sorry. I didn't mean it like that."

"You know what, Michael? I barely slept this weekend thinking about how
you may have been hurting. Julian tried to touch me but I wouldn't let him
because all I could think about was you. I should have let Julian have his way,
that's all that matters, anyway, huh?"

"You need to calm down so that we can talk about this rationally."

"Too late for that, Michael! Don't say anything to me unless it's dealing
with Upskon!"

"I'm afraid I can't do that, Alicia."

"Just leave me alone!"

"No, I care about you and I want to apologize for hurting your feelings,
okay?"

"Your apology is accepted," Alicia said, with a big smile across her face.

I thought to myself, *good, now she's not mad at me anymore*. Then I thought
a second time, and asked myself what the hell had happened? Why was I
apologizing after I was the one who had been abused? Sneaky-ass woman
had duped me and duped me good!

❖❖❖

For the next couple of days neither Alicia nor Cynthia had much to say to
me. On the other hand, Pam and I were meeting in every nook and cranny
we could find. On one occasion, I asked Pam to meet me in the men's bathroom. We met after lunch when everybody had made their afternoon bathroom runs. When she came in, the lights were off, and I immediately
pounced on her. She had taken her bra off in preparation for our meeting.
And I was already unzipped, hard, swinging and waiting for her. Knowing

how spontaneous our meetings were, I had learned to keep a few condoms stashed in my lower drawer. So if we were really heated, there would be nothing to prevent us from getting a quickie.

I went straight for Pam's breasts, and started sucking on them as if I had not eaten in a month. I turned her around, then lifted her skirt from the back. She gripped the sink, lowered her shoulders, and raised her ass in the air.

"Come on, baby, hurry up!" Pam whispered. "I need it."

I wasted no time pushing myself deep inside, then grabbing her hips and pulling her back to me.

"Oh yeah, baby, faster!" Pam cried.

"Shh! Quiet, baby."

"I can't help it, baby! I can't help it! Faster, baby, I'm almost there!"

I reached around and covered Pam's mouth. When she reached her orgasm, she grabbed the sink to brace herself, then rammed backward so hard, I lost my balance and almost slammed into the door. She continued to ram backward until her orgasm subsided.

"Oh God, that's some good shit, baby!" Pam whispered.

"Shhh!"

"Ooh, baby! That felt so good," Pam moaned, reaching back and rubbing my thighs as she slowed her grinding to a halt. "I can't believe you got me doing it all over this office like this, Mike."

I pulled my pants up and Pam arranged her skirt. As we were sharing the sink cleaning ourselves, we continued to whisper.

"We can stop if you like," I said.

"Yeah, like you wanna stop."

"Hey, you know, it's up to you," I said with a wicked smile.

"You talk too much. Look out the door and see if the coast is clear," she suggested.

I cracked the door, and peeked out. Tazzy and Susan were standing in the hall having a discussion. Meanwhile, Pam was being paged over the speaker, which created a dilemma.

"You can't go out there, Pam."

"Why not?"

"Tazzy and Susan are standing right there in the hallway."

"I got to go, they're paging me."

"What are you going to tell them? 'Excuse me, Tazzy and Susan, I'm coming out of the men's bathroom because I just had sex with Mike'?"

"Look, I'm leaving!" Pam opened the door and walked out.

"Pam! Pam!" I whispered nervously. "Get back in here!"

She walked past Tazzy and Susan, and I overheard her ask them to come to her desk for a second. She needed to show them something. They quickly followed her back to her desk, giving me an opportunity to escape.

"Brilliant!" I said.

When I walked out, Ms. Virginia was walking into the women's bathroom that was only inches away. In the midst of pushing the door open, she paused, then looked at me. She turned and looked in Tazzy, Susan, and Pam's direction and looked at them. She looked at me again, turned up an eyebrow, and went inside.

On my way back to my desk, I past Susan and Tazzy standing at Pam's desk. I overheard Pam tell them that her computer was functioning properly now and their assistance was no longer needed. They walked away and Pam looked over her shoulder and gave me a smile. I smiled back and mouthed the word, "Brilliant."

❖❖❖

For the remainder of the week Alicia and Cynthia spoke to me sparingly. By Friday, I was so excited to be getting my girls it didn't matter, anyway. They lived on opposite sides of the city: Brimone lived in Lithonia, on the eastern side of town; and Alexiah lived in the Buckhead district, north of downtown. I lived in Lawrenceville, which is located northeast of Atlanta. When you factor in the Friday evening traffic it's like we all live in different parts of the country.

By the time we got home it was after eight. I fixed some popcorn and we watched movies until they fell asleep. The girls had become pretty close to

Cynthia over the past months, and they had planned a busy day of shopping and doing other girlie things the next day. This arrangement had been planned prior to her meeting her wonderful new boyfriend. She wasn't talking to me, so I was going to tell the girls that something had come up and she couldn't make it. But I didn't have to do that because Cynthia called bright and early and told me to get the girls ready.

"Hey, what's up?"

"I'm surprised to hear from you," I said.

"Why?"

"Because you're not speaking to me."

"What does that have to do with my girls?"

"Oh, nothing, I guess."

"Put Brimone on the phone, please."

"All right, hold on." I yelled, "Bri-mone! Pick up the phone!"

"Hello," Brimone said.

"How's my big girl?"

"Hi, Ms. Cynthia, are you still going shopping with us?"

"Yes, Ma'am. I'll be over in an hour to pick you up."

"Can you comb our hair? I like it when my daddy comb my hair, but I want you to do it."

"Bri, I'm still on the phone," I said.

"Sorry, Daddy."

"You don't like the way I comb your hair?"

"Yes, Daddy, but I want to see if Ms. Cynthia can do something different."

"Leave that girl alone, Mike, before I come over there and slap you upside your bald head."

"See, Cynt, you need to go back to not speaking to me again."

"Like you always say, 'I can do that.'"

"Ms. Cynthia, can we have a sleepover tonight?"

"A sleepover?"

"Yes, Ma'am. Can you bring your night clothes and spend the night with us?"

"That may not be a good idea, sweetheart. We will have so much fun when we go shopping, you won't care if I spend the night or not."

"I still want you to spend the night with us," Brimone pleaded. "Daddy, tell Ms. Cynthia to spend the night with us."

"I can't make her spend the night, Bri."

"Ms. Cynthia, can you spend the night with us? Pleeeeeeeeease?"

"We'll see, Bri," Cynthia said. "Right now, Mike, get my girls ready to go. I'll be over there in an hour."

"All right, see you when you get here." I hung up the phone.

"See you in a minute, Bri."

"All right, bye."

"Bye."

"All right girls, get in the tub!" I yelled.

"Dad," Brimone said.

"Yes, baby."

"I don't take baths anymore. I'm thirteen, I take showers."

"What are you talking about? You take baths with Alex all the time."

"Dad, I give Alex baths all the time."

"What the hell?" I said.

"Daddy, stop cussing!" Alex said.

"I'm sorry, baby," I said, smiling at Alex. "I meant, what the bleep?"

"Dad, I'm not a baby anymore."

"Well, you're my baby."

The girls took their baths and waited for Cynthia. I kept looking at Brimone and thinking how much she'd grown. Then I would look at Alex and think that one day she would be the same age. Taking showers on her own, talking to boys, and not needing me as much. I cringed at the thought. I picked her up and kissed her on the cheek. I put on Stevie Wonder's "Isn't She Lovely," and we danced. To my surprise, Brimone told me to put Alexiah down so that she could get her dance.

"Dad, have you spoken to Mama lately?"

"No, why?"

"Uh, I think she better tell you."

"No, you tell me," I said, putting my hands on my hips, "now."

"Da-ddy, Mom's gonna tell you."

As if on cue to save Brimone, Cynthia, rang my doorbell precisely one hour from the time she'd hung up the phone. As soon as she stepped through the door, the girls attacked.

"Can you do our hair, Ms. Cynthia?" Brimone asked.

"Yes, can you do our hair, Ms. Cyn-tia?" Alexiah repeated.

"Go get your hair stuff, we got to hurry up!"

They ran and grabbed their hair items and jetted back into the den. Cynthia combed their hair in a matter of minutes, whereas, it takes me an hour to braid one ponytail. They looked in the mirror to view their hairstyles and hugged her with their stamps of approval. While they were admiring themselves, the phone rang. I answered in the kitchen.

"Hello."

"Can I come over?"

"Now is not a good time."

"Too late, I'll be there in five minutes."

"Alicia, don't do that. My daughters are with me this weekend."

"So what? You don't have a problem with Cynthia coming over while they're there!" Alicia snapped. "I think now is a fine time to meet them."

"No. Not today."

Alicia was quiet momentarily, and then she spoke in a very needy voice that gave me reason to be concerned.

"Please, Michael, I really need to see you. Julian and I broke up."

"All right, Alicia. My daughters are about to go shopping with Cynthia. Give me a few minutes and I'll call you back."

"Okay, baby, I'll wait for you to call back."

"Okay, bye."

"Bye-bye."

I hung up and went back into the den.

"Is everybody ready to get out?" I said jokingly.

"Yup," Brimone said.

"Yup," Alexiah repeated.

"Here's my credit card. Don't let them go crazy, Cynt."

"Girls, that means we can get anything we want, now thank Daddy."

"Thanks, Daddy," Brimone said.

"Thanks, Daddy," Alexiah repeated.

"All right, get out!" I opened the door.

"Bye, Daddy!" the girls shouted in unison, kissing me on the cheek and running out of the door.

"Bye, Daddy!" Cynthia said, kissing me on the cheek.

"Take care of my kids, Cynt, especially that grown Bri!"

"Better than you would, knucklehead."

I closed the door and went upstairs to take a shower. In the middle of my shower my doorbell rang. I jumped out with nothing but a towel, thinking Cynthia and the girls had forgotten something.

"I'm coming! I'm coming!"

I looked through the peephole and saw Alicia.

"What's up, come in." I opened the door and stepped to the side.

"Thanks for the return call."

"I was trying to get my girls out of here and it slipped my mind."

"What are you doing?"

"I'm taking a shower."

"Looks like I came at the right time," Alicia said, squeezing my penis in her hand.

"Not quite," I said, moving her hand and wrapping my towel tightly around my waist. "Well, I got to get back in the shower."

"Don't let me stop you."

I showed Alicia to the den and went back into the shower. Within a matter of minutes my shower door opened and Alicia was standing, butt naked.

"Scoot over."

"Alicia, this is not a good idea right now."

"There's nobody here but us."

"Yeah, but we don't know when they're coming back."

"They're not here now, so let's enjoy ourselves."

"I can't, Alicia. My kids might come back here!" I said, becoming very annoyed.

"Come on, Michael, you don't want me anymore?" Alicia said, rubbing my chest.

"Right now, no!"

Alicia grabbed my penis, which was harder than Chinese arithmetic, and squeezed it tightly.

"Well, I think you better tell your little head, 'cause he's saying something different."

"Alicia, please, get out and put your clothes on! Please!"

"Come on, Michael!" she responded, kissing me on my chest.

"Look! Don't you understand? My kids could come back at any time, Alicia!" I shouted.

"Is it your kids, or Cynthia, you're worried about?"

"Let me tell you something! I don't give a damn about you, or any other woman, when it comes to the welfare of my kids! Now go put your damn clothes on! NOW!" I yelled, extremely pissed off.

"All right, Michael." Alicia was embarrassed and realized I was not going to give in to her temptation. Alicia stepped out of the shower and put back on her clothes. I rushed my shower and went to talk to her.

"Look, I didn't mean to be rude, but I can't jeopardize my children finding me in an inappropriate situation like this." I found myself apologizing once again. But this time she wasn't going to manipulate me in to feeling as if I had done something wrong.

"I understand, Michael, you don't have to explain."

"Maybe we should go get a bite to eat or something."

"That's fine, I just need to be with you."

I turned to go into my bedroom, then turned around to her. "It's ironic that you only seem to need me when Julian is not around."

"That's not true, Michael."

"Yes, it is. But it's okay. Because at least now I know where we stand."

I got dressed and we left to have lunch. Cynthia called me every couple of hours to let me know that everything was going superbly with the girls on their day out. Alicia and I went to the park and walked and talked for a while. I listened patiently to her go on and on about her breakup with Julian. Afterward, I told her we could continue to see each other but it would be a platonic relationship. I kissed her good-bye and went home to wait for Cynthia to bring my daughters.

They didn't get home until the late evening and I was going out of my mind. I know how badly they wanted their girls' day out, but it was taking time out of my weekend with them. However, if that made them happy, it made me happy, too.

When I opened the door to let them in, it was as if they had brought back something from every store in the mall.

"Cynt, how much money did you spend?"

"Shut up, Mr. Thurston Howell the third, I didn't even use your card."

"Then how did you pay for all this stuff?"

"I ain't broke, boy."

"I know you didn't spend your money on my kids?"

"No, Mike, I spent my money on my kids."

"Daddy, please tell Ms. Cynthia to spend the night with us," Brimone asked.

"Yeah, Daddy, please tell Ms. Cynthia to spend the night with us," Alexiah repeated.

"All right," I said, "Ms. Cynthia, would you please spend the night with us?"

Cynthia went into one of the many bags and pulled out matching T-shirts, shorts, and socks for her and the girls.

"Ta-dah!" Cynthia said, holding the T-shirts in one hand, and the shorts and socks in the other. "I accept your invitation, oh bald king of the castle."

"Are you three the Bobbsey twins?" I said, holding up the matching outfits.

"Twins are two people, Daddy; there are three of us." Brimone laughed.

"Whatever! You know what I mean."

"Daddy, can we sleep down here on the floor?"

"I don't care, Bri."

"You too, Daddy," Alexiah said.

"I think you girls should sleep down here, and Daddy should sleep in his room, Alex," I said.

"Daddy, please!" Brimone said.

"All right, girl, stop whining."

"Go get your stuff, Daddy."

"I'll be back in a minute."

I changed into my ESPN attire and joined the girls in the den. Cynthia had bought the girls matching sleeping bags, and they had them spread out and were ready for bed by the time I returned. They started to sing songs and I did what any red-blooded American man would do under the circumstances. I turned on the television and watched ESPN. They were having so much fun with each other they forgot all about me. As it turned late, Alexiah found a comfortable spot with her head on my chest and fell asleep. It wasn't much longer before Brimone had rested on my shoulder in deep sleep as well.

"You wore them out today, Cynt."

"They wore me out, too. I couldn't get up if I wanted to."

"Do you want a cup of coffee?"

"It's kinda late for coffee, Mike."

"This is our first slumber party; we can't go to sleep this early."

"Okay, but hurry up."

"Yes, Ma'am," I said.

I laid my girls in their sleeping bags, then went into the kitchen and put on a pot of coffee. The aroma from the coffee drifted throughout the house and the outdoor cool weather made the moment that much more comforting. When the pot was finished, I fixed cups of coffee for Cynthia and me. We sipped and we talked.

"So, Cynt, I thought your new friend was coming to stay with you this weekend."

"I told him I thought it would be better if we waited a while for a big step like that."

"Hey, look, Cynt, if I offended you at work about him coming to visit you, I apologize."

"You did offend me," Cynthia said, then flashed that big pretty smile, "and I accept your apology."

"I was about to tell my girls you weren't going to make it."

"Even if he had come, I wasn't going to break my promise to those babies."

"Let me ask you something, Cynt. I know I'm your boy, but why are you so nice to my children?"

"Well, I love them and..."

Cynthia's Story

I was born and raised in Savannah, Georgia. Savannah is an old city rich with antebellum culture and history. In the summer we used to always go to Tybee Island and hang out on the beach. We used to try to get summer jobs at one of the hotels but when we did, we didn't make a lot of money.

After I graduated from high school, I attended college at the University of Tennessee in Knoxville. I met a boy from Shreveport, Louisiana and we dated a couple of years. I had never been the type of woman to date a lot of men. As a matter of fact, before my husband, I had only been with one other man in my entire life. So, I was quite content with being in a monogamous relationship.

My husband was quite a different story. He was a lady's man who chased every pretty thing in a skirt. He knew that if he wanted this skirt, he had to stop chasing the others.

He tried to court me the first day I stepped foot on campus when we were both freshmen. He told me he wanted me and I told him that if he wanted me, he was going to have to marry me. He continued to pursue me our sophomore and junior years. I ran from that man for almost three years, eventually I gave him a chance.

We started dating our senior year, but nothing physical. Once we got our degrees, we figured it was time to get married and start our lives as mature responsible adults. We both found great jobs making more money than we had ever seen in our lives.

Our first couple of years of marriage were magical. It was everything I'd expected and more. I became pregnant with twins, two beautiful girls. Then we bought a house in the suburbs. After the twins were born, it brought us even closer together; it was like a fantasy come true.

My fairytale turned into a nightmare on a Sunday afternoon when we were on our way home from church. We had the twins strapped in the backseat and we were maybe a mile from our home when the car in front of us slammed on its brakes trying to avoid hitting an animal. This made my husband slam on his brakes which made the driver behind us slam on his brakes, and although he tried, he couldn't stop and rammed into us from behind.

The impact caused my husband to lose control of the car sending us head on into the oncoming path of a semi-truck. My husband and children were killed instantly. I was ejected from the car and knocked unconscious. When I regained consciousness I was lying in a hospital room. My injuries were not life-threatening but I was pretty banged up. My family came to visit me and tried to lift my spirit, but all that I could think about was the loss of my family. No one could explain why I had survived a horrendous accident like that. Frankly, after losing my family, I wished I would have died that day.

I haven't seriously dated since my husband died and I haven't been intimate with a man at all. But when the right man comes along, I'll give him everything I got.

After the accident, I couldn't continue to live in Knoxville. It was too painful. And I wasn't going back to Savannah. So Atlanta seemed to be the logical choice.

I worked a few places and then I got the job at Upskon. It paid very well. I love the girls from the office. But I only hang with them outside of work if we're in a group. I don't have time to become a part of their cliques.

Ms. Virginia, on the other hand, is a different story. She is nothing short of an angel. She, Tina, and I go to lunch and have dinner together sometime. She helped me get settled when I started working there. She was the supervisor when I first started. I don't know how much longer I'll be working there because I'm starting a public relations firm and it will be off the ground real soon. When I do leave, I'll miss that office because they've been my family here in Atlanta.

❖❖❖

"I never knew you had children, Cynt."

"No one does. It's not anything I talk about, brings back too many sad memories."

"I'm so sorry to hear about your family."

"Thanks, there's not a day that goes by I don't think of them and that accident. There's not a day that passes when I don't think that maybe if we had stayed at church a little longer, or left church a little sooner, everything would have been different. And I would still have my family."

"Why haven't you told me this until now?"

"I don't know, being with these girls today really allowed me to open up and want to talk about the accident. These girls know that I'm not their mother, but they love me, Mike. They love me. Just like my babies would have loved me. Don't think I'm crazy, but being with these girls fills an empty space in my heart."

"I don't think you're crazy at all, Cynt. I think you're the most incredible woman I've ever met."

"Don't take this the wrong way. You're a wonderful father and you love these girls as much as any woman can love her child, but you're a man. But by being a man, you're not going to understand some of the little things that make a little girl happy. But if there's anything I can do to help out with these girls, please don't hesitate to call on me."

"I can do that."

"Have they told you what they have planned for tomorrow?"

"Uh, no."

"Just giving you a little heads-up. Tomorrow is hair and makeup day. I'm going to let them play with makeup and wash their hair for them. They're going to extend an invitation to you so that you won't feel left out."

"I think I'll pass on that one."

"See, this is one of the times when you don't understand what it's like to be a little girl. I know that's not your thing but if you don't play with the girls, they won't enjoy themselves because they'll feel like they're leaving you out."

"Oh…oh, I didn't think of it that way."

"Well, now you know."

"I'll play, but I won't be putting on any of that makeup crap. And need I remind you of the hair situation?"

"I can see where we stand on the hair situation, bald man."

"Very funny!"

"Um, I spoke to Brimone today," Cynthia said. "I was surprised you said she could go on a date?"

"What date?"

"Oops, my bad! I'll let her mother tell you."

"Cynt, don't play with me, what date?"

"Well, if I tell you, you have to promise you won't say a word…promise?"

"You know I can't keep that promise."

"Well, I'm not going to tell you."

"Okay fine, I'll wake Bri up and ask her!"

"Mike! You can't do that! We were having a girl talk!"

"Well, you better tell me, then."

"Okay, bald man, but this is blackmail."

"Okay, I am a black male, now let it out!"

"It's nothing major. A boy has asked her to their spring dance and she wants to go with him."

"Not gonna happen."

"Mike, don't do her like that. She likes this boy."

"Do you think talking like that is going to help her case? And why is that boy asking about a spring dance in December?"

"That's how they do nowadays."

"Well, the answer is still, no."

"Come on, Mike. She's going to be very disappointed."

"Life is full of disappointments."

"She may wind up resenting you for not letting her go."

"That's okay, I have another daughter!"

"Mike, please don't mention it. It may ruin her trust in me."

"Shit, man," I said, "all right."

"Thanks, and Alex is right, you curse too much."

Cynthia and I talked for a little while longer, the conversation fizzled and she fell asleep. The next morning, I was the last to wake up, but not on my on accord. Cynthia and the girls were jumping on top of me. We wrestled around the room and at one point, I happened to look down at Cynthia's feet and notice that she was wearing no socks. If this was any other woman it would be nothing, but of all the times I'd spent with Cynthia, I had never seen her feet. Not at work. Not at home when we're just relaxing, not ever. I presumed it was because her feet were so hideous she was simply too embarrassed to show them publicly. And had they been, I would have continued about my business. But her toes were so perfectly manicured. And her feet were unblemished.

"Cynt, you have very pretty feet."

"Stop looking at my feet, you perv."

"No, I'm serious. I thought your feet had calluses by the way you're always hiding them."

"I don't hide my feet and stop looking at 'em," Cynthia said, trying to hide her feet.

"They're pretty, man, why are you ashamed?"

"I'm not ashamed. Do you have a foot fetish, or something?"

"Daddy, what's a foot fetish?" Brimone asked.

"It's someone who likes feet."

"I like my feet. Do I have a foot fetish?"

"Look at what you've done, Cynt, you turned my baby into a freak," I joked.

"Daddy, what's a freak?"

"Bri, stop asking so many questions."

"Daddy, I'm hungry," Alexiah said.

"I'm about to cook breakfast. What do you want?"

"I want some bacon. And I want some cookies. And I want some…"

"Alex, you know you're not getting any cookies."

"Can I have some candy?"

"No."

"Can I have some donuts?"

"Alex, no! You're going to have eggs and bacon, okay?"

"I don't like bacon and eggs, Daddy."

"Alex, you love bacon and eggs."

"Not anymore, I don't."

"I have an idea!" Cynthia shouted. "Let's go to McDonald's and get breakfast!"

"McDonald's is cool!" Brimone shouted.

"I want some McDonald's, too!" Alexiah screamed.

"McDonald's? You're going to get the same food at McDonald's as you're getting…"

"Mike!" Cynthia shouted, interrupting me.

"All right, hurry up and put some clothes on before I change my mind,"

The girls zoomed in the bathroom. Cynthia took a shower in one of the guest bedrooms we never used while I cleaned up their mess in the den. Afterward she walked around for a few minutes in only a long T-shirt that revealed her legs. Her feet were not the only attractive feature below her waistline. I couldn't take my eyes off of her legs. I had never imagined Cynthia having sexy feminine attributes. But, lo and behold, there she was right before my very eyes. I complimented her on her legs and she blew me off as if she didn't hear me. That was the end of that.

Later that day, the girls asked me to play beauty shop with them. Having already been briefed by Cynthia about the girls' invitation, I accepted with great enthusiasm. I was pretty much the assistant passing items from one to the other. Seeing my girls have so much fun really put a smile on my face.

It was Sunday, so when the evening fell upon us, I took the girls home and Cynthia left as well. The house felt so lonely after they were gone. I went to my computer and started to work on the office girls.

I was really making progress with the book. I had gotten Alicia, Pam, and Cynthia to open up and tell me their personal stories. The real face of the office girls was beginning to show. Perhaps they weren't as close as they appeared to be. At first, I had believed I'd discovered the lost Amazon tribe. They seemed to get along so well. But the reality of a group of women working together without their petty little female issues was only a fantasy. Day by day—no, hour by hour—they began to fill the pages of my book with their emotional office antics. Three down and the rest to go!

chapter 5

I regretted going to work on Monday. The office girls were going to do their diet contest and I wanted no part of it. They were buzzing around one another's desks like flies so I knew it would affect me in some manner. We had high traffic passing through our zone because Alicia was the biggest fan of this contest. At one point it looked like the entire office was at her desk.

"Everybody ready for the diet contest?" Alicia asked.

"I don't need a diet contest to tell me how beautiful my butt is," Darsha responded, patting her butt.

"The scale can't tell one ass from another," Valerie said.

"I think I did pretty good last week," Alicia said, looking at her own behind.

"Alicia, you know better than to be struttin' yo' butt in front of Val like that." Darsha laughed.

"Alicia's not my type."

"Well, what's your type, Val?" Darsha asked.

"You, babygirl," Valerie said sarcastically.

"Oh, hell nawl !!!" Darsha shouted.

"Stop talking to Darsha like that, Val, before you scare that girl to death," Alicia said.

"I don't know! Babygirl young, but she looks like she might be a little freaky," Valerie said.

"I'm freaky. But I ain't that damn freaky!"

"Would you ever date a woman, Darsha?" Alicia asked.

"HELL TO THE NAWL !!!"

"Y'all don't know what you're missing," Valerie said.

"I got the same thing any other woman got, so it ain't nothin' a woman can do for me!" Darsha said emphatically.

"A woman can satisfy another woman like a man can't because she knows what it takes to satisfy herself," Valerie responded.

"Man, I don't even want to hear that crazy-ass shit, Val," Darsha said. "What about the di..."

"Watch that mouth, girl," Alicia said, interrupting her.

"Hell, we can buy the necessary attachments," Valerie said.

"If it ain't attached to a man, I don't want it," Darsha said, waving her hand.

"Darsha, you too young to know what you want."

"I know what I wanted last night, Val, and I got mine," Darsha said, "twice!"

Ms. Virginia, Lisa, Wanda, and Pam walked over to Alicia's desk and joined the tail end of the conversation.

"I know what I wanted last night, and I got mine, too. Twice!" Valerie shouted.

"I know what I wanted last night, too. And if my husband hadn't been sniffin' all up my ass I woulda got it," Wanda said.

"If it wasn't your husband you wanted, what was it? Or *who* was it, Wanda?" Lisa asked.

"Me! Butt naked and horny as hell!" Wanda shouted. "A little privacy, a little nakedness, and a little candlelight can be a little heaven."

The girls laughed and Alicia quickly interrupted.

"Hey, let's do the diet contest right quick," she said with enthusiasm.

"Let's do this weight contest befo' Alicia drive me crazy!" Wanda snapped.

The office girls chatted as they walked to the break room, the place where the infamous weight contest was held. On their way, Pam and Wanda grabbed me by both of my arms and pulled me with them. I sat down and prepared for the entertainment.

"You get on first, Val," Alicia said.

"I don't wanna get on first, Alicia. You get on first."

"Lisa, you get up there then."

"What's wrong with you getting up there first, Alicia?"

"Because I wanna go last."

"One of you get up there before our break is over," Ms. Virginia said.

"Okay, I'll go first." Alicia jumped on the scale.

"Alicia, you knew you wanted to go first, anyway," Valerie said, patting Alicia on her behind, "now get on up there, baby."

"All right now, Val, you better cut that out," Alicia joked back.

Ms. Virginia waited for Alicia to stop moving and looked down at the scale.

"What's the verdict?" Alicia asked.

"Alicia, you have lost a total of fifteen pounds of your goal weight of twenty. Putting you at seventy-five percent and also putting you in the lead right now," Ms. Virginia said.

Alicia jumped off the scale, pointed her finger in the faces of the women, and shouted, "I told you! I told you I was going to lose the most weight! Didn't I?"

"Alicia, you've only lost a few pounds, not won the lottery," Lisa responded.

"Don't hate," Alicia shouted again, holding up her hands. "Don't hate on me!"

I was surprised to see Alicia exhibiting so much excitement. She was normally so quiet and reserved.

"I don't mean to brag, ladies, but it's not easy to maintain this. But don't hate!" Alicia gave high-fives to everybody and sat down.

"Chick probably don't even know what the word 'hate' means," Wanda whispered to Pam.

"Probably don't. Funny how people can go from acting professional to ghetto fantabulous in a matter of seconds," Pam whispered back.

"Let me get this out of the way." Valerie sighed, stepping on the scale.

Ms. Virginia adjusted the scale and said, "Val, you've lost five pounds of your goal weight of twenty-five, putting you at twenty percent."

"Damn! That's it?"

"I'm sorry, Valerie, that's it. Tina, you're next." Ms. Virginia gestured for her to get up.

Tina stepped on the scale, and covered her eyes with her hands. "What is it, Ms. Virginia?"

"You've lost fourteen of your twenty-pound goal, putting you at seventy percent. That's great, Tina!"

"That ain't fair," Wanda whispered to Pam. "She gotta trainer."

"Yeah, Curtis keep her in shape by chasing her ass all around her house." Pam laughed.

"Lisa-Lisa, you're next," Tina said.

Lisa stepped on the scale and dropped her arms by her side. "Well, Ms. Virginia?"

"Lisa, you have lost ten of your goal weight of twenty pounds, putting you at fifty percent."

"That's not too bad. I can do better, but that's not bad."

"Wanda, come on." Ms. Virginia pointed to the scale.

"I bet y'all can't wait for me to get up here, huh?" Wanda stepped on the scale and stared at each office girl one at a time. "Y'all think I ain't a lost a damn pound, don't you?"

"I'm sure you have," Ms. Virginia said, then looked down at the scale. "Oh my God!"

"What?" Wanda shouted.

"Wanda, you've gained five pounds, baby."

"Damn! OH HELL NAWL!!! It's something wrong with this thang, man! I know I ain't gained no five pounds!"

"The machine doesn't lie, Wanda," Alicia joked.

"The hell it don't! Y'all need a new scale."

"It's working fine for everybody else," Alicia continued joking.

"Shut your skinny ass up before I bite you in half, Alicia!" Wanda said, stepping off the scale.

"Pam, you're next," Ms. Virginia said, pointing to the scale.

"I wouldn't get on that thang for all the rice in China!" Pam said, walking with her arms folded out of the break room.

The rest of the office girls, along with me, watched as she stormed out.

"Pam done lost her damn mind," Wanda said.

"You ain't lyin'." Valerie laughed.

After our break we went back to our desks. On our side of the office were Tina, Alicia and me. Pam, Wanda and Ms. Virginia were kind in the middle and Lisa, Valerie, and Darsha were on the other side. Cynthia's desk was in the corner. We didn't have the high cubicles, making our voices reverberate all over the place. So not only could you hear what people were saying, you could see what everybody was doing at all times. That made it easy, or should I say easier, for everyone's business to travel throughout the office.

Once we sat down, Tina pulled a napkin she had gotten from the break room and started writing down numbers. Ms. Virginia saw her, and couldn't help but inquire.

"Tina, what are you doing with that napkin?"

"I'm trying to write down everybody's weight number from the diet contest but I can't remember."

"Why on earth are you doing that?"

"I need those numbers for my lottery tickets. I swear those are some good numbers. When y'all were being weighed I felt my heart beat faster and faster every time Ms. Virginia called out a number."

"Tina, maybe you need to save that lottery ticket money you're about to spend for your bills," Ms. Virginia said.

"But I only use a dollar or so when I play the lottery. If I ever hit, WHOO! Lord, have mercy!"

"You better listen to Ms. Virginia, Tina, and save that dollar," Alicia said.

"I know, Alicia," Tina agreed, "but it's like the lottery is a drug and I'm addicted. I can't help myself. Like when I came in, I was looking at your license tag number, Wanda, and it had the numbers 8-1-0-7. I dreamed about those numbers last night. I'm going to box that number."

"Leave my license tag alone, you might be puttin' a mojo on it."

"Now, how much weight did you lose again, Alicia?"

"Not gonna tell ya!"

"Ms. Virginia, give me something to work with. Were you born on an even or an odd day?"

"Neither!"

"Okay, Pam, you're my good luck charm," Tina said, standing up so that the entire office could hear, "what's your waist size?"

"Girl, I ain't tellin' you my waist size!"

"Wanda, I'm back to you, what's your fo'head size? That oughta be a good solid number right there."

"I ain't givin' you my fo'head size! You scarin' me, Tina. You actin' like you on crack, for real!"

"Well, what time did we go to break?"

"Almost ten o'clock, Tina," Ms. Virginia said.

"That's it! 1-0-0-0! If I hit, I'm going to give you something for that number, Ms. Virginia."

"Don't worry about it, Tina."

"If Tazzy comes in here, tell her I had to go to the restroom." Tina stood.

"Go 'head, man, Tazzy get on my damn nerve tryin' to watch our every move, anyway," Wanda said angrily.

"She means well," Ms. Virginia said.

"But still, it's like...damn!" Wanda said, struggling to get her sentence out. "We are grown-ass women! Give us a damn break!"

"See, Ms. Virginia, if you would have made me supervisor, I would have a more casual office," Pam said sarcastically.

"And maybe that's why you're not the supervisor, dear."

"I would be the supervisor if you hadn't helped Tazzy get that job."

"One had nothing to do with the other, Pam, and you know it."

"You gave up the supervisor position and then hired Tazzy in your place. You hired that girl from off the streets."

"My opinion had nothing to do with you versus Tazzy. They asked me to give them my choice on the next supervisor, and I did. I gave them my answer and that was that. Why are you complaining? You never even applied!"

"I didn't apply because I didn't know there was outside competition!"

"It doesn't make sense for a person to think they have a job they didn't even apply for, Pam! No sense whatsoever!"

"It made sense to me because you were supposed to be my best friend!"

"So you thought that because I was your best friend, you didn't have to apply for a promotion that was being offered to several people? That wasn't my decision to make."

"I worked my ass off for that position, Ms. Virginia, and you know it!" Pam said, looking as if she was on the verge of tears. "How could you stab me in the back like that?"

"I did not stab you in the back! Pam, you weren't ready to be a supervisor because you wanted to be everyone's best friend. The two just don't go together. You think that if you're friendly with everyone, everyone is going to be friendly with you. And that's just not how it is."

"It worked for you, didn't it?"

"There is a difference between being friendly with everyone and being everyone's friend. The latter requires a commitment."

"Let me tell you something, Ms. Virginia! You think you can…"

"No dear!" Ms. Virginia interrupted. "Let me tell *you* something. If you want to speak to me I'm more than happy to listen, but you're not going to talk to me like I'm one of these young women around here who's going to yell and scream like we have no sense! Now, if there's something you want to say to me, say it like you have some decency about yourself."

"You don't want to hear what I have to say to you."

"Darling, please, there's nothing you can tell me that I haven't heard before."

"Hold it! Hold it! Hold it! Now I was too late to save Biggie Smalls and Tupac," Wanda said, trying to soften the mood, "but I be damned if I stand back and let you two kill each other. This east desk-west desk rivalry stuff has got to stop!"

"I am fine. And one day Pam will be, too," Ms. Virginia said.

Ms. Virginia turned and started to work at her desk. Pam stared at her as she rapidly tapped her feet on the floor.

"Now that y'all stopped arguing it's boring in here. Somebody turn on the radio," Wanda said.

Ms. Virginia was the closest, so she cut on the radio.

"I don't wanna hear no oldie but goodie, Ms. Virginia," Wanda said, "can you put it on 103?"

"Girl, you're going to listen to whatever station I put it on."

"Okay, Ms. Virginia," Wanda said. "I don't won't no trouble!"

Ms. Virginia cut on the radio and started scanning the stations until she found the radio station they'd requested.

"Can you cut it up, Ms. Virginia? It's time for the 103 giveaway."

"If you don't shut up, I'm going to cut this thing off, Wanda."

Ms. Virginia turned up the sound on the radio and the DJ was talking to a winner.

"We have our lucky one hundred-and-third caller on the line. Hey, what's your name?" the DJ asked.

"Do I have to give my name?" the caller whispered.

"If you want to win you do," the DJ whispered sarcastically. "Why are we whispering?"

"Because I'm not supposed to be on the telephone. I'm at work."

"Hold up! Don't that caller sound familiar?" Pam asked, walking closer to the radio.

"Okay, we won't tell anyone. But before you win your one hundred-and-three dollars, you have to tell us where you work."

"Where's Tina?" Tazzy asked, walking around the office.

"I think she said she was going to the bathroom, Tazzy," Wanda answered.

"Tell her to come to my office when she gets back."

As she turned to walk away she noticed the volume of the radio. "That radio is too loud, somebody cut it down a little?"

"I work at Upskon," the caller whispered.

"ALL RIGHT!!! YOU HAVE JUST WON YOURSELF ONE HUNDRED AND THREE AMERICAN DOLLARS!!!"

"Can we please hurry? I have to get back to my desk."

"If you're not at your desk, caller, where are you calling from?"

"I'm in the bathroom sitting on the toilet."

Tazzy stopped in her tracks and angrily said, "Wait a minute! That's Tina on that radio!"

"Ooh, TMI! We didn't need to hear that. I guess we need to let you get back to work before you get fired."
"Excuse me, Mr. DJ, what's your address number?"
"Excuse me?"
"What's your address number?"
"Why? Are you some kind of stalker?"

"That fool done lost her mind!" Wanda said, shaking her head.
"She's going to lose more than that when she gets back in here," Tazzy said.

"No, Mr. DJ, I'm not a stalker. I just think your address might be good luck and I want to play your address numbers for my lottery number. Come on, Mr. DJ, help a sis..."
CLICK!
"Good-bye!" The DJ disconnected the call. "Hey, hang that caller up, she's too crazy to win a hundred and three dollars!"

"Cut that radio off, please! I think I'll wait for our caller to *'come on down,'*" Tazzy said, sitting at Tina's desk.
A few seconds later Tina rushed in. She slowed down once she saw Tazzy sitting and waiting.
"Been on a little break, Tina?" Tazzy asked.
Wanda and Pam gestured to Tina that Tazzy had heard her on the phone but she didn't notice them.
"Yeah, you know how that is, Tazzy. It's one of those women things. You feel me?"
"No, I don't feel you, but I did hear you," Tazzy said, "on 1-0-3!"
"That ain't true, Tazzy, somebody lyin' on me!" Tina shouted nervously.
"Tina, I heard you on the radio myself."
"What you think you heard?"

"I know what I heard, now come to my office. This is not the place for this conversation."

Tina lagged behind pretending to straighten up her desk.

"Okay, Tazzy, here I come."

"Can I have your liquid paper if Tazzy fire you?" Wanda laughed.

"Can you kiss my liquid ass?"

"One hundred and three times!" Wanda said, blowing Tina a kiss.

"Come to my office now, Tina!" Tazzy shouted.

"You better get on in there, and stop playing before Tazzy fire you for real," Wanda said.

"You ain't lyin'!" Tina said, picking up the pace. "Let me get on in there."

Tazzy gave Tina a written reprimand and sent her back to her desk. No one asked her what happened at first because her silence spoke volumes. Wanda couldn't stand the silence and started asking questions.

"All right, we've been quiet long enough. What did Tazzy say to you in her office, Tina?"

"She told me I had one foot out the door and if I didn't straighten up the other one would follow."

"That thang is little, but she don't take no junk."

"I'm hot! I'm about to turn the air on," Pam said, walking over to the thermostat.

"Don't do that, Pam. Tazzy told us not to touch that thing. Now give her, her respect and not touch it," Ms. Virginia said.

"Shit, I'm hot."

Tazzy and Susan were walking from Pam's rear while she was adjusting the thermostat, and she couldn't see them coming.

"I wouldn't do that if I were you," Susan said.

"Look, I'm hot! I want some air."

"Look! People in hell want ice water! Now please take your hand off of that thermostat," Tazzy said.

"Who do you think you talking to like that?"

"I'm talking to you!" Tazzy shouted, and then quickly calmed down. "Pam, it's like this. I'm tired of you and your attitude. If you don't want to work for me, get your hat, get your coat, and get the hell out of my office!"

"Oh my God, Tazzy!" Susan said, putting her hands on her chest.

The rest of the office looked in disbelief with our mouths wide open.

"That's fine with me, Tazzy! This ain't the only job in the world!" Pam said, gathering items from her desk.

"So do I take this as your resignation?"

"Do you take what as my resignation?" Pam said, pondering quitting, or backing down. She looked at me and I shook my head no. "No, Tazzy, as much as you would like me to quit, I'm just going to lunch. Is that okay?"

"Yeah, Pam, that's fine with me!"

Pam snatched her purse and walked out.

"Tazzy, I keep telling Pam to stop running off at the mouth so much," Wanda said.

"Oh, do you, Wanda?" Tazzy said sarcastically.

"That girl needs to go to some of them anger management classes Upskon offers," Wanda responded.

"She'll be fine, Wanda, leave her alone," Ms. Virginia said.

"Yeah, she'll be fine," Tazzy said. "Well, we were coming out here to tell you all that since we've processed all of our claims for this month, you ladies—excuse me, and you too, Michael—can take an extra fifteen minutes for lunch for doing such a fine job. If you happen to see Pam, Wanda, tell her she has fifteen extra minutes."

Pam was standing in the entryway of the office waiting for Wanda to go to lunch. She knew Wanda was waiting until Tazzy left the area before she left so she kind of put a rush on her by yelling to her.

"Wanda, Tazzy knows I'm waiting on you so come on so we can go. And oh, I'm going to show you just how much I can't manage my anger when you get yo' ass out here, too!"

"Well, y'all, it seem like the silence of the lamb done got rowdy so I'm outta here," Wanda said. She stood up and yelled back to Pam, "Here I come, girl. I was only playin'! You know you don't need no anger management!"

❖❖❖

At lunch, I was sitting in the break room, trying to avoid the afternoon rush, when Lisa, Darsha, and Valerie walked in while in mid-gossip.

"I'm not supposed to say anything but did y'all hear about Tammy in collections?" Valerie asked.

"Naw, what happened to her?" Darsha asked.

"Nothing happened to her. But do you remember the big IT guy who used to work here and then he moved to Michigan, Mississippi, Missouri, somewhere like that? I know it started with an 'M.' Anyway, they used to mess around," Valerie informed.

"Who?" Darsha asked.

"Tammy and the big ol' IT man. They used to mess around."

"Little bitty Tammy used to mess with that big ol' man? Don't that big ol' man have a big ol' wife?" Darsha asked.

"Yeah, girl," Valerie answered.

"Stop interrupting her, Darsha," Lisa said. "Finish what you were saying, Val."

"Anyway, he came back down here a couple of weeks ago to see her. He told his wife he was going to Florida or something like that."

"And?" Darsha asked.

"And he met Tammy in a hotel so they could get their freak on. Tammy said he got to drinking and taking so much of that Viagra he passed out."

"Passed out?" Darsha asked.

"That ain't even the tripped-out part. When she tried to wake him up, he wouldn't wake up. She got scared and called me. I told her to call an ambulance and I would be there in a minute."

"Da-yum!" Darsha shouted.

"Hold on. I'm not through. By the time I got to the hotel, the ambulance was there. The police was there, and they were detaining Tammy."

"I know that scared you to death, Val," Lisa said.

"Hell yeah! I started to turn my ass around and run, but I knew my girl needed me."

"Is he all right?" Lisa asked.

"That's the tripped-out part, the man is dead!"

"Dead?" Lisa and Darsha said in unison.

"Yup. The dude died, girl!"

"I know that freaked Tammy out," Lisa said.

"Let me tell you. When I got there I couldn't even talk to her. The police had detained her for questioning. She told her husband she had to work Saturday morning until three o'clock. Can you imagine what he must've been thinking when he didn't hear from his wife until late that night?"

"Now that's a story for yo' ass right there!" Darsha said, shaking her head.

"I ain't through. Her husband had to go pick her up from the police station."

"How did she get out of that?" Lisa asked.

"She told him the truth, Lisa."

"The truth? And he didn't kill her?" Darsha asked.

"Well, the truth mixed in with little lies. She told him a guy who used to work with her had passed out in a hotel and he was with another friend who worked with her. Guess who was the friend? *ME!* I was supposed to have called her while she was at work because I was scared and she came to the hotel to check on me. She said we called the police and the police detained us for questioning until she called him. First of all, y'all know you ain't gon' find me in a hotel with no man. But her husband believed her."

"Men will believe anything!" Darsha said.

"So was it the Viagra or the liquor that killed him, Val?" Lisa asked.

"It was a combination of things," Val responded, counting on her fingers. "He was taking some heart medication, drinking liquor, and taking Viagra. All that just to keep his shit hard."

"Well, he ain't gotta worry about it no more 'cause his shit gon' be hard from now on," Darsha said.

"Fa' sho'!" Val laughed loudly.

They were starting on a new story when I walked past them on my way to lunch.

"Where you going, Mike?" Valerie asked.

"Finish my lunch, you wanna come with me?"

"Mike, if I was straight I'd put somethin' on yo' black ass, man."

"Oh, is that right, Val?" I asked, standing in the door, waiting for her to say her last smart statement so that I could leave.

"I might try you one day, Mike."

"Just let me know, I'll mark my calendar."

"Get on out of here, boy," Valerie joked.

❖❖❖

I couldn't wait to get home and work on the book. I cut on my computer and microwaved some leftover pizza in the process. I was so anxious to get started it felt like it was taking my computer forever to start. Once I logged on, I went to my email to retrieve some of the notes I had sent from work. I was almost finished eating my pizza before I heard those familiar words, "Welcome! You've got mail!" I pulled up the office girls file, and went straight to work.

Around eleven that night, my telephone rang.

"Hello," I said.

"Can I come over?"

"Pam, what's up?"

"They're driving me crazy at work, Mike."

"What's going on?"

"You saw how Tazzy tried to go off on me today."

"Pam, come on now."

"Come on, what?"

"She didn't go off on you."

"Yes, she did Mike, in front of everybody in the office, too."

"Come on now, Pam." I was trying to get her to admit that she deserved what she'd gotten.

"What, Mike?"

"Look, I'm about to get off the computer. Why don't you come over so we can talk?"

"You sure?"

"Yeah, bring some clothes. You can go to work from my house."

"Okay, I'll be over in a little while."

I cut off my computer and waited for Pam to arrive. When she said "a little while," she meant a little while. Within minutes she was knocking on my door. I let her in, and led her to my den.

"Are you all right?" I asked.

"I don't know, Mike. I'm so tired of those people at work!"

"Hey!" I said, surprised to see tears coming from Pam's eyes. "Hey, are you crying, Pam?"

"No, I'm so tired of them!" Pam shouted, trying to fight back her tears.

"Pam! Pam!" I held her face close to mine. "Calm down and talk to me."

"Mike, if that had been anyone else messing with that thermostat today, Tazzy wouldn't have gone off like that."

"Pam, do you want the truth?"

"No."

"Do you want me to bullshit you, or be straight up with you?"

"I want you to pacify me, boy." Pam smiled, trying to prevent from crying.

"Well, I can't do that because I care too much for you. Now, I didn't ask you to come over here to baby you. I asked you to come over to get this shit over and done with."

"What?" Pam reclined on the couch and folded her arms.

"Stop acting like a baby."

"You stop acting like a baby!"

"You ready to hear what I got to say?"

"Go 'head, Mike."

"You were wrong today. And I don't know what happened between you, Ms. Virginia, and Tazzy before I started working at Upskon. But since I've been there, Pam, you've been the one initiating all of the hostility. Tazzy has bent over backward trying to prevent from arguing with you, but you keep pushing her. Whatever problem you have with her, you need to let it go."

"You don't understand, Mike."

"Okay, if I don't understand, explain it to me."

"Ms. Virginia was like a mother to me. I mean she took me under her wings and looked out for me. Then when that supervisor position opened up, I knew she was going to hire me for that job. Mike, when I found out she had given the job to Tazzy, I went home and cried my eyes out. That hurt me so bad. It wasn't the job itself, it was the betrayal that hurt so bad."

"Pam, I'm listening to you, but I'm not hearing how Ms. Virginia betrayed you."

"She gave the job to Tazzy, Mike."

"Maybe she felt Tazzy would make a better supervisor."

"Maybe you're right. And maybe that's why it hurts so much."

"I always try to avoid this, but can I give you some advice?"

"Go 'head."

"Talk to Ms. Virginia."

"No, too much has happened."

"That's pain talking."

"Ms. Virginia probably doesn't even want to talk to me."

"That's not the Ms. Virginia I know."

"You're right." Pam smiled.

"Pam, I see how you act at work, and I see how you act when you're not at work. It's like a three hundred and sixty-degree turn. At your place of business, all that you do is use slang, but outside of work, you're an articulate bright woman. Why?"

"I guess I want to rebel against them."

"Let them see what I see. If you do, you'll get everything you want from Upskon."

"You think so?"

"I know so," I said, "now can we get some sleep?"

"You sleepy? All that talking has made me kinda horny."

"Don't do this to me Pam, it's late."

"Do what?" Pam said, taking off her clothes as she walked over to me.

"Have we ever done it in a bed?" I asked.

"I don't think so."

"Do you want to do it in my bed?"

"No, I want to do it right here and right now!"

"No bed, no sex!"

"Boy, please, I bet you wish you do have a choice in this. Now lay on your back and let me do my do so I can go to sleep."

"This is kind of like rape, Pam."

"For real?"

"For real."

I got comfortable on the floor and Pam straddled me. It wasn't long before she was rocking back and forth on top of me. She squeezed my chest, and maneuvered her hips in different motions until she was near her orgasm. She lowered her face to my chest, and started biting ferociously when her orgasm exploded.

She held on to the back of my head and bucked her hips as fast as she could until her orgasm was over. I flipped her on her back, and spread her legs wide. I placed my hands under her knees and folded her legs backward until they were almost touching the floor. I went as deep as I could inside of her and without taking it out, continued to grind, and push until I felt my orgasm approaching.

When I began to release my juices I started to pound as fast and as hard as I could. I was moaning so loudly, she pulled me down to her and stuck her tongue in my mouth to hush my groans.

"Damn, I said this wasn't going to happen anymore!"

"Mike, come on, you know once you saw this fantabulous body, there was no way you could resist."

"Whatever, Pam. Let's go to bed."

"Yeah, we can get in the bed 'cause it's time for sleep-sleep now."

Pam and I slept as if the other was not even in the bed. There was no post-coitus tenderness. We went out like a light, she stayed on her side, and I stayed on mine.

When I woke up the next morning, it felt strange. It was a totally different situation from all the previous times. I'd never woken up with her after sex, so how would we react?

I woke up first feeling more and more uncomfortable trying to figure out what my first words would be. I didn't know if she wanted me to be affectionate, or if she wanted us to act like buddies.

Pam answered all questions when she woke up, and went into her bag and got her things for the day. I was still in the shower at the time. She poked her head in the bathroom and said, "Hurry up, Negro; I got to go to work."

I knew then I would always feel comfortable around Pam because we would always be more friends than lovers.

We laughed and joked while we were getting ready for work. When we left to get in our cars, Pam playfully kissed me on my cheek and said, "Have a nice day at work, honey."

"You, too, sweetheart," I joked in return.

chapter 6

T hat morning at work, Jaline called me into her office right before lunch for my sixty-day review. It was almost sixty days overdue. I went in and sat down waiting for some kind of break in our monotonous business relationship, a break that would give me an opportunity to get some kind of information on this woman.

"Good morning, Michael, how are you?" Jaline asked.

"I'm fine, how are you?"

"I'd like to apologize for our delay in your sixty-day review."

"That's all right, I understand."

"Good! A good attitude can get you far in this department."

"Thank you."

"How are things going out there?"

"Things couldn't be better."

"Great! I apologize for not being here to help you get settled but we just opened an office in San Francisco and I've been getting things together out there. How does it feel to be the only man in an office full of women?"

"I feel as if I'm one of the office girls."

Jaline stood up and walked around to my side of her desk and placed her hands on my shoulders. She proceeded to give me a quick, three-second massage, and then sat down on top of her desk directly in front of me. She exposed her long legs, and a good portion of her thigh.

"We don't want you to feel too much like one of the girls around here. It's good having a man in the office."

"Oh, I see."

"Let me ask you a question, Michael." Jaline opened her thighs a little more. "Do you like to go dancing?"

"Yeah." I laughed.

"What's so funny?"

"I'm just curious to know why you would ask me that question."

"You look like you could be a great dancer."

"Looks can be deceiving in some cases."

"Interesting. My instincts are normally very keen, Michael," Jaline said, walking behind me and rubbing on my shoulders. "I bet you can move your body in all kinds of different ways, can't you, Michael?"

"What do you mean?"

"You know what I mean, Michael. I've been managing this office for a long time. Once we officially open the San Francisco office, I will be over the entire building, which will leave my position open here."

"And how does that affect me?"

"If you be a nice boy to me, I promise you'll get my position."

"But I'm the last to be hired, plus I lack the experience. How can I possibly get that job?"

"Because you have a Harvard degree. You're an attorney. And you're a man."

"Um," I said, still in disbelief, "what do you think the rest of the office 'women' will think about that, Jaline?"

"Frankly, who gives a shit what they think?"

"I'll still be here, so I do."

"Well, Michael, if you want my job, I'll make sure you get it. But you have to keep me happy until I leave."

"And how do I do that?" Michael asked.

"Sex!"

"I see."

"And as far as your sixty-day review, I gave you a big fat raise. I'm sure you'll be more than happy with what you've received."

"I don't know what to say, Jaline."

"You don't have to say anything. Now you just have to earn that money."

"I thought I had earned it."

"That's potential interest, Michael. You'll have to prove your true value at a later date," Jaline said, opening her legs wide, and then closing them quickly as she stood to go back to her chair. "That's all. We'll chat later."

"Okay, I guess I'll be getting back to my desk."

"All right, Michael, and let's keep this conversation strictly confidential."

After I stepped outside of her office door, I jumped up and clapped my feet together.

"I got that bitch!"

❖❖❖

On my way back to my desk, I heard a loud commotion coming from outside of the office doors.

"How did you get in here?" a woman's voice shouted.

"None of yo' damn business!" a man's voice shouted back.

I could hear the sound of scuffling, as if people were fighting. I was on my way out of the door when I heard Wanda's screaming voice.

"Get yo' hands off her, you sorry-ass bastard!"

I ran as fast as I could and burst through the doors. When I got outside I could see Wanda, Ms. Virginia, Valerie, and Pam trying to stop a man from strangling Tina. Alicia, Lisa, Cynthia, and Darsha were all shouting and screaming hysterically.

"What are you doing, man?" I shouted, moving the ladies out the way, and grabbing the man.

"Get outta my face, man! I'm gon' kill this bitch!"

The "bitch" he was referring to, happened to be Tina!

"Hey, man! Let go of that woman, man!" I shouted.

"You ain't got nothin' to do with this, man! Step off!"

"Get him off her, Mike!" Pam yelled.

Without thinking rationally, I grabbed the man and wrestled him to the ground.

"Call security!" Jaline shouted, as she saw me wrestling with the man.

"Mike, look out, he got a gun!" Cynthia shouted.

The words, "he got a gun," echoed in my head. I didn't see a gun and I didn't know where it was. I was still struggling to keep the man on the ground. His hands became free several times. I was hoping that he could not see the gun as well. But being that he was the person who dropped it, odds were with him to locate it first. Kind of like a missed shot in basketball, the shooter always have the better insight on which direction the ball will fall from off the rim. So what, I like using sports as metaphors.

"Get back! Back up!" I yelled to the women.

"Michael, look out!" Alicia screamed.

I could hear the women screaming, but the whole experience seemed surreal. I gave up trying to locate the gun, and focused on the man's hands. If he could've shot me with anything other than his hands, like his feet or his ass, I could not have stopped him, anyway.

Out of nowhere, I heard a calm serene voice say, "Michael, get off him. And Curtis, you better not make a move."

I looked over my shoulder to see who was speaking and there was Ms. Virginia standing with a gun in her hand. She was calm and composed, and she was holding on to that gun for dear life. With the threat of being shot, the once out-of-control maniac suddenly became a rational-thinking human being.

I stood up, and straightened my clothes, and I could see that his gun was still lying on the ground where we were once fighting. I kicked the gun to the side, and then Ms. Virginia walked right on top of the man and pointed it at his face. The man remained on the ground with his hands blocking as much of his vital organs as possible.

"How dare you put your hands on her?" Ms. Virginia shouted to the man. "I'll kill you, you son-of-a-bitch!"

I had never heard Ms. Virginia use profanity until that day. I know he was afraid, because she scared the hell out of me. She aimed the gun at his chest and cocked it. The women scattered, running to and from one another's arms.

"Ms. Virginia! Ms. Virginia!" I shouted.

"Please, don't shoot me, Ms. Virginia!" the man shouted.

"I told you to leave her alone! I will kill you dead!" Ms. Virginia screamed.

I slowly reached over Ms. Virginia's shoulder and grabbed her wrists. "Ms. Virginia, let the gun go!"

"Get the gun from her, man!" the man shouted.

"Ms. Virginia, it's okay," I said, gripping her hands and the gun tighter.

"Don't let her shoot me, man!"

"Ms. Virginia! Please! Give me the gun! Please!" I said, slowly taking the gun out of her hands.

Security arrived, along with the police, at the moment I was taking the gun out of her hands, and turned their weapons on me.

"Put the weapon down! And get down on the ground!" they shouted.

"Wait a minute, he's the one who attacked us!" I shouted, before they screamed at me again.

"Put your weapon down! And get down on the ground! NOW!" they shouted again.

"Mike, drop the gun!" Cynthia screamed.

I dropped the gun, and then fell on the ground with my face to the side. They commanded me to spread my legs and arms in the position of the letter "X." I was embarrassed and humiliated. Never in my life had I ever been in such a situation. On the other hand, I could understand their position not knowing the victim from the perpetrator.

The police immediately rushed me, and put me in handcuffs for questioning. Upon the mass cries from the women to subdue the other man, he, too, was handcuffed for questioning.

"What's going on, here?" one officer asked.

Everybody started speaking at once. And like in the movies, the police had to tell them the classic line, "one at a time, Ma'am." They had to tell everybody but Ms. Virginia, who was still standing and staring at the man. The police had sat him up, with his hands in cuffs behind his back. After the police deciphered through the madness, and found out I was actually the good guy, they took the handcuffs off of me.

Throughout the hysteria, no one had noticed that Ms. Virginia seemed to be in a catatonic state. I whispered to one of the police officers to check on her, because I believed she was in shock. It took her several minutes to respond, but eventually she came around. They took the man to jail, and Jaline gave us off the remainder of the afternoon.

My house was chosen to host the afternoon tea party. With the exception of Jaline and Ms. Virginia, the entire office piled into my home to discuss the events of the day. We ordered Chinese food, and rented the movie, *The Mirror Has Two Faces.* There was so much estrogen floating around I almost put on a bra. No one actually watched the movie. With all of the conversations being thrown in so many different directions, I was surprised I finally found out who the man was, and why he was there.

"Tina, you've got to do something about Curtis before he kills you," Pam advised.

"What can I do? Every time I try to leave him, he acts crazy!"

"We have to do something. Jaline called me in the office and told me to fire you," Tazzy said.

With all of the commotion of Tina's affair, I had completely forgotten my own little affair with Jaline until Tazzy mentioned her name. I made a note to go buy a miniature recorder. The next time I had a private meeting with her, it wouldn't be private.

"Fire me?" Tina asked.

"Tina, everybody's life is at risk as long as Curtis continues to come to the office and terrorize you."

"He could have killed Mike today with that gun!" Alicia added.

"Mike, I'm so sorry, Mike!" Tina said, as she started to cry.

"No apology necessary. He didn't bring that gun there for me and you can't stay under a rock because that fool don't want to let you go."

"I just feel so bad for y'all!" Tina whimpered, and then burst into tears.

Cynthia and Wanda consoled her by hugging her tightly.

"Baby, it's not your fault!" Wanda said.

Wanda was known for her acidulous remarks, but she was always the first to offer consolation.

"Don't feel sorry for us, Tina. You're the one who has to deal with this shit," Lisa said.

"Tina, listen to me," Tazzy added. "Things like this happen every day. I know it's going to be hard, but you have to get your life back. Believe me, I know exactly how you feel. I've seen this from all angles."

Pam pointed to Tazzy and said, "It was you."

No one in the room knew what she was talking about. We thought she was using this unfortunate situation as an opportunity to attack Tazzy away from the job.

"Tazzy, may I speak with you for a second?" Pam asked.

"Pam, this is not the time, nor the place," Tazzy answered.

"Tazzy, please," Pam said, "I need to speak with you."

It looked like Tazzy had opened her mouth to repeat her first response, but when she looked at Pam and saw the sincerity on her face, she agreed to speak with her.

"All right, Pam. Let's talk."

Tazzy followed Pam out onto my patio. As soon as they closed the door, Darsha shouted, "Mike, you better go out there before they tear yo' shit up!"

"That's a good point," I said, running to the patio. "I can't have them breaking my stuff. I just got it all paid for."

Although they had a little head start, I caught them at the beginning of their conversation.

"Tazzy, I know it was you."

"You know what was me?"

"I know that you were the jogger that Ms. Virginia was talking about."

"Why do you say that, Pam?" Tazzy took a seat.

"I just feel it."

"What if I said that you're right, then what?"

"Then I would say that it all makes sense."

I was under the impression that Tazzy and Pam didn't realize I was standing behind them, so I tried to make my presence known.

"Excuse me, ladies, but I think I need to go back in the house," I said.

"No, Mike, please stay," Pam said.

"Is that all right with you, Tazzy?" I asked.

"It doesn't matter to me, maybe you can referee?" Tazzy chuckled.

"Please, Mike, stay," Pam repeated.

"All right, I'll stay," I said, pulling up a chair and sitting next to Tazzy.

"Tazzy, for the sake of my sanity, can you explain what happened?" Pam asked.

Tazzy's Story

I was born and raised in Warrensville Heights, Ohio, a suburb of Cleveland. I had two older brothers. Having always been very small, my brothers felt the need to protect me. My boyfriends were always getting in to scuffles with them over the slightest arguments. Sometime the arguments would lead to physical altercations, especially with my college sweetheart, Terry. He was physically abusive and as much as I would try to keep our fights between us, my brothers would always manage to find out.

They would make the two-hour drive, from Cleveland to Columbus, whenever my mother told them she had a feeling something was wrong. Most of the time, my mother was right.

After I graduated from Ohio State, I packed up my bags and moved down here. Leaving my boyfriend, mother, and brothers back in Ohio. My life was going well, I started off with small jobs here and there, but eventually I got a fantastic job as an office manager in a small office.

Not soon after I got the job, my ex-boyfriend came to visit and decided he didn't want to leave. I begged him to go back home, but he wouldn't. I tried to have him removed but that only made him angrier.

One day, his temper flared and he beat me up pretty bad. Out of all the nurses in Atlanta, I happen to have a nurse who was from Cleveland and knew my family. Only God knows how she got in contact with my brothers but she managed to get the word to them that I had been beaten up.

They jumped in their car to come to my rescue once again. But this time they brought a couple of my rowdy cousins who had been raised by the penal system of the state of Ohio.

They banged on my door at three in the morning, and of course, that scared my boyfriend and me. He jumped up and ran to the door to see who it was. He looked out of the window and saw that it was my family and ran and got his gun. I didn't even know there was a gun in my house. I begged him to stay in the bedroom until

I got the situation under control. I talked to my brothers through the door and I told them that I would call the police if they made any trouble. They agreed to only talk to him, and I let them in.

"Hey, baby girl," my oldest brother, Randy, spoke.

"Hey, big brother, don't forget your promise." I hugged him.

"I can't get a hug, baby girl?" my other brother, Calvin, spoke.

"Come here! I missed you so much!" I said, hugging Calvin.

After I hugged my brothers, I hugged my two cousins. We sat down and I made my brothers promise again, not to cause any trouble.

"Please, don't you all start trouble with him, please," I begged.

"We won't. We just want that niggah to get his shit and get out!" my cousin Larry said.

"Straight up!" my other cousin, Cordell, said.

"That's all we want, baby girl. We just want him away from you," Randy said.

"I'm fine though, Randy."

"No, you not, Tazzy. You lettin' that niggah push you around," Calvin said.

"Hey, Tazzy, where he at?" Larry asked.

"He's in my bedroom sleep."

"Hey, Terry! Get out here, man! We need to holla at you!" Larry yelled.

"Larry, you all agreed there wasn't going to be any trouble."

"Babygirl, I'm not going to do anything in here, because I promised you. But if that niggah don't leave tonight, he can't leave tomorrow. It's simple as that."

"Larry, leave him alone, please."

"Don't worry, Babygirl, there ain't gon' be no violence in here."

"No violence, Larry?"

"No violence," Larry said, and then smiled, "in here."

"I'll go get him if that will get you all back to Cleveland. But you promised Larry. No violence?"

"No violence," Larry said, throwing his hands in the air, "no violence."

As soon I stood up to go to the bedroom I heard a flurry of gunshots. They whisked right past my head. My brother Randy jumped from the table to shield me from the bullets. We fell on the floor and the bullets continued to fly. I saw my cousin Larry's shirt instantly become stained with blood and I screamed at the top of my lungs. He fell backward in his chair with his arm still in the air from our talk. Randy pushed my head down to the floor, as a second gun began to fire.

When the firing stopped, Randy stood up and ran to Larry. He tried shaking him, and shaking him, but he wouldn't get up. Then we saw Calvin lying in a puddle of blood with his eyes open. I ran over to him hollering and screaming and laid my entire body on top of him. Randy tried to pull me off of him, but I somehow thought I could cover the open wounds in his chest.

"Get up, Babygirl! You gettin' blood all over you! Get up!"

"Babygirl," Calvin panted, "Babygirl, you all right?"

"NO! NO! NO!" I screamed.

Though my cousin Cordell had been shot, too, he managed to tackle Terry in the yard. They were fighting when Randy ran outside, reached in the glove compartment of their car, and pulled out a gun. He walked on top of Terry from behind and at point-blank range, fired three shots into his head. Terry slumped over, and fell to the ground. I was lying on the floor on top of my dying brother, watching my other brother kill my boyfriend.

Later that week I attended the funeral of my brother Calvin and my cousin Larry. I wanted to attend Terry's funeral, too, but it would have been awfully awkward. His family blamed me for his death.

My brother Randy was charged with second-degree murder, and my cousin was charged with accessory to murder. We were pretty confident they would get off by pleading self-defense, but my brother received seven years, and Cordell got two.

After the sentencing I began to feel guilty for what had happened. I didn't feel like going to work so I lost my job. I didn't have a job so I couldn't pay my rent, so I was about to be evicted. That is when I started to feel like I didn't want to live anymore.

I woke up one Sunday morning and said this would be the day it stopped. I put on my jogging clothes and I ran. I didn't know where I was going, I just ran. When I got to this big park, I was trying to decide how I should kill myself. I had brought a bottle of pills, and by using them I knew that I could slowly see the end of my life and it wouldn't be painful.

Before I could decide, I heard horrific screams coming from behind some tall trees. I ran behind the trees and saw this man pounding on this woman. I started to scream for help, but no one would come. After he pulled out a knife I knew I had to do some-

thing. I jumped on his back and he flipped me on the ground. I jumped back up and climbed on his back again. The next time, instead of flipping me, he started stabbing me, over and over again. The last thing I remember is that I fell on the ground and he was on top of me, still stabbing me. I knew I was going to die, and I was angry with God that instead of letting me die peacefully like I wanted, I had to die in this hideous manner.

When I woke up, I was in the hospital and Ms. Virginia was sitting by my side. I had no identification on me so they couldn't notify my family. Ms. Virginia explained to me that she was the lady in the park. She made me feel like a hero describing how I had saved her life. She apologized every hour of every day. I told her that God had placed me there for a reason. It was a blessing because two lives were saved that day—hers and mine.

She stayed by my side day and night until my mother came down. We did a lot of talking. Once she found out I was about to be evicted, and I had no job, she told me she wanted to help me as I had helped her. She told me that as much as she would like, she couldn't switch places and absorb all of my pain, but she could make my life as comfortable as possible. I didn't know until later but she gave up her job as supervisor so that I could have it. I had managerial experience, so with Ms. Virginia's recommendation, I became the supervisor at Upskon.

❖❖❖

"I'm glad you told me that, Tazzy," Pam said, "that sounds more like the Ms. Virginia I know."

"I hope we can put this to rest now."

"I have to apologize to you and Ms. Virginia. I have been acting like a butt-hole all this time because I felt like Ms. Virginia betrayed me, for you. I didn't want to admit it, but a good friend made me realize it."

"The good friend was me, Tazzy!" I said jokingly.

"I didn't know where the animosity was coming from. The only reason I could come up with, was that you felt a little animosity toward me because I was a young girl coming into a position that you all felt you deserved. But everybody loves Ms. Virginia. I couldn't understand what your problem was with her. I thought maybe your problem happened before I got there, but not when I got there."

"So, do you forgive me, supervisor?" Pam asked.

"Why, of course."

"And I'm sorry about your tragedy. I don't know if I would have been able to handle all that, Tazzy."

"You would if you had to."

"Is it safe for me to go back in my house now?" I said.

"Yeah, Mike," Pam said.

I grabbed both of them by their waists and escorted them back into the house.

"You two beautiful ladies need to come with me. I still don't trust you around my good furniture."

Everybody in the house had calmed down and started to relax until Tina realized she had forgotten to get her children from school.

"Y'all, I forgot all about my kids! I got to get 'em!" Tina said, jumping up.

"We'll go get 'em, Tina!" Valerie voluntereed.

"What if Curtis is out of jail and he's already picked them up?"

"Tina, Curtis ain't getting out of jail no time soon," Darsha said.

"He's looking at some serious time, Tina," Susan said. "We're going to prosecute him to the fullest extent of the law."

"I have to get to my children!"

As they were discussing Tina's children, the doorbell rang. Ms. Virginia walked in with all three of Tina's children.

"Look at what I found," Ms. Virginia said with a wide grin on her face.

"Come here!" Tina said, running to her children. "Thanks, Ms. Virginia, you're an angel. I'm glad they let the kids leave with you."

"When a grandmother is mad, she can pretty much get anything she wants." Ms. Virginia laughed.

"You told them you were their grandmother, Ms. Virginia?" Tina asked.

"Yes, dear."

"Look at Ms. Virginia with some game," Darsha joked.

"Tina, you can't go back to that house. I'll have your things picked up and you can stay in a hotel." Ms. Virginia wrapped her arms around Tina.

"Ms. Virginia, I can't afford no hotel."

"I'll help you out."

"Yeah, but for how long?"

"As long as it takes."

"No. You've done enough."

"Tina, you're not going back to that house!"

"I know, Ms. Virginia, but I can't take your money, either."

"You can stay with me, Tina!" Cynthia suggested.

"Cynthia, your house is not big enough for me and my three children."

"It'll be cozy, but we can make it work."

"Thanks, but I can't impose on you like that."

"I got room!" Pam said.

"You also got boys, Pam," Tina responded.

"And?"

"And boys and girls at their age don't mix."

"I can try to squeeze you in my house, Tina," Alicia volunteered.

"Alicia, you squeeze me in now, and Julian will squeeze me out as soon as he gets back."

"I tried!" Alicia said, shrugging her shoulders.

"How about here, Tina?" I said.

Everybody stopped the multiple conversations to listen to Tina's response.

"Thanks, Mike, but I can't ask you to do that."

"Why not? My girls are only here every other weekend. Other than that, I'm here all by myself."

"Tina, I'm his best friend, he's telling you the truth," Cynthia joked. "He does kind of have that lonely Maytag repairman thing going up in here."

"How much would you charge me for rent?"

"Rent's on the house as long as you wash your own dishes, and cook a home-cooked meal every once in a while."

"Mike, are you sure about this?"

"It makes perfect sense, Tina. Your husband knows nothing about me, with the exception of our little scrap, so he'll never think to look here. And in the event that he does find you, I think it's safer to have a man around if that nut acts the way he did today."

"Yeah, it might be better if you hide out with a dude!" Wanda agreed. "I ain't gon' lie, if that fool come around me acting crazy, it's every woman for herself, and God for us all."

"Thank you so much, Mike!" Tina said, hugging me tightly.

"We still have to get your things out of your house without a confrontation," I advised.

"I just want our clothes. He can have everything else," Tina said.

"I'll call the police," Wanda said. "Curtis ain't comin' nowhere near the po-po!"

"Throw me your keys, Tina," I said.

Tina went into her purse and tossed me her keys.

"Do you remember how to get there, Mike?" Tina asked.

"Nope, but Cynthia can show me. Cynt, let's go!" I said.

"Are you asking me, or telling me?"

"Whichever you prefer, let's ride!"

"I can't stand you, bald man."

"Hey, roomie, make sure they don't wreck the house while I'm gone."

"I won't," Tina said, "not as sharp as this house is."

When Cynthia and I walked outside of my house, Alicia invited herself, and rode along. She followed us in her car so that she wouldn't take up space. When we got there, the police were waiting for us. They stayed outside until we had everything loaded and we left.

Surprisingly, the three of us actually had fun. Alicia started to put me on the spot about my feelings for Cynthia. And I really believe she was doing it because she wanted me to be happy. On one of our trips from the car back to the house, Alicia jokingly said, "I got a feeling we'll be doing this for you two in the not-so-distant future."

Cynthia stopped in her tracks and looked at Alicia. "You two, who?"

"You and Michael."

While they stood and talked, I continued to load the car as if I didn't hear a word they were saying.

"Me and Mike?" Cynthia said sarcastically, because she always called me Mike.

"Yeah. I believe you two are destined to be together."

"Mike, do you hear Alicia over here?"

"No, I don't. And you can't make me!" I said, still loading the car.

"You can't be more wrong, Alicia."

"You know you two are in love with each other."

"Mike's not my type."

I stopped and looked at them when Cynthia said I wasn't her type. I made a smirk, but I dared not say a word.

"Yes, he is, Cynthia."

"You're more Mike's type, than I am."

"Mike, do you find me attractive, Mike?" Alicia asked.

Without stopping, I answered Alicia's question in full stride, "I think all women are attractive, Alicia."

"Look, we're embarrassing him, Cynthia."

"That clown's not embarrassed, he's just being stubborn."

"You see?" Alicia said.

"See what, Alicia?"

"You see how you talk to Mike? You talk to Mike like you guys have been married for years. You're so comfortable with each other," Alicia said.

"Why are you trying to play matchmaker?" Cynthia asked.

"Because I want Mike to be happy," Alicia said, removing the smile from her face and staring directly into my eyes as I walked by. I returned a smile to let her know I appreciated her unselfishness.

"Well, if you want the bald man to be happy, Alicia, why don't you drop that pretty boyfriend of yours and give him a chance."

"Believe me, I would if I could."

Cynthia looked at Alicia, and then looked at me. She made a strange face as if to say, *what was that all about?* I tried not to make any direct eye contact with her, as I loaded the last trip to the car. That conversation ended as abruptly as it began. We piled into our cars and headed back to my house.

By the time we got back everybody had left but Ms. Virginia and Tina. While Cynthia and Alicia were taking a load into the house, Tina pulled me to the side because she didn't want the others to see her cry. She thanked me again.

"Mike, you don't know how much I appreciate this," Tina said.

"No problem, Tina."

"No, I'm serious. Outside of Ms. Virginia, I don't know who else would be this kind."

"You had a room full of women earlier who would have done the same thing I'm doing."

"Yeah, they were asking, but I bet they were also hoping I would say no, too."

"Oh, in that case, they weren't hoping for anything more than what I was hoping for," I joked.

"Ha! Ha! Very funny, Mike!"

"Seriously, Tina, if you were my sister, or one of my girls, in the same situation I would want someone to look out for them."

"You know some people may call you crazy for letting a woman you've only known a few months, and her children, move into your home."

"They might. But then I don't care what those people think. The people who matter the most will know that what I'm doing is what I should be doing."

"How do you think your daughters will feel about your new roommates?"

"Like it's Christmas every day. They love me with all of their hearts, but I know they like to do girly things. They are only going to get so many girly things out of me. So it'll be nice to see them playing with girls their own age, and not just me, nice for all of us!"

"All right Mike, I can't help feeling like I'm imposing."

"Tina, you are imposing! But if you can't impose upon a friend, who can you impose upon?"

"MIKE! TINA! Are y'all going to help or what?" Cynthia shouted.

"Here we come!" Tina shouted back.

Tina grabbed me by the arm and we walked over to the cars.

"Hey, Tina, don't get too comfortable in there. Mike's my best friend, and I'm not going to let you take him from me!" Cynthia said.

"Oh girl, you can forget that, he's mine now! I'm going to have him reading romance novels, watching Oprah, and polishing my toes by the time I leave here."

"That's all right. As long as I don't come over here and catch you two watching a football game, I'm cool."

"Oh, you don't have to worry about that." Tina took the last small pile of clothing from Alicia's car.

"I'm glad you decided to help." Alicia closed the trunk.

"I don't want to mess up your rhythm, so here!" Tina said, handing the small pile of clothes to Alicia, then running into the house.

"Girl, you better get these clothes! Tina! Tina! Tina, come get these damn clothes!" Alicia yelled.

chapter 7

Once we had Tina's things inside the house and in their proper places, we huddled in the kitchen where Ms. Virginia was cooking dinner. The aroma of down-home food filled the house. I could hear the crackling of oil cooking fried chicken. The smell of greens, whichever ones they were—collards, turnips or mustard—I had not a clue, but they smelled delicious. There was also a pitcher of iced tea sitting on the counter, asking me to drink it.

"Ms. Virginia, what is the aroma I smell up in here?" I asked.

"Probably something your mother used to cook for you."

I went to the stove and peeked in one of the pots, and Ms. Virginia smacked my hand and made me put the lid back on.

"Sit down somewhere, boy, before you can't eat in your own house."

"All right! I'm sitting down, Ms. Virginia."

"You better stay out of my pots."

"Can I have some tea?" I asked.

"Yes, but don't drink it all up."

"You should let him dehydrate, Ms. Virginia," Cynthia said.

"Do you ever get tired of running your mouth, Cynt?" I asked.

"Nope!"

"You two act like little children who like each other, but you too scared to tell, so you pick on each other."

"That's what I told them, Ms. Virginia, but they ignored me," Alicia said.

"Oh Lord, here we go," Cynthia said.

I sat silently and sipped on my tea and didn't say a word.

"I'm glad somebody brought that up. I thought I was the only one who could see it," Tina added.

"See what, Tina?"

"See that you and Mike would make a good couple, Cynt," Tina said.

"Michael, what do you have to say about that?" Ms. Virginia said, wiping her hands on her apron, but still carefully watching the pots on the stove.

"Say about what, Ms. Virginia?"

"You know what I'm talking about, boy."

"Seriously, what are you talking about, Ms. Virginia?"

"Well, let me make myself clear. Do you think that you and Ms. Cynthia would make a good couple?"

"Cynthia and I have never thought of each other as nothing other than friends. We're good friends, and that's how we see it."

Ms. Virginia walked over to me, and wrapped her hands around my head.

"Now look at that girl, Michael," Ms. Virginia said, grabbing my chin and turning my head in Cynthia's direction. "Now that's a pretty girl, isn't she?"

"Yes, Ma'am, she is."

"She's smart, too, huh?"

"Yes, Ma'am, she's smart."

"Has good morals, too, doesn't she?"

"Yes, Ma'am, she has good morals, too."

"Then why are you sitting up on your butt like a fool, and not asking that girl to marry you?" Ms. Virginia said, playfully slapping me in the back of my head.

"Ms. Virginia, before you ask someone to marry you, shouldn't you be in love with them first?" I asked.

"Wait a minute!" Cynthia interrupted. "Everybody is talking to Mike as if you all know for sure I have feelings for him."

"We don't have to ask you. Michael's name is written all over your face, Cynthia," Alicia said.

"Everywhere! All up in here!" Tina said, moving her hands in different directions in front of Cynthia's face.

"Girl, please!" Cynthia said, moving Tina's hands out of her face.

"I'm going to the basement," I said, standing up to leave.

"Sit down, Michael," Ms. Virginia said, pushing me back down. "It's time to eat dinner, anyway."

"Ms. Virginia, you remind me so much of my mother," I said.

"I hear that all the time. I guess I have those motherly instincts."

"How many children do you have?"

"I don't have any children, Michael."

"I'm sorry, I didn't know."

"What are you sorry for?"

"I don't know, Ms. Virginia. I was apologizing."

"No need to apologize."

"Did you ever want to have children, Ms. Virginia?" Tina asked.

"Tina, that's rude," Alicia said.

"There's nothing wrong with asking that question," Ms. Virginia said, "as long as we've been knowing each other, I'm surprised it hasn't been asked before now."

"Well?" Tina asked, urging Ms. Virginia to talk.

"Okay, but this better not ever go beyond these walls."

Ms. Virginia's Story Begins...

I was born and raised in Anniston, Alabama. At birth, I was given the name of Cora, after my grandmother. I have three sisters, and four brothers left. My oldest brother who moved to New York City died a couple of years ago. Anniston is a small town located about fifty miles east of Birmingham. I was born in the nineteen forties when black people weren't treated as equals, and black women were treated even worse. I graduated from high school and went to college at Jackson State College in Jackson, Mississippi. After I graduated, I went back to Anniston and got a job working at the county courthouse. I was one of the first blacks to work for the government in Anniston.

While I was working at the courthouse I ran into a boy named Willie I knew in high school. He was known for breaking the law, and going in and out of jail. He never gave me the time of day in school, but after he saw me at that courthouse he was on me like white on rice. I eventually gave in, and we started dating. I lived with my mother and father and they were awfully strict. They bumped heads with Willie all the time. They felt he was influencing me to sneak out of the house and get in trouble. If they only knew, I was the one making him meet me most of the time.

I was a twenty-five-year-old virgin when I met Willie at the courthouse. I went away to college to get from under Mama's and Daddy's watchful eyes. But I came home the same way I left—a virgin. Willie was my first. Once I got comfortable with doing it with him, it's like I couldn't control myself. I had discovered a new-found happiness and we did it whenever we could. I fell head over heels in love with the man and he knew it. He asked me to marry him, and I said yes before he could get it out of his mouth.

My father was so mad at me for marrying him he stopped speaking to me for a while. My mother talked him into coming to my wedding, which was at the court-house, but he let it be known that he wasn't happy with the marriage. He told me in front of Willie that he loved me with all of his heart, and his door was always open to me, but he would never cross the threshold of any house where Willie lived.

"Cora, you know I love you with all my heart. And you know I'll do anythang you wont me to do. But this piece of shit right here ain't nothin' but a no-account man who ain't gon' never do right by you," my father said, pointing his hand in Willie's face.

"Daddy, all I want is for you and Willie to get along."

"I can't! I just can't do it, baby!"

"Not even for me?"

"Baby, like I said, I'll do anythang to make you happy. But I don't think you should marry Willie! He ain't good enough fa you! And that's all it is to it!"

"Come on, let's go, baby," Willie said, pulling me away from my father.

"Get yo' damn hands off my daughta while she talkin' to me, niggah!"

Although Willie was known as a troublemaking bully in Anniston, he knew better than to mess with my daddy. I'm not just saying that because he's my father, but my father didn't care about dying and he didn't let anybody intimidate him or his family. Not even the white folks. He always seemed to be in a bad mood, except to me, Mama and my sisters. Even my brothers had it bad with Daddy. My father was a big man—I don't exactly know how tall he was—but he was an enormous man. And he *proved himself to be as big as his bite. Willie knew this, and he wasn't foolish enough to try to challenge Daddy all by himself.*

"We gotta go, Mr. Cooper," Willie said.

"My daughta ain't goin' nowhere 'til I'm through talkin' to her."

"Daddy, I'll be over tomorrow to talk to you, all right?"

"Leave them kids be, Shiny," my mother said, calling my father by his nickname.

"I'll see you tomorrow, Cora. Come on, let's go, Sha'lett!" Daddy said, with Mama following in his big footsteps. My mother's name was Charlotte, but my father could never pronounce it correctly.

Willie wouldn't let me visit my parents the next day, or the day after that. He thought that if I visited them, they would talk me into leaving him. After three months, my father did what he said he would never do, and that's come to my house. He was so mad that I hadn't come to see them he was coming to put me in my place.

I sat and listened while my father yelled and screamed how much I was hurting my mother. I told him I would start visiting more. He gave me a hug and a kiss, then lowered his voice as he always did when he spoke to one of his daughters. Then he went back home.

When Willie came home, I told him that Daddy had come by and he was upset. I told him that I would have to start visiting my family more and that set Willie off. He started yelling and throwing things all over the place. I was scared to death. He calmed down only when I said I wouldn't go visit them.

Almost a year passed before I saw my parents again. I was nine months' pregnant, and had not told them. I knew they would find out through third party, and that was not how they should have found out. And I also knew that would hurt them badly, but I was trying to be loyal to my husband.

One afternoon while I was walking in town I saw my mother on the opposite side of the street. She called my name and I ran over to her. When she noticed I was pregnant, she started crying. I apologized but it didn't seem to help. I hugged her and then held her. Even while we were talking, I held on to her tightly.

"How can you do this to us?" Mama asked.

"Mama, I'm so sorry, but I don't mean to hurt you and Daddy."

"If you don't wanna hurt us, why won't you come see us?"

At that time, Willie walked up and stood beside me and stared at my mother.

"I'm sorry, Mama, but I can't. I just can't!" I said.

Willie grabbed me by the arm and I let my mother go. My mother called me several times, but I didn't turn back.

Not talking to my family was upsetting me so much it started to make me physically ill. Willie didn't care that I was becoming sick. All that he cared about was that I never left him. If I died, fine, so long as I never left him.

When the baby was due I told him I was going to see my family whether he wanted me to or not. We argued, and he forbade me from seeing them. But I went anyway. I surprised them by visiting them on Christmas Day. I apologized, and explained to them that I was only trying to keep my husband happy, and I would never intentionally hurt them. They accepted my apology, and we enjoyed ourselves.

When I got back home, Willie was furious. He started yelling and screaming again, but this time he didn't stop at throwing things. He started to hit me. Then he threw me down on the floor and kicked me. When he was finished, he ran out of the house. He left me lying there on the floor in a puddle of blood. I crawled to the telephone and called one of my brothers. He called my father, and they took me to the hospital.

I lost the baby, and I almost lost my life. When I got out of the hospital, I moved back in with my parents. Nobody could find Willie, not even the police. My father and brothers went looking for him, and if they would have found him, there's no doubt in my mind, they would have killed him. The word was that he moved to Chicago with some of his relatives.

After I was back on my feet, I went back to work. About six months later, Willie showed up at my job crying and begging me to get back with him. He told me he had a house in Chicago, and we could start all over again. I kept telling him no, but he wouldn't give up. He was so convincing that he was sorry, and he seemed to really regret what he had done to me. He was my husband and I felt like it was worth giving him a second chance. But before I agreed to go with him, I made him promise not to be angry if I came back to Alabama to visit my family from time to time. He promised, and we made plans to move to Chicago. We would have to sneak because if my father found out, he would never let me leave with Willie.

I quit my job, but my parents didn't know. I got up the day after I quit as if I was going to work and I met Willie at the bus station. I left my mother a note explaining that I was all right and I had left on my own accord. I told her to tell the rest of my *family I loved them and I would miss them very much. I tried to ease her mind by saying that Willie was sorry for what he'd done, and he promised never to do it again. I cried all the way to Chicago. Willie consoled me by hugging me and telling me everything would be fine once we got there.*

When we arrived I found our nice family home was actually the basement of one of his relatives. At least Willie did have a job working at the bus station. I got a job my second week there, and Willie treated me like I was a queen. It seemed I had made the right decision to come to Chicago.

He took me to big nightclubs that were even larger than the ones in Birmingham. I liked Chicago until the winter came. I had never seen real snow in my life. It was the first time Willie had seen it, too. As it got colder, he got tired of working outside at the bus station. He quit his job, and I had to take care of us. He stopped looking for work, and the first time I asked him when he was going to start looking, he slapped me and told me not to ever ask him anything like that again. I cried and told him I would not.

His cousin, Vivian, who owned the house, was one of the kindest people you could ever meet. Vivian was a widow and her children were grown and had moved out. She noticed that I was paying all of our bills, while Willie stayed in and out of pool halls. She let me pay whatever I could for rent. She told me that I needed to make Willie work or he would have to leave.

I didn't want to tell her Willie would beat me if I talked to him that way, but I didn't want her to tell him, either because that would make him beat me, too. I made up some ridiculous story about Willie hurting his back, and not able to work. She asked Willie about his back, and he told her there was nothing wrong with him. She knew I had lied to her, and she jumped on Willie about not taking care of his family. After they argued for a while, he came down to the basement and started beating on me. He told me that if I screamed he would beat me even worse.

I took a couple days off from work to give time for my black eye and fat lip to heal. I had to avoid Vivian, too, so that she wouldn't ask any questions. After that, Willie started to drink more, and he started to beat me more. I wanted to leave him, but I was afraid.

A year later, I became pregnant again and Willie still didn't have a job. I was making decent money, but not enough to take care of us and a baby. Vivian was so excited for us she started to buy clothes for the baby. We would go shopping, and we were really enjoying ourselves. Willie had cut back on drinking, and stopped beating me. We were finally coming together as a family.

I was so happy, I wanted to call and tell my mother. I didn't know how they would feel after not hearing from me for two years, so I wrote her a letter instead. I received a letter back from my family within a couple of weeks. They wanted me to come to Alabama to have my baby. I asked Vivian for her opinion, and she told me I should go.

I was nervous about telling Willie, but I wanted to go home and be with my family. I was almost nine months' pregnant, and I knew that he wouldn't be crazy enough to try to hit me then. I was wrong. He was lying on the couch, and as soon as I told him, he jumped up and threw me on the floor. Once again, he began to kick me, and throw chairs and other things on top of me. This time I knew he would kill me.

He was screaming and shouting as usual, and fortunately Vivian heard him. She called the police first, then came and tried to stop Willie from beating me. "What is wrong with you, Willie? Stop beating on that girl!" Vivian shouted.

"Get away from down here! This my biz'ness!" Willie shouted back.

Vivian threw herself on top of me, shielding me from Willie's rage. I don't know how the police got in the house, but they ran down the stairs and saw Willie kicking Vivian and me on the floor. They roughed him up first and then took him to jail. An ambulance came and rushed me to the hospital. I passed out on the way, and I remember waking up with my mother and father sitting at my bedside.

They were both sleep. I stared at them, and noticed how they had aged over the last four years. I called for them, and they woke up. Neither one of them mentioned the baby, nor that I had not contacted them for nearly two years.

They stayed in Chicago until I was healthy enough to travel back to Alabama. Vivian was also still in the hospital. She had suffered a spinal injury from a stern kick to the back. She was kind enough to let my parents stay at her house. Her prognosis was that she would be paralyzed in her lower limbs for the remainder of her life. She called me every day to reinforce my decision to press charges against Willie. She told me she would be by my side the whole way, and she did just that.

I took her advice, and I became a witness for the state of Illinois. Willie was found guilty and sentenced to ten years in prison. He had to go to jail for assault on Vivian and me, but his most severe charge was causing the death of an unborn child.

And as for Vivian's prognosis, she proved science wrong and walked into the courtroom to see Willie face-to-face with the assistance of a walker and my arm. She, too, was a witness for the state of Illinois.

Willie only served six of his ten-year sentence. During those six years he was in prison, a lot of things happened. Most importantly, both my mother and father died. I moved back to Alabama, to Birmingham though, and not Anniston.

My brothers and sisters weren't too excited about visiting me in the big city, so I started to lose contact with them. But on the brighter side of things, I met an attorney named Howard, whom I fell in love with, and we became engaged. I was still married to Willie, but Howard was going to make sure I got my divorce.

Howard took me places I had never seen before, and encouraged me to go back to college. We planned a huge wedding and we were going to be married in his home-town of Richmond, Virginia. He took me home to meet his family and I fell in love with them and Virginia.

On one evening, Howard and I were eating dinner, and just like something scripted from a horrible nightmare, Willie showed up. He was wearing raggedy clothes, and his face was unshaven. He came to our table, and stared at us with a menacing smile. I was so scared, I couldn't speak. I didn't know what to do, or what to say. Howard had no idea who he was, but Willie quickly made himself known.

"Good afternoon, good people, how are y'all doing today?"

"We're fine," Howard spoke, "how are you, sir?"

"I'm fine. I just wanna know one thang?"

"What's that, sir?" Howard asked.

"Do you always run around with other men's wives?"

"I don't know what you're talking about," Howard said.

"I'm talkin' 'bout you sittin' up here with my wife, like she yo' wife!"

"Do I know you, sir?"

"You don't know me, but you gon' know me!"

"Sir, I don't know what your problem is, but I don't want any trouble."

"Oh, if you don't stay away from my wife, you gon' get more trouble than you can handle!"

"I don't take kindly to threats, mister."

"That ain't no threat, that's a promise."

"Let's get out of here, baby," Howard said, going into his wallet.

"Did I just hear you call my wife 'baby'?"

"No, sir, you didn't. You heard me call my future wife, 'baby.'"

"I'll kill you, you son-of-a-bitch!"

"I told you, sir, I don't take kindly to threats, mister," Howard said, standing up and looking Willie straight in the eye.

Willie took a wild swing, and Howard ducked and punched him once in the face. Willie fell incoherently to the floor. Howard was not an incredibly big man, so I don't know what was behind the punch to send Willie to La-La Land like that. Howard paid for the check and any damages which may have occurred during his brief boxing career. He apologized for the incident, and then we stepped over Willie and left the restaurant.

We were preparing to move to Richmond the next week, but I was still kind of nervous that Willie may be lurking in the shadows somewhere near. Howard told me I was being paranoid, and I tried to forget all about it.

The next evening I was supposed to meet Howard for dinner, but he never showed. I drove to his house in Bessemer to see if he was home. When I got there, his door was ajar, so I walked in. I called his name several times but he didn't answer. I walked down the hall to his bedroom and I stopped in horror when I saw his feet lying in his doorway. I didn't want to take another step, but I knew that I couldn't just stand there.

I slowly stepped around the corner and I could see his entire body. He was lying face down. I started screaming and ran out of the house. I was halfway down the street when a man stopped me and asked me what was wrong. I told him my fiancé had been hurt, and he was still in the house. I wasn't for certain if Howard was dead, but I felt it in my heart.

The man followed me back, and we called the police. When the police and medics arrived, they confirmed my worst fears. Howard was dead. He had been murdered by a gunshot blast to the back, and I knew exactly who'd done it. I told the police about the incident the previous night. But they were unable to find Willie. I, on the other hand, was hoping that Willie wouldn't find me.

After Howard's funeral, I was lonely and depressed. All that I had to remind me of our love were sweet memories and an engagement ring he'd spent a small fortune on to make me happy. It was probably worth more than everything I own combined.

I couldn't stand living in Birmingham without Howard. After I finished getting my master's degree, I moved back to Jackson, Mississippi where I went to college. I found a job at an insurance company, but shortly thereafter, Willie showed up, and tried to get me to talk to him. I wouldn't do it, and security took him away. He kept coming every day, causing more and more problems. One day he stopped coming and I thought maybe he'd finally decided to let me go. But after two years of Willie-free horror, he showed up again and beat up a security guard who was trying to stop him from coming into my office. The next day, I received my pink slip.

I left Jackson, and moved to Dallas. Finding a job wasn't as easy as it once was. I was getting older, and my job history did not reflect that I could stay on a job for an extended period of time. Persistence prevails, and I was blessed with the best job of my life. It was my first position as manager. After ten years of working out there, Willie showed up at my job and tried to forcibly put me in his car.

John, the supervisor who worked under me, and I were the last two employees to leave work that day. He saw Willie forcing me into the car and he tried to stop him. Willie beat him to a pulp. Do you hear me? To a pulp! They didn't have to fire me. I left. I tried to stay in contact with John to make sure he was all right, but his wife was very bitter and angry and she wouldn't let me speak to him, and I don't blame her. He was in bad, bad, shape the last time I saw him.

After that I changed my name from Cora to Virginia, the state that Howard was from. The state I was going to be married and start my family. From Dallas I moved here to Atlanta, and started working with Upskon. For eleven years I looked over my shoulder. I was afraid to get close to any man, thinking that would pull Willie out from under the rock he was hiding. I often wondered if Willie ever loved again. I couldn't understand why after all of those years, he still wanted me to be his wife. Anyway, after years and years of moving from city to city, I decided to make Atlanta my home.

I was happy, and I was free, and I didn't know what to do with myself. As badly as I wanted children, I knew that a fifty-something-year-old woman shouldn't be having children. I said that I would just love everyone else's.

I met a deacon in my church and we started to go out every now and then. At our age we were happy to find spiritual companionship. One day, somebody vandalized his car, and my first thought was that Willie had found me again. But they found a couple of children who admitted to the crime.

A few weeks later, I was leaving church and as I pulled out of the driveway, Willie pulled up and blocked my path. It had been almost eleven years since I had last seen him, and I barely recognized him. I stared at him, but this time, I wasn't afraid. I felt that if it was my time to go, then Lord, take me home. He jumped out of his car and told me to follow him. I didn't want to cause a scene at church, so that's exactly what I did.

I followed him to a park and he started to explain that it was not too late for us to have a family. That we could have everything we always wanted. Every time he mentioned getting back together, I would tell him that it was too late. I could see the rage start to build in his eyes, but as I said, I wasn't afraid this time. He grabbed me by my arm, and demanded that I get in the car with him. I knew that if I got in that car, he would surely kill me.

I started to scream, and he began to beat me, and beat me. I continued to scream until a little angel came out of nowhere and leaped on his back. I don't remember what happened after that. I know that I woke up in the hospital, and the young lady who saved my life was in critical condition. It's like she was heaven-sent; nobody knew who she was, or where she'd come from.

Unfortunately, Willie turned his rage on her and stabbed her several times. The young lady survived but she was near death in an unconscious state.

When she woke up, I was right there by her side to greet her. After my attack, I stepped down from being supervisor. I decided two things that Sunday afternoon: I was not afraid of Willie anymore; and I was not going to run from anyone ever again. I know he may be waiting around the corner for me at any moment, but I shall not be intimidated or afraid of any man again.

❖❖❖

"Well, that's been some time ago and you haven't heard from him, so let's pray to God you never see him again," Alicia said.

"I know exactly how you feel, Ms. Virginia," Tina said, "always having to look over your shoulder to see if he's coming to get you."

"I can't even imagine how that must feel," Alicia said.

"That man has cost me a life of happiness. It's too late for me to have children. Most of my memories as an adult are of running from him, and seeing him hurt the people around me. And after all that pain, I'm still married to that man," Ms. Virginia said. "You know what? Sitting here complaining is not going to change a thing. Let's eat some dinner."

"I second that emotion!" I said, going to the stove.

"When I'm here we're going to say grace around here before we eat, Michael Forrester," Ms. Virginia said.

"Ms. Virginia, you are aware that this is my house, aren't you?" I joked.

"And you are aware that I am old enough to be your mother, aren't you?"

"Point taken," I said, kissing her on the cheek.

I had really grown to be quite fond of Ms. Virginia. I didn't know what it was, but she seemed to have a kindred spirit which could relate to everybody. We all sat down at the kitchen table, and our conversation turned much more upbeat as we ate dinner. After dinner, Ms. Virginia invited all of us to attend her church on Sunday.

"Now Michael, I want to see you at my church this Sunday."

"Sorry, I'd love to go but I'll have my girls this weekend, Ms. Virginia."

"So what? Bring them with you."

"That'll be a lot of work."

"What kind of work, Michael?"

"Ms. Virginia, I'll have to comb their hair and that's an all-day job for me."

"Get up early then."

"Yeah, man, just get your lazy butt up and go to church," Cynthia said.

"You can come with him, Ms. Runaway Bride," Ms. Virginia said.

"Hold on, Ms. Virginia, I haven't been to church in God knows when."

"Well, he'll know when on Sunday, when you walk through the door."

Ms. Virginia turned and looked at Tina, but Tina cut her off before she could get started.

"I'll be there!"

"That's what I'm talking about, Tina."

"What about Alicia?" Cynthia asked.

"Ms. Pretty-Pretty comin', too. I better see *all* of your faces in church this Sunday."

"You had to put my name in there, didn't you, Cynt?" Alicia asked.

"You got something against God, Ms. Alicia?" Ms. Virginia asked.

"Oh, no, Ma'am, I'll be there!"

"Okay, young people, I've got to go. Tina, you relax tonight, and let Ms. Runaway Bride and Michael wash the dishes. Maybe that will make them come to their senses," Ms. Virginia said jokingly.

We all laughed, then we walked her to the door. Alicia left about an half-hour later. Cynthia, Tina, and I walked her to the door and then I walked her farther to her car so that we could speak privately.

"Alicia, what is this all about?"

"What?"

"What's up with your crusade to get me and Cynthia together?"

"Michael, I really do care a lot about you. If I was sure Julian and I were not going to make it, do you think I'd be trying to hook you up with anybody else? Thing is, I don't know. And I don't want to keep bouncing from man to man to find out. I know that you are a good man, and Cynthia is a good woman. And if I can't have you, I want you to have the next best thing."

"And the next best thing is Cynthia?"

"I think so, yeah," Alicia said jokingly.

"Well, if you say so, Alicia."

"I say so."

Alicia sat in her car, and rolled her window down.

"Mike, Cynthia is not going to wait forever."

"Whatever, Alicia," I said, putting my hands in my pocket as she pulled off.

I waved good-bye to her, and once she was out of sight I went back into the house. Cynthia left about an hour later. I worked on my book, while Tina and her daughters continued to settle in.

I was more than halfway through and today's notes had best-seller material written all over it!

chapter 8

Tina did not go to work for the next couple of days. She managed to get herself settled in, and we talked unlike we talked at work and I got to know her much better. She was comical and down for anything at work. But at home, she was much more serious and spent plenty of time with her daughters. She did their homework with them every night, ironed their clothes, and prepared them for the next day. She fed them, and me, every evening.

In three days, all of my dirty clothes were clean. She left a little note on my stack of underwear that read, *Wipe a few more times after doing the number two.* I don't know how my *"drawers"* got mixed with my regular wash, anyway. It was a surprisingly, yet comfortable, feeling to have her as a roommate.

Her children were well mannered and respectful. They played and made noises like all children, but they played where you asked them to play, and they didn't run all over the house destroying everything in sight. The whole family was a pleasant surprise.

The night before my daughters arrived, Tina and I were sitting in the den watching television. I was lying on the couch, and she was relaxing in my recliner. She told me she was nervous to meet my girls because she didn't know how they would react to another family moving into their father's house. I told her that she didn't have to worry and that they would love making new friends.

"Mike, you sure it's okay?" Tina asked.

"Tina, if you don't be quiet, I'm going to kick you out and keep your kids."

"I'm serious, Mike. Little girls are very sensitive."

"It seems like big girls are very sensitive, too."

"I just don't want to come between you and your family, that's all."

"You won't come between me and my family, now can I watch television?"

"No. I'm not through talking," Tina said, throwing a pillow at me from my favorite chair, the recliner. It was the first piece of real furniture I'd ever bought.

"All right, Tina, I'm letting you sit in my chair, I don't normally do that. If you keep throwing my pillow, it'll be your last time sitting in it."

"Mike, this chair has to be a hundred years old. It don't even match your other furniture."

"So what? It's comfortable, that's all that matters."

"Hey, Mike?"

"If you don't stop calling my name, I'm going to scream!"

"Say what, Mike?"

"Okay, keep joking."

"Mike, what is your opinion of me?"

"I don't have an opinion, Tina."

"Tell me. If someone was to ask you your opinion of me, what would you say?"

"Tina, I know better than to answer that question."

"It must be because you have such a negative opinion of me."

"That's not it. It's because if I answer that question, it's going to lead to a hundred more questions."

"Just answer that one."

"You're not going to stop harassing me until I tell you, huh?"

"Correct."

"Now if I tell you, I'm going to tell you the truth, you sure you want to hear it?"

"Yeah, I wanna hear."

"Well, I think you are a frightened, embarrassed woman who's hiding behind laughter."

"What am I embarrassed of?"

"The fact that you have a husband who comes to your job threatening you, physically abuses you, and everybody in your life knows he does it."

"So are you saying I'm the classic clown who sheds tears behind her painted-on smile?"

"That would be a great analogy."

"Yes, I am embarrassed. I'm embarrassed that all of my friends think that I am some fool who doesn't have the sense to leave a man who tries to beat her to death. I'm embarrassed that my children watch him beat me to the ground sometime. I'm embarrassed that my friends at work have to ante up money to get me out of a situation that I can't get myself out of because my husband takes all of our money and spends it on his girlfriend. I'm embarrassed when I go to a family affair and everyone asks me how I am doing, because they think Curtis may have beaten on me again. I'm embarrassed that my husband brings his girlfriend to the same church where we worship, right where my children and the whole congregation can see. So yes, I am embarrassed, Mike," Tina said, "how in the hell can I not be?"

"Tina, all you have to do is decide that you want to change your life, and then make strides toward those changes."

"It's not that easy. I didn't get to where I am overnight, and it's going to take me a while to get back to where I was."

"Maybe so. But until you take that first step, you're not going anywhere."

"Thank you, Mike."

"Thaaaat's why I'm here, Tina," I said jokingly.

"Mike, can I talk to you about something personal?"

"Sounds deep, I'm listening." I sat up giving Tina my full attention.

"This is really personal, Mike, so it has to stay between us, okay?"

"Okay, you know I wouldn't tell your business."

"Okay," Tina sighed, "here we go."

Tina's Story

I was born and raised in New Orleans, Louisiana. I was the youngest of six children. I had five older brothers. My biological father died when I was six, and after that I felt an overwhelming sense of emptiness that needed to be filled. My mother remarried when I was ten. It felt like we had a whole family again with the addition of my stepfather, and that seemed to fill the emptiness for a while.

When I was fourteen my brother Paul and me had to move to Mississippi with my mother and stepfather. We moved to a poverty-stricken area called Tunica. Up until then, my life was perfect.

My mother worked nights and my stepfather worked days, so he would be home with my brother and me while my mother was at work. Mississippi was quiet and rural. I hated it. We never had anything to do, and the houses were so far apart it was hard to meet other children. As soon as my brother turned eighteen, he moved back to New Orleans with my other brothers. That left me home alone with my stepfather.

One night when I was lying on the couch in my underwear and T-shirt, my stepfather walked in and sat down on the couch with me. He asked me to raise my head, and I did, and he laid my head on his lap. He started to rub my face, and then he started to raise his hips very slowly. He was moving so slowly. I could barely tell he was moving at first.

I wanted to get up because it just didn't feel right, but I didn't want to embarrass him. He started to raise his hips higher and push my head a little harder into him. At that point, I could feel his penis through his pants. It scared me, and I jumped up and ran in my room. He walked in and sat on the edge of my bed and told me that if I told my mother he would leave. And Mama would blame me for breaking up the family. I should have been old enough to know that it didn't matter what he said, but I didn't want to be responsible for breaking up our family. My father had left me. My brothers had left me, and now my stepfather was talking about leaving me. I didn't know if I could handle it and I didn't want Mama to be alone. I promised him that I would never tell anyone. He kissed me on my cheek and left the room.

On another night, I was lying in my bed sleep, and I woke up to him sliding his penis between my legs. I pretended I was sleep until I knew that he was finished doing what he wanted to do. He didn't put it inside me; he rubbed it between my legs until he relieved himself. After he finished, he slid out of bed, and acted as if nothing had happened the next day.

He kept slipping into bed with me, and I kept pretending to be sleep. One night, he came into my room, and he slid my underwear down. He opened my legs, and tried to force himself inside of me. It wouldn't go in at first, and it was so painful I couldn't pretend that I was asleep. After a while he stopped trying to put it in and he left me alone. A few nights later, he slipped in my bed again. That time when he opened my legs, it wasn't as hard for him. I suppose he used Vaseline, or something oily, because I could feel the stickiness.

Even though it wasn't as hard for him to get in, it was still excruciatingly painful for me. That was my first experience with sex. After that night, he began to come into my room more and more. Sometime on nights when my mother was home he would wait for her to fall asleep, and then sneak into bed with me.

When he would come in, he never used any form of protection. So, one morning I woke up sick. I was nauseated and vomiting. My mother took me to the emergency room, and they told her that I was pregnant. She took me home and demanded I told her who the father was. I lied on this boy that I had a crush on, and said it was him. We had fooled around but we'd never had sex. When my mother went to his house and told his mother, his mother went ballistic on him. And when he finally saw me he cursed me out. In the meantime, my stepfather didn't say a word.

My mother took me to have an abortion. She paid half, and the boy's mother paid half. Not only was I considered a whore, but a rat as well. When I went back to school, the boy started pushing me around for lying on him. Then other kids started to pick on me, too.

It got to a point where my mother had to transfer me to another school for my safety. I felt bad for lying on the boy, and I wanted to tell the truth, but I couldn't tell on my stepfather.

A little time passed when he left me alone, and then he started coming into my bedroom again. Now I didn't pretend I was sleep. Nor did I keep my back turned to him. I turned around on my back and welcomed his touch. He would climb on top of me and we would have sex. I had learned to enjoy it, even though it made me feel sick afterward.

Some nights when my mother was home, I could hear them having sex. As I listened, I wished that it was me in there with him instead of her. I remember him sneaking in my room one night after he and my mother had finished having sex. He waited for her to fall asleep and then came to me. I could hear my mother only moments earlier, moaning from pleasure, and that made my body sizzle. When I saw the door crack open, I pulled my underwear off and started moaning before he even touched my bed. He climbed between my legs, and this time I took hold of him and forced him inside of me.

I wanted him so bad that night. It felt like he was actually my husband and not my stepfather. As he was pounding inside of me, I kept moaning, "I love you', I love you." I remember later that he never once said it back.

When my mother was home, we would always try to do it as fast as we could before she woke up. I think the thought of getting caught made it more exciting for both of us. That night I needed and wanted more than a quickie. Every time I felt his orgasm coming, I would shift my hips and pull him out. My moans and sighs were much louder because I wanted to feel as if we were really making love. In the midst of it all, my mother woke up, and walked in on us. I remember the light from the hallway slowly entering my room and my mother's shadow stretching like a mean angry giant. She pushed the door open and screamed, "What the hell are you doing? Get off my baby!"

He jumped off of me, and tried to grab his underwear. I covered up my head with my blanket and started crying. He and my mother fought and argued until I called the police. My mother made him leave and I never saw him again. My mother never yelled at me, or showed any anger. She sent me back to New Orleans with my brothers, who raised me until I left for college. Since then, she, nor I, have ever told my brothers why she sent me back. Since then, she, nor I, have never discussed that night. And since then, she and I have not been mother and daughter.

❖❖❖

"How do you and your mother get along now, Tina?"

"We don't call. We don't write. We occasionally see each other at rare family gatherings; we speak, but that's about it."

"That's messed up."

"I've learned to deal with it, though."

"But still, it has to be difficult."

"I am only concerned about my children now. I had to get them out of that dysfunctional household before it was too late."

"Well, you're out and they're out. You're all safe, so let's try to keep it that way."

"Okay, Mike." Tina walked over and kissed me on the cheek. "I got to get in the bed. See you in the morning."

"Good night."

❖❖❖

The next day after work I went and picked up my girls. I told them that Tina and her daughters would be staying with us, and like I thought, they were very excited. I picked up Brimone first, and she began to drill me with questions.

"Daddy, what are their names?"

"The oldest is Sasha, who's twelve. The next is Kiya, who is ten. And the youngest is Ariel, who is five."

"Are they going to live with us forever?"

"No, dear. Only for a little while."

"Aw, that's too bad."

"You haven't even met them yet, why are you saying that?"

"Because I know we're going to have a lot of fun."

"I'm sure you will, too," I said, pulling into the driveway of my second wife's house.

"Daddy, can I come in?"

"Yeah, but when we get in here, we're just going to stand at the door and wait for your sister. Don't go running up to her room and playing, you hear me?"

"Yes, sir."

I knocked on the door, and my ex-wife's husband answered. A white guy named Brent Jamison. He just happened to be her ex-attorney in our divorce. Outside of the divorce case, Brent was a pretty nice guy who treated Cecelia, my aforementioned ex-wife, and my daughter very well.

He was slightly older than she was, but then so was I. Cecelia was thirty-two, but looked as if she was twenty-two, maybe even younger. She had long wavy hair, light-brown eyes, which matched her golden-brown skin. An hourglass figure that was accentuated in almost everything she wore. The experience of having a child only added much needed weight to her slender hips which made her look more mature. She was an extremely attractive woman.

She was spoiled and couldn't cope with not having her way. That made a proud man like me even more stubborn toward her, and I refused to let her have her way about anything. That's why we were divorced. It had nothing to do with falling out of love. We simply didn't have patience with each other.

After our divorce was final, Cecelia and Brent kept seeing each other, but not for business. Brent was about six feet two inches tall, clean-shaven, with black hair that was graying at his sideburns and temple. He was quite wealthy and well known in the metro Atlanta area. I have to say, she seemed happy with him. And as long as her love life was doing fine, she and I were doing fine. Brent was always nice; even after he destroyed my lawyer in our divorce case, he apologized. Whenever I went to pick up my daughter, he was very courteous.

"Hey, how are you doing there, Mike?" Brent asked, shaking my hand and stepping to the side to let Brimone and me enter the house.

"I'm doing fine, Brent, how about you?"

"I can't complain."

"Hi, Mr. Brent," Brimone said, waving to him.

"Hey, pretty little girl, how are you doing today?"

"I'm doing fine. Where's Alex?" Brimone asked.

"She's upstairs getting ready."

"Okay."

"Hey, Brent, is 'Celia around?"

"Yeah, she'll be down in a minute. She's getting Alex's stuff together."

As if on cue, Cecelia and Alexiah came down the stairs. As soon as Alexiah saw Brimone and me she dashed over and hugged us both.

"I love you, Daddy!"

"I love you, too, baby."

"I miss you, Daddy."

"I miss you, too, baby."

"Now give me a hug?" Alexiah said, then jumped in my arms.

This was a ritual I performed with my daughters every time I picked them up, and dropped them off. When we were saying good-bye, we would change it from "now give me a hug" to "bye-bye!"

"Dad, can I show my sister my new doll you bought me?" Alexiah said to Brent.

When I heard her say those words I felt like someone had taken a knife and stabbed me straight in my stomach, and twisted it around.

"Sure. Sure you can," Brent answered.

Alexiah grabbed Brimone by the hand and they ran upstairs to her room. I stood there and looked back and forth at Cecelia and Brent. Before I exploded, I wanted them to give me an explanation of why my daughter was calling another man, "Dad."

"What's that all about, guys?" I asked sternly.

"Does it bother you that she calls Brent, Dad?" Cecelia asked.

"Does it bother me? Hell yeah, it bothers me!"

"Mike, we ask Brent to treat Alex as if she was his child, and then when he does, you have a problem with it."

"I never asked Brent to do anything, you did. And I don't have a problem with Brent and Alex's relationship, but I am her father, and he is her stepfather. The objective word in that sentence is '*step*,' 'Celia."

"It is difficult for her to understand the difference between father and stepfather, Mike, especially when she goes to school every day hearing children talk about their experiences with their fathers in the home. When she mentioned the experiences she shares with Brent, she doesn't want to call him stepdad or stepfather. She wants to call him daddy, like all the other kids."

"Unfortunately, when people are divorced things become difficult. Children suffer some consequences just like the adults. I have no problem with Brent, and I think he knows that, but I can not, and will not, allow my child to call another man, '*Dad.*'"

"So what do you want us to do, Mike? Tell her to stop calling Brent, Dad?"

"Yes!"

"That will only confuse her more," Cecelia said. "I don't see why you are saying anything when you have a woman living in your home."

"That's none of your business! But you can rest assure neither of my daughters will be calling her, Mom!"

"If you haven't noticed, I'm not complaining about what's going on in your house," Cecelia said.

"'Celia!" I said, trying to stop the bickering. "This is not a request. I am telling you, I am not going to accept my daughter calling Brent, 'Dad.' There's nothing you can say, or do, to make me change my mind. Do you understand me?"

"You're being unreasonable, Mike."

"Sometimes in life, you have to be unreasonable."

Brent was standing between us, as he often did, waiting for the right moment to mediate. I respected his opinion because it was always unbiased, and most of the time logical and on point. Despite my constant arguing with Cecelia, Brent never saw my hostility as a threat toward him. First of all, he'd sue the hell out of me if I ever thought about any physical altercation.

He would hear the problem from the sideline and then step in to let us know which one of us needed to alter their perspective a little. Cecelia listened to him, and could communicate with him better because he was much more patient with her than I was.

"Guys! Guys! Guys! Calm down before the girls hear you. Now, you don't want that, do you?" Brent asked.

We both said no, and Dr. Brent took over with his counseling session.

"Cecelia, I think Mike has a point."

"So you're taking his side again, Brent?"

"No, honey," Brent said, "I'm just putting myself in Mike's shoes. If I had a little girl living in the house with another man and she started to call him *Daddy*, I would feel threatened like Mike does."

"Well, I wouldn't say threatened, Brent," I mumbled quietly.

"Well, what would you say, Mike?"

"I feel disrespected."

"Who's disrespecting you?"

"Well, you," I said, and then retracting the statement, "well, I guess not you, per se."

"Then whom? Is it 'Celia? Or is it Alex?"

"I guess it's not a matter of disrespect," I conceded.

"No matter what the specific matter is, Mike, you don't feel comfortable with Alex calling me, *Daddy*, and I think that I would feel the same as you if I was in your shoes."

"Look, Mike, if you feel that insecure about it, then you tell Alex not to say it," Cecelia said, folding her arms.

I knew that Cecelia was trying to play on my ego by saying that I was insecure, hoping to draw an adverse reaction. I realized it but I didn't take the bait.

"It will be my pleasure. I'll talk to her this weekend. Can you go get the girls for me?"

Cecelia turned around and stomped her way upstairs.

"No hard feelings?" I asked, extending my hand to Brent.

"Of course not," Brent said, shaking my hand.

The girls came running down the stairs with Cecelia still stomping behind them. I opened up the door and before we walked out, Alex said, "See you, Mom, see you, Stepdad."

Brent looked at me and shrugged his shoulders. "I guess that's that." I smiled and winked my eye at Cecelia, and she playfully pushed me out of the door.

❖❖❖

Alexiah, younger than and not as inquisitive as her sister, asked me a couple of questions about the new people living in our home, but that was it. I looked in the mirror and I could see her staring out of the window. I was curious to know why she'd called Brent, "Dad," when we got there and also curious to know why she'd called him, "Stepdad" when we left. I was concerned she and Brimone had overheard our conversation.

"Alex, why did you call Brent, 'Dad,' sweetheart?"

"Because I call Mommy, Mommy, and I call you, Daddy, and I don't call him anything. I don't want him to feel bad."

"I understand, but I'm your daddy, baby."

"I know, Daddy."

"Okay, what made you call him Stepdad when we were leaving?"

"Brimone told me that I hurt your feelings when I called him Dad. And she told me that I should not say that. Did I hurt your feelings, Daddy?"

"Just a little, but I know you didn't mean to."

"I'm sorry, Daddy."

"That's all right, sweetheart."

"I told her not to call Mr. Brent that, Daddy!" Brimone shouted.

"Shut up!" Alexiah shouted back.

"I want the both of you to stop yelling at each other right now!"

"Okay, Daddy," Brimone said.

"Okay, Daddy," Alexiah repeated.

"Stop repeating everything I say!" Brimone shouted.

"You stop saying everything before I say it then!"

"Look!" I said, raising my voice. "Both of you be quiet!"

They both stopped screaming in mid-sentence, and turned their heads away from each other.

"You two can sit back there and act rude to each other if you want, but if you do, when we get home you're going straight to your room."

They knew that I meant exactly what I said. If we made it home and they hadn't apologized to each other, they would spend their weekend in the slammer. Just before I turned on my street, Brimone whispered, "I'm sorry, Alex."

Alex displayed a great big smile and said, "I'm sorry, too, Bri."

I could see their excitement grow, as we got closer to the house. As soon as I parked the car, they opened their doors and ran to the front door.

They were telling me to hurry to unlock the door and let them into the house.

I teased them by taking my time opening the door. I finally unlocked it and let them in. They walked in to our regular, huge, lonely house. They walked around the house inconspicuously looking through every room for evidence of new inhabitants.

After they put their bags in their rooms, they solemnly came in the basement with me and sat down. I looked at them and laughed.

"What's the matter?"

"Nothing," Brimone said.

"We want somebody to play with," Alexiah said.

"You can play with me," I said.

"You're a boy. We want to play with a girl," Alexiah said.

"What's wrong with playing with a boy, Alex?"

"I don't like playing with boys."

"You don't like playing with Daddy, sweetheart?" I asked.

"I do like playing with you sometime, but sometime I want to play with girls."

"Okay," I said, "are you girls hungry?"

"Yes!" they yelled in unison.

"I'll order a pizza and we'll have a pizza party, all right?"

"Yeah!" Brimone shouted.

"Yeah!" Alexiah shouted.

"Stop repeating everything I say, Alex!"

"No! You stop saying it before I do, Bri!"

"Are you arguing again?"

"No, Dad, we're not arguing," Brimone said quickly.

"That's what I thought. I'll go order the pizza. You girls go change into your bed clothes."

The girls ran upstairs, and I called Cynthia to see what was keeping her and Tina so long to pick up the pizzas. We had made arrangements to surprise the girls with a sleepover pizza party with Cynthia's and Tina's daughters. They told me they were running late because they had to stop and pick up something else along the way.

Tina had a key, so I wouldn't have to open the door, but I asked them to ring the doorbell, anyway because I wanted my daughters to think it was really a pizza delivery person.

Ding-dong! the doorbell rang.

I announced to the girls that the pizza had arrived and they should hurry and come downstairs. When I opened the door, not only were my girls surprised, so was I. Coming through the door were Tina and her children, along with Cynthia, Pam, Alicia, and Valerie. They were followed by Wanda and her two girls, Darsha and her daughter, and Lisa and her daughter.

My mouth dropped to the floor when I saw Susan walk in with her daughter. Then my tongue rolled out even farther when I noticed that Susan's daughter's features had *Negro* up in her somewhere.

"What the hell?" I whispered to Cynthia and Tina.

They ignored me, and the entourage began to chant, "Slum-ber Par-ty! Slum-ber Par-ty! Slum-ber Par-ty!"

"Hey, Susan, how are you?" I asked.

"Hi, Mikey!" Susan responded with enthusiasm.

"You didn't give the rest of us a warm welcome like that, Mikey," Wanda said, poking me in the side.

My daughters went nuts when they saw all of the people filing in one by one. The only person they knew was Cynthia, and they ran to her and wrapped their arms around her. They didn't stop there. They hugged everybody who walked into the house. Tina formally introduced herself and her three girls to my daughters, and then the rest of the group introduced their children as well.

I pointed to Cynthia and Tina and said, "In the kitchen."

They followed me into the kitchen and I asked them what was going on with the office coming over unannounced.

"What's up? Whose idea was this?" I asked.

"It was mine," Cynthia answered.

"What are you doing?"

"Go out there and look at Brimone's and Alexiah's faces, and ask that question to yourself."

"But I only have them every other weekend; you guys are cutting in on my time."

"Mike, stop being so selfish. If you don't spend every second with them they won't love you any less. Let them enjoy themselves, and you, at the same time. Those girls worship the ground your bald head walks on. If they enjoy themselves tonight, this will only make them enjoy you more tomorrow."

"Whatever, Cynt," I said, knowing she was right.

"Whatever, my butt," Cynthia responded.

"You two need to just say, 'I love you,' and get married," Tina said.

"Mike is afraid of me, Tina," Cynthia said, walking out of the kitchen.

"I'm not afraid of her, Tina," I said, after she was gone.

"If you say so, Mike." Tina walked out of the kitchen.

"What do you mean by that?" I said. Tina kept walking and I repeated the question, but louder. "What do you mean by that, Tina?"

She waved her hands in the air, and I yelled to her one more time, "I ain't scared, man!"

chapter 9

They were having so much fun I let the women and girls use the theater room in my basement, while I was content to watch television in my den—alone. I told them to be careful because every item down there was sacred to me. I could hear the screams and playing and I knew my children were really enjoying themselves.

I was thinking that in the future, maybe this night would make them want to visit because they had fun at my house, and not only because I am their father.

Ever since Cynthia had come into our lives, my girls seemed to laugh more. The idea of having a slumber party for them touched me. I could hear them downstairs, and when the other children sought their mothers, my girls sought out Cynthia.

The children started to go to sleep one by one. By midnight, they were all out. The big girls, however, were still up and ready for some big-girl fun. I was lying in my den and I could hear the footsteps of what seemed like a thousand feet coming up the stairs at one time.

"Mike, get up!" Wanda said.

"The slumber party is downstairs," I said.

"We bringin' it up here!" Wanda said. "Get up before we pants you."

"Man, I'm sleepy, go back to the dungeon, witches," I said, rolling on my stomach and covering my head with my pillow.

"Mike!" Valerie said, jumping in the air, then landing on me.

"Oh!" I shouted from the impact of Valerie slamming on top of me. "Val, have you lost your freakin' mind?"

"Get up then!"

"Do you chicks realize that I am not a woman? I don't want to hang with you. Get lost."

"*Get lost,*" Wanda said, mocking me, "stop whining, you sound like a girl."

"You ingrates!" I shouted, "I let you into my home and what do I get? I get a bunch of wild high school girls who won't take their butts to sleep."

"Tonight we are high school girls!" Wanda shouted. "And we gon' have some high school fun!"

"Hey, Mike, where's the liquor and the cards, man?" Darsha said.

"You sound like a bunch of drunken men," I said.

"I don't give a damn! Where's the liquor, Mike?" Wanda said.

"I don't drink, you have to go get some yourself."

"Is the liquor sto' still open around here?" Wanda asked.

"There are no liquor stores around here," Alicia said.

"I should have known there wasn't no liquor sto' around this boogee place."

"I think that's bour-geoi-se," I said.

"Niggah, you know what I'm talkin' 'bout!" Wanda said.

"Hey, you don't see Susan sitting over there?" Lisa whispered to Wanda.

"She one of us tonight, dammit!" Wanda added.

"There's no need to fear, liquor woman is here!" Tina said, walking into the den holding up three brown bags.

"What you got to drink, Tina?" Darsha asked.

"I got some vodka, Kahlua, and some rum," Tina said.

"I think I may have some Hennessy in my trunk," Lisa said.

"Sweet, innocent Lisa got some liquor?" Wanda asked.

"Shut up, Wanda," Lisa said, "it ain't mine. It's this guy's that I'm seeing. He used my car last night, and left all that crap in there. I started to throw it out."

"I tried to tell all of you that Lisa isn't as innocent as she claims," Alicia said.

"It's about to get crunked up in here!" Darsha shouted. "Hey, Mike, cut that damn television off, and cut on some music."

Alicia walked over to Mike's stereo and turned it on.

"Alicia, you act like you been up in here befo'," Valerie said.

"I'm telling you," Darsha said, giving Valerie a high-five.

"Lisa, let's go see what you got outside," Wanda said.

"Come on, let's go," Lisa said.

"I'm comin', too," Darsha said.

Darsha, Lisa, and Wanda walked outside while the rest of the office girls went into the kitchen to make drinks. This left Cynthia and me alone in the den.

"Mike, I think we need to talk," Cynthia said.

"All right, about what?"

"Us."

"What about us?"

"Don't play dumb, Mike. You know what I'm talking about. There's something going on with us, and I want to know what it is."

"I don't know what's going on with you, Cynt, but there's nothing going on with me."

"It seems like the only way we're going to get to the bottom of this, is if I come right out and ask you. Mike, do you have feelings for me?"

"Feelings? What kind of feelings?"

"That's what I'm asking you, ding-dong!"

"I mean, I think you're nice and all, and you're probably the best friend I have in Atlanta, but I don't think there's any romantic feelings between us, do you?"

"If you have to ask, then I guess the answer is no, Mike. There are no romantic feelings between us," Cynthia said, standing up and walking into the kitchen with the rest of the office girls.

"Cynt, wait a minute!" I tried to stop her by grabbing her hand. She snatched away from me, and continued into the kitchen. "If one more person walks out on me tonight, I'm going to stick my foot up their ass!"

While the girls were in the kitchen it struck me that this could be a wonderful opportunity for me to fill the rest of the pages of my book. I went into my office and found a miniature tape recorder I had bought but never had an opportunity to use. I tested it, and it worked perfectly. I put on a pair of warm-up pants and placed the recorder in my pocket. I tested the recorder from the inside of my pocket and the sound once again was perfect. I brought an additional tape for back-up. I went back to my den and posted up on the couch.

After mixing their drinks, the girls piled back into my living room.

"Who made this? This is some good-ass shit!" Wanda said, holding the drink up and looking at it.

"What you drinkin', Wanda?" Darsha asked.

"I don't know what the hell this is."

"Who fixed it?"

"That damn Susan."

"Susan, what's that Wanda drinkin'?" Darsha asked.

"That's a White Russian."

"What the hell is a White Russian?"

"A White Russian is Kahlua, cream and vodka," Susan said.

"How does it taste, Wanda?" Darsha asked.

"Y'all ghetto heffas have never heard of a White Russian?" Pam asked.

"Hell nawl!" Darsha answered. "I ain't been drinkin' as long as you old-ass women."

"It tastes like coffee a little bit." Wanda smacked her lips.

"Coffee?" Darsha said, "I don't want none of that. What you drinkin', Alicia?"

"I'm drinkin' a Mudslide."

"What does that tastes like, Alicia?" Darsha asked.

"It tastes good. It has like a coffee taste, too."

"Why y'all keep makin' these drinks that taste like coffee?" Darsha asked.

"It's the Kahlua, Darsha," Susan said.

"Please keep that away from me, I don't need no coffee tonight."

"I haven't taken a drink in years; can I have a Pina Colada?" Cynthia asked.

"Cynt, you gon' drink?" Wanda asked.

"Hey, I'm hanging out with my girls."

"Cynt, you know you don't need to be drinking," I said.

"Like you care," Cynthia said, taking the drink from Susan's hand.

"Hey! Hey!" Wanda said. "It's time to chill out and tell some secrets."

"That's what I'm talkin' 'bout!" Darsha said, standing up and stomping her feet.

"Sit yo' drunk ass down, Darsha, before you wake up them kids," Valerie said.

"All right, everybody grab a spot, cut the lights down so a niggah won't be embarrassed, and let's get to talkin'," Wanda said, "who first?"

"Val, you go first. Tell us somethin' you haven't told nobody else in here," Darsha said.

"Why y'all always want me to go first? I wouldn't normally tell my business, but whatever the hell this is I'm drinking is telling me to spill my guts. They say shit like this is therapeutic, anyway, so here we go, gotdammit!"

Valerie's Story

"I was born on the island of St. Lucia, in the city of Castries. I have three brothers and three sisters. I am the oldest child. I lived in St. Lucia until I was seventeen. My mother and father made me come to the States because I was an embarrassment to our family. They were devout Catholics, and I was the spawn of the devil in their eyes. They had priests pray over me. They made me sleep in a room with lit candles and Bibles surrounding me. They made me promise that I would never tell anyone my evil secret. And then when all of that didn't work, they made me say that I was no longer their child, and they sent me away.

"I tried my best to be the precious pretty little girl they wanted me to be. But after meeting a girl one summer, I knew I was hooked. She was visiting the city of Soufri re. It's a town located further south of Castries. I met her between the mountains of Petit Piton and Gros Piton. All summer long we would meet and talk.

"One night, she kissed me. It was a little peck on the lips, but it was so exciting. The next night we kissed using our tongues. After that, we started fondling each other. One night, we were so caught up in our exploration of each other's bodies we didn't notice the police. They caught us naked, and told our parents.

"My parents drove down from Castries to pick me up. When the police told my mother what they had seen me do, my mother cried. She cried all the way home. I saw how bad I had hurt her, and I told myself that I would never be with another girl again.

"I tried to like boys. I mean, I really, really tried. But I couldn't. When I was with a boy, I felt uncomfortable. It was like I was lying to myself. I tried to have sex with

this boy in St. Lucia, to see if maybe, just maybe, there was some kind of an attraction. But no matter what he did, it felt sickening.

"*I asked him to do oral sex on me, and he did. I did have an orgasm, but it was because I was imagining a woman going down on me. After I was finished with my orgasm, he wanted me to have sex with him but I couldn't do it. He demanded that I have oral sex on him, and it seemed that he was about to get violent, so I did. I felt so disgusted afterward, I literally threw up. I have not had another sexual encounter with another man since.*

Once my parents realized I was going to like women, no matter what, they got rid of me and sent me to stay with my cousins in Far Rockaway, New York. It's on the outskirts of Queens. It took me a while but I learned to disguise my island accent, and speak as the native New Yorkers.

When things didn't go right for me there, I moved down here to Atlanta and started working at Upskon. I learned how to speak with a Southern dialect, and made everyone think I was born right down here in College Park, Georgia! I've acquired the knack of learning to get in where I can fit in.

It seems like ever since I've been an adult I've been lying about who I really am, or where I'm really from. I'm so used to lying to myself, I've even convinced myself.

If you were to ask me the question, "who are you?" In my native tongue I would say, "qui je suis je ne sais pas!"

❖❖❖

"Have you seen your parents since you left the island?" Wanda asked.

"No," Valerie said, "Because they have not found peace with who I am."

"I know the feeling, Val," Tina said.

"You know y'all are my family as far as I am concerned," Valerie said.

"We think of you as our family, too, Val," Darsha said.

"Nobody is gon' top that, but whose next?" Wanda asked.

"The person who went last selects the person who goes next," Alicia said.

"Val, who do you want to go next?" Wanda asked.

"Your turn, Lisa," Valerie responded.

"Okay, but my story ain't nearly as exciting."

Lisa's Story

I was born and raised in Los Angeles, California. I lived in the suburb of Rowland Heights. We were considered wealthy for black people who weren't entertainers or athletes. I went to a private Christian school where I was the only black until my senior year of high school.

I hated that school and I couldn't wait to get out of there. It's been fourteen years, and I haven't stepped foot inside of those doors. After high school I went to the University of California at Los Angeles, or UCLA, for short. I lived with my parents my entire four years of college. I met a guy named Derrick, and we dated off and on all the way through college.

During one of our breakups, I met a guy, we had sex, and I had my daughter. It was a one-night stand, and I didn't even know how to get in contact with him to tell him he had a child on the way. Hell, I didn't even know his last name. Of course Derrick was angry, but we managed to work things out.

We decided to move to Atlanta after that to start over. The move to Atlanta rejuvenated our careers, he found a great job, and I got my master's degree, but it could not save our relationship. But we're cool as hell. We agreed we grew up and grew apart. He's one of my best friends to this day. He is happily married and has two children with his wife.

Now me, I've been through bad relationship after bad relationship since then. It seems every man I get, is either cheating on me, or lying to me, about something else.

One said he was a music producer, but he was actually a drug dealer. One said he owned a club but he was only a bouncer at the club. Another one couldn't leave the state or couldn't get a job because he was a felon, just a run of bad luck with men. I'm just tired of waiting on something, and I'm tired of always moving on to nothing."

"I feel you, Lisa," Darsha said.

"Choose somebody to go next, Lisa," Wanda said.

"Let's hear your story, Darsha," Lisa said.

"Y'all wanna hear my story?" Darsha asked.

"Can't wait," Susan said.

"All right," Darsha said.

Darsha's Story

I was born and raised in Lake Charles, Louisiana. I never knew my father. I have one brother. My mother and I get along like sisters more so than mother and daughter. We moved to Atlanta a year after I graduated from high school. I never made an attempt on going to college. I was happy to just get out of high school. Not that I was bad a student; college didn't appeal to me.

After we moved here I met Quinton. We had fun and we shared common interests. We both loved hip-hop music, going to clubs and hanging out and having fun. We started going together and then, moved in together. The next thing I knew, I was pregnant with my daughter.

Quinton was happy as a kid in a candy store when I told him he was going to be a father. It's like it affected his ego. He was running around telling everybody like that made him a man. All of that changed when my daughter was born and he had to step up and be a man.

He couldn't keep a job. He couldn't handle keeping the baby while I worked. It was just crazy. We had to move in with my mother. My mother wasn't feeling him working every other month and she told me that something had to change if we planned on staying there. My mother gave me an ultimatum, and then I passed it on to him. Either get a job, or get out!

He got a job, and then another job, and another job. But between jobs he wasn't bringing home anything. He had to go! We sat his clothes outside, and he moved in with somebody else. He stood outside my mama's house, cussing and yelling so loud we had to call the police. That really made that fool mad. I got a restraining order put out on his ass, and he stopped trippin' then 'cause he wanted to see his baby.

He grew up quick then. He's a supervisor now, and he bought his own house. I'm thinkin' about movin' in with him. He got a woman, and I got a man, but we still kinda kick it every now and then. We gon' always be tight because that's my baby's daddy.

I don't think we gon' ever get married. For one, I'm in school now, and I'm about to get my degree. I think that intimidates him and would cause too many problems. If it wasn't for that I probably would move in with him 'cause we know that no matter who we with, we are going to always hook up on the side."

❖❖❖

"Um!" Wanda said. "You young girls are a trip now'days. I ain't sayin' we ain't used to do it, but we just didn't have the balls to brag about it."

"Who's next, Darsha?" Alicia asked.

"Wanda!" Darsha said.

"I can't go yet, I'm the facilitator. I got to keep this shit going!"

"Well, pick somebody for me, Ms. Facilitator!"

"Y'all don't even have to ask me who I want to go next," Wanda said. "I wonts the white shadow, formerly known as Susan."

"Don't you call me that, Wanda," Susan said, elbowing Wanda jokingly.

"Susan! Susan! Susan!" Alicia said.

Wanda looked at Alicia. "Girl, you have a gift, don't you?"

"What gift?"

"The way you can turn yo' white personality on and off, like it's amazing!"

"Wanda, shut the hell up!" Alicia said, laughing.

"See!" Wanda said. "Back in black!"

"Will ya'll shut up and let Susan talk?" Valerie asked.

"Okay, ladies," Susan said, "mine may not be as interesting as yours, but I'll give it a whirl."

Susan's Story

I was born and raised in Hartford, Connecticut. I am the middle child of three children. I have one younger sister, Cindy, and one older brother, Richard. My parents are from what is called, "old money," and we have a tradition of socializing only with other families of old money. There are those exceptions when we allow ourselves to socialize with the rich contemporaries who have more money than us.

We have the family home in Hartford, the summer home in the Hamptons, and we have a plush apartment in Manhattan. My parents are both graduates of Ivy League schools. My father went to Yale and my mother, Princeton.

Imagine their dismay when I told them I wanted to attend New York University. We fought and fought over it. They demanded that I attended an Ivy League school, even thought NYU is a great school.

I talked to my older brother and asked him if I should just listen to Mom and Dad, and not go to NYU. My brother, Richard, was a Harvard Law graduate and a successful corporate attorney. He told me that Mom and Dad had every right to suggest which college I should attend. And he also said that I should respect their opinions and listen to them.

Then after I've listened, make my decision based on what is best for me. I took my brother's advice and I stopped arguing with my parents. I listened to what they had to say, and then I thanked them for their advice. But I attended NYU in the fall.

They were outraged, and threatened to cut all financial ties with me. We both did what we said we were going to do. I went to NYU, and they cut all financial ties with me. That meant no bank accounts. No credit cards. No access whatsoever to my family's fortune. That in itself, turned out to be a blessing in disguise. It made me independent. I had to earn everything I got from that point on, including my degree.

Richard showed me how to apply for government grants and loans and that's how I went through five years of college at NYU. I worked every year I was in college. I paid my own rent, paid my own utilities, bought my own food. Everything I got, I got on my own.

My sophomore year I met a guy named Trent, a black guy. He was beautiful to me. The way he looked, the way he spoke. I was instantly attracted to him. We were at a poetry reading, and he was reading a poem about making love to a woman. It was so seductive. So enticing, I had to meet the man, even if it was only to explain what was going through his mind when he wrote that poem.

Prior to NYU, I had never been remotely attracted to any man who was not white. I was never exposed to any other culture. But when Trent read his poem, I didn't even notice his color. All that I could see was this beautiful man speaking the words that I wanted a man to say to me.

He stood there with his dark-brown skin. His shirt clung to his muscular shoulders. He was about six feet tall. His chest was bulging. His hair was cut in the old afro-style. It was so neat, round, and precise. He had on black shades, and his moustache and goatee were manicured so well it didn't seem like a hair was out of place. His lips were full, and they were moist from licking them so frequently. I will never forget the poem he read. I still remember every single word that came out of his mouth. The name of the poem was called; Making Love is Something Pure…

Making Love is Something Pure
So reassure your heart is sure
But never be too insecure...
For-Love
Your body is a spectacle
My eyes say unbelievable
That one can be so beautiful…
To-Me
Naked in my mind you stand
Skeptical that this romance
Can last a lifetime take a chance…
On-Me
Your body's begging to be pleased
Face your sexuality
Denial's no security...
For-You
Oh, Making Love is Something Pure
So reassure your heart is sure
But never be too insecure...
For-Love
Kisses gently to your neck
Then trickle to your pointed breasts
The sweetest taste is tongue to flesh...
For-Sure
Bite your lips to hush the cries
Of passion screaming from your thighs
Take a breath then open wide…
For-Me
Wrap your legs around me twice
Squeeze my love with all your might
Baby, it's so good and tight...
In-Side
Yeah, Making Love is Something Pure

So reassure your heart is sure
But never be too insecure...
For-Love
Your hips move right on time with mine
Pleasure pain you can't define
Your fingertips rip at my spine...
My-My
Sounds of pleasure fill the air
Passionate screams for all to hear
All your fears have disappeared...
Bye-Bye
Our bodies shake from head to toe
Once unsure but now we know
Our juices start to overflow ...
Don't-Cry
Oh, Making Love is Something Pure
So reassure your heart is sure
But never be too insecure
For Love!

...After the poetry reading I introduced myself. Something I had never in my life been as bold as to do. He told me his name, and invited me to a coffee shop to talk. He was a native New Yorker from Harlem. We started to see each other more and more as friends only. Until one night we accidentally slept together. My first time with a black man, well, it was nothing short of amazing. The myth was no longer a myth. He made love to me in ways no man had ever made love to me before. It was spiritually and physically satisfying.

It wasn't too long before we were seeing each other monogamously. He took me to parts of New York that I would have never visited on my own. We even went to the Apollo. Learning his culture, and seeing black people from a realistic perspective and not from the television, really opened my eyes to the disparaging differences between white and black America.

I met his family, and they were very kind to me. I was the first white woman he had brought home to mom, so this was something new for him, too. It seemed like his entire family was there to meet me. His parents, his three older sisters, two uncles, two aunts, and so many cousins I couldn't count.

I was nervous about meeting them all, but his father took me by the hand and sat me down. And his warmth made me feel a little more comfortable. He made me laugh telling stories about Trent. The fact that I was white wasn't even a factor. Well, not that I could see, anyway. I'm sure there were conversations circulating behind my back, but from what I could see, they were very kind people.

His sisters and I became very close. They were considerably older than Trent, and even though he was a grown man, they still seemed to see him as their baby brother. They wanted him to be happy and that was all that mattered. And I made him happy.

They invited me along on their shopping ventures, and I would go and have the time of my life. They were like being with my aunts, instead of my boyfriend's sisters. I became so close to his family, I would visit even when he wasn't there.

Eventually, the time came for him to meet my parents. I had delayed it as long as I could, because I wasn't very optimistic my parents would support my decision to date a black man. I was correct in my assumption because they hit the ceiling.

My father told me that Trent wasn't welcome in his home, and I'd better not ever bring him there. My mother was not necessarily against it but she wasn't going to take sides against my father.

Once again, I went to Richard for help. He talked to my parents and convinced them to meet Trent before they made a decision on his character. My parents would never admit to being racists, that's being politically incorrect. On the other hand, they had no problem admitting they were elitists. In their opinion there's nothing wrong with being elitists.

We decided to meet them at a restaurant in lower Manhattan. They were there when we arrived. Trent wore a nice black suit that made him look very professional. As I introduced them, Trent stuck out his hand to shake my father's, my father looked him up and down, and then firmly shook his hand. My mother didn't even bother to shake his hand. When Trent extended his hand to her, she smiled, and gave a half-hearted wave.

"Oh, it doesn't come off," Trent said jokingly.

"Excuse me," Mom said.

"He was only joking, Mom," I said, trying to ease the tension.

"You think that embarrassed them?" Trent whispered in my ear.

"Yes," I whispered back.

The rest of the evening went pretty much the same way—uncomfortable conversation when we weren't talking that much, and embarrassing conversation when were talking. The introduction did nothing to change my parents' view of our relationship; although they did say that Trent dressed very nicely to be an African-American fellow.

They met a few more times, like at my graduation and my graduation dinner. But my parents didn't exhibit warmth in any of the meetings. They were particularly cold when they found out shortly after my graduation that I was pregnant.

This infuriated them, and they blamed it all on Trent. They told me that his people were used to going through situations like that, but I wasn't. They adamantly expressed that they were not going to be party to any financial assistance for my illegitimate child. They suggested that I have an abortion or get on welfare. I told them that I hadn't asked them for a dime since I was eighteen, and I didn't want anything from them then.

Trent graduated the year before and he was already making waves in his career. He had an advertising job, and two promotions in his first year. He had a great apartment that most people would kill for in New York. And I was pretty confident that once I had my baby, I would find a good job as well.

Shortly before my daughter was born, Trent asked me to marry him, and I said yes. I invited my parents, but they declined the invitation.

Richard told me he would give me away at my wedding. My sister, Cindy, was my maid of honor. My parents told her that if she attended the wedding she was only perpetuating the false belief that Trent and I could somehow make our marriage last. Cindy was a senior in college herself and she was old enough to make her own decisions. She basically told Mom and Dad to go screw themselves.

Although we had the financial situation under control, with Trent's family paying for everything, my brother felt obligated to contribute. He told Trent that he wasn't contributing because he had to, but out of love for his sister. And just as I thought, Trent had no problem with Richard helping out.

The wedding was fantastic! To my surprise, Cindy got along with Trent's sisters even better then I did. Well, I guess I wasn't that surprised on Cindy's part. She has always had black friends, and dated black men. Dad and Mom's opinion never meant anything to her. She was raised on MTV, VH1, and hip-hop music. She didn't care about race, politics or any of the political or social divisive issues in this country. When it came to men all that she cared about was if he was, or was not, a good lay.

Cindy sung and danced with Trent's sisters the night before the wedding as if she was born and bred in Harlem. They played the karaoke. It was a blast. They absolutely loved each other.

The next day, our wedding was even more beautiful than I expected. It was the most special day of my life. Richard sent my parents a tape of the wedding and they sent it back to him. He made a special visit to their house to let them know how he felt about their attitude toward my marriage. I heard it was pretty ugly. My parents stopped speaking to him for a while after that, but they couldn't go too long; he was their pride and joy.

Cindy didn't have a close relationship with them, anyway, so not speaking to her didn't matter much. She loved Trent, and a couple of his cousins I heard, and she visited us quite frequently. I tried to keep in contact with my parents but they only responded on holidays when they corresponded with all of their associates.

When my daughter, Kala, was born I sent them pictures of her. I'm assuming they got them; they've never mentioned it, so I really don't know. Christmas is coming up soon so I look forward to getting one of their Christmas cards with no personal message.

Luckily, my daughter has brought so much joy to my life. She makes me so happy I don't waste time feeling sad over my parents' ignorance. Hopefully, they'll come around and see the wonderful experiences they're missing with their grandchild.

As far as Trent and I are concern, we are just as in love now, as we were on our wedding day. He is in love with our daughter, and loves being a family man. He grew tired of the hustle and bustle of the city and wanted to raise Kala in a more provincial area.

After his father died, he couldn't stand living in New York anymore so we moved down here to Atlanta with my mother-in-law. We haven't been down here that long, but so far we love it.

I put Kala in summer school our second week here. The next day I went looking for a job and found one at Upskon. If I could change anything it would be that my co-workers start treating me more like one of the girls in the office and less like management.

❖❖❖

"Susan, if you can spend the night with us, *'Black Girls Gone Wild,'* you have to be one of the girls," Wanda said.

"Yeah, Susan," I said. "After tonight, you and I both will be full-fledged office girls."

"Who's next?" Alicia said.

"Who are you, Alicia, the story police?" Wanda said.

"Yes, I am! It's your turn next, Ms. Facilitator!"

"Oh, y'all think y'all ready for me? I'm just gon' come on out and tell you, you ain't ready!" Wanda said.

"We'll see, start talking," Alicia said.

"Gimme a minute, half-pint."

Wanda's Story

I was born and raised on the South Side of Chicago, Illinois. I have six brothers and two sisters. Both of my parents are still living, and still living together. We grew up close in my family. My sisters and brothers were my best friends. We had friends outside of us, but when we hung out, the brothers of the family hung out with the brothers, and the sisters of the family hung out with the sisters. Sometimes we even hung out together.

I graduated from high school, but I didn't go to college. I got married young. And when I tell you I loved that man, I loved the hell out of that man. But we were young and stupid. Well, he was young and stupid, anyway. He couldn't take care of his family. Well, he could have, he didn't want to. He cheated on me so many times I stopped counting. But I was so in love with him, I couldn't let him go. But when he started having kids with other women, I had to cut it off. He had about three kids outside our marriage, but the bastard couldn't manage one inside our damn marriage.

It took me a while to get over him. We broke up a few more times before I could get that niggah outta my system. Actually, I came down here to Atlanta to visit my cousins, and we were hanging out on Old National Highway. I met this black, country-ass niggah, and we kept in touch when I went back to Chicago. I talked about his Jethro ass the night I met him, but when I got back to Chicago and he started talkin' that country shit to me, I had to uproot and come back down here permanently.

He's a mama's boy, but that's a good thang. He'll do anything for his mama, but he'll also do anything for me and my girls. We go at it now, we ain't perfect, but we know how far to go, and we know when to back up.

I started working at Upskon not too long after I moved down here, and been here ever since. I think I like working there so much because it's all women, and we don't have to put up with that macho-man bullshit.

People say I got a big mouth, and a bad attitude, and I like to talk shit. That ain't it, I don't like to talk shit, I like to bullshit. I like to start fun, not trouble. Sometime people don't understand that, but oh well. If they misunderstand and want to get an attitude with me, they can kiss my ass.

❖❖❖

"Whoo! Tell 'em, Wanda!" Alicia said. "Who's next?"

"Mike! That niggah always sitting around listening to us, and we don't know none of his deep dark secrets," Wanda said.

"And that's where my secrets are going to stay, deep and dark."

"Wanda's right, let's hear from Mike," Valerie said.

"Move along busybodies, there's nothing to see here."

"Truth or dare, Mike, you havin' an affair with somebody in the office, or are you a gay?" Wanda said.

"A gay? I'm offended by that comment," Valerie said.

"Why? I'm a black!" Wanda said.

"In that case, Mike, are you havin' an affair, or are you a gay?" Valerie asked.

"Leave Mike alone, it's almost four-thirty in the morning, the sandman is next," Alicia said.

"My daddy always said the first hen that cackled laid the egg." Valerie laughed.

"Yeah, leave that niggah alone. He ain't squealin' and I'm sleepy as hell," Wanda said.

"Come on, it's still early," Darsha said.

"Girl, it's almost time for daylight to come again. That means it's the next damn day. Now lay your ass down somewhere and go to sleep," Wanda said.

"Wanda, one day I'm going to pay a crackhead to come up to you and whoop you good. Do you hear me?" Alicia said.

"Send her!" Wanda said. "I ain't scared of no crackhead! I'll whoop a crackhead's ass and won't think twice about it."

"Wanda, how did you get to be so tough?" Susan asked.

"Susan, Wanda's not tough," Valerie said. "In the black community you have three types of people. You have those who are tough and don't give a shit about nothing and will tear yo' ass up just for looking at 'em. You have those who don't bother people and don't want to be bothered and won't mess with you unless you mess with them. Then you have those who are bullshitters. Bullshitters try to bullshit the other two types into thinking they're tough when they're not. Or they may say they have this or that, when they ain't got shit. That's what Wanda is, a bullshitter!"

"A bullshitter?" Wanda shouted. "Val, you can get yo' ass whooped up in here for talkin' to me like that! And that ain't no bullshit!"

"Get my ass whooped by who?" Valerie shouted back.

"Me!" Wanda shouted. "I'm going to introduce you to my two weapons of ass destruction! My left fist, shock, and my right fist, awe!"

"Don't y'all start playing in here; you're going to wake up those kids!" Cynthia said.

"If you're feeling froggy, bitch," Valerie said, "leap!"

"Aaaaah!" Wanda said, hitting Valerie in the head with a pillow.

"Oh shit! Yo' ass is mine!" Valerie said, chasing Wanda.

Wanda crouched behind Alicia and used Alicia as a shield. Valerie didn't stop or slow down. She swung wildly and hit Alicia.

"Ow!" Alicia screamed. "You hit me, Val."

"Sorry, but there's always casualties in war, baby," Valerie yelled, "move the hell out the way!"

"It's like that, huh?" Alicia said, picking up her pillow and striking Valerie in the face while she was in mid-sentence.

"Yeah, it's like tha…," Valerie said, before being struck in the face by Alicia's pillow.

"What?" Valerie said, addressing Lisa and Darsha. "Y'all ain't gon' help me?"

"You were handling it," Lisa said, "but I got yo' back."

Lisa and Darsha attacked Wanda and Alicia in a pillow fight. Pam and Tina joined Alicia and Wanda and it was a free-for-all. Cynthia jumped on the couch with me out of harm's way. Susan picked up a pillow and started swinging with the fury on an angry bee.

"Susan, I thought you were on my side," Wanda said.

"Well, I'm on no one's side," Susan said, hitting Wanda in the back with one of the pillows. "It's just that there are four of you against three of them, and that's not fair!"

They continued to chase one another upstairs, and all around my house. I tried to gather them in one room to get them to stop, but it was like catching greased chickens. Finally, the alcohol took its toll, and they began to drop like flies, every last one of them. They were in different rooms of my house—in the den, both of the living rooms, upstairs, everywhere.

chapter 10

Cynthia and I stayed up cleaning the house. We didn't want the girls to know that their mothers were drunkards so we put the house back in ship-shape condition. We threw away the liquor bottles to remove all signs of the drunken fiesta from the previous night.

The women were a part of the cleanup. Cynthia straightened out their clothes, and I put blankets on them. Mostly all were in rooms on the first floor except for Lisa and Valerie. We went upstairs and checked out the bedrooms. That's where we found Lisa sleeping in Valerie's arms. We slowly backed out of the bedroom, and closed the door.

"I didn't see nothing," Cynthia said.

"Me neither," I whispered back.

"Let's get out of here before they hear us," Cynthia said.

We tried to get a quick nap before the children woke up. But before we could close our eyes, the little ones started to come upstairs. Before we knew it, we had ten screaming girls begging for breakfast. We reluctantly threw our blankets to the floor and marched into the kitchen.

"You get the eggs and bacon, I'll get the sausages and pancakes," I said. "And I don't care how much those kids beg, it's not going to be any McDonald's this morning."

"Affirmative!" Cynthia said.

After the children bathed we put in a movie to entertain them while they waited for breakfast. Meanwhile, Lisa and Valerie woke up and came downstairs one at a time. They had no idea we had spied on them in their sleep.

"Hey, what time did you two get up?" Lisa asked.

"We haven't been to sleep," Cynthia said.

"What? Y'all been up all of this time?" Valerie asked.

"Yes. We had to clean up the aftermath from the party last night," I said.

"Oops! Sorry 'bout that, Mikey," Valerie said, "let's get the rest of them up to help feed their own kids."

"Can you please wake 'em up?" Cynthia asked.

Valerie grabbed a skillet and a big spoon and banged them together making enough noise to wake the dead.

"Damn, my head hurts," Darsha said, lying face down with her head in the pillow.

"Mine too," Wanda said, lying with her blanket covering her head.

"What happened?" Susan asked.

"We got drunk, that's what happened," Wanda said.

"Oh my God, my head is killing me," Alicia said.

"Where are the kids?" Susan asked.

"They're downstairs watching a movie," Cynthia said. "Maybe you ladies need to go wash up before your children see you looking like Ned the Wino."

"Who's Ned the Wino?" Susan asked.

"Don't ask me," Darsha said.

"He's a drunk dude that used to be on *The Waltons*," Wanda said.

"Oh, I never watched that show."

"I got first dibs on a shower," Darsha said.

Darsha, Lisa, Valerie, and Susan dashed to find available showers.

"Hey! Hey! Hey! No running! There are enough showers to go around," Cynthia said.

"If I didn't know no better, I'd swear up and down that this was your house, Cynt," Wanda said.

"I spend enough time over here," Cynthia said.

"Naw, I think it's a little more than that," Wanda said.

"Oh, is it deeper than that, Mike?" Pam asked, looking at me.

I ignored Pam and kept flipping my flapjacks!

"Are y'all still drunk? Stop being so nosy!" Cynthia said.

"I think we hang around each other too much," Pam said, walking and scratching herself. "We work together, party together, and now we're sleeping together."

"I know, right?" Cynthia said.

"That's too damn much," Wanda said. "Here come Darsha, which means there's a free shower."

"Here comes, Lisa," Pam said. "I got that one."

The more the sun came up, the more hectic my household became. The children were anxious to see their mothers. The mothers were anxious to get cleaned up, and I was anxious to get them all out of my house and spend some time with my own children.

Cynthia and I finally finished cooking breakfast, and Darsha and Lisa set the table. We called the children upstairs to the kitchen. They made so much noise stomping on the stairs they sounded like a pack of wild animals. All that I could think about was my sacred basement being ripped apart. We got them all seated and fed in a well-organized manner.

They sat and played while they enjoyed their breakfast and the mothers ate happily in the den. I had a feeling they were not going to leave immediately following breakfast so I prepared myself for the worst. The worst was realized when Tina asked Cynthia about the arrival time for the bouncy ball booth.

"What bouncy ball booth?" I asked, looking at Cynthia.

"Shhh!" Cynthia said. "It's a surprise for the girls."

"What's a surprise for the girls?"

"The bouncy ball booth."

"What is a bouncy ball booth, Cynthia?"

"That's when they get in a booth and jump around on bouncy balls."

"Where are they going to do this?"

"In the backyard."

"Cynt, it's two weeks before Christmas, they're not going outside in the cold to play."

"Mike, it's sixty degrees outside and it's not even nine o' clock yet. They'll be fine."

"I don't care about that! Cynthia, it's time for these people to go home!"

"They'll be gone by noon," Cynthia said. "I promise."

"Cynt, I need some sleep, man. We got to get them out of here!"

"If you're sleepy, go get in the bed. I'll look after the girls."

"I can't ask you to do that."

"Man, go get some sleep."

"You sure?"

"Mike, get real. Go get in the bed."

"You're not sleepy?"

"I'm having too much fun to be sleepy."

"Since you're being nice, I'm assuming you're not upset with me anymore."

"Life's too short to hold grudges, Mike," Cynthia said. "Now go get some sleep or come outside and help."

"No way," I said. As I walked off, I looked back at Cynthia and saw how she was working hard to make sure these people had a wonderful time. I wanted her to know that I really appreciated the effort she puts forth to make sure my daughters enjoy themselves when they visited me. I walked back to her and stood in front of her.

"Cynt," I said.

"Yeah, what's up?"

"You're an amazing person."

"Okay, looks like somebody needs some sleep."

"No, I mean it. You're really an amazing person."

"Go get in the bed, Mike, you're tired."

"You see, when I try to open up to you, you always blow me off."

"I didn't mean to blow you off, Mike, but would you be so open to tell me how amazing I am if the girls weren't involved?"

"I can't win."

I stared at her again, and then I went to my bedroom and took a short nap. When I woke up everybody was gone, even Tina and her daughters had stepped out. I looked outside and the bouncy ball booth was still in the backyard, and so were Brimone, Alexiah, and Cynthia. I put on my robe and walked outside with them.

"Have you had any sleep, Cynt?"

"Not yet. I've been having fun with the girls."

"Well, it's my shift now, you can go get some sleep."

"Daddy, can I take a nap, too?" Alexiah asked.

"Sure, sweetie."

"I got an idea, Daddy," Brimone said, "how about we all take a nap in your room?"

"I don't know, Ms. Cynthia may want to go home and take a nap," I said.

"Ms. Cynthia, can we take a nap in Daddy's room?" Brimone asked.

"That's up to your daddy, Bri," Cynthia said.

"Can we, Daddy?" Alexiah asked.

"Sure, if it's all right with Ms. Cynthia," I said.

"We're not getting anywhere like this," Brimone said. "Ms. Cynthia, Daddy said it's okay. Daddy, Ms. Cynthia said it's okay, so let's go take a nap already."

Brimone grabbed me by one hand, and grabbed Cynthia by her other hand. I picked Alexiah up in my arms and we all went into the house for a nap. I slept on the edge of the bed, Cynthia slept on the other edge, and Brimone and Alexiah slept in between. Before long they were all sleep and I lay there quietly watching television, careful not to disturb them. I looked at Cynthia and I couldn't help but kiss her for being so nice to my children and me. At that moment I knew that I loved her, I just didn't know how much.

They woke a couple of hours later and we watched some more movies. It wasn't long before they had passed out again, this time for the evening. Tina and her girls came back, and they, too, made it an early evening and went to bed.

I woke up during the night and went to work on my book. I had so much information from their slumber party I couldn't get it out fast enough. I played the tape and wrote down every word and every emotion. I now had personal confessions from every single woman in the office, except for Jaline.

While I was writing, that familiar sense of guilt started to take over my conscience. These women's lives were going to become an open book, literally speaking. And there were going to be repercussions to the exploitation of our confidential conversations, regardless of whether I wanted to admit it or not. I thought about the disappointment they would feel, the pain, and the betrayal. Then I thought about the frustration, the anger, and the murder. My murder!

However, I knew my purpose, and I promised myself that no matter what relationships formed during this project, I would not deter from that purpose. Still, the words I was writing did not bring a feeling of gratification, but betrayal.

After typing for a few hours, my fingers and eyes became exhausted and I dragged myself upstairs to go to bed. Cynthia and the girls looked so comfortable I didn't want to disturb their sleep by rearranging the sleeping format. I grabbed a blanket and stumbled back down to the basement. I cut on the television and instantly fell asleep. In what seemed like only a minute, I was awakened to Tina tapping me on my feet.

"Hey, sleepyhead, it's time to rise and shine."

"Huh?" I said, still dazed from the lack of sleep.

"We let you sleep as late as possible. Get up and get ready for church."

"Church? Who's going to church?"

"We are. We promised Ms. Virginia, remember?"

"Shit," I said, rubbing my eyes.

"It's Sunday morning, man, watch that profanity."

"Oh yeah," I said. "Damn, I'm tired."

"Mike, get up now." Tina dragged me onto my feet.

"Hey, the rest of you can go to church. I got to get some sleep."

"Mike, get yo' ass up, and put yo' clothes on, boy!" Tina shouted.

"Damn!" I rubbed my entire head.

I made my way upstairs, and fell into the shower. I stood there with my head down and let the water run on top of me. I was trying to wake up, but I couldn't. I lifted my head to let the water splash in my face to see if that would help, but that didn't work, either. It seemed nothing I did could spring me from my state of drowsiness. That was until I heard the door to my shower open, and Cynthia tell me to speed up my pace.

"You holding up the whole team here, Mikey. Everybody's almost ready to go but you." Cynthia ignored that I was standing in front of her stark naked.

"Cynt, what are you doing? I'm in the shower!"

"And?"

"And? And I'm naked!"

"Please, Mike, I'm not impressed." Cynthia laughed and slid the shower door closed.

"You're not 'impressed'?" I said, as she was walking out of the bathroom. "What do you mean, you're not 'impressed'?"

As usual, she kept walking and ignored me. So I yelled louder, knowing I would not get a response, "What do you mean you're not 'impressed,' Cynthia?"

As expected, she didn't answer.

I was alert then, and hurried to get out of the shower. I quickly put on a suit and quickly I was ready for church.

Cynthia had combed my daughters' hair, and they looked so beautiful wearing their dresses. I was so moved I uncontrollably displayed my affection by talking in baby talk to them.

"*Oh, you two look so cute,*" I said.

"Let's go, Michelle," Cynthia sarcastically remarked.

"See, men are doomed if we do, and we're doomed if we don't. If we don't express our emotions, we're called machismo, and if we do, we're called effeminate names like Michelle. We're doomed if we do, and we're doomed if we don't."

"Finished whining?" Tina asked.

"Let's go before I curse one of you out," I said.

"You're an office girl, Mike," Tina said. "You are beginning to act like us."

I wrapped my arms around my girls and we started to walk out of the door. I leaned over to Tina and whispered in her ear.

"Bullshit! I will never be an office girl."

Tina laughed, and punched me in the shoulder.

Cynthia and I rode in Tina's car, and the girls rode with Tina in mine. Tina wanted to drive her own car but there wasn't enough room to fit all five girls. They wanted to ride together and the only vehicle that would hold all of them was my Navigator. I refused to drive around with five screaming girls so Tina was the next available candidate. She was intimidated at first to drive the Navigator, but once she turned her first corner she was spitting dirt the remainder of the way.

Cynthia and I followed closely, because we didn't have the directions.

"That chick is driving like a madman," Cynthia said.

"She better not do any damage to my truck," I responded.

"What about your kids, Mike?"

"Them, too."

"Priorities! Priorities!"

"You know what? You've been awfully sarcastic lately, Cynt."

"Who?"

"You!"

"How so?"

"It's like, every time I say something, you have a smart reply."

"Mike, that's always been our relationship."

"No, not always. Yeah, we are sarcastic with each other, but we still manage to have conversations without the sarcasm."

"Poor baby, is little Mikey's feelings hurt?"

"See, what I mean. Stop doing that!"

"Calm down, Mike, I'm only joking."

"That's it, Cynt! You joke too damn much!"

"Stop raising your voice to me, Mike."

"Stop trying to make stupid-ass jokes every time I say something to you then, Cynthia!"

"If you can't take it, don't dish it out!"

"There's nothing to take! I'm just tired of these childish jokes!"

"Stop acting like a woman, Mike!"

"That's what I mean, right there! Why do you keep making remarks just to make me mad?"

"I don't say things to make you mad."

"You do! Everything is, I'm 'acting like a woman' this, or I'm 'acting like a woman' that! I'm tired of that bullshit!"

"First of all, stop yelling and cursing at me, Mike!"

"Well, stop trying to emasculate me!"

"You're just being sensitive."

"You damn right, I'm sensitive! Stop trying to refer to me as a woman before you get your feelings hurt! I'm tired of hearing that shit!"

"Mike, I saw you in the shower this morning." Cynthia smiled. "You are far from being a woman."

"Oh yeah?" I said, lowering my voice and smiling.

"Yup!"

"So were you impressed?"

"Very much so."

"Did you get a good look?"

"Yes, sir, front and rear."

"And?"

"And my eyes opened wide when I saw the rear view, and they nearly popped out when I saw the frontal view."

"That's what I thought."

The rest of our conversation on the way to the church was pleasant and borderline seductive. We lost Tina a couple of times and had to use the technology of cellular phones to find her. We arrived at church late, and we had to sit in the overflow room. There were eight of us so it was still a little difficult to find seats together. However, we were seated as before the minister began to speak.

"Good morning, God's beautiful children."

"What the hell?" Tina said, reaching over the children to tap Cynthia on the arm. "That's Ms. Virginia!"

"Tina, stop cursing in church!" Cynthia whispered back.

"What? I cursed?"

"Yeah girl, you better watch your mouth."

"I'm sorry, Lord, but you can't throw surprises in front of me like that and not expect some crazy outburst," Tina said, looking above.

"Oh my God, that is Ms. Virginia," Cynthia said.

"Did either of you know that she preached?" I asked.

"Not me," Cynthia said.

"Me neither," Tina added.

"Man, there are too many secrets floating around that office. Lisa's a lesbian. Susan's husband is black, too many secrets."

"Shh!" Alexiah whispered, placing her finger to her lips.

"All right baby, we'll be quiet," I said.

❖❖❖

"Hallelujah, sisters and brothers!" Ms. Virginia said. "It is so good to see you all looking so beautiful this fine morning. I would like for you all to turn your Bibles to the book of Numbers, Chapter Thirty-Five, and Verse One."

Ms. Virginia continued to give a heartwarming sermon that made all of us thankful for coming out and hearing a wonderful message. After church we stayed behind to talk to her. We weren't the only ones present from the office. All of the office girls, along with Susan and Tazzy, hugged and congratulated her.

We stood and talked for a while and then we all went our separate ways. Tina, Cynthia, and I took the girls out for a late lunch. After that we went to the park. Then Tina and her girls headed home. I asked Cynthia to ride with me when I dropped the girls off at home and she said she'd love to go. We went home and packed their things. I dropped Brimone off first, and we kissed and said our good-byes.

I don't know why, but when I dropped Alexiah off, she cried. It was the first time she had ever behaved that way. She didn't want me to leave and it broke my heart to have to say good-bye. I assured her that I would pick her up for Christmas and we would spend a whole week together. After a while she stopped crying and I felt comfortable leaving.

I've always loved both of my children with no favor, or difference. But Brimone and I have always had a special connection, a connection that I didn't have with Alexiah. I suppose it's because I never felt that Alexiah needed me as much as Brimone. And I never felt that I needed Alexiah as much as I needed Brimone. Brimone was with me through two divorces, and through-out it all, I remained her hero.

Alexiah has never really lived in the household with me for an extended period of time, so I guess that's why I felt our connection was not as strong. On the other hand, Brimone had cried for me more times than I can count and never have I ever felt as badly as I did the day Alexiah cried. My love for one is no greater than my love for the other. I can honestly say that in situations like mine it's possible to love your children differently, but the same.

❖❖❖

The following Monday, the buzz was about Ms. Virginia's sermon. We were all impressed and sincerely happy for her going into the ministry. Although it was a surprise, I could see where she could serve as a minister to most people. She had a reverent personality that emanated from her soul.

Tazzy held a special meeting to congratulate her in front of the office and presented her with a gift. There was hardly any work done that day, but we knew we were going to make up for it the next day.

As expected, we were loaded with claims the following morning and Tazzy started with a meeting to stress that we needed to process as many claims as possible to get caught up. She also mentioned that we were going to have a new employee starting to work our Call Orders.

Call Orders is a process where customers call directly into our office to file their claims. They normally have to go through customer service to file their claim, but when it is an extremely expensive insured claim, they are exempted and forwarded directly to us. We really needed help this area.

Around nine o' clock Tazzy walked in with our newest employee. My jawbone almost dislocated itself after dropping so fast to the floor. A bombshell! Alicia had competition! I thought that beauty didn't come in packages wrapped more exquisitely than Alicia, but now I wasn't so sure.

Tazzy introduced the new lady, Cherie, to everyone and showed her to her desk. Cherie had to be in her late twenties or early thirties. She had a caramel complexion with beautiful eyes that were shaped like a cat. Her body was absolutely perfect, small waist, with nice firm legs. A perfectly round bottom that wasn't too big, or too small. She had a nice smile with sparkling white teeth. Her voice sounded like a nightingale. It wasn't only her physical features that were so magnetic. This woman had an inner presence that superseded anything physical.

After Tazzy gave Cherie her utensils, Cynthia took over from there and began training. I was thankful that Cynthia worked closely with Cherie. That way I could try to control my animalistic male instincts.

Cynthia and Cherie formed a bond and they started to go to lunch together. The first week I spoke to her in passing, but I didn't hold an extended conversation with her. Cynthia told me that she was happily married and had two children, so that made me feel a little more comfortable around her.

I felt even more comfortable when I found out she was married to a minister. If I couldn't control myself after finding out that information, the Lord needed to strike me down. On her breaks, she would talk to the rest of the office girls, but then she would also take time to read the Bible. I went from wanting to jump her bones to wanting to give a confession. I figured one day we would have to say something to each other. One day while we were in the break room alone, she broke the ice.

"Good morning," Cherie said.

"Good morning, how are you?"

"I'm fine. How does it feel to be the only guy working in an office full of women?"

"I'm just one of the girls."

"What church do you belong to?"

"I'm not a member of any church in Atlanta."

"Well, where is your home church?"

"My home church?"

"Yeah, where is the church you call home?"

"Oh, it's in my hometown of Buena Vista, Michigan."

"Good. When was the last time you attended?"

"Do I have to answer that?"

"You don't have to, but now you've got me curious."

"It was about twenty years ago."

"Twenty years ago? That's no longer your home church, Michael."

"I'm working on finding a church here."

"Well, you've found one. I want you to come to our church this Sunday."

"I would love to come to your church sometime, but can I have a rain check on this Sunday?"

"I understand, but even if it's not our church, you still need to find a church somewhere."

"I'm sure I will."

Pam walked in as we were talking and nudged me with her hip. It had been a while since we were together, but we never officially broke it off.

"Good afternoon, Pam," Cherie said.

"Hey, Cherie, good afternoon."

"May I ask you a question?"

"You sure can."

"Where is your home church?"

"I haven't found a home church."

"Well, you have now. I want to invite you to my church this Sunday."

"Oh, sweetie, thank you, but I went to Ms. Virginia's church last Sunday. And I want to give the Lord too much, too soon. You know?"

"Believe me, the Lord can handle anything you bring, Pam."

"That's so true," Pam said.

"Well, it's an open invitation, you're welcome any time."

"I promise to take you up on it, Cherie."

"You, too, Michael," Cherie said, walking out of the break room.

"All right." I waved as she left.

"Hey, it's been a long time. I want some of this," Pam said, grabbing my crotch and everything inside.

"Pam, I thought we weren't going to do this anymore."

"Niggah, you must be crazy, I'm addicted."

Pam slipped her tongue into my mouth, and I grabbed her by her waist and we started our wild passionate kissing. We normally had a grip on our groping of each other while focusing on the door at the same time. But we were so caught up in the moment, we couldn't react fast enough. Cherie snatched the door open before we could break free of each other and she saw Pam standing there with a hand full of my penis.

"Oopsies!" Cherie said. "I'm so sorry."

"It's not what it looks like," I said nervously.

"Yes, it is, Cherie!" Pam said boldly. "Mike and I are having an office fling and we don't want anyone else to know. Can you keep this to yourself?"

"It's none of my business," Cherie said. "I'll get my Bible and you can go back to doing whatever it is I didn't see you do."

"Thank you, dear," Pam said.

Cherie walked out, and Pam resumed her assault.

"Come on, baby," Pam said, rubbing me up, down, and in the middle.

"Pam, we can't do this. Cherie almost caught us!"

"All right, meet me in the men's bathroom."

"What if we get caught, Pam?"

"I'm horny as hell! Come on, Mike, shit!"

"Okay, you go first. I have to go get the latex."

"Okay, baby, hurry up!"

I went to my desk and grabbed a condom and started on my way back to the bathroom. On my way, Cherie looked at me and smiled. I could tell that she knew what I was going to do. But I returned a wholesome smile and proceeded to the bathroom.

The last time Pam and I'd had one of our episodes it was Ms. Virginia who looked at me peculiarly. I was beginning to think that the Lord was trying to tell me something. But I wasn't sure, so I went to the bathroom to have wild sex with Pam. When I walked in, Pam was standing in the dark in her heels, totally naked.

"Pam, where are your clothes?"

"Over there," she said, pointing at a dark spot in the corner.

"You're a freak!"

"You damn skippy!"

"Come here!"

"How do you want me, Mike?" Pam said, already moaning.

"Sit on it," I said, sliding my pants to my ankle, and sitting on the commode.

"Okay, baby!"

Pam stood over me, and squatted down slowly. I could feel her wetness as soon as I became close to her hole. When the tip of my penis touched her hole, she let out a loud moan and started to slide up and down. I covered her mouth with one hand, and I grabbed her hips with the other. She grabbed my shoulders with her hands, and leaned back. I let go of her hips and grabbed her butt, still covering her mouth. I could feel my orgasm nearing, so I pulled her close to me and started to pump as fast as I could.

"You ready, baby?" I asked.

"Oh yeah, baby, give it to me! Give it to me!" Pam whispered in my ear.

My orgasm triggered hers, and we slid off the commode and onto the floor. I ended up on top of her and I kept drilling until the last shiver went through my toes. Pam was lying on the floor breathing and moaning so loudly I knew that someone had to have heard us. I cleaned myself, and left Pam still lying and panting on the floor. A few minutes later, Pam came around the corner as if nothing had happened. I looked up, and Cherie was looking at me.

I told Pam later that Cherie knew what we were doing in the bathroom but she refused to believe me. She thought that I was panicking as I normally did when we snuck a quickie at work. Pam and I had sex the next day, and then the next week right before Christmas.

Cherie was watching every move we made, and I was becoming annoyed. Pam didn't care one way or the other. I was her sex buddy and nothing more, and she liked it the way it was. If people knew, fine. If people didn't know, that was fine, too. She simply didn't care. I had a lot more at stake. I had been with Alicia, and I was starting to develop feelings for Cynthia. I didn't want them to know that I had been having wild sex with Pam all over the office. If they were to find out, I wanted to be the one to tell them.

chapter 11

As fate would have it, I got my chance to find out how much Cherie knew about Pam and me when we were one of only five people at work the day before Christmas Eve. Susan, Valerie, and Lisa were the other three.

Susan was the only supervisor and she was only going to be there until noon. The four of us had to alternate lunch two at a time, to make sure the office had someone to man the phone at all times. Of course Lisa and Valerie went together at twelve, and Cherie and I went at one.

Cherie asked if she could go to lunch with me and I said yes. I seldom went to lunch with anyone at work, even Cynthia. So this was a rare occasion. We went to an Italian restaurant close to the job.

"So Michael, do you eat Italian food?"

"Actually, it's okay, but I'm not a big fan. You suggested this place, and I wanted to see if you had good taste."

"I must have good taste, I chose you, didn't I?"

"Chose me for what?"

"I want you, one time, no strings attached."

"Uh, you want me, to do what?" I asked.

"I want you to make love to me like you make love to Pam."

"You're joking, right?"

"Does it sound like I'm joking?"

"I know those office girls put you up to this."

"Nobody put me up to this. I'm lonely, I'm sad, and I'm aroused. That's it. Pam doesn't have to know. Nobody ever has to know."

"I'm flattered, but I think you're setting me up, Cherie."

"Michael, this is a one-time opportunity. If you think I'm setting you up, let's just forget it!"

That was the moment when I should have taken the high road and let the temptation pass. But, I couldn't do it.

"I want to make love to you, Cherie. Boy, do I want to make love to you. But you're a preacher's wife. This is adultery, plus a whole lot of other stuff."

"You're right. I am a preacher's wife, that's what has driven me to the point where I am now."

"Your life should be perfect. You have a rich, God-fearing husband."

"Nobody's life is perfect, Michael."

"But you have the life every other woman in that office would kill to have."

"They can have it. Within a year they'd want to give it back."

"Forgive me, Cherie, but this is some phenomenal shit happening here. Oops! I didn't mean to use profanity."

"Michael, look, I understand if you don't want to make love to me."

"Believe me, that's not it! I'm fighting the temptations of hell to keep from leaping over that table on you, right now! I just feel like you'll regret it later."

"I won't regret it. And I would like to explain why, Michael."

Cherie's Story

I was born in Omaha, Nebraska, and I was raised in Dallas, Texas. I have two brothers and one sister. We moved from Omaha when I was two years old and never went back. Not even to visit. We moved because my father became one of the ministers of the Greater Ebenezer Temple in Fort Worth, Texas.

After he took over the pastorate, he spent almost every day of his life in that church. The only days he was not there, were on the days when he was visiting some other church on its behalf. My mother loved being the first lady of the church. People treated her as if she was the first lady of the United States. My father was a good, good devoted minister. He always thought of the church first. The decisions he made were always predicated on what was best for the church.

He spent a lot time away from us, his family, and his children. He tried to make up for it, but there weren't enough hours in a day. I used to sit by the window and wait for him to come walking up the stairs to the house. He would always pick me up and carry me around the house.

I grew up idolizing my father. I had nothing but respect for the man. And he never disappointed me. When he had to leave us, he always explained that he had to do God's will. And he explained that he missed us more than we could ever know.

Eventually, my father became sick and I prayed and prayed and prayed that God would spare his life. After all, my father was not an old man; he was only forty-five years old. But he didn't. He took my father away, and my mother explained that death comes to us all. And I asked my mother why didn't God answer my prayer and let my father live. She told me he did answer my prayer; he told me that it was time for him to go to Heaven.

I started to drift away from the church after another man became the pastor. He was single and so was my mother. He needed a first wife, and my mother was the reigning first wife so they married less than two years after my father's death. My mother said it was in God's blessing. I never bought that.

After high school, I moved away and went to a theology college in my home state. I never lived with my mother again. She seemed to enjoy being the preacher's wife more than a mother. Even though I didn't live with my mother, she and Pastor Washington still financed my living expenses.

When I finally found the courage to be totally on my own I moved away from Texas, and moved here to Atlanta. Not soon after that I met a man who was becoming a minister. And being that I was also becoming a minister, I thought I had met the perfect man. We made plans to start our own church where we would co-pastor and start a new generation of believers.

We got married and not too long after that we rented out space in a shopping center for our church. It was difficult at first getting people to show up consistently every week. But once the word started to spread the rental space wasn't big enough. We had to find a place to accommodate the members of our congregation.

We took out a loan and had our own church built from the ground. The building was huge. It could accommodate our members and more. We were afraid that it may be a bit premature, but it turned out to be a fantastic idea. Our congregation grew with our building. It grew so much that we had to add on to it to accommodate additional membership.

But as the membership grew, our co-pastorship diminished. It diminished to the point where I wasn't doing sermons on Sunday anymore. I wasn't even an assistant pastor. I had become the recruiter for the church. His name was on our sign. His picture hung in our church. And me, I moonlighted as the preacher's wife. The thing I despised more than anything else.

I tried to just be quiet, and let God lead my husband where He wanted Him to go, but in my heart, I knew I was supposed to be spreading the gospel myself. The church became a place of horror, instead of a place of contentment for me. I am so tired of pretending to be happy, when I am feeling such anguish in my heart.

Day by day, I grow tiresome of this charade. I came to work at Upskon just to get away from our church and the loneliness of being a preacher's wife. It is said that a preacher often commits adultery right in front of his wife's face and she never even knows it. It's because he doesn't cheat with another woman, he cheats with the church. It gets all of his time, all of his love, all of his affection. And everything else that he has to offer. And all the while, we sit back and pretend everything is okay. Unless of course, you're my mother, then you truly enjoy being the first lady.

❖❖❖

"Michael, do you realize that I haven't made love to my husband in nearly a year."

"That's insane."

"He hasn't held me in his arms. He hasn't kissed me, or caressed me. Nothing, in nearly a year."

"So why are you with him?"

"I love him."

"My next question is, if you love him, then why are you here with me?"

"Because I feel like I can't live another day of my life without being touched by a man."

"If you do this, you will probably feel guilty tomorrow."

"Maybe I will. Maybe I won't."

"Perhaps you should think this through, Cherie."

"This is not something I am rushing into, Michael. This is something I have been imagining for the past year."

"Why don't you tell your husband what you are telling me? You are a very beautiful woman; I can't imagine any man refusing to make love to you."

"I have talked to my husband. My husband doesn't even realize how long it has been. When I try talking to him, he tells me that it hasn't been that long and he accuses me of being some kind of nymphomaniac."

"Have you been with another man since you and your husband haven't been together?"

"Michael, I haven't been with another man in my entire life."

"What? Your husband is the only man you've ever been with sexually?"

"I haven't even kissed another man. Ever!"

"Okay, I'm in!" I said, responding before she could get all of her words out.

"What a turn of events!" Cherie said, laughing at my quick response.

"One question, why me?"

"I guess after seeing you and Pam in the break room. Then seeing you two sneak in the bathroom, it aroused me and gave me the courage to fulfill my own fantasy."

"Hypothetically speaking, if we were to do this, when and where would we do this?"

"We would do it at a nice hotel, already reserved, down the street from the job immediately following work today."

"You were pretty confident I would do this, huh?"

"No. But even if you don't go, I'll spend time with myself."

"All right, I'll go with you to the hotel. But let's see how you feel when we get there."

"I won't change my mind."

"All right, it's a date. We better be getting back to work."

"I'm ready when you are."

Cherie and I returned to the office and stared at each other until it was time for us to leave. She gave me the directions and room number to the hotel and we left in different directions. I nervously knocked on the door as if I were back in high school picking up my prom date. She opened it, still wearing the clothes she'd worn to work.

"I haven't had time to change. Make yourself comfortable while I go take a shower," Cherie said.

"Okay," I said, sitting on the edge of the bed.

I sat and waited for her to come out of the shower and when she did, I was not disappointed. She had a towel wrapped around her and dropped it only when she was safely underneath the blanket. I wanted to join her so badly, but it was my turn to take a shower.

I jumped into the shower and cleaned the essential portion of my anatomy and then dried myself off quickly. I brushed my teeth and applied the scented deodorant I'd purchased on my way to the hotel. I was ready for action. By the time I walked back into the bedroom, Cherie had fallen asleep. I slowly slid into the bed beside her and wrapped my arms around her. It worked out great that I didn't have to get my girls until the next morning because I had nowhere to go or nothing to do but hold Cherie.

When she woke up, she rubbed her body against mine and I instantly became aroused. She noticed the massiveness, and moved away from me.

"Are you okay, Cherie?"

"Yes, I'm fine. I've never felt another man before."

"Do you want me to slide back?"

"No, please. Come closer."

I slid closer to Cherie and she slid backward into me. I started to kiss her on the back of her neck and she purred like a small kitten. She took my hand and placed it on her breast. I began to squeeze her nipples and grind into her. She turned around and faced me and we started to kiss.

I could tell that she hadn't had a lot of sex with men because she was very apprehensive about using her tongue. I forced my tongue into her mouth and that seemed to really arouse her. She started to grind into me harder, and caress my back. I turned her on her back and slid between her legs. We rolled on each other until I couldn't take it anymore.

"Cherie, are you sure you want to do this?" I asked.

"Yes."

I rolled over and pulled out the condom I had strategically opened and placed in the drawer next to the bed while Cherie was showering. I put it on, and positioned myself between her legs again.

"Please, go slow, Michael."

"You put it in, and we'll go as slow as you want."

Cherie grabbed me by the head and placed it at the entrance of her hole. She barely put the head in before she grimaced and stopped. We waited for a moment until she became used to me, then slid in a little more. I patiently allowed her to take as long as she needed to make herself comfortable. For some reason, her innocence made the wait that much more exciting.

"Oh, Michael, this feels incredible."

"It feels incredible to me, too."

"I can't take anymore; can we just do it like this?"

"Of course." I stared into her eyes.

We moved slowly as I went in and out of Cherie. She squirmed and turned adjusting her body. After what seemed like forever, I felt myself slip deep inside of her and she wrapped her legs around me tightly and scratched at my back with her fingernails.

"Oh, my God, Michael. This hurts so badly."

"Do you want me to stop?"

"No, please don't stop. It feels good, too."

"Okay, let's move like this," I said, slowly pushing myself inside.

"That feels wonderful. Keep doing it like that. Please."

"You like it like that, Cherie?"

"Yes! Oh yes!"

"Open your eyes, and look at me."

Cherie opened her eyes, and looked at me while I slowly made love to her.

"Oh, my God, this feels wonderful. Absolutely wonderful."

"I want you to come for me, Cherie, can you do that?"

"Oh yeah, Michael, oh yeah!"

"Does it feel good?"

"It feels wonderful! Don't stop!"

"Do you want me to go faster?"

"Oh yes, please, faster!"

"Like this?" I said, driving deeper and faster inside of her.

"Oh yes! Yes! Yes!"

"You like that, Cherie!"

"Oh, yes! What's happening to me?"

I grabbed Cherie's feet and put them on my shoulders and drove deep inside of her, faster and faster until her legs started to kick wildly.

"Oh God! Oh God! Oh God! Oh God!"

"Are you coming, Cherie?"

"Oh my God, yes! Yes! Yes! Yes!"

"That's right, let it out! Let it all out! Let out your pain! Your loneliness! Everything! Let it out!"

"Owwwwwwwww!" Cherie yelled.

"That's it Cherie, I'm here for you, let it out."

Cherie's sounds of pleasure quickly turned to tears of heartache as her hips stopped moving and her eyes began to water.

"What's the matter, Cherie?"

"I'm sorry, Michael. My marriage! My life! I hate it!"

"Go on and cry, that's why I'm here."

"Please, Michael, don't stop. I want you to experience what I experienced."

"I'm satisfied. I enjoyed watching you."

"But I'm not satisfied. I want to watch you."

That was all I needed to hear. I started to stroke Cherie again with deep and long strokes. I grabbed her face in my hands and kissed her very slowly. She used her hips to grind with me with every thrust, and then I sped up. She reached behind me and punched her fingernails deep into my skin. I started to raise my hips to get an even deeper thrust, and she matched me stroke for stroke. My orgasm was strong and powerful.

I did my normal deep and loud groan, followed up by a series of lower moans. This apparently turned Cherie on, because as I was concluding my orgasm, she was in the middle of her second. Not wanting to ruin the party, I continued to stroke her until she was finished.

"Oh, my God, that was unbelievable, Michael."

"Did you enjoy yourself?"

"I'm, I'm speechless! That was amazing! There was so much passion, so much affection!"

"So, how do you feel now?"

"I feel like I can go home to my husband and wait another two years for him to make love to me."

"What happens if it's more than two years?"

"Then I'll have to find another, Michael."

"I hope not."

"Me too," Cherie said, with me still inside of her, "me too."

For the next three hours we talked about everything under the sun. We didn't bother to put on any clothes because we were still caressing and touching as we conversed.

We started playing around and it led to another round of hot sex. This time Cherie was much more animated. She suggested that she get on top, and I was more than happy to oblige. After the second round we showered and got dressed, and then we went and had a late cup of coffee. She told me that instead of breaking up her marriage, I probably had saved it. I walked her to her car, gave her a hug and she drove away. That was the last time I saw Cherie.

chapter 12

When I got home, Tina had decorated the downstairs and the sound of Christmas carols were being played throughout the house. Her girls were asleep, and she and Cynthia were drinking unplugged eggnog.

"Where you been?" Tina asked.

"I was out with a buddy."

"What buddy? We're the only buddies you have." Cynthia said.

"I have friends all over Atlanta, Cynt."

"Then why haven't I met any of them?" Cynthia asked.

"Because I don't want you men-starved women to embarrass me."

"Nobody wants your stale friends, Mike."

"Speak for yourself, Cynthia," Tina said.

"I tell you what, I'll have them come over next week for New Year's Eve and we can have a little party."

"I got to get in shape before next week then," Tina said.

"Tina, do you actually think you can get in shape in one week?" I asked.

"Hell yeah!"

"You see the things we have to do to make men happy, Mike?" Cynthia asked.

"You're not doing that because we're asking you to, you're doing it because you want to."

"Dressing for a man is hard, Mike. We have to wear high heels, put on makeup, wear uncomfortable clothes. It's not easy."

"Cynthia, first of all, I have never seen you wear high heels. I have never seen you wear makeup, and your clothes consist of slacks at work, and warm-ups at home."

"I wear heels all the time and they hurt," Tina said.

"Well, don't wear them."

"But that's what men like, Mike!" Tina shouted.

"Men don't give a damn about the type of shoes you're wearing if your ass looks good in a nice tight dress. How many times have you had sex with a man without your shoes on? Now compare that to the amount of times you've had sex without your ass on! As long as you have a nice ass, a man will forgive you for your shoes, makeup, and anything else."

"That's so sexist," Tina said.

"We're talking about sex, so it's all right for me to be a sexist."

Tina broke the conversation when she heard the Temptations' version of the Christmas carol, "Rudolph the Red-Nosed Reindeer."

"Oh shit! That's my jam right there!"

"Sang it, Tina!" Cynthia shouted.

"*Rudolph, the red-nosed reindeer, had a very shiny nose. And if you ever saw it. You would even say it glows. All of the other, other, other reindeer. Used to laugh and call him names. They never let poor Rudolph, join in any reindeer games,*" Tina sang loudly.

"What the hell is in that eggnog?" I shouted.

"Nothing, don't pay no attention to Scrooge.Tina, sang it!"

"*Rudolph, the red-nosed reindeer. You'll go down in HIS-TO-REEEY! Hey Rudolph! Come on and guide my sleigh! Hey Rudolph! Come on and guide my sleigh!*" Tina shouted, dancing with a cup of eggnog in her hand.

"I hope you are happy. You have destroyed an American Christmas classic!"

"I added my own flavor to it."

"That you did."

"Forget you, Mike," Tina said.

"Mike, what time are Bri and Alex going to get here tomorrow?" Cynthia asked.

"I'm going to get them first thing in the morning."

"I'm going, right?"

"That's up to you."

"I'm about to go home," Cynthia said. "Mike, call me when you're on your way to pick me up in the morning."

"Yup."

"See y'all tomorrow."

"See you, Cynt," Tina said. "Mike, go walk her to her car."

"I'm going, shut up, Tina."

I walked Cynthia to her car, and without even thinking, I kissed her on her lips.

"What was that?" Cynthia asked.

"What was what?"

"What was that kiss for?"

"I was trying to kiss you on your cheek but I mistakenly caught your lips."

"Oh, so that's what happened?"

"That's my story, and I'm sticking with it!"

"Well, in that case," Cynthia said, pulling me to her and giving me a long passionate kiss, "we don't want any mistakes, now do we?"

"Uh, no. We don't want any mistakes."

I closed her car door, and she waved and pulled off. I swear my knees shook when she kissed me. I had just had wild passionate sex with an extremely beautiful woman most men would give their life savings to have, but Cynthia had me standing in my front yard wanting to chase her down the street like a dog. What the hell was going on?

I went back in the house and Tina and I stayed up for hours listening to Christmas carols, and preparing the house for Christmas Day. In the short time Tina had lived with me she'd become like a sister. I didn't know when she planned on moving, but I was in no hurry for her to leave.

When the house was still and I was the last soldier standing, I got on my computer to complete the last chapter of *The Office Girls*. It began with Jaline and it had to end with Jaline. I had enough information on her, but I wanted more.

My publisher was anxious to read the manuscript. I promised to have it to him before the New Year and I was going to do it. I made a few edits, then paused. Finally I pressed "send." And there it was, my book was now at the mercy of my publisher.

❖❖❖

The next day, I woke up bright and early and left to pick up my daughters. On the way I had to meet with my publisher, Jerry Greenbaum, to discuss my book. Greenbaum was a short, fat, balding man who had a loud mouth. His sport coats were too small, and so were his shirts. One of his buttons was always popping open, or falling off.

He had a gap between his two front teeth and a thin moustache. He was totally tactless and incapable of caring for anyone other than himself. He smoked cheap cigars that left a horrible lingering smell in the air. It smelled even worse when it emanated from his clothes.

But outside of those character flaws, the man was a multi-millionaire genius when it came to publishing bestsellers. My first three books were his few failures. He released me from my contract and wouldn't accept another book until I came up with more contemporary concepts. I sold him on *The Office Girls* and he was eager to read the manuscript.

Greenbaum had called me bright and early to arrange a meeting as soon as possible. I told him that it would have to be a quick meeting because I had plans for the day. I rushed into his office preparing to explain how this book would be different from the others. However, as soon as I walked in, he greeted me with a cigar and an enthusiastic handshake.

"Michael! Michael! Michael! You have a bestseller on your hands here, my man!" Greenbaum shouted.

"You've read it already?" I asked.

"I couldn't put the son-of-a-bitch down, my friend!"

"What did I tell you, Greenbaum?"

"If I would've known you had these kinda books in you, I would've never gotten rid of ya! Just kiddin'," Greenbaum said, whispering in my ear, as if there was someone else around that may hear him.

"So I take it you like it?"

"Like it? I freakin' love the son-of-a-bitch! It's got bestseller written all over it!"

"Good, I'm glad you like it."

"People are going to eat this shit up! A man telling the secrets of his female co-workers! A true story based on women's real-life heartaches! This is some unbelievable shit you got here, my man!"

"Thanks."

"You got to get this finished! Quick!"

"I still have one more chapter to go but I should be finished in a couple of months or so."

"A couple of months? No, my man, I need this thing within a week!"

"A week?" I shouted. "That's impossible, Greenbaum!"

"I got to get this thing in the stores as soon as possible! This thing is hot! Go home and get to work!"

"It's Christmas, Greenbaum. I'm going to spend time with my family."

"That's right, for a minute there, my man, I thought you were Jewish! In that case, go home, eat ya chitterlings, ya black-eyed peas, or whatever it is you people eat for ya holiday. And then get to work on that book first thing in the morning!"

"I can't promise that I'll have it finished by next week, but I'll try."

"Trying is not good enough! You got to do it! You got to get this son-of-a-bitch finished, Michael!" Greenbaum walked me to the door.

"I'll try."

"All right, all right, my man," Greenbaum said, closing the door with me halfway out. "Say hello to the wife."

As I took a step away from the door he opened it back up quickly and said, "Sorry about that, my man, I forgot about the wife situation. Ya got kids, don't ya?"

"Two girls."

"Well, say hello to the girls for me, and have a Happy Christmas!"

Greenbaum closed the door, and I walked off smiling. He hadn't changed a bit. As a matter of fact it looked like he was wearing the same suit he had on the last time I saw him. The last time we met in person he told me he was pulling my books off the shelf and advising me to go into law. This meeting had gone much better.

I called Cynthia as soon as I got in the car to tell her I was on my way to pick her up, but like always she was waiting for me. We stopped and ate a quick breakfast, then we were on our way. We picked up Brimone first. This time, Cynthia got out, and went up to the door with me. I knocked on the door, and Tonita answered.

"What's going on, Mike?" Tonita said, then yelled upstairs. "Bri, your father's here!"

Tonita stepped to the side and let Cynthia and me inside.

"Mike doesn't have any manners. I'm Brimone's mother, Tonita."

"Good to meet you, I'm Cynthia."

"I was wondering when I was going to get a chance to meet you. Bri talks about you so much I was beginning to get jealous."

"Don't worry about it, she talks about you all the time, too."

"Would you like a cup of coffee while Bri gets ready?"

"Sure, that sounds nice."

"Mike, go upstairs and help your daughter get ready," Tonita said, taking Cynthia by the hand. I knew that she was about to give her a thorough interrogation.

"Where's Rob?"

"Downstairs putting together Bri's toys."

"When Bri gets ready, tell her I'm downstairs."

I went downstairs and found Rob sitting in his recliner watching Sportscenter. Rob was a short stocky guy, about five feet seven inches tall. He was light-skinned, with a skinny pointed nose, and a bald head.

He worked as a detective for the Atlanta Police Department. We got along great. We even hung out sometimes. I actually knew Rob before Tonita. We played on the same team in a semi-pro football league for one year. Like Brent, he loves my daughter, and treats her like she's his own.

"Hey, what's up my brother?" I said.

"Hey, what's up, Big Mike?"

"Putting the toys together, huh?"

"Yeah, I'm on my break."

"I hear you, man. So how long have you been on your break?"

"Ever since I came down here."

"And what time did you come down here?"

"About seven o' clock this morning."

"Dude, you've been on break for three hours?"

"Yup, and I still have thirty more minutes left."

"That's my boy!" I said.

"I've been meaning to tell you, we got to do something about Brimone," Rob said.

"What's up?"

"Her grades are dropping. Bri has never gotten anything less than an 'A' grade on her report cards. Now she's gotten two 'B's."

"What's going on, Rob?"

"Man, you know what's going on, Mike."

"What? Some little knucklehead boy?"

"You know it, man."

"Man, I'm going to have to break my foot off in somebody's child's ass!"

"I got this one taken care of. I went up to the school in my patrol car and had a little talk with Mr. Mannish."

"Is this the boy who asked her to the dance?"

"One and the same. Tonita was scared you wouldn't take the news very well."

"She knows me well, Rob, I'm not ready for that!"

"Hey, that's our baby girl, and I feel the same way, but you're fighting a losing battle, Mike."

"Yeah, I know, man. I have Cynthia on my back, and you already know what type of fight I have coming with Tonita, but man, that's my baby."

"Hey, that's my baby, too! But we have to come up with a better plan than we're not going to let her and that's that."

"Well, what you got?" I said, sitting back.

"Nothing!"

We stopped talking and started to watch Sportscenter. Then simultaneously, we both sang the ESPN song, *"Da-da-da! Da-da-da!"*

❖❖❖

Upstairs in the kitchen, Tonita and Cynthia were sitting at the table drinking a cup of coffee.

"That Bri is crazy about you, Cynthia," Tonita said.

"And I'm crazy about her, too."

"She told me that she wants you to marry Mike."

"Oh, she did."

"Yeah, she did," Tonita said, "so when is the big day?"

"Mike and I are only good friends, Tonita."

"Oh Lawd, Cynthia. Don't sit back and wait on that man. If you want him, go get him."

"Mike's a great guy, but I think we will do better as friends."

"Cynthia, let me tell you something, girl. You may be a nice lady. And there is no doubt in my mind that your intentions, and your feelings, for my child are sincere. But no woman is so nice that she devotes so much time to another man's child without there being some romantic feelings involved."

"I love those kids, Tonita."

"I'm sure you do, but you also love Mike."

"Of course I love Mike."

"No dear! You are *in* love with Mike."

"Are you always this outspoken?"

"No. Sometimes I say what's really on my mind."

"If I didn't know any better, I'd think you were trying to set us up."

"Let me make you know for sure. My little girl does not get attached to too many people. And if you were able to get her to open up the way you did, there has to be something special about you."

"Thank you."

"Have you met the Wicked Witch of the West yet?"

"Who would that be?"

"Mike's second wife."

"Not yet, we're going there next."

"She's something else."

"She is?"

"Yeah, she's a stuck-up little something."

"I take it you guys don't get along that well."

"Not really," Tonita said, "when the little princess Alexiah was born, she told Mike he needed to stop spending so much time with Bri, and spend more time with Alexiah because she was younger. That pissed me off, and I told her exactly what I thought about it. I told Mike when he married her that he was marrying a nut, but he didn't believe me. Well, he believes me now."

"From what I've heard Brimone really loves Cecelia."

"Yeah, she does. And she is crazy about her sister, too."

"Yeah, I know. You would think that they were raised in the same household the way they get along."

"I wish they could see each other more often. Alexiah loves to come over."

"Why don't they visit each other more often then?"

"Cecelia doesn't want Alexiah to spend the night over here. And that pissed me off too, so I stopped Brimone from going over there. I know I'm just as wrong as she is, but I can't see myself sending my baby over there when she doesn't want to send Alex over here."

"It seems like the mothers not getting along, is affecting the sisters not being together."

"You know what, you're right. But if that stuck-up heffa would talk to me, we could resolve this issue."

"It hurts Mike to know that his children only see each other when they are with him every other weekend."

"I know it does. Mike loves those girls more than anything in the world. You couldn't ask for a better father. But until Cecelia wants them to establish a relationship, there's nothing I can do."

"Maybe together we can work on her."

"That woman is the devil."

"Tonita, I need to apologize."

"Oh girl, what have you done?"

"I accidentally let it slip to Michael that a boy asked Bri to their spring dance."

"Oh my God, did he put a chastity belt on her and lock her in the room?"

"No." Cynthia laughed. "I got him to calm down, and not mention it to her but he still hasn't decided if he's going to give his permission."

"I'm not mad at you, girl. You saved me the stress of having to tell him."

"Don't worry," Cynthia said, "I'll get him to change his mind."

"Hmm!" Tonita grunted. "You must have something powerful in your panties to get that man to let his girls do anything with boys."

"I don't think so," Cynthia said, "just a little female persuasion."

"That's what I just said." Tonita stood up from the table. "Let me go get this girl, it's taking her all day."

"Where's Mike?"

"He's in the basement with my husband. My husband thinks he's fooled me into thinking he's in the basement putting Brimone's Christmas toys together. But if I know him, he's down there watching sports with Mike."

"Can I go down there and get him?"

"Girl, *mi casa es su casa*."

"What's up with you and Mike and this Spanish thing?"

"Girl, I got that mess from him. Yuck!"

As Cynthia walked down the basement stairs, we heard her and grabbed some toys as if we had been putting them together.

"Hey, guys, what's going on down here?"

"Just fixing toys, Cynt."

"Hello, how are you?" Cynthia said.

"Excuse my manners. Cynthia, this is Rob. Rob, this is my friend, Cynthia."

"Good to meet you, Cynthia," Rob said.

"Tonita is getting Bri. Are you almost finished down here?"

"Yeah, I'll be up in a second."

"Mike, can I speak with you for a minute?" Cynthia asked.

"Yeah, hold on," I replied, following Cynthia upstairs.

Cynthia stood there for a second silently, and then held me by the hands.

"Mike, Bri is upstairs crying because she thinks you won't let her go to the dance. She is embarrassed because all of the other girls are going but her. Now, I'm with you. These boys don't know how to treat a young lady and she could become misled with her first experience."

"Where are you going with this?"

"Perhaps if she had a positive experience with her first date, she would know what to expect from dates as she gets older."

"Yeah, yeah, I'm glad you agree with me," I said, rubbing my chin. "I'll take her out on her first date to show her how a young man should treat her and she should never expect anything less from any other man who asks her out."

"Uh, yeah," Cynthia said sarcastically, "I'm glad you agree with me. I'm done. I'll wait for you up here."

"All right, I'll be back in a minute."

I walked downstairs and sat next to Ron and tapped him on the leg.

"I got it, bro."

"Got what?"

"The plan, man!" I said, holding both of my hands in front of me as if the plan was lying in them. "I'm going to take Bri out for her first date to let her know how these young knuckleheads should treat her and she should expect nothing less."

"Damn, Mike, I should have thought of that. That's clever as hell."

"I'm good now."

"Well, I gotta tell you, Mike, I'm not too happy about it."

"What's up, it's the perfect plan, man!"

"Why do you get to be the one to go out on the date?"

"Because she's my daughter, Rob."

"But she's my stepdaughter, Mike!"

"Okay, we'll both take her out," I said, trying to be diplomatic, "I'll go first."

"Nope, bad plan."

"Rob, I'm letting you take my daughter out on a date, man. I can't let you take her first; she's my daughter."

"But if I did take her out first, how would you know?"

"Rob, I know you're the law, but don't make me break it on your ass."

"Ha! Ha! Ha!" Rob laughed. "All right, man, we got a plan. We'll both take her out."

"Two things, though," I said, "I go first and you tell Tonita about the agreement."

"Damn, I'm getting the short end of both sticks," Rob said. "But it's a deal."

We shook hands and Rob quickly switched subjects.

"So who is that chick, man?"

"She's just a friend."

"That friend is fine as hell."

"Her?" I said, pointing in the direction of the upstairs.

"You can't see?"

"I can see, but I don't see fine. I see friend."

"Bullshit!" Rob said. "You ain't gay, are you Mike?"

"All right man, I'm out!" I said, standing up to avoid further conversation.

"All right, Mike, be cool."

I went upstairs and Brimone gave me her usual hug and kiss.

"You ready to go?" I asked.

"Yes, sir!"

"Come on, let's go."

"Thank you for bringing Ms. Cynthia, Daddy!"

"No problem, baby."

On our way out the door Tonita pulled me back into the house.

"Can I speak with you for a second, Mike?"

"Oh Lord," I said half-heartedly. "What's up?"

"That is a nice woman you got, don't mess it up."

"Shut up, Tonita, please."

"Oh, we know you can mess up a good thang. So don't mess this one up."

"Bye, Tonita."

"Don't mess it up."

Our planned ten-minute stop to pick up Brimone turned into an hour and a half. That put us behind schedule to pick up Alexiah. I told her mother that

I would be there by nine-thirty. It was a quarter of eleven when we pulled in their driveway. Cynthia and Brimone got out of the car and went to the door with me. I knocked on the door and Alexiah opened it with hugs for us all.

"Brimone!" Alexiah shouted.

"Come here, Alex!" Brimone shouted back. "I've missed you so much." Alexiah grabbed Brimone by the hand and pulled her upstairs.

"What's up?" I said to Cecelia as she passed from one room to the other.

"Nothing much," Cecelia said, "her stuff is over there in the corner."

"'Celia, I'd like to introduce you to my friend, Cynthia."

"I thought you said you would be here by nine-thirty," Cecelia said, ignoring my introduction to Cynthia. "Brent and I had an appointment for breakfast with the Whittendales at ten. Unfortunately, he had to go alone which doesn't look good for business."

"Who has a business meeting on Christmas Eve?" I asked, and then I remembered my little appointment with my publisher earlier that morning.

"Businessmen!" Cecelia snapped.

"Anyway, I was introducing you to my friend, Cynthia."

"How are you, Cynthia?"

"I'm fine, how are you?"

"I'd be doing a lot better if Mike had gotten here on time."

"Oh," Cynthia said, arching her eyebrows.

"Bri! Alex! Come on!" Cecelia yelled to them upstairs.

They both ran down the stairs and stood next to Cynthia by the door. I picked up Alexiah's bag and walked outside to my car, not saying good-bye to Cecelia. Brimone and Alex were right behind me. I was highly pissed off. But I was going to make an effort to not let it spoil our Christmas.

"Bye, Mommy."

"Bye, baby."

"Bye, Ms. Celia," Brimone said.

"Bye, dear," Cecelia said. Once Brimone turned her back Cecelia whispered to Cynthia, "Mike must have a stick up his ass."

"Um, I don't know," Cynthia said, feeling uncomfortable, "it was a pleasure to meet you though, bye-bye!"

"Bye-bye, dear." Cecelia waved.

As soon as we got in the car I forgot all about my little dispute with Cecelia, and we started to sing Christmas carols. It really helped us to get into the Christmas spirit as one big happy family.

chapter 13

When we got home Tina was fixing Christmas cookies. Sasha, Kiya, and Ariel were in the kitchen with their mother as well. Tina had invited my girls to help make the cookies. They were more than happy to join them.

Cynthia and I snuck in the basement to get my daughters' gifts ready to put under the tree later that evening. Then we went upstairs and told Tina that we would prepare her gifts as well since she had them all occupied.

"Tina, can we talk to you for a second?"

"Sure, Mike," Tina said, wiping her hands on her apron, and then following us into the den.

"Where are your girls' gifts? Have they been wrapped, already?" Cynthia asked.

"I've explained to my girls that Santa may not bring their gifts until after Christmas this year. This year he wants us to share the gift of family."

"You mean, they don't have any gifts?" Cynthia asked.

"No, not yet."

"Tina, why didn't you tell us?" I asked.

"There's nothing to tell, Mike. They'll be fine."

"How are they going to feel when Bri and Alex open their gifts tomorrow morning?"

"They'll be a little sad, but they'll get over it."

"Tina, I understand your financial situation. So let me go get them something?"

"I have to stop depending on other people so much, Cynthia."

"This is not about you, it's about those kids," Cynthia said. "Please let me get them something."

"Tina, look," I said, "everybody is not fortunate to have financial resources, but in most cases they have other important resources. I am fortunate to be able to offer you a place to stay until you are back on your feet, but look at what you give to me and my children. You turned this house into a home. You have us eating meals instead of eating snacks. You and Cynthia made me realize that my relationship with my daughters can be something exciting and not just ordinary. That is an invaluable gift. Let me give to your children what you have given to mine, and that's a little happiness. "

"I don't know, Mike," Tina said, in deep thought, "I have imposed enough."

"Look! We'll be going back and forth all night like this. I'm going out before the stores get too packed," Cynthia said.

"Here, take my card," I said, going into my wallet and handing her my credit card.

"That's okay, Mike. This one's on me."

"I'll go with you, Cynt," I said.

"Not this time, buddy, you'll only slow me down."

"I'm offended by that comment."

"You should be," Cynthia said, grabbing her purse and running toward the door. "Mike, I need your keys, buddy."

"If it wasn't for the kids I'd make you walk." I tossed her the keys.

"If it wasn't for the kids, I wouldn't be here."

"Get out!" I said, closing the door behind her.

About four hours later, Cynthia called, asking Tina to take the children upstairs while she and I sneaked the gifts inside.

As soon as Cynthia pulled up, I ran outside to meet her. She opened the passenger rear door and gifts, already wrapped, fell out of the car and onto the ground.

"Cynt, where did you get all this stuff, man?"

"Santa Claus."

"This must have cost a fortune."

"No, not really."

"Let me give you something on this, Cynthia. This had to be way over your budget."

"It's Christmas Eve. Mike, there is no budget," Cynthia said, filling my arms with gifts, "one more trip and that should do it."

We took the first load of gifts into the basement and dropped them off, then came back and got the second. Both of our arms were full each trip.

For the remainder of the evening we sang Christmas carols and watched old classical movies. The three youngest girls went upstairs early and played until they fell asleep. Sasha and Brimone were stubborn and stayed awake past midnight. They no longer believed in Santa Claus but we made them promise not to spoil it for the other kids. They stayed up as long as they could, but eventually the Sandman came and made his Christmas visit.

I carried both of them up to my room where they all were sleeping for the night. Cynthia, Tina and I spent the rest of the night putting the gifts under the tree, and filling their stockings. Tina was speechless when she saw all of the gifts with her children's names on them. Then she came to tears when she noticed they were signed as coming from her.

"Oh my God!" Tina said. "Oh my God! You didn't have to do this, Mike!"

"I didn't." I pointed at Cynthia. "She did."

"Oh my God! Come here, girl!" Tina hugged Cynthia tightly.

"It's no problem, Tina."

"This is unbelievable, Cynt!"

"It's nothing, Tina." Cynthia patted Tina on the back.

"Oh my God! This is unbelievable!"

"Merry Christmas, Tina," Cynthia said.

"Merry Christmas to you, too, Cynthia!" Tina said, still hugging Cynthia tightly.

"Are we going to finish filling these stockings or are we going to hug all night?"

"Shut up, Mike," Tina said, "we're having a special moment over here."

"Hurry it up, we got work to do."

"He's just mad because nobody's hugging him," Cynthia said.

Tina finally let go of her bear hug and ran to me.

"Come to mommy, baby," Tina said, charging at me with her arms wide open.

"Tina, get back!" I said, playfully running behind Cynthia.

"Don't you run from me, boy!"

"I got him!" Cynthia grabbed me by the waist.

Tina jumped on my back and started kissing me on the cheek.

"Um! Um! Um!" Tina said, making smacking noises every time she kissed me.

"Yuck!" I wiped my face.

"Merry Christmas, Mike," Tina said, giving me a kind hug.

"Merry Christmas to you, too, baby." I hugged her back.

"Aw!" Cynthia said, covering her mouth. "That's so sweet."

"That's enough, let's get back to work," I said.

We resumed our Christmas work and finished at about four o' clock in the morning. We got a couple of hours of sleep right there in the living room. I lay on the floor and the two women slept on both of the couches.

Cynthia woke up first, and then woke up Tina and me. We ran upstairs and dove on the bed to wake up the children. They were so excited, once they realized it was Christmas morning they ran past us, and headed downstairs for the tree.

We made them stop while Tina said a thank-you prayer. As soon as they heard the word, "Amen," they charged underneath the tree.

Paper and boxes were being tossed all over the place. Even though it was Christmas, I was still in my damage surveillance mode for my house. I made sure the festivities wouldn't leave a post-celebration call to the carpet cleaner.

Sasha, Kiya, and Ariel were extremely surprised because Tina had told them not to expect gifts this year. Ariel, the youngest, kissed Tina repeatedly when she opened the gift with the doll she had asked Santa to bring her.

"Mama, I thought you forgot to send my letter to Santa, but you didn't! Thank you so much!" Ariel shouted.

Tina was so overwhelmed by her daughters' gratitude she had to excuse herself from the room. Cynthia and I stayed in the living room helping the girls open their gifts. After she shed a few tears she came back and played with them.

Later that morning, Ms. Virginia came over with a bag of goodies, and helped Tina make Christmas dinner. Alicia, Lisa, and Valerie came over later and joined us. My house had become the central spot for all of the outside office girls' activity.

Lisa and Valerie arrived together around four o' clock. Alicia came about an hour later when dinner was almost ready. We all sat in the kitchen and marveled over Ms. Virginia's ability to entertain us with great stories while she watched the chicken and dressing, cooled the sweet potato pie, and fried a skillet of chicken.

"Do you all realize that we work in a predominantly black office and the only two women who are not black, are the manager and assistant supervisor?" Ms. Virginia asked.

"You *were* the supervisor, though," Valerie said.

"Yes, I was," Ms. Virginia agreed, "but Jaline was still the manager."

"You got a point, Ms. Virginia," Cynthia said.

"When they opened this department, I applied for the job along with Jaline. I had more experience. I had more education. But I didn't have what really mattered to them, so they made her the manager, and me the supervisor."

"Do you think they should have made you the manager?" Alicia asked.

"I'll say this; I am still doing most of Jaline's work."

"Doesn't that make you angry?" Alicia said.

"No, baby," Ms. Virginia said, "things like that don't bother me. That's the way of the world. It's a small sacrifice for what I get back in return."

"And what do you get back?" Lisa asked.

"Sometime you have to give a little to get a lot. Outside of the two managerial positions, everyone else in the office is a black woman. That's not by coincidence, that's by design."

"What about Mike?" Cynthia asked.

"Who do you think pulled his resume from the printer?" Ms. Virginia asked.

"I think what she means, Ms. Virginia, is that Mike is a dude," Valerie said.

"I know what she meant, sweetie. God told me not to toss Michael's resume to the side because he can make a difference in that office."

"God told you that?" Valerie asked.

"What kind of difference?" Lisa asked.

"Cynthia!" Alicia said.

"Bite me, Alicia," Cynthia said.

"All right, Cynt!" Alicia hugged her around the shoulders.

"Susan must have slipped by you, Ms. Virginia," Valerie said.

"Nobody slips past me," Ms. Virginia said. "I'm going to tell you all something and it better not leave this room. If it does, I know one of you squealed. Susan's married name is my maiden name."

"I'll be damned!" Valerie shouted. "That black dude Susan is married to is your brother, ain't he?"

"No, girl," Ms, Virginia said, "she's married to my nephew. His father was my brother."

"Damn!" Valerie said.

"If you let one more curse word come out of your mouth, Val, I am going to put some Lysol in it."

"Ms. Virginia, I'm sorry," Valerie said, "pray for me, hear?"

"I'll pray for you, all right."

"It's hard to stop cussin' when you on a roll, ain't it, Val?" Tina asked.

"Damn sho'll is," Val said.

"VALERIE!" Ms. Virginia said, smacking her with a big plastic spoon.

While the women chatted, I sat on the kitchen linoleum floor and listened. I had learn to keep my mouth shut whenever there were three or more gathered in one sitting. They tended to lose all thought for reason and logic about the issue at hand and gang up on me. That rarely happened when Ms. Virginia was around because she was wise enough to not make every issue a man-versus-woman issue. So I remained in my snug little corner until the announcement was made for dinner.

The adults sat at one table and the children sat at the other. Ms. Virginia made me lead the prayer, and then we enjoyed a great meal. After dinner, the girls played until they fell asleep and the adults sat around talking about different subjects.

As it became late, Alicia, Lisa, and Valerie went to visit other people before the day was out. Ms. Virginia and Cynthia ended up spending the night as our guests. Cynthia hadn't technically been a guest for months but because we made special arrangements for Ms. Virginia, we also made them for her.

It wasn't easy convincing Ms. Virginia to stay. She was determined to sleep in her own bed. She made it perfectly clear that she wasn't in her twenties or thirties anymore and she didn't want to jump from house to house like we did. Tina, Cynthia, and I combined our pleading powers and she reluctantly agreed.

After everyone went to bed for the evening I went into my study and began to work on my book. While working, I heard the television in the den, and I walked in to see who was suffering from insomnia. It was Ms. Virginia sitting on the couch with a blanket wrapped around her legs.

"Are you all right, Ms. Virginia?" I asked.

"Oh yes, Michael. Don't mind me."

"Can I get you anything?"

"Oh no, I'm fine."

"Well, if you need anything, I'm over here in the study, just let me know."

"There is something I would like to discuss with you, Michael," Ms. Virginia said, patting a spot next to her. "Please come sit down and talk to me for a second."

I went over and sat down beside Ms. Virginia and waited for her to hit me with the heavy news.

"First of all, I really appreciate you all asking me to spend Christmas with you. That was very sweet."

"It's great to have you here."

"I kinda get the feeling that it was a pity invitation, but that's all right, too."

"It was more like an invitation of adoration than anything else. We all love and respect you and we like to include you in some of our get-togethers. The innocent get-togethers, anyway."

"It's a pleasure being around you all."

"Well, the pleasure is all ours."

"Well, that's not even why I called you over here," Ms. Virginia said. "Michael, when are you going to ask that girl to marry you?"

"What girl?"

"Boy, if you sit up here and try to play dumb with me I'll pop you upside your head!"

"All right, Ms. Virginia." I smiled and moved my head out of harm's way. "I have feelings for Cynthia but I just can't seem to get past our friendship."

"Friendship, smendship! You need to let that woman know you care about her before somebody else swoop her up."

"It's not that easy, Ms. Virginia."

"Why not?"

"Cynthia and I don't know how to talk to each other unless we are being sarcastic."

"Well, change that. Talk to her seriously, and make her understand how you feel."

"If only it was that easy."

"Judging by this conversation, it sounds more like you're the one who can't communicate."

"Me? Why do you say that?"

"Because you keep coming up with excuses why you can't talk to her. She's not in the room right now and you still have problems communicating to me how you feel about her."

"All right, if you want to know the truth, I do think that I am in love with Cynthia but I don't know if she feels the same way."

"You don't know if she feels the same way? That girl is upstairs sleeping in the same bed with your children and you don't know if she feels the same way."

"Cynthia is a naturally kind person, and that could be all that it is, and besides, she loves being around my kids."

"Wake up and smell the roses, Michael. Cynthia is a kindhearted person but nobody is that kind. She spends mostly all of her time over here and most of the time she's here, your children are not."

"Well, we have fun watching football and just hanging out."

"All right, how would you feel if another man came into the picture and Cynthia stopped coming around so much? What if she stopped hanging out and watching football, as you put it?"

"I guess I'd miss her."

"You guess?"

"I suppose I'd miss her a lot."

"Michael, you have to stop taking that woman for granted before it's too late. She's not going to wait on you forever."

"What do you suggest I do, Ms. Virginia?"

"You tell her you love her and that you want to marry her."

"But I haven't known her that long."

"Are you saying that you've known her long enough to spend almost every waking second of your free time with her, but not long enough to spend every waking moment of your free time with her as her husband?"

"No, I'm not saying that, I'm saying…"

"Ask that child to marry you, boy!" Ms. Virginia interrupted.

"What if she says no?"

"That's a chance you have to take."

"Yeah, that's a big chance."

"I have the perfect wedding gift!"

"You sure you don't want to wait until after she says yes?" I asked sarcastically.

"Well, I'll give it to you and you can give it to her when she's ready."

"Okay, well, I'm getting ready to go to bed."

"Okay, sleep tight!"

"Good night."

❖❖❖

The next morning, I was the last to wake up. A rare occurrence because I was usually trying to steal a moment of tranquility before the guests and locals arose. They were enjoying themselves so much, I don think they missed me, anyway. Ms. Virginia was anxious to get back to her house so I took her home early.

When I got back, I had to take my daughters home so that they could open their gifts from their mothers. They would spend the rest of the week with me. But we had an arrangement of sharing the girls every other Christmas, and Thanksgiving. If I had them for Thanksgiving, their mother had them for Christmas, and vice versa. The agreement was that the visitation began the day before the holiday, the day of the holiday, and the following day we would let the other parent open their gifts with the child. We also agreed that they would return to stay with me the remainder of the week.

Cynthia rode with me to drop them off. She and Tonita sat in the kitchen and had an extended conversation while Rob and I sat in the basement and watched sports. On the way home I wanted so badly to tell Cynthia how I felt, but for some reason, I couldn't.

chapter 14

When we went back to work the following Monday after Christmas, there were only five of us: yours truly, Pam, Cynthia, Susan, and Tazzy. Once again we really didn't get a lot of work done. But then there really wasn't a lot of work to do. We weren't getting a lot of claims because most corporations had the intelligence to enjoy the holiday.

The day went by fast and we shucked and bucked the time away.

The next day was an entirely different story. The office was back in full swing and it was business as usual. Cherie, Lisa, and Valerie were the only people off for the day.

The girls made me promise to have the New Year's Eve party and invite some of my friends. I had forgotten about it, but I managed to contact enough of them to have a legitimate party. The guys I invited weren't just my buddies, they were my Masonic brothers. They were excited when I told them I worked in an office full of women who wanted to meet some of my friends. They were all for it!

The office girls pressured me every day about having that party, so much that I wanted to have it a day early simply to get it over.

The day of the party, Tina, Cynthia, and Alicia went shopping for all of the party supplies. Tina took her daughters to spend the night with her mother-in-law. Their grandmother had been asking to see them, but Tina had been too afraid to let them visit in fear that Curtis may take them. She didn't know if he had gotten out of jail or not, but she wasn't comfortable with the girls visiting. Her mother-in-law repeatedly told her that Curtis was still in jail and he would not be a threat.

She began to feel guilty because she thought she was punishing her mother-in-law for Curtis' crimes. This would be the first time the children had seen their grandmother since Curtis' arrest at the office. Everybody thought it was a good idea, especially the girls.

Tina, Cynthia, and Alicia got back to the house around seven o' clock, then went upstairs to get dressed. Around eight, people started to show, but it was only the office girls. They showed up dressed to kill. Even Valerie was dressed in sexy attire, and you know she wasn't looking for a man. They made themselves comfortable and waited for Tina, Cynthia, and Alicia to get dressed.

When the office girls didn't see any men, they started to chew me out. They thought my Masonic brothers weren't going to show. But before they got too far in their verbal attack, the door rang and all five of them walked in together.

"Hey, what's up, Square?" Todd asked. Todd was a six-foot-two, light-skinned bald guy. He was a little overweight but he had the charisma that brought him plenty of attention.

"Todd, what's up, Square?" I said, hugging him and giving him our secret Masonic handshake.

"Oh, you gon' act like you don't know a niggah no mo' up in yo' litto' mansion, huh?" Kenny Wayne yelled.

Kenny Wayne was about six feet one or two inches tall, light-skinned, very outgoing, slightly overweight, with a gold tooth in his mouth, and country as hell. He was also very popular with the ladies.

"Oh shit! Where they find you at?" I shouted.

"Mane, I came all the way from Jackson, Mississippi for this ol' bullshit-ass party, it betta be somethin' I can have breakfast with in the mornin'!" Kenny Wayne whispered, trying to keep the women from hearing him.

"Whaddup, Square?" Antonio shouted. Tony, as we affectionately called him, was about five feet ten inches tall, dark-skinned, and slightly muscular. I could not understand it, but he had an uncanny knack of stumbling into meaningless sexual affairs with extremely beautiful women.

"You, boy!" I shouted back to Tony, as he stepped to the side to let me greet the other brothers.

"What's up, Square?" Reggie said. Reggie was about six feet even, brown-skinned, and neatly shaven at all times. Women found him irresistible.

"Nothing, Square. Nothing at all!" I hugged Reggie. I was surprised to see him because we had a misunderstanding a year back and he stopped speaking to me. I accidentally had sex with a girl he was dating. She was not his steady girlfriend, only a girl he was dating.

"Glad you could make it, Reg," I said.

"I'm glad you called me, Mike," Reggie said. "Where the women at?"

"The women are here, bro. Just go get you one."

"Sheeiiiiiiitt!" Reggie said, looking over my shoulder, "you got some fine-ass chicks up in here, man."

"Yeah, and available too, bro."

"Which one you hittin'?"

"I'm not hitting anything man, they're all up for grabs."

"You know why I asked, don't you?"

"No, not really." I pretended not to know what he was talking about.

"Because I don't want to do to you, what you did to me," Reggie said.

"So are we through with that or what, Reg?"

"Bro, if we can't laugh about it, we'll have to fight about it. Now I know you don't want me to whoop yo' ass in front of all these chicks up in here, do you?"

"No bro," I said, smiling and wrapping my arm around his shoulder. We turned to walk into the living room to the party when suddenly I felt a sharp punch to my side.

"You ain't gon' holla at us, niggah?"

"Oh hell, no," I shouted to Melvin and Marc. I grabbed them both and the three of us hugged right there. We were so animated we were bumping into furniture. I was not expecting Marc to come at all. He was a total surprise. Melvin lived in Atlanta, but I hadn't seen or spoken to him in five years.

Melvin was dark-skinned. His hair had been receding ever since he'd come out of the womb. If given a poll, I would say that Melvin would be voted the least physically attractive out of all of us. However, there is no poll needed to say that Melvin would also easily be voted the most successful in reference to women.

Melvin played the numbers when it came to women. He felt that if he approached enough women, law of average would take effect. And more times than not, he was correct. The rest of us had pride, and egos. For Melvin, there was no place for such things in the game of love and sex. Rejection, humiliation, embarrassment, fear, none of those emotions existed in Melvin.

I once saw Melvin turned down by six women at once, but by the end of the night he left the club with one of the sexiest women in attendance, thus, proving the law of average theory to be successful on that night.

Marc was light-skinned, slightly husky, about six feet, or six one. He used to dance on a teen show in Jackson when we in college. I think the show was called *Black Gold*. The guy was a living legend in his collegiate days. He was the only married brother in the group. Marc, Melvin, and I chatted among ourselves for a moment to get caught up.

"What's been up, Mike?" Melvin said.

"Mel, just staying out of trouble!"

"You still holding it down, I see," Marc said.

"No, I work with these sisters, that's all. But how's married life with you and Marci?"

"You know, we're doing good."

"Tell her I send my love, man."

"Damn, it's good to see you, Mike."

"I'm tripping, Mel. I can't believe you brothers are in my house, man!"

"Enough of the small talk," Melvin said, walking past me. "Where them honeys?"

We walked into the living room where I introduced the girls to the boys. On our way to the living room I realized that I had assembled the most sexually notorious female-assassinating group of all time with the most opinionated, independent, feministic group of all time, a recipe for disaster.

It didn't take my brothers long before they started their assault on the office girls. Valerie was curious to find out the mystery behind Masonry and that got the conversations flowing.

"Why y'all keep calling each other 'Square,' are y'all nerds?" Valerie asked.

"If I told you, I'd have to kill you," Todd replied.

"That's just what we call each other," Tony added.

"Why?" Wanda asked.

"It represents something sacred to us as Masons," Marc answered.

"What?" Wanda asked.

"None of yo' dam' bus'ness, baby!" Kenny Wayne joked. "We told you that if we give you that information, we gon' have to kill yo' ass!"

"My daddy was a Mason! He used to act secretive, too!" Wanda said.

"Are you guys a secret fraternity?" Lisa asked.

"No, baby, everybody knows who we are," Todd said. "We're not a secret fraternity, we're a fraternity of secrets."

"I don't give a damn! We just wanna know why y'all call each other 'Square'!" Valerie shouted.

Everybody was getting along, but it was still too much talking, and not enough dancing.

"Is this a party or what?" I said. "Somebody dance with somebody!"

"You ain't said shit!" Melvin said, walking over to Valerie and taking her by the hand. They started to dance and that led to the others dancing.

At the time, Wanda, Valerie, Lisa, and Darsha numbered up almost evenly with my Masonic brothers, but when the other three ladies walked in, it threw the numbers off tremendously. But when you think of it in a broader scope, Wanda was married and not looking for anything but a night out. Cynthia was not looking for anything but a night out with the girls as well, and Valerie was a lesbian. That put the numbers back at even.

When Cynthia, Tina, and Alicia walked into the room, my eyes nearly popped out of my head. I was used to seeing Tina and Alicia dressed up, but not Cynthia. She had on a short dress that exposed her legs, and her curvaceous figure. My chin almost dropped to the floor.

My Masonic brothers realized there were a new batch of women added to the party and that made it that much more delightful for them.

"Mike," Reggie said, "you work with all these women, man?"

"Yeah, bro."

"Damn! How do you do any work?"

"It's not easy, believe me."

"Hey, who is that right there?" Reggie said, pointing at Cynthia.

"Oh, that's my girl, Cynthia."

"You hittin' it?"

"No, man, we're just friends."

"I'm gon' ask you again, niggah, which one of these sisters you hittin'?"

"None of 'em, bro! Strictly business!"

"Sheee-iit! It ain't no way in the world I could work around all these fine-ass chicks and not hit one of 'em. And you neither, niggah! Somethin' is up!"

"I know you couldn't handle it, Reg," I said, "that's your M.O."

"It's a dirty job, but somebody got to do it," Reggie said, laughing and taking a drink.

"Enjoy yourself, Reg."

"I see Mel over there trying to get on ol' girl, so let me put a halt to that shit right now," Reggie said, referring to Cynthia.

"She's not going to give either one of you the time of day."

"She won't give who the time of day?"

"You *and* Melvin. You're not her type, Reg."

"Who's not her type?" Reggie asked emphatically.

"Cynthia is a laid-back type of sister, bro; she doesn't fall for those lines you throw at women."

"Care to make a little wager, Mike?"

"Not on her."

"Hey, you sure you don't have some kind of feelings for that chick, bro?"

"No, bro."

"All right then, Square," Reggie said, patting me on the back, "now when I tap that ass, I don't want to hear no shit from you."

"If you get the ass, you get the ass, Reg," I said, becoming annoyed with the conversation.

"Damn!" Reggie said, covering his mouth. "What the hell is that?"

"That's Alicia."

"That's the most beautiful creature I have ever laid eyes on. I'm going to marry that chick, Square."

"Reggie, calm down, man. You can't have them all."

As we were talking, the doorbell rang. I looked around the room because everybody I was expecting was already there. I went and opened the door, and to my unbelieving eyes, my brother Johnny was standing there with a smile and a bottle of wine.

"Surprise!" Johnny said.

Johnny was a little taller than me, around six-four, or six-five. Broad shoulders, not quite as dark as me, but still had a dark complexion. He was clean-shaven. No moustache. No beard. No signs of hair anywhere on his face with the exclusion of eyelashes and eyebrows. His hair was cut very short but as always, it was fresh.

Throughout our lives I had been the prodigy, and he had been the problem child. No one expected much of him, especially my parents. He stayed in trouble as a youth. The police were constantly visiting our home. He was in and out of juvenile facilities until he reached his senior year of high school.

He told us that he was tired of hearing about me being so great, and him being so awful. He told us that we were the reason he stayed in so much trouble. He said he was trying to get some of the attention everyone was giving to me.

But during his senior year of high school he told us that he didn't care what we thought about him anymore. He said he was going to straighten up and do the best he could, and if that wasn't good enough for us, then too bad. He graduated from high school with honors, and went to the University of Michigan where he played football.

He graduated from the University of Michigan with honors as well. Then he went to the National Football League where he played nine successful seasons, with six trips to the Pro Bowl, attaining his master's and Ph.D. degrees along the way. After football, he launched his own practice becoming a psychologist, or psychiatrist. And while he was fulfilling his second lifelong dream of becoming a doctor, I was waking up from my nightmare of being a writer.

"Man, what the hell are you doing here?" I asked, excited and surprised.

We hugged each other and I asked him to come into the house. I took him into the living room.

"Hey, everybody, I want you all to meet my little brother, Johnny."

"Good to meet you all," Johnny said, waving at everyone.

I took Johnny into the kitchen where we could talk privately.

"Come here, boy, let me look at you. How long has it been?"

"About seven years, Mike."

"So how are things going, Johnny?"

"Pretty good. I was passing through on my way to Florida and I decided to stop by. I hope it's not a problem."

"No problem at all. As a matter of fact, you couldn't have picked a better night."

"Hey, how's Tonita?"

"She's doing fine," I said, "she's married again."

"How did you take that?"

"Oh man, her husband and I get along well."

"How's your second wife? What was her name again?"

"Cecelia," I said, "she's doing fine, too."

"And how are my beautiful nieces?"

"They're doing fine."

"I bet Brimone has gotten so big now. The last time I saw her she was pulling on my legs trying to follow me everywhere."

"Yeah, she was crazy about her Uncle John."

"Do they still live here in Atlanta?"

"About twenty minutes away from here."

"What about your youngest daughter," Johnny said. "Does she live here, too?"

"Yeah, she lives here, too."

"If we can arrange it, I'd like to see them before I leave."

"When are you leaving?"

"The day after tomorrow," Johnny said. "I was supposed to catch a connecting flight heading on to Florida, but I don't need to be there until next week, so I decided to spend a little time here and get caught up with my big brother."

"Do you have any children yet, Johnny?"

"Yeah, Johnny Junior, he's five years old. You would know that, if you kept in contact with the family, Mike."

"Come on, Johnny, don't go there, man."

"I have to, Mike," Johnny said. "When was the last time you spoke with Mom and Dad?"

"I don't know, why?"

"Because they're your parents, that's why!"

"Johnny, let's not forget who's the big brother here, okay?"

"It doesn't matter who the big brother is, you need to pick up the phone and call us sometime."

"It's not that simple, Johnny."

"Why not? What is so difficult about calling your family?"

"You know what, Johnny? This is not the time for this conversation. Let's talk about this tomorrow."

"No, Mike, this is the time."

"No, it's not! I promise, if you let me off the hook tonight, I will sit down and talk about this for as long as you like in the morning."

"You promise?"

"I promise."

"All right, I'll let you get back to your party," Johnny said. "I'm about to go back to my hotel and catch me some winks."

"You're not going to a hotel. You're staying here with me."

"Too late. I've already paid for my room."

"Oh, I know your cheap ass is not going to let that room go to waste."

"You better believe it," Johnny said, with a huge grin across his face.

Seeing his smile reminded me of when we were children. Johnny wanted to follow me everywhere I went, but I would never let him. Looking at where we were now, it might have served us both better if I had followed him instead.

"Well, at least stay and enjoy yourself at the party."

"Sure, why not?"

We stood up and walked back into the living room. My guests had started to pair off by that time—Melvin and Darsha, Todd and Tina, Tony and Pam,

Kenny Wayne and Lisa, while Reggie and Marc entertained the other women. No one had actually declared themselves an item, but it was getting close to midnight and the threat of not bringing in the New Year with a kiss was looming on every boy and girl.

Wanda had to leave early to make it home in time to bring in the New Year with her family. My Masonic brothers loved her wild and crazy humor and did not want her to leave. We all gave her our New Year's kiss and she left. Johnny was sitting alone in a corner, and then he called me over.

"Who's that?" Johnny asked.

"That's Alicia," I answered back.

"Is she married?"

"No, but aren't you married?"

"No, I am happily divorced."

"What kind of psychiatrist are you if you can't handle your own marriage, Johnny?" I said jokingly.

"First of all, I'm not a psychiatrist, I'm a psychologist."

"What's the difference?"

"A psychiatrist messes people's heads up, and a psychologist fixes them."

"Of course you'd say that."

"Back to Alicia. Does she have a boyfriend?"

"Yeah."

"Is it serious?"

"That's what she says. He's a model, but he's never in town."

"So what you're telling me is that she's a lonely woman, who feels neglected by her man. She hides behind her own beauty to perpetrate a fraudulent scheme of happiness. She pretends nothing bothers her, when she's as fragile as the wet piece of tissue she uses to wipe her crying eyes. She makes it seem as if she's everything to her man, when she feels as if she's nothing to him at all," Johnny said, with his hand resting beneath his chin.

"Man I got to tell you, you hit it dead on the head."

"One more question!" Johnny said.

"What's that?"

"When did you have sex with her?"

"What makes you think we had sex?"

"There are only two ways you could have known the answer to that question: one, you had sex with her and she confided in you; or two, she trusted you as a friend, and she confided in you. And we both know you're much too selfish to listen to someone else's problems unless you had an ulterior motive. Don't we, big brother?" Johnny said to me, looking back over his shoulder as he walked over to where Alicia was sitting.

"Excuse me, Alicia, do you mind if I sit here?"

"Sure."

"It's kinda noisy in here. Can we go somewhere and talk?" Johnny asked.

"That's fine."

Johnny reached for her hand and they walked into another room for privacy. I was a little jealous, but I felt my brother deserved to get the prize sometime.

On the other hand it left the door wide open for Reggie to make his move on Cynthia. I was pretty confident he would get nowhere with her, anyway so I didn't think too much about it.

As it approached midnight everybody began to huddle together to bring in the New Year. As we sang, and hugged one another, I noticed Reggie and Cynthia were not a part of the celebration. I thought Reggie had perhaps asked her to join him away from us to prove to me that she was interested in him. And knowing Cynthia, she would go just to prevent hurting his feelings.

Midnight struck, we all shouted, and resumed our prior activities. Cynthia and Reggie were still missing in action, so I went to rescue her from Reggie's assault. I looked in several rooms before I went into the basement. I walked down the stairs, and I could see Reggie with his arms around Cynthia, kissing her. I was so stunned I missed the last two stairs and fell on my butt.

"What's up, bro?" Reggie asked, laughing as I looked up at them.

"Oh nothing," I said, embarrassed. "I was just looking for you guys."

"We right here," Reggie said.

"Are you all right, Mike?" Cynthia asked, embarrassed for me.

"Yeah, I'm fine."

"We fine, too, Square," Reggie said. "You can go back upstairs, if you want."

"Oh, okay," I said, not believing what I had seen.

My jealousy of Johnny and Alicia was nothing compared to this catastrophe. I went back upstairs and sat down in a chair in the corner. I watched as everyone seemed to be having a ball. I was miserable. I was in love with Cynthia, and I wanted to marry her. No matter how long, or short, we may have known each other, I wanted to marry her. But she was in my house in the arms of another man.

I couldn't concentrate, or enjoy myself, knowing she was downstairs with Reggie. I wanted to go back down there and tell her how I felt, but I would have only made a bigger fool out of myself. So I sat there agonizing, wondering what they were doing. I watched the clock as it ticked second by second, oblivious to anything other than my basement door opening, and Reggie and Cynthia walking through it.

Around one o' clock, they did just that. I took a deep sigh of relief, but before I could breathe again, Reggie announced that he and Cynthia were going to go to another party. The office girls shouted, urging Cynthia to finally loosen up and enjoy her life. They had never seen Cynthia with another man, and they were excited for her. I, contrarily, wanted to strangle her and Reggie for torturing me.

On their way out of the door, Reggie whispered, "I'm about to tear this ass up, Square!"

I almost collapsed. I couldn't even respond. All I could do was look at them and wave good-bye.

"My girl is about to get that monkey off her back!" Valerie shouted.

"It's about time!" Pam said.

"It ain't no way in the hell I could go that long wit' out gettin' some!" Darsha said.

"You keep talkin', you gon' get somethin' tonight!" Melvin added.

"That's okay, too," Darsha said, sitting on Melvin's lap.

"Excuse me, I'll be right back," Alicia said to Johnny. "Mike, can I talk to you for a second?"

"Sure," I said, dazed and heartbroken. I followed her into the kitchen and she turned around with questions coming one hundred miles a minute.

"How do you feel about me dating your brother?"

"I really haven't thought about it, but I guess it wouldn't bother me."

"Good, because he seems interesting and I would like to get to know him."

"What about your boyfriend, Alicia?"

"What about my boyfriend? I'm willing to see where this can go with Johnny. He is a very nice guy."

"But he doesn't live here in Atlanta. You're putting yourself right back in the same situation you were with Julian."

"I thought about that, Mike. We're not talking marriage, we're talking dating. If we're meant to be, we'll get together. Right now, I just want to get to know him."

"I don't have a problem as long as you don't do to him, what you did to me."

"I will never do that again. Not to you, not to any man."

"Then, I don't have a problem."

"Thanks, I wouldn't feel right unless it was all right with you."

"To be honest, I think you two make a much better couple than you and I ever could have made."

"You think?"

"Without a doubt."

"Now," Alicia said, hitting me on the arm, "how could you let Cynthia leave with that piranha?"

"She's a grown woman, she can do what she wants."

"Come on, Mike, it's me! Be honest, how do you feel?"

I stood in silence and stared, because I couldn't truly explain the pain and disappointment I was feeling. But I tried gallantly to express myself.

"I really don't know how I feel, Alicia. I know that I don't like it, and I wish I had stopped them but what can I do now? They're probably somewhere having wild sex by now."

"Hold on."

She pulled out her cell phone and dialed. When Cynthia answered I wanted to shout for joy. That meant that they weren't having sex, and if they were, it was so horrible she was willing to hold a conversation, so that was still a good sign.

"Hey, Cynthia, where did you take your butt to, girl?"

I couldn't hear what she was saying, but my heart was beating so fast I could hear it through my shirt.

"Hold on, Cynthia, Mike wants to say something to you," Alicia said, handing me her cell phone. "Here, handle your damn business!"

Alicia walked out of the kitchen to leave me alone to talk to Cynthia.

"Cynt," I said nervously.

"Hey, what's up, man?"

"We need to talk."

"Go 'head. What's up?"

"Not on the phone, face to face."

"Well, I'm kinda in the middle of something right now, Mike."

"Cynthia!" I said, frustrated and hurt.

"What? What's so important that it can't wait until tomorrow?"

I paused, and then I whispered, "I love you, Cynthia."

"I love you, too, Mike, and?"

"No, you're not listening to me. I love you. I mean, I am in love with you! And it's killing me to know that you are with Reggie right now, when I know that you should be here with me."

Cynthia paused, and didn't respond.

"Cynthia! Cynthia! Are you still on the phone?"

"Yeah, I'm here." Cynthia said.

"Then say something."

"Mike, I'm shocked. I don't know what to say."

"Don't say anything until I talk to you face to face."

"Why are you telling me this now, Mike?" Cynthia said with a long sigh.

"Because seeing you with Reggie is killing me."

"Oh, I got it now. Another man finally shows me attention and you want to make sure your football buddy is not taken away from you!"

"That's not it, Cynthia, and you know it."

"Then what is it, Mike? If you don't want me, leave me the hell alone and let someone who does have me!"

"Cynthia, can you please come back over here?"

"Reggie and I are having a cup of coffee and that would be rude."

"What's open on New Year's Eve, Cynthia?"

"My house."

"What? You have Reggie in your house?"

"Yes, he is."

"Can he hear me?" I shouted. "Can Reggie hear me?"

"No, I'm in another room."

"Well, Cynthia, if you want to stay over there with Reggie, then stay over there with Reggie. Bye!" I hung up the line when she was about to speak.

I gave Alicia her cell phone and noticed she was sitting very close to Johnny, but I didn't have the time to concern myself with that issue. I had to handle the fact that after all this time, Cynthia decides to date a man, and he happens to be one of my closest friends, the same friend that stopped speaking to me because I did the same thing to him.

Then, there is the fact that Cynthia, a woman who has all but come out and told me that she loved me, a woman who put her life on hold for me, and I refused to reciprocate her feelings simply because I thought I could get away with it. I know I didn't deserve sympathy from Cynthia and Reggie, but I didn't want to be revenged, either. Not by those two people.

"So what happened?" Alicia asked.

I saw Johnny sitting there, and I thought how he had never seen me in this condition. Things had always gone well for me. But after seven years he sees me in a way he has never seen me, vulnerable and weak.

I was hurting so badly, I didn't give a damn what Johnny thought of me. I needed comforting, and I needed it quickly.

"I asked Cynthia to come back, but she wouldn't, Alicia."

"What was your response?"

"I hung up the phone in her face."

"Bad move, big brother," Johnny said.

"I don't know what to do, you guys."

"Go get her," Johnny said.

"I've already made a fool out of myself with them once."

"What do you mean?" Alicia asked.

"I went to the basement to check up on them and caught them kissing."

"Oh, in that case, Mike, you better run over there," Johnny said.

"I want to, but I can't."

"Mike, listen to me. Go over there and tell her how you feel," Alicia said.

I lowered my head, and kneeled down in front of them.

"All right, I'm going over there, but if I humiliate myself, I'm coming back here and kick your ass, Johnny. And Alicia, you and I are going to have some sex, rough sex!"

"Get!" Alicia said, laughing and pushing me away.

I threw on a coat, and jumped in my car. I probably ran a few stop signs and red lights because I don't remember making one stop. I jumped out of my car and quickly walked up to her door. I banged on it hard to interrupt any activity they may be enjoying. Cynthia came to the door, and cracked it open. She left the chain on the latch as she spoke to me from behind the door.

"What are you doing over here, Mike?"

"We need to talk."

"Talk about what?"

"Us."

"Well, talk."

"Cynt, it's cold as hell out here. Let me come in."

"Why?"

"Cynt, open the damn door!" I said, raising my voice.

She laughed, and then took the chain off of the door.

"Come on in, ol' crazy boy."

I walked in looking around for Reggie. "Where's Reg?"

"He's gone."

"Oh, okay."

"Were you jealous?"

"We've already been through that, Cynt."

"Well, I want to hear it, anyway."

"Okay. I was jealous! And I think I was hurt!"

"Oh, poor baby."

"Cynt, how could you kiss Reggie, after only knowing him for a couple of hours?"

"You have no right to judge me, after you've been with almost every woman in that office!"

"Huh," I said, wondering if she was calling my bluff.

"Huh? Huh, my ass, Mike! You think you're so slick! You think those women weren't going to talk about you and them?"

"What are you talking about, Cynt?"

"You know exactly what I'm talking about!"

I couldn't tell if Cynthia was pulling my leg, or if she actually knew the truth. I instantly went from anger to fear.

"Uh, I don't know what you're talking about."

"Why are you so nervous?"

"I'm not nervous."

"It's true, isn't it?"

"What's true?"

"You know what I'm talking about! I tried to tell your dumb ass from the beginning they were playing you. But your nasty ass played right along with them!"

"I don't know what you're talking about, Cynt!"

"Stop lying, Mike! Tell me the truth right now, or get the hell out of my house!"

"Cynt, what have they told you?"

"It doesn't matter! Don't try to salvage your good-boy reputation with me because you're a fake-ass selfish man who only cares about himself! You knew I loved you and you slept with those women, anyway. Women that I work with! How do you think that makes me feel?"

"Cynt, I can explain!"

"No, you can't! I'm hurt, Mike! Now tell me the truth, or never speak to me again!"

"Okay! All right! I slept with them! But Cynthia, I swear to God I didn't know that I was in love with you! I would have never hurt you intentionally!"

"Well, you did," Cynthia said, walking to her door, "now please get out of my house, Mike."

"Cynthia, please," I said.

"GET OUT!" Cynthia screamed.

I could see her eyes begin to fill with tears, and I wanted to wipe everyone, but she wouldn't let me. I walked past her, and once I was outside, I turned around to ask her one more time to talk to me, but she slammed the door in my face.

I sat in my car for a while, and then I drove back home. I wanted to give the party time to end so that I wouldn't have to talk to anyone. By the time I got there everyone was gone, including my brother. Tina had gone to bed as well. I stayed up the remainder of the night pushing redial to Cynthia's phone. She never answered. I fell asleep just before dawn with the phone still clutched in my hand.

chapter 15

The next morning I got up as soon as day broke and treated myself to a nice breakfast on the town. My brother had left his contact information to the hotel where he was staying, so after breakfast I went to pay him a little visit. I didn't bother calling, to tell you the truth, I was so out of it, I didn't think about calling him. I knocked on his hotel door and apparently he was still asleep because it took him forever to answer.

"Who is it?" Johnny yelled from inside the door.

"Room service," I said, stepping to the side so that if he looked out of the peephole he wouldn't see me.

"Oh," Johnny said, opening the door.

"Get up, boy!" I said, walking past him.

"Mike!" Johnny reached for me.

As I walked in, I saw Alicia reaching for the blanket to cover herself.

"What are you doing that for?" I said angrily. "It's not like I haven't seen you naked before."

"It's timeout for those type of jokes, Mike," Johnny said.

"I'm serious, why are you covering yourself, Alicia? Have you told my brother how you and I had sex? You seem to tell everything else."

"Mike, are you joking or what?" Johnny said, not wanting to overreact.

"Hell no, I'm not joking! Did you tell my brother about how we had sex, Alicia?"

"Why are you acting like an asshole, Mike?" Alicia asked.

"Asshole? I know all about your asshole, don't I?"

"Mike, I think you need to leave, man," Johnny said.

"I'll leave, but answer one question first, Alicia!"

"Michael, what's the matter with you? I asked you, and you said you were all right with this!" Alicia said.

"I don't give a damn about you and Johnny, Alicia! You were supposed to be my friend!"

"I am your friend, Michael, what are you talking about?"

"If you're my friend, Alicia," I said, sitting on the bed, "why would you play your little office girl games? Huh?"

"What game? What are you talking about?"

"You told everyone in the office about us! All the time I'm thinking you and I are such good friends and all the time you are making a fool out of me behind my back!"

"Michael, it's not like that!"

"Cynthia knows, Alicia! You told Cynthia!"

"Mike, I didn't tell Cynthia anything!"

"Then how does she know?"

"I don't know, Michael, but I didn't tell her!"

"You had to tell someone, because she knows!"

"I'm sorry that Cynthia knows but I didn't tell her anything! I swear to God!"

"That's bullshit, Alicia! From now on, don't you say anything to me! You don't know me as far as I'm concerned."

I stood up, and started to walk out, and then Johnny grabbed me by the arm. "Mike, what's this all about, man?"

"Johnny, you're my brother and I love you, but please take your hands off of me before I forget who you are." I stared straight ahead and didn't look at him in his face.

He released my arm and I walked out.

By the time I got home Tina was awake. She was in the kitchen fixing breakfast. She had not gone to get her children so she made breakfast for only the two of us. I was trying to subdue my anger, but I felt that every woman in the office was a part of the scam Pam and Alicia had pulled on me, including Tina.

I wanted to avoid a conversation with her so when I walked in the house I went straight to the basement. A few moments later she came down to tell me she was finished.

"Breakfast is ready, Mike," Tina said, standing on the bottom stair.

"No thanks, Tina."

"What? You're passing up a cooked meal?"

"I'm not that hungry right now."

"Well, it's up here when you get hungry," Tina said, walking back up the stairs.

For whatever reason, halfway up the stairs, she turned around and came back, bad mistake.

"What's wrong, Mike?"

"Nothing's wrong, I'm waiting for the Bowl games to get started."

"Mike, I know when there's something wrong with you, and there's something wrong with you."

"Tina, there's nothing wrong with me; now can you please, please, leave me alone?"

"I'll leave you alone once you tell me what's wrong."

Tina's persistence only added fuel to my already burning fire, and I exploded.

"Look, I told you there's nothing wrong with me. Now get the hell out of my damn face, man! Shit!"

Tina stared at me, but did not respond. I could see that she was shaken by my outburst, but I felt no compassion at the time.

"Did I do something, Mike?"

"Tina, just leave me alone!"

"I don't understand. Are you still comfortable with me living here?"

I kept turning the channel on my television and pretended I didn't hear her.

"I'll take that as a no."

"Take it however you like."

"All right, Mike. I appreciate your hospitality, and I will move out as soon as I can."

"Hasta la vista!" I said angrily.

Although I heard the words come out of my mouth, I couldn't believe that

I was saying them. I wanted to apologize but my anger wouldn't let me. I know she thought I was a nut because she had no idea why I was reacting that way.

Tina walked back upstairs and closed the door gently. I knew she was terribly hurt but I couldn't bring myself to apologize to her. I figured I would talk to her later and let her know I was just blowing off steam.

The longer I sat in the basement thinking, the angrier I became. I wanted to get even with the office girls, and I knew how to bring them to their backstabbing knees. I called my publisher and told him I could get the manuscript to him immediately. He told me to bring it right over.

I jumped on my computer and added some spicy ingredients to the book. I gave explicit details of the torrid love affairs I'd had with each of the women, even Cherie. If her husband found out, he found out. In the end, I had written the story I was looking for in the beginning.

I copied the book to a disc and headed over to Greenbaum's house. We sat down and he was extremely excited to have the completed product.

"Let me tell you something, my Afro-American friend. This is going to buy me a small villa in the Caribbean!"

"How long will it take to have it on the shelves?"

"I've already got their mouths salivating! They want it, and they want it bad!"

"I think this is my best work, Greenbaum."

"Come on, now my man, I'm not trying to hurt ya feelings but um, what do we have to measure this book against?"

"Funny, Greenbaum."

"Don't go gettin' all sensitive on me now. You artists are such sensitive people. Take a pill, and chill, Bill. Hey, you like that rhyme?"

"Greenbaum," I said, ignoring his question, "how soon can we have the books on the shelves?"

"I don't know, should take a couple of weeks to edit it and get it ready for print, another six to eight weeks for promotions, and then BOOM! Your name will be as big as that other black author. What's his name, Spike Lee?"

"Spike Lee is a director, Greenbaum, not an author."

"Oh, whatever." Greenbaum stood and reached for my arm, giving me my cue to leave.

"So we have a good one, huh?"

"This will be bigger than Clinton's book?"

"Which Clinton?" I asked.

"All of 'em! Bill, Hillary, hell, even George! Sign this little contract, and we're ready to go."

I looked over the contract again. "Why do I feel like I'm selling my soul to the devil, Greenbaum?"

"Well, if the devil doesn't like your soul, he'll sell it back to you at half-price!"

"I'd like to have my attorneys go over this contract before I sign it!"

"What's the matter? You don't trust me?"

"I can't afford to trust you, Greenbaum. But I'll have my attorney go over it and get it back to you as soon as possible. Let's sell some books!"

"That's the spirit, let's sell some books, Mikey boy!" Greenbaum politely patted me on the back, then walked me to the door. "Merry Kwanza, my man!"

When I drove up to my house there were two cars sitting in the driveway: Alicia's car, and I assumed the other was my brother's. I wasn't in the mood for one of his psychological analyses but I tried to mentally prepare myself for it just in case. As I walked to my front door I could see the door was ajar, so I quickened my steps to see what or who was the reason.

When I walked in, Alicia and Lisa were sitting next to Tina on the couch. She was crying, and naturally, I thought it was the result of our earlier conversation.

"Tina, I didn't mean what I said. You don't have to go anywhere until you are ready." I slid between Alicia and Tina, and then put my arms around her.

"Michael, what are you talking about?" Lisa asked.

"I was upset about something this morning, and I kind of took it out on Tina. But I didn't mean to make her this upset."

Tina put her head on my chest, and continued to cry.

"Michael, I don't know what you said, but that's not why Tina is crying," Lisa said.

"What happened? What's the matter?"

"When Tina went to pick up her daughters, they were not at her mother-in-law's. We think Curtis has taken them and disappeared."

"What?"

"We've called the police, and they're on their way."

"Do you think your mother-in-law has anything to do with this, Tina?"

"I don't know, Mike, I don't know!" Tina said, sobbing.

At that time, Cynthia walked in the house. Alicia stood up and hugged her, and then she kneeled in front of Tina on the floor.

"Tina, baby, I'm so sorry!" Cynthia said.

"You okay, Mike?" Alicia asked. I knew her question was not referring to Tina's situation, but ours, and I answered it the best way I could.

"No, not really. But I'm sure I will be."

"Good, now let's see how we can help Tina."

The police arrived and Tina gave them a statement about her abusive relationship with her husband. They told her that since he is also the girls' legal guardian, and she gave them permission to spend the night with his mother, he had not broken the law. That may have been the law, but that certainly didn't bring any comfort to Tina.

We tried to ease Tina's tension, but to no avail. Once the other office girls got wind of Tina's recent crisis, they piled into my house. This time, I felt too uncomfortable with them to stay and pretend I was a part of their circle.

I told Johnny if he wanted to see his nieces he'd better come with me while he had the chance. He was excited and anxious to go. We stopped to visit Brimone first. We didn't have to tell her who he was; she instantly remembered him and called him by his affectionate nickname, Uncle John. For Johnny, that alone was worth the pit stop in Atlanta.

They enjoyed themselves for a while, and when it was time to leave Brimone wanted to go with us. Johnny suggested we take her with us to see Alexiah. He had never met her, and Brimone might be able to help break the ice. Tonita thought it was also a good idea.

While I was there I also mentioned Tina's situation to Rob, and he told me that if I needed him to give him a call and we could get right on it. He also explained that cases like this one normally go straight to the file room unless the children are not returned for an extended period of time. And by that time, the trail is so cold it's difficult to track them. I told him to expect a call from me later.

Alexiah warmed up to her uncle quickly. We took them for a ride; we didn't have a variety of places to take them on New Year's Day, but we still enjoyed ourselves.

They were very disappointed when we had to drop them off. They wanted to spend the remainder of the day with Johnny, and he wanted to stay with them.. But I felt that despite my anger toward the office girls, Tina needed me and I had to get back to her. Johnny told the girls he would stay an extra day to spend solely with them and they were satisfied for the moment.

On our way home Johnny touched on the subject of my outburst earlier in his hotel room.

"Hey, Mike, what was that all about this morning?"

"Didn't Alicia tell you?"

"No, man, she made me take her home as soon as you left."

"It's a long story, Johnny."

"I got time. Give it to me."

"Oh boy," I said, "I don't even know where to begin, man."

"How about the beginning?"

"All right," I said, taking a deep breath, "I am going to make this quick."

"Quick is good, Mike."

"Well, since I've been working at Upskon, I've had sex with three women in the office. You know about Alicia, and then there's this sister named Pam, and another sister named Cherie. Cherie is the wife of a preacher."

"Mike, you hit a preacher's wife?"

"Hey, bro, she needed it, and I let her have it."

"Damn! Was it good?"

"Oh God, yes."

"What about this Pam chick? Wasn't the lady at your party last night named, Pam? Is it the same woman?"

"One and the same."

"I see why you hit that, Mike, she looks sexy as hell."

"And you talk about being a freak? Good God!"

"She's a freak?"

"Man, freak's not the word for it."

"Well, now that we have the characters, let's get a little of the story."

"Oh yeah," I said, "well, to make a long story short, while I was having sex with these women, they were agreeing to keep our office romance a secret. But all the while I was hush-hush, they were blabbing our business all over the place bragging about how they coerced me into having sex with them."

"And?"

"And what?"

"Mike, tell me that's not why you were mad at Alicia this morning?"

"Hell yeah, that's why I was mad."

"Mike, you've been hanging around these women too long, man. You're acting like a woman."

"What do you mean 'acting like a woman'?"

"Because if a woman is going back bragging that she had sex with you, how can that ever be a bad thing?"

"It's the principle of the thing, Johnny. If it was one of them and I went behind their backs discussing our sexual relationship, they would be mad, too."

"Mike, what the hell are you talking about, man? Didn't you tell me you had sex with Alicia?"

"Yes, I did.

"Then what's wrong with her telling her girls?"

"That's different, Johnny."

"What's the difference?"

"The difference is that you're my brother, and you two were interested in each other. And you needed to know the truth, and besides, you don't know them. Now Alicia and Pam told the people I have to work with every day, man."

"Mike, you had your reason, and they had theirs."

"I don't agree with you on this one."

"Mike, if you don't stop acting like a little bitch, I'm going to push you out of this car, man."

"I'm serious, Johnny, that shit they did was foul."

"Maybe so, but they did nothing men don't do on a daily basis. And certainly nothing you haven't done. Quite frequently, I may add."

"Johnny, they told Cynthia, man. And now she hates me."

"You need to stop acting like a victim and understand that all is fair in love and war, my brother."

"Whatever, man."

We drove a few miles in silence, then Johnny remembered to finish our conversation from the previous night.

"Hey, we have some unfinished business, Mike."

"What 'unfinished business'?"

"We need to finish our discussion from last night."

"What do you want to discuss, Johnny?"

"Why haven't you been in contact with the family?"

"There's no way I'm going to get around this, is it?"

"Nope!"

"Johnny, man," I said, "my life was in place. I had everything in order just as I planned. I went to law school, passed the bar, and could have been a great attorney. But noooooooo! I had to be writer. Follow my heart, and not my head."

"So what's wrong with that?"

"I barely sold one thousand books. That's horrible, man. I wrote three books and they all bombed. That was my first experience at failure in my life."

"Mike, is that your problem? Do you know how many times I've failed at things in life?"

"But that was your thing, Johnny," I said, laughing under my breath, "you failed, and I succeeded."

"Your little joke wasn't funny at all," Johnny said, "but back to the subject at hand. We both failed, and we both succeeded."

"But look at you now. You're a successful psychiatrist, who…" I said, before being interrupted by Johnny.

"Psychologist, man!" Johnny interrupted.

"Well, you're a successful psychologist, and I am an unsuccessful writer, turned columnist, turned claims worker. My life is very disappointing."

"That's your life, not Mom and Dad's. They don't deserve to suffer because you're feeling pity for yourself."

"I am embarrassed to talk them and tell them I have been reduced to working in a claims department."

"Reduced? There are women working in that office that I have known for one day, and I have nothing but the utmost respect for them."

"I'm not putting them down. I'm just saying that working in that office is nothing I thought I'd ever be doing."

"That's your problem, Mike. If things don't go the way you intend for them to go, you don't know how to handle it. You have a great job that most people would kill for, and you're complaining about not having your dream job. Your house is almost twice as big as mine. You played two years in the pros and I played nine. But you probably don't ever have to work again in your life if you choose not to do so, but you're worried about not being a successful writer! You can't have it all, man! That's life! Stop whining and accept the life you have. And stop making the people you claim to love miserable because you are."

"Are you finished, Johnny?"

"Yes!"

"Good. Now I have a question?"

"Shoot."

"This session is free, right?"

"Sorry, you'll be receiving a bill in the mail."

"One more question, bro."

"What man?"

"You don't, uh," Johnny said, rubbing his nose, "you don't still talk to your little friend, Bernice, do you?"

"Shut up!" I shouted.

"I'm serious! You still confide in ol' Berny Bern?"

"I don't know what you're talking about!"

"I'm glad." Johnny laughed. "After you start to get some real ass you didn't need ol' Berny Bern anymore, huh, big bro?"

"Man, that ain't funny!" I said, pushing him.

"Hey, boy! Keep your hands on the wheel, now!" Johnny said nervously.

The rest of the drive to my house was a more pleasurable conversation. We discussed Mom and Dad, and our lives growing up as brothers. Looking back on our lives, despite being dirt poor, we had a great family. My brother, within a few minutes, had resolved a lot of my issues that I had refused to resolve on my own. I didn't know if he was an excellent psychologist, or if I was so desperate to finally accept the truth, I just needed to hear someone else say it.

The truth being that I was an egotist and I had to face the fact that I was not going to be successful at everything. My self-pity caused me to alienate people from loving me: my parents, my brother, Cynthia and me.

❖❖❖

When we got back to my house, the office girls were still there. There had been no word on Tina's girls and the mood was even more solemn than when we had left. I called Rob, and asked if he could come over and help us out. It didn't take long before he was knocking on the door.

"Hey, what's up, Rob? Glad you could come."

"No problem, where's your friend?"

"She's in here," I said, leading him into the den.

"Tina, this is Detective Robert Baniels from the Atlanta Police Department. He is here to help us."

"How are you doing, officer?" Tina asked.

"You don't have to be so formal, Tina. Call me, Rob. My stepdaughter, Brimone, has told me an awful lot about you and your daughters. She loves coming here to visit you guys and I will do everything I can to make sure we get those girls home safely and as soon as possible."

"Thank you, Detective Baniels. I mean, Rob."

"No problem, I need to ask you a few questions just to know where I need to begin, all right?"

"Okay."

"When was the last time your daughters were seen, and who were they seen with?"

"They were over to my mother-in law's house visiting. After she put them to bed, she said their father came in and made them leave with him."

"Are you and the father divorced?"

"No, we're separated at the time."

"Did she tell you where they might have gone?"

"She said she had no idea."

"Do you know any of his hangout spots? Or any relatives who may be willing to help hide the girls?"

"His whole family is willing. You can start with any of them."

"I'll start with his mother, and go from there. Can I have her address, please?" Rob pulled a pad and a pencil from his inner coat pocket, just like on television.

"Please, Rob, please find my girls. I'm afraid he may hurt them."

"Don't worry, Tina, I'll find them." Rob patted her hand.

Although I knew Rob was a good cop, I had no idea that he was so efficient when it came to addressing victims or those critical situations where he had to be sympathetic.

All that I had ever seen or heard of the man was an occasional scream at the television when a football play did or did not go his way. Listening to him talk to Tina, I actually believed he was going to find the girls. He started to walk out of the door but I stopped him.

"Hey, Rob, I want to go with you, man."

"I don't know, Mike."

"I can't stay here knowing those girls are out there with that maniac."

"I'm only going to ask questions so I suppose it'll be all right. But you can't get out of the car, man."

I snatched my coat from out of the closet, and on my way out of the door Johnny insisted that if I was going, he was going to go, too. Along the way, Rob told us he thought he knew where Curtis and the children were hiding.

"Where do you think they've gone, Rob?"

"You'll find out soon enough." He pulled into Tina's mother-in-law's driveway.

"Rob, can we get out?" I asked.

"That's not a good idea, Mike."

"Come on, Rob, we won't say a word," Johnny added.

"Come on, Rob, this guy attacked me with a gun, man! You can say I'm here as a witness to identify him."

"Man, damn!" Rob said. "Get out the car, but keep your mouths shut. And if anything happens, get your ass on the ground and cover up. Do not try to be a hero."

Rob knocked on the door and the three of us stood and waited for someone to answer. Rob had to knock three times, each time louder than before, until someone answered.

"Who is it?" a woman's voice came from inside.

"I'm Detective Robert Baniels with the Atlanta Police Department. May I come in?"

"What do you want?" the voice shouted again.

"I need to speak to you for a minute, Ma'am. It won't take long."

"The police done already came over here. What you want now?"

"Are you Curtis' mother, Ma'am?"

"Yeah, I'm Curtis' mama, and Curtis ain't here!" the mother-in-law shouted.

"I know, Ma'am, I need to talk to you just to get this thing cleared up."

There was a long silent moment, and we stood there and looked at one another waiting to see if she would open the door. Finally the door opened, and the chain came off.

"Come on in. I only got a minute; I got somethin' cookin' on the stove."

"It won't take long, Ma'am," Rob said. "When was the last time you saw your son Curtis?"

"I already done told the police this, and I ain't sayin' it no mo'."

"Ma'am, if you cooperate with me, this matter could be resolved."

"Look, I don't know where Curtis is, and that's all it is to it!"

Rob looked at Johnny and me and then looked back at the lady and said, "Okay, Ma'am. I'm sorry for disturbing you, and I appreciate you letting us in."

Rob turned around and walked out with Johnny and me following behind. Once we were in the car, Rob drove around the block and parked.

"Listen, fellas, I can't jeopardize your safety, so at this point, I need you to drive around for about ten minutes and then pick me up in front of the old lady's house."

"Why are you going back there?" I asked.

"To get Tina's kids," Rob said, stepping out of the car and jogging back toward Curtis' mother's home.

I slid into the driver's seat and drove around the neighborhood for ten minutes as Rob instructed. Actually it was more like twenty minutes because I was lost for a while. When we pulled up, Rob was standing on the porch with the three girls, and Tina's mother-in-law was yelling hysterically.

"Get yo' hands off my kids!"

"Ma'am, you're going to have to take this up with the authorities," Rob yelled back, standing between the children and the mother-in-law.

"Damn!" Johnny said.

"Mike, call Tina and tell her to come pick up her children," Rob said.

"I'm on it!"

I called Tina and told her that Rob had her children and she could come pick them up. She was understandably happy and she drove over with a caravan of the office girls. Meanwhile, Rob had called the police to keep the situation under control. Throughout the entire ordeal there was no sign of Curtis.

The office girls arrived in two cars with wheels screeching and brakes slamming. It was like a scene from a James Cagney gangster film. Even the police looked at them with amazement. Tina slung open the car door and ran to me screaming.

"Mike! Mike! Where they at?"

"They're in the police car over there." I pointed to a patrol car surrounded by police officers.

I tried to stop her, but she took off before I could grab her. I followed her to make sure the police knew she was the children's mother. Before she could get to the car, Rob stopped her to get her under control.

"The girls are fine, Tina," Rob said, "they're in the car."

Rob opened the door to the car and Tina pulled the girls out one by one and hugged them tightly.

"Thank you! Thank you, God!" Tina said, hugging and kissing her daughters repeatedly. "God bless you, Rob!"

"You probably need to get them out of here, Tina," Rob said.

"Okay! Okay, Rob! God bless, you!" Tina hugged Rob and kissed him on the cheek.

"No problem."

"Thank you! Thank you, Lord!" Tina sighed.

Tina's mother-in-law was still screaming and yelling at everyone standing around, including Tina.

"You can't take my grandkids from me! You don't deserve them!"

"Who is that?" Wanda asked.

"That's Tina's mother-in-law," Cynthia answered.

"She's going off, ain't she?

"I'm telling you, Wanda," Alicia said.

"I ain't gon' just stand here and let her go off on my girl like that," Wanda yelled to anyone listening, "they better restrain that ol' woman before she get her ass whooped out here!"

"Calm down, Wanda," Lisa said.

"Tina, you ain't nothin' but a lowlife tramp! I hope my son never, ever take you back! And he gon' get those kids! Believe dat!" the mother-in-law shouted.

"Shut the hell up!" Wanda yelled to the old woman.

"You shut the hell up! And get off my property!"

"Make me!" Wanda said, walking toward the old woman on the porch.

"Bring yo' ass on up here!" The mother-in-law shouted, walking down the stairs as fast as her legs would carry her.

"Oh, I'm coming! And when I get there I'm gon' slap the dentures out of yo' mouth!"

"Wanda," Cynthia said, trying to restrain her, "calm down!"

"Girl, have you lost your mind?" Alicia said, helping Cynthia restrain Wanda.

"This ol' bitch is about to get a old-fashioned ass whoopin'!"

"Is she serious?" Rob asked, pointing at Wanda.

"Serious, as a heart attack, Rob," I answered, chuckling and shaking my head.

"Dude, what kind of people you hang out with?" Rob asked.

"Crazy-ass women!" I said. "Let me go get her before she ends up in jail."

"Let me go!" Wanda said.

"Wanda," I said, picking her up off of her feet and taking her over to Rob's car, "you're riding back to my house with us."

I slid her in the rear passenger side door, and she jumped out of the rear driver's side door and ran back toward the house before being restrained by the police. Rob explained to the officers that he had the situation under control to keep them from arresting her. We finally got her into the car and calmed her down.

"Wanda, what in the world is wrong with you?" I asked.

"That woman was out there goin' off on my girl, man! I don't play that shit, Mike!"

"That lady look like she is almost seventy years old, though, Wanda," I said.

"I don't give a damn! If you gon' talk shit, you better be ready get yo' ass whooped! I don't care how old you are! Ass whoopins don't discriminate! Anybody can get one!"

"Dude, what kind of people you hang out with?" Rob asked again.

"I told you, man," I said, "some crazy-ass women."

"Wanda," Rob said, "your name is Wanda, right?"

"Yeah, it's Wanda."

"You weren't going to fight that old lady for real, were you?"

"Man, I was going to whoop that ol', no-teeth-havin', bald-headed, stankin', grandma bitch's ass!"

"Then we would have had to take you to jail."

"I don't give a damn! I been to jail befo'!"

I cut Wanda off by changing the subject.

"Rob, how did you know the girls were in the house?"

"It was obvious the lady was hiding something. I'll be honest and say I didn't know exactly what it was, but I did feel that whatever it was, it would lead me to the girls."

"Another baffling case solved," I said.

"Mike?" Wanda asked.

"Yeah, baby."

"Shut the hell up!"

chapter 16

By the time we got back to my house, Tina and the rest of the office girls were already there. The office girls stayed until they were satisfied with Tina's state of mind and then they left. Alicia and Johnny left together, I'm assuming to have one more rendezvous before he left town, and Cynthia left without saying a word to me.

Rob advised Tina on what she should do to prevent that situation from happening again. Once they had all left, Tina and I had our own conversation.

"Tina, I can't apologize enough for my childish behavior this morning."

"What was wrong, Mike? I have never seen you act like that before."

"Well, I found out that all of you ladies in the office knew that I had slept with Pam and Alicia, and it was just a game you play on men."

"You slept with Pam and Alicia?" Tina asked, covering her mouth in shock.

"Don't tell me, you didn't know?"

"Are you crazy, ol' silly boy? Everybody knew."

"Tina, well if you knew, why didn't you tell me?"

"Because it was none of my business."

"That's messed up, Tina. That's why I was so pissed off this morning."

"Wait a minute," Tina said, "answer this for me, you're the one trying to be a player, and have sex with different women in the office, but you're mad at us because we all knew your game?"

"I'm not mad because you knew, I'm mad because you didn't tell me you knew."

"Mike, listen to how you ridiculous you sound. On one hand you're trying to keep your sexual relationships on the down low, and not tell anyone. And then on the other hand, you expect for us to tell you if we find out. Get a grip, man."

"Hmmm. That does sound a little hypocritical, doesn't it?"

"Uh, yeah"

"Now this is very important to me, Tina," I said, "who told Cynthia?"

"Cynthia don't know, Mike."

"She is the one who told me, Tina."

"I'm telling you, Mike, if Cynthia knows, no one from the office told her. Once Alicia and Pam found out how Cynthia felt about you, they promised to back off and they made everybody in the office promise to forget it ever happened. They love Cynthia and they would never want to hurt her."

"Somebody had to tell her."

"I don't think anybody from our office would tell Cynthia something like." Tina added, "Unless of course, it was you."

"Why would I tell her? That doesn't make sense."

"Mike, did she specifically give you names?"

"Dammit! She called my bluff!"

"Dammit! You're right!"

"Look, I'm sorry, Tina."

"Mike, you've already apologized, let's just forget it."

"Dammit! I have to apologize to Alicia, too."

"Yeah, Mike, you are in some deep doo-doo, my brother. First things first, call Cynthia and get things straightened out with her, then get things straightened out with Alicia."

"Cynthia won't talk to me."

"I can get Cynthia to talk to you. But if I do, you better get down on them ashy black knees of yours and beg her to forgive you."

"No problem, I'll do it."

"Let me see you practice."

"What do you mean?"

"Get down on your knees and beg like you're going to beg to Cynthia."

"I'm not getting down on my knees in front of you."

"I guess you don't want me to fix things with Cynthia."

"All right! But if you tell anybody, Tina, it's your ass, you hear me?"

"Boy, get on your knees and beg!" Tina said, pointing to the floor.

I kneeled down. "I'm sorry for acting like a jerk, and I hope you can forgive me."

"That's it?" Tina asked.

"What's wrong with that?"

"That's not personal enough, try again."

"All right," I said, sighing heavily, "I'm sorry for acting like a jerk, I didn't mean to hurt you, and I hope you can forgive me."

"First of all, Mike, you're talking to a black woman. Don't even use the word, jerk. Tell the woman why she should forgive you."

"How do I do that?"

"Why should she forgive you?"

"Well, I don't know, because I'm truly sorry for what I did."

"So you think calling yourself a 'jerk' will make her believe that you're truly sorry?"

"Stop asking me what I should say, and tell me, Tina!"

"No, you're going to tell me, Mike! Why should she forgive you?"

"Because I love her, and I miss her, and I can't stand not talking to her, and seeing her laugh."

"See, that didn't hurt a bit, did it? That's what you need to tell her, and maybe she'll forgive you."

"Maybe?"

"Man, I ain't God!"

"Okay, I'm ready, let's get Cynthia on the phone."

"Get them knees ready, boy."

Tina told Cynthia that she was feeling depressed and she needed to talk to someone. Cynthia rushed over as expected to comfort her. They went into the den for privacy, but I stood at the door listening to find out how much damage I had caused, and how much damage control it would take to fix it.

"Hey, still upset over the girls?" Cynthia asked.

"Yeah, but that's not the only reason I asked you to come over."

"What's up?"

"I called you over to talk about Mike."

"I'm not ready to talk about him right now, Tina."

"Come on now, why not?"

"Because he's a jerk!"

"Mike was right about you! You have to be the first angry black woman I know to refer to a man as a 'jerk' when she's mad at him."

"Well, he is a jerk!"

"Maybe he is, but even a jerk deserves an opportunity to be forgiven."

I looked at the door in reference to Tina's comment about me being a jerk wondering if she was going to help me or get me in deeper trouble.

"I don't know, Tina, this man has slept with some of my closest friends, and then he tells me he's in love with me. I don't know if I can handle that."

"I know what you mean," Tina said. "That would be hard for me to swallow, too, Cynthia."

She's killing me in there, I thought to myself. I used my cell phone to call Tina, and when she answered I told her to keep Cynthia in the room until I returned. I warned her that it would take about an hour to an hour and a half. But for Tina, that's nothing. She's good for several hours of pure meaningless conversation.

I ran a few errands, and called on a few favors, and a little over an hour later I was back at my house. I walked into the den where Tina and Cynthia were, and kneeled on my knees.

"Cynthia, listen to me. I apologize for being a jerk," I said. I looked over at Tina. "I mean I apologize for being stupid."

"Turns out, 'jerk' is fine with Cynthia, so go 'head with your apology."

"Anyway, I'm sorry for hurting you, Cynthia. I was a fool for not realizing how much I cared for you. But it's only because I never thought a sweet, magnificent woman like you would ever be interested in a man like me. You are everything a man wants in a woman. I respect and adore you so much. The only reason I never made a move on you is because I didn't think I deserved your love. I still don't! It's just that I love you so much, I'd rather you break my heart, and tell me no, than to sit back and let some other man take you out of my life without a fight. I know you may never forgive me but if I had known for one second that there was a chance you would be interested in me for anything other than friendship, I would never have looked at either one of them. You are the most incredible person I have ever met in my life. And I swear, if you don't let me try to make you happy for the rest of my life, I don't know what I'll do with myself."

"What are you trying to say to me, Mike?"

"I'm saying that," I bowed my head, and then I stood up to look Cynthia straight in her eyes, "I'm saying that I love you, and I want to spend the rest of my life with you as my woman. I'm saying that I want to marry you, and spend every second making you the happiest woman on earth. Because just knowing that you're my woman, makes me the happiest man in the world. What I'm saying is, will you marry me?"

"I will!" Tina wiped tears from her eyes.

"I don't know what to say!" Cynthia sat down.

"I will!" Tina said, raising her hand.

"Say what's really in your heart, Cynthia."

"Mike, look, over here!" Tina shouted.

"Tina, will you be quiet?" I mumbled out of the side of my mouth.

"I'm surprised," Cynthia said. "No, I'm shocked."

"Hold on," I said.

I returned with a friend who played the saxophone. He played several love songs as I held Cynthia in my arms. She resisted at first, but my persistence paid off and finally she relaxed. She laid her head on my shoulder and danced with the rhythm to the music.

"This is so romantic." Tina waved her hands in front of her eyes as if she was drying her tears.

"Hold on, there's something else," I said, leaving the room again, and returning with dozens and dozens of white tulips.

"Oh, Mike," Cynthia said.

"Hold on, one more thing." I left the room again and returned with a small box.

"Mike, what is this?" Cynthia asked.

I opened the box and showed her the engagement ring.

"Oh my, Mike. I don't know what to say."

"Say you'll marry me, and that's all I need to hear."

"Mike, I don't know," Cynthia said, shaking her head, "I just don't know."

"Listen, this is only the beginning. If I have to do this every day until you say yes, I will."

"Damn, Mike, you got loot like that?" Tina said.

"Tina, what do you think?" Cynthia looked over my shoulder past me.

"It's your decision," Tina said, "but you better say yes before he changes his mind."

"Yes, Mike! I'll marry you!" Cynthia wrapped her arms around my neck and kissed me.

"Hey, saxophone man," Tina said, "what's your name?"

"Kym."

"You married?"

"No, Ma'am."

"Got a girlfriend?"

"No, Ma'am."

"Gay?"

"No, Ma'am."

"Then what's your problem?"

"I don't have any problems, Ma'am. I'm a musician; I don't need a wife or a girlfriend."

"I heard that!" Tina said.

"Thanks for the favor, Kym," I said, as I showed him to the door.

Kym and I were friends because I frequented his jazz club. He used the unisex Kym as his stage name because he thought it was sexy to women. He also used French, the language of love, as his dialect. Most people thought he was French-born and bred. His real name was actually Roosevelt Jackson, and he hailed from Pascagoula, Mississippi.

Anyway, I once wrote him a favorable review in my column and he told me that if I ever needed the favor returned to let him know. The first day of the year is always a busy day for his club, but luckily he is as big of a romantic as I am, and he left his club to do me this favor. Now I owed him.

When I walked back in the den, Tina and Cynthia were admiring the engagement ring.

"Girl, I didn't know Mike had it going on like that," Tina said.

"Me neither!" Cynthia said.

I stood in the doorway and listened to the two of them go on and on about me and the ring until Cynthia finally noticed me.

"I'm sorry, Mike, I didn't see you standing there."

"I'm just listening, that's all."

"Tina, can I have a second alone with Mike."

"Yeah, you can have a second alone with your fi-an-cé," Tina said, making funny faces.

After Tina closed the door, Cynthia walked over to me and held my hands.

"Mike, are you sure you want this and you're not overreacting to seeing me with another man?"

"I have never been more certain of anything in my life. And I won't say that seeing you with Reggie didn't make me jealous, but that's not it. All of this time I felt that you were the perfect woman, but not the perfect woman for me. I truly never thought I was good enough for you, Cynthia, but after seeing you with Reggie, that didn't matter anymore. All that mattered was me telling you that I loved you."

"Well, do you want to remain engaged a while before we get married to see how things turn out?"

"I don't have to wait a while. I don't have to wait another day, Cynthia. I know who you are, and now, I know who I am. And I know that with you in my life I can only be a better man."

"So," Cynthia said, "what are your plans with me, Michael?"

"So now it's 'Michael,' huh?"

"Yes, Michael," Cynthia said sarcastically.

"I plan to marry you as soon as you let me, and create a family with you."

"We already have two children; how many more do we need?"

"See, that's why I love you. You love my children. That's special. I believe that if you and I never would have spoken again, you would still love and care for my daughters."

"You're right there, Mike. I am drawn to those girls, despite the fact that they have a knucklehead for a father."

"You know we are going to be the talk of the office, don't you, Cynt?"

"You've been the talk of the office, playboy."

"Let's not go there again."

"Believe me, I don't want to go there."

"How do you think that will affect our relationship?"

"I don't know. I have spoken about it with Pam and Alicia already."

"What do you mean you've spoken with Pam and Alicia?"

"Mike, you were the only person in the office who didn't realize I was in love with you. Today, I spoke with Pam and Alicia about your relationships with them. They were both apologetic. Not because they did something wrong, but because they didn't want to hurt me. Alicia told me, you and she broke it off a while back. And ever since she realized there may be a chance for us she has been campaigning to get us together. And I think we both can vouch for that."

"Boy, can we vouch for that."

"Pam told me that you are a wonderful guy that she shared special moments with, but you and she never had anything serious. She also said that once she realized there may be something between us she backed off as well. She has backed off, hasn't she?"

"Oh yeah! Oh yeah! There's nothing going on between us anymore."

"Is there anyone else I should know about, Mike?"

I immediately thought about Cherie, but my mouth still said, "No, nothing at all."

"Good."

"Cynthia, how did you know about Pam and Alicia?"

"Actually, I didn't," Cynthia said. "I started off teasing you to get you off of me and Reggie but you were acting so nervous I knew something was going on."

"Dammit! You bluffed me."

"Never play poker, buddy."

"Not with you, anyway."

"Sooooo…" Cynthia looked for me to say something.

"Sooooo," I said, "where do we go from here, Cynt?"

I had asked that question to many women and none had ever given the answer I wanted to hear.

"We go all the way, Mike!"

I smiled a broad smile because that was the answer I'd been waiting to hear.

"How are you going to feel working at Upskon under the circumstances?"

"Under the circumstances, I'll be turning in my two-week notice."

"Cynthia, you can't quit your job."

"Mike, don't worry. I'll be fine. That will make me get off my butt and start this firm."

"We can discuss that later."

"You know what, Mike?"

"What's that?"

"You have a lot of people who genuinely care about you."

"Why do you say that?"

"Your friend, Reggie."

"What about Reggie?"

"Now he wasn't going to get anything from me last night, anyway, but he didn't know that. But once he saw your reaction in the basement, he totally backed off. He realized you cared for me, and told me that he had recently been through the same thing. He said a woman had broken his heart. He said he never told the woman how much he cared for her, and she got with another man. He said he would never want you to go through what he's gone through."

"Reggie said that?" I asked, knowing that I was the man responsible for breaking his heart.

"Yes, he did. I have much respect for the man."

"But you did kiss him, right?"

"No, silly. When you came downstairs we were laughing, not kissing."

"But your faces were like, right in front of each other's."

"He was wiping tears out of my eyes. That boy is a fool."

"No, Reggie's not the fool, I am."

"Aw, ain't that sweet."

I know Cynthia thought I was referring to my sleeping with other women, but I was actually referring to thinking Reggie would do to me, what I had done to him a year earlier.

"So, what do we do with the remainder of our evening?"

"Let's talk," Cynthia said, "let's sit and talk."

"Talking sounds good to me."

Cynthia and I spent the remaining portion of the evening talking. Later that night, Alicia and Johnny called and asked if it was too late for them to stop for a visit. Johnny has never been one to leave situations unresolved. He wanted Alicia and I to discuss our issues and resolve them before he left the next day. He had no idea of the bomb I was about to drop on him.

Tina and the girls were asleep by the time they arrived, so we all went into the basement, not to disturb them. Johnny was the last person downstairs and when he reached the bottom step where he could see the entire basement, he stopped in his tracks.

"Man, what is this, Mike?" He looked from wall to wall.

"It's my favorite Michigan Wolverine."

"Mike said he knows that guy, Johnny, does he?" Cynthia asked.

"Yeah, he does." Johnny lowered his head.

"Do you know him, too?" Cynthia said.

"Oh, I know him very well."

"Who is it?"

"It's me," Johnny said.

"Johnny, that's you?" Cynthia shouted.

"Yup, that's me."

"I don't get it, Mike," Cynthia said.

"Don't get what?" I asked.

"Why didn't you just say that these posters were of your brother?"

"Because I didn't want to get into the why's, and the where's, and the what's that would follow."

"What why's, where's and what's that would follow?" Alicia asked.

"Well, my big brother hasn't really communicated with his family for a while and I suppose he doesn't know enough about us to maintain a conversation," Johnny said.

"That's not true. The truth is that I am so proud of my little brother, and when I talk about his successes to others, it only reminds me of my own failures. So, the less I speak of my family, the less I'm reminded of the many embarrassments I've caused them. I've failed as a husband! I've failed as a father! A brother!"

"You may have failed as a husband, but maybe it was because you were married to the wrong wife. And you can't fail as a brother because I won't let you. And after seeing you with my beautiful nieces, there's no way I'm going to let you stand in front of me and say that you're a failure as a father. Stop feeling sorry for yourself and get off your ass and do something if you're not happy with your life. Otherwise, shut the hell up!"

"You can't talk to my fiancé like that," Cynthia said, smiling and holding up the engagement ring I had given her, "but thank you for doing it, Johnny."

"Congratulations!" Alicia said, grabbing Cynthia's hands, and jumping up and down with her.

"Thank you, Alicia, thank you so much!"

"I want to tell you guys that if there are two people who are meant to be together it is you two. And I am sincerely happy for you." Alicia kissed me on the cheek.

"Thanks, Alicia, it means a lot coming from you."

"Hey," Johnny said, shaking my hand, and hugging me at the same time, "I'm proud of you, big brother."

"I'm proud of you, too, Johnny."

"This causes for a toast," Johnny said, "what do you have to drink?"

"Sorry, Cynthia and I don't drink, Johnny," I said.

"I do!" Tina said, running down the stairs with five glasses, and two brown bags in her hands. "Wine, for the grown-ups, and Coke for the children."

"I should have known you were somewhere around here listening," I said.

"Yeah, you should have, but you didn't."

"A toast to my brother, his future wife and many, many years of happiness to come," Johnny said.

We all lifted our glasses, and drank a toast.

"My turn," Tina said. "I'd like to toast my sister, Cynthia, and my brother, Mike, on announcing to themselves what the world has known for a long time now, and that's that they're meant to be wife and husband. Notice I said wife first."

"Amen!" Cynthia said.

"I would like to add that sometime things happen unexpectedly, which makes for better things to happen. If I had not been going to Florida, I would never have stopped here in Atlanta to see Mike and my nieces. Nor would I have met Alicia. So thank God for all things, great and small." Johnny said.

"Good speech, Tiny Tim!" Tina said. "I'm sitting up here thanking God and getting drunk at the same time. Now you know I'm wrong!"

"I'd like to add to that, I'd like to drink to Mike finally having the guts to fight for me instead of acting like a high-school boy," Cynthia said.

"I'll drink to that, too! Oh, and if Mike would never have come to Upskon, I wouldn't have had a place to get away from my nutty-ass husband," Tina said. "Turn 'em up!"

"Yeah, and Mike, would not be, as he calls us, one of the office girls," Alicia added.

"Office Girls! Oh shit!" I said.

"What's the matter, Mike?" Cynthia asked.

"Nothing, I'll be right back!" I said, running upstairs to the telephone.

I called my publisher and woke him from what sounded like a dead sleep. I asked him to hold off the book until I edited some of the chapters. He told me he had read the book and felt that it needed no editing, except for punctuation and grammar. I pleaded and pleaded, but to no avail. He would not give an inch.

Johnny left the next day as planned, but he did get the chance to visit with my daughters on his own.

❖❖❖

The following Monday, we were all back at work as scheduled. Tazzy made the announcement that Cherie had decided to no longer work, and resume her duties back at her church. I smiled and thought that maybe some good came out of our evil.

Cynthia and I couldn't keep our eyes off each other the whole morning, and neither could Tina. She smiled or winked at every opportunity. Alicia wasn't as bad, but she too joined in the exultation of our engagement. Right before lunch Tina admitted that she was going to boil over and she would give us until after lunch to tell the office or she would have to do it herself. Cynthia told her that she would tell Tazzy and let Tazzy tell the office.

This was on one of the mornings Jaline happened to be in the office, so everyone would find out at the same time. As promised, Cynthia did tell Tazzy, Tazzy did tell Jaline, and then Jaline congratulated us and asked to speak to us privately before they told the rest of the office. She asked to speak to Cynthia first, and so as she requested, she went first. While Cynthia was in Jaline's office she kindly turned in her two weeks' notice. Before I went into her office I grabbed a couple of items out of my desk drawer and placed them in my pocket.

"Good afternoon, Michael, I hear congratulations are in order," Jaline said.

"Yes, thank you."

"I never knew you two were even seeing each other."

"Well, we didn't have a clue either until recently. It was kind of sudden."

"Anyway, congratulations!"

"Thanks again." I stood to leave.

"Don't be in such a rush," Jaline said. "There is one thing I would like for you to do for me before you get married."

"And what's that?" I asked.

"One lay." Jaline held up one finger.

"Excuse me?" I said quickly, sitting back down and fumbling around in my pocket.

"One lay," Jaline said again. "One good, hard, rough, exciting round in the hay, and I'll make you the supervisor."

"What about Tazzy?"

"What about Tazzy? I'll give her another title."

"I'm very flattered, but I don't think I can do that."

"Well, there is another alternative."

"And what's that?"

"You can become unemployed if you tell me no."

"So are you saying that if I don't have sex with you, you're going to fire me?"

"That doesn't sound nice, Michael. Let's say that if you do sleep with me, there could be some great benefits in it for you. And you can use some extra benefits with starting a new family and all."

"To tell you the truth, I really don't need the extra benefits."

"Come on now, Michael. You don't find me sexy?"

"I find Cynthia sexy, Jaline."

"What about these?" Jaline said, pulling her bra down, and exposing her breasts. "They cost me over fifteen hundred dollars, apiece."

"I think what you're doing is very unethical."

"Unethical or not, what do you say? Keep your job, and have some great sex to top it off, or lose your job and have no money to take care of your new wife? Which is it?"

"Do you not understand that Cynthia and I are going to be married?"

"I also understand that she was at the bottom of the totem pole when it came to selecting your sex partners in the office."

"You understood wrong, Jaline. And how could she have ever been at the bottom, anyway? You always held that spot."

"Sarcasm, I love it!" Jaline said, walking around the table, and kneeling on her knees in front of me. "Let's see how funny this is."

Jaline took my zipper and begin to slowly unzip my pants. I pushed her hand away. But each time she smiled, and continued to unzip my pants until the zipper was completely down. I jumped up and pushed Jaline off of my lap.

"Get the hell off of me, you despicable excuse for a woman!"

"What did you say to me?"

"You heard me! You use your position to exploit people. You've been doing it for so long you don't even have a conscience anymore!"

"And what about you? You're no better than I am!"

"If I wasn't, you'd have your mouth between my legs right now!"

"Get out of my office, you black son-of-a-bitch!"

"And for the life of me, I can not understand why anyone would ever allow you to write a column. Did you earn that privilege on your knees, too?"

"Who are you to comment on my column?"

"Who am I? I am Cyrus."

"Who the hell is Cyrus?"

"Do you remember a diatribe you wrote called, "Black Women: The New Civil Rights Movement!" Well, after that garbage you called an article, I wrote you back asking you to edit some of the content, but you refused."

"Yes, I remember. That was you? You were a big talker; now look at you working for me!"

"On the contrary, I don't work for you and I never have." I reached into my pocket and played the recorder. Jaline could hear her voice asking me to have sex with her. "I didn't come here because I needed a job. I came here to bring your ass down off your white horse, BITCH!"

I cut the tape off and stuck in back in my pocket. When I walked out of Jaline's office, Tazzy was waiting for me.

"Mike, what's going on?"

"Nothing," I said. "I just quit."

"Gimme that tape!" Jaline shouted from inside of her office.

I walked out of the office and didn't bother to clean my desk. I left all of my items, condoms included, and left the way I came, with nothing but a penis and a smile. I took a deep breath and sighed as I walked to my car. I had lost my job but I had gained something much more valuable, my dignity.

On my way home, I received a call on my cell phone from an unknown number. I looked at it, and didn't recognize it, so I didn't bother to answer. The caller left a message, so I checked my voice mail. The voice was soft and sweet. Here is what it said:

❖❖❖

"Hello, Michael. Bet you never thought you'd hear from me again, huh? Anyway, I don't want to fill your voice mail up so I'll make it quick. Who would have ever thought that an act of infidelity could actually save a marriage? I don't know what you brought out of me, but when I went home, I was able to tell my husband how I felt about the church, making love, and the other issues that were driving me out of my mind. Surprisingly, he listened and then apologized for taking me for granted.

This Sunday, I will preach my first sermon as assistant pastor. He was supposed to preach at another church, but he cancelled it to make this Sunday special for me. That's why I had to quit Upskon so abruptly. Sorry, I didn't get a chance to say good-bye in person, but thank you for being a friend when I truly needed one. Love ya!"

❖❖❖

I held the telephone close to my face, and thought briefly about that wonderful night we shared. I was happy that she had found the strength to confront her husband on their issues and work things out. I smiled and played it several times before I erased it, never to hear that sweet voice again.

chapter 17

I got home a little after one o'clock. I loosened my tie, and sat down in my recliner in the den. But as soon as I cut on my television I heard the sound of a car pull into my driveway. I looked outside my window and I saw Cynthia getting out of her car. Then, I saw Ms. Virginia getting out of the passenger side. I knew it was something serious at that point. I met them at the door and before they could ring the doorbell, I opened the door.

"Why aren't you two at work?" I asked.

"After you left I told Tazzy, I had to leave, too," Cynthia said, walking in, and putting her purse on the couch.

"Never mind why I'm here," Ms. Virginia said.

"What happened between you and Jaline, Mike?" Cynthia asked.

"How are you doing, Ms. Virginia?"

"I'm fine, Michael, how are you, dear?"

"I'm fine."

The three of us walked into my den and sat down.

"This is what happened in Jaline's office." I pulled the miniature tape recorder out of my pocket and set it on my coffee table. I pushed the play button, and sat back.

❖❖❖

Click.
"Anyway, congratulations!"
"Thanks again."

"Don't be in such a rush. There is one thing I would like for you to do for me before you get married."

"And what's that?"

"One lay."

"Excuse me?"

"One lay. One good, hard, rough, exciting round in the hay, and I'll make you the supervisor."

"What about Tazzy?"

"What about Tazzy? I'll give her another title."

"I'm very flattered, but I don't think I can do that."

"Well, there is another alternative."

"And what's that?"

"You can become unemployed if you tell me no."

"So are you saying that if I don't have sex with you, you're going to fire me?"

"That doesn't sound nice, Michael. Let's say that if you do sleep with me, there could be some great benefits in it for you. And you can use some extra benefits with starting a new family and all."

"To tell you the truth, I really don't need the extra benefits."

"Come on now, Michael. You don't find me sexy?"

"I find Cynthia sexy, Jaline."

"What about these? They cost me over fifteen hundred dollars, apiece."

"I think what you're doing is very unethical."

"Unethical or not, what do you say? Keep your job, and have some great sex to top it off, or lose your job and have no money to take care of your new wife? Which is it?"

"Do you not understand that Cynthia and I are going to be married?"

"I also understand that she was at the bottom of the totem pole when it came to selecting your sex partners in the office."

"You understood wrong, Jaline. And how could she have ever been at the bottom, anyway? You always held that spot."

"Sarcasm, I love it! Let's see how funny this is."

"Get the hell off of me, you despicable excuse for a woman!"

"What did you say to me?"

"You heard me! You use your position to exploit people. You've been doing it for so long you don't even have a conscience anymore!"

"And what about you? You're no better than I am!"

"If I wasn't, you'd have your mouth between my legs right now!"

"Get out of my office, you black son-of-a-bitch!"

"And for the life of me, I can not understand why anyone would ever allow you to write a column. Did you earn that privilege on your knees, too?"

Click.

❖❖❖

"Oh my God," Ms. Virginia said, covering her mouth.

"So she called you in that office to proposition you?"

"I'm afraid so, Cynt."

"She's not getting away with that!" Cynthia said, standing up and pacing the floor.

"What do you think I should do with this tape, Ms. Virginia?" I asked.

"Oh! You're going to sue her for sexual harassment!" Cynthia said.

"I had no idea Jaline would do something like that," Ms. Virginia said.

"Listen, Cynthia, before we go any further with the tape or anything else dealing with Upskon, there's something I need to tell you."

"Please don't tell me you've slept with Jaline, too, Mike!"

"No! No! No! Nothing like that, but it's just as important."

"Do I need to sit down?"

"I think you both need to sit down."

I sat between them and held their hands.

"Okay, when I first started to work at Upskon, it wasn't because I was in desperate need for a job."

"I figured that out once we started to hang out, Mike!" Cynthia smiled.

"Well, the reason I took the job there was to compile research for a book I was writing, a book called *The Office Girls*. My intent was to prove that if given a position of authority in corporate America, women would behave the same way as men."

"So, what are you trying to tell me, Mike?"

"Well, my reason for working at Upskon was to write about women."

"What's so bad about that?"

"I kind of used your confidential conversations and situations from the office girls as the research for my book."

"So, were we just a game to you, Michael? A joke?"

I knew she was highly pissed off because she only called me Michael when she was upset with me.

"Oh no, baby!"

"So you heard the dirty little secrets of women in corporate America! Now what do you do? You get your own talk show? Does your book become a best seller? Huh?"

"I will do whatever you want me to do, Cynthia!"

"Mike, you know what? I only have so much patience. I've accepted the fact that you ignored my love for you! I've also accepted the fact that you've slept with some of my friends! But this, this is too much for me to accept! I can't do it!" Cynthia said, grabbing her purse and walking towards the door. "Let's go, Ms. Virginia!"

"No."

"Excuse me?" Cynthia stopped in her tracks.

"I'm not leaving and neither are you," Ms. Virginia said, "now you two sit down and talk this out!"

"What is there to say, Ms. Virginia?"

"Listen to him, and find out! You young people nowadays, every time you have a little disagreement you want to pack it up and call it quits. Love is not easy. So if you love this man, listen to what he has to say before you go running off!"

"Okay, Michael. What do you have to say?" Cynthia said, throwing her purse in a chair and slamming herself down on the couch.

"Cynthia, when I decided to write this book it wasn't to hurt anybody in the office—nobody but Jaline, that is. She once wrote an article depicting black men as ignorant savages, and glorifying black women for maintaining the integrity of the black race. She said that as minorities, black men couldn't handle the pressure of leadership in corporate America, nor our communities, like women.

"I took offense and asked her to retract the article. She wouldn't do it, so I wrote an article in response to hers. My article received a lot of negative feedback from women accusing me of being a misogynist. I was eventually fired and I set out to seek my revenge by writing the book. Along the way, I found a deeper understanding and appreciation for women. Especially the women I've worked with at Upskon. I still believe that power and money often dictate behavior. But it's not about that. It's about men respecting women, women respecting men, and people respecting people."

"But Michael, why us?" Cynthia said, softening just a tad.

"It wasn't about the office girls, it was about Jaline. But you women have made me realize that this battle of the sexes is dangerous for us. I don't give a damn about this book anymore. I don't care if I sell a million copies, or just one copy. If I don't have you, I don't have anything! Do you believe me?"

"Yes, Michael. So how do you fix this?"

"I don't know, Cynt," I said, "but I can't hurt the office girls."

"Don't publish the book, Michael! That's how you fix it!"

"It's not that easy, Cynt."

"Did you use our actual names?"

"Yes," I said, very humbly.

"Why? Why would do that?" Cynthia said, tapping me in the head.

"I thought that would make it more authentic."

"Mike! Mike! Mike!" Cynthia shook her head.

"I'll fix it. I'll do something."

"You have to."

"How about I use a pen name or an alias for the author of *The Office Girls*? And I change the names of the characters in the book. That way, I keep the juicy content, the girls' names remain anonymous, and none will be the wiser."

"Sounds good to me!" Ms. Virginia said.

"If that's what you've got to do to correct this mess, then fine! But we're not through by a long shot," Cynthia said. "And you know that if you do it that way, you will not be able to receive any public notoriety or accolades for this book, right?"

"I guess that's a fair trade."

"Are you sure, Mike?" Ms. Virginia asked. "What happens if this book becomes a bestseller?"

"Then I'll know I've finally written a good book. Cynthia, how are you going to feel working with the girls knowing about the book?"

"As of today, I no longer work there."

"What?" I pushed her slightly away from me to look at her in the face.

"After you walked out, I walked out behind you. I told Tazzy that I resign, and walked out."

"So, I guess somebody will be moving in here sooner than expected."

"No, I'll be fine. I'm not moving in until I'm *Mrs.* Cynthia Forrester. And after today I don't know if that's ever going to happen."

"I promise I'll make it up to you, Cynt."

"Mr. Forrester, my name wasn't in that book, was it?"

"Ms. Virginia, I can neither confirm nor deny those allegations," I said, running into another room.

❖❖❖

I called Greenbaum later that evening to discuss my new idea for the book. I really didn't know how he would take it, so I tried to break it to him gently.

"Greenbaum? This is Michael Forrester, how are you?"

"Hey, my man!" Greenbaum shouted into the telephone.

"Greenbaum, what do you have for me?"

"Good news, my man! You have twenty-thousand copies of your books already pre-sold!"

"What do you mean, pre-sold? The book hasn't been released yet."

"Where you been, Mikey boy? The book doesn't have to be released in order for us to sell it!"

"Oh," I said, confused on whether or not it was too late to make the necessary changes.

"You've pre-sold more copies in one day than you did with all three of your first crappy books combined!"

"Crappy?"

"Sorry, my man! I don't mean 'crappy,' I mean misunderstood."

"So, what's up next?"

"Booksignings! Seminars! Speaking engagements! Whatever you want, it's yours!"

"I can't believe it, Greenbaum!"

"You better believe it!"

"I need to tell you something about the book, Greenbaum."

"Speak, my Afro-American brother."

"I need to use a pen name for my book."

"For what? Your name is about to go international, my friend!"

"I can't use my name, that's all!"

"You know what? For you, we'll use a different name. But I'm telling you, you don't write mystery books, my man; it's best to use the name on your birth certificate!"

"Perhaps it is. I also need to change the names of the characters in the book."

"What? Ya killin' me here, Mikey! It's too late in the game to change names!"

"We have to, Greenbaum!"

"No can do, Mikey boy!"

"Why not?"

"I've already put the capital into having the manuscript set up and prepped for print, and I can't get that money back! That's why!"

"Then every woman in that office is going to sue the pants off of the both of us for slander, Greenbaum."

"Slanda'?"

"Yes, slanda'!" I said, sarcastically mocking Greenbaum.

"You think they can do that?"

"This is definitely a case of defamation of character. We used their names. And then we put out negative propaganda on them. We're in trouble!"

"We? Where do you get this 'we' stuff from? I'm just an innocent publisher here."

"Not if you don't let me make the necessary changes to that manuscript, Greenbaum. You're just as liable as I am because you've been made aware of the content."

"Dammit to hell! In that case, make those, uh, necessary changes and get that new manuscript to me yesterday."

"That's only a matter of swiping a keyboard key."

"Well, start swipin', Mikey," Greenbaum said, "and uh, no more talk about lawsuits, okay?"

"Okey-dokey!"

"Now go finish that book, my man!"

"I'll have it completed by next week."

❖❖❖

Over the next couple of months, our lives changed drastically. Ms. Virginia took the tape I had recorded of Jaline's sexual proposition to their regional manager and Jaline was fired. Ms. Virginia was offered the manager's position, but she respectfully declined. Tazzy was promoted to manager, Susan became the supervisor, and Pam became the assistant supervisor. Everyone else remained in the same positions. The purpose of writing *The Office Girls* was to avenge Jaline Dandy. I had looked forward to that day for so long, but when it arrived, it didn't matter. As a matter of fact, there was no mentioning of my account with Jaline at all.

❖❖❖

Cynthia and I were married in early February, and Tina and her children moved into Cynthia's house. My girls were just as happy as I was to have Cynthia become a part of our family.

Brimone was Cynthia's maid of honor, and Alexiah was our flower girl. The girls visited more than ever, and Cynthia somehow got Cecelia to let Alexiah spend the night with Brimone. My brother Johnny flew in to be my best man. I'm sure Alicia was ecstatic about that. My parents surprised me by coming.

Our wedding night was the most incredible night of my life. There had only been two other occasions when my heart felt so light, and so full at the same time, and that was the births of my children.

After the celebration Cynthia and I had to rush to the airport to catch a plane to St. Croix where we would spend our honeymoon. We knew how romantic the island was, but Cynthia insisted that we took our entire family to enjoy our coming together as a family. So Alexiah and Brimone went with us. Tonita, who attended the wedding, called us both crazy for taking the children along with us, but Cynthia didn't feel comfortable leaving them behind.

When we finally got settled in St. Croix, it was late so we all passed out from exhaustion. The girls had their own room, so Cynthia and I still had our privacy. I would not get to make love to my wife for the first time until the second day of our marriage.

We stayed up late until the girls fell asleep, then we went to bed ourselves. Cynthia had on a sheer nightgown that revealed her toned curvaceous figure. I leaped in the bed and waited for her to join me. She slid in beside me, and held my hand.

"I'm ready, Mike."

"Me too."

"Well, come here," Cynthia said, pulling me on top of her.

"Oh, okay."

As I rested myself on top of Cynthia, she opened her legs, and we started to kiss very slowly. I didn't have to tell her to open her eyes because she was already looking at me. As we caressed and kissed in the darkness, I could hear her begin to moan. The only light that shined in the room was coming from the moon shining through the window. Her face seemed so beautiful to me that I rubbed my hand against it, to see if she was real.

My heart was beating so fast, I thought it was showing through my chest. I pulled off my clothes, and climbed back into bed. I slowly kissed her lips, as I took off her bra, and then her panties. As we lay naked, I rubbed her face again several times. I started to kiss her neck very gently. I would take her neck in my mouth and bite down with my lips. Then I would twirl my tongue in circles before I bit her slightly again.

Cynthia started to grind her hips into me and my pole was jerking right at the edge of her hole. I lowered myself, and cupped both of her breasts in my hands. I placed my mouth on her nipples, and I went back and forth to each breast sucking the nipple sternly.

Cynthia began to shake and moan out loud.

"Oh, baby, you feel so good."

I moved down further and kissed her stomach. She started to wiggle and tried to pull away. "Oh, Mike, baby, I can't take that."

"It feels good to you, baby?" I asked.

"Oh, it feels so good I can't take it!"

I held her down and started to kiss and bite her inner thigh. She arched her back, and wrapped the pillow around her face to muffle her sighs. I continued to kiss between her thighs. She lifted her butt off of the bed, and squirmed trying to get away. But I clamped down on her hips to pull her back down to the mattress.

"Oh, Mike, what are you doing to me, baby?"

"I'm making love to you, baby!"

"Oh, baby, I can't stop shaking!"

"Don't try to stop, just enjoy it, baby!"

"Oh, God, Michael, I can't stop shaking!"

"Shhh, baby!"

I did this for what seemed like forever and she began to jerk and kick like a fish out of water.

"OH, GOD, BABY! OH, GOD! OH ,GOD!"

While Cynthia was having her orgasm I climbed up and placed my pole inside of her. She was so wet and moist that I had no problem entering her. She opened her legs wider and I started to push my pole deeper. She wrapped her feet around the back of my legs and gripped my ankles with her toes. Then she wrapped her arms around my back and her fingertips met at my spine.

We lay staring each other in the face, and enjoying every moment. What I was experiencing was so much more than a sexual feeling. It was spiritual, and emotional. What I was feeling was Cynthia's soul. As we continued to grind to our sexual rhythm and look each other deeply in the eyes, Cynthia reached up and wiped my eyes.

"What are you doing, Cynt?" I asked.

"You're crying, baby."

"What?"

"You're crying, baby." Cynthia wiped my eyes again.

"I'm sorry, baby, I didn't know."

"Oh please, don't apologize, I love you, baby," Cynthia said, crying herself, and squeezing me tightly. "I love you so much."

"I've never felt this way before in my life, Cynthia."

"Neither have I, baby, neither have I."

As we talked, we continued our rhythmical love-making. Each thrust deep and pleasurable. And with each thrust Cynthia met me stroke for stroke.

"I want to come inside of you, baby," I said.

"I'm ready, sweetheart, I'm ready."

I could feel my orgasm approaching and I closed Cynthia's legs so that I could feel her entire body, her breasts, her thighs, her feet, everything. And as she ground nothing but her hips, my orgasm hit, and I completely lost my mind. It had been a while since I'd had an orgasm and this one hit with the magnitude of a number seven on the Richter scale.

I pushed so deeply inside of Cynthia that she had another orgasm. We lay and stared each other in the eyes, holding each other tightly as we shook and jerked until our orgasms subsided. The only words to come out of our mouths during our euphoric moment were, "I love you."

I feel asleep, still nestled inside of Cynthia. And when I woke up the next morning, though flaccid, I was still inside of her. We kissed, and lay there holding each other until the girls knocked on the door.

"Can we come in?" Brimone shouted.

"Hey! Do you guys want to go get some breakfast?" Cynthia shouted, as I kissed her on the neck.

"YEAH!" the girls shouted.

"Well, give us time to take a quick shower and we're on our way!"

"Thank you, Ms. Cynthia!" Brimone shouted.

"No, Bri," Alexiah whispered, "she's our stepmommy, now!"

"You're right, Alex," Brimone whispered back, "thank you, Stepmom!"

"Yeah, thank you, Stepmommy!" Alexiah said.

"Oh, Mike," Cynthia whispered to me, "they called me Stepmommy!"

"I heard, and nobody is thanking me for shit!"

"Shut up, bald man!"

"Daddy, stop cursing!" Alexiah shouted.

"I'll shut up, but I don't like it!"

"Well, I'll make up for it later."

The rest of our honeymoon was a family vacation where Cynthia and I had to sneak to make love. Turns out that although Cynthia hadn't had much sex, she did love to have sex much, very much, but only with her husbands.

When we were settled back in Atlanta, I had to explain to my new bride that I had committed to a date prior to our union. She gladly dressed me, selected the restaurant and sent me on my way.

❖❖❖

Ding-dong.

"Ah, look at you; you look like you're in high school."

"Very funny, where's Bri?" I asked.

"Bri, your father's here!" Tonita said, yelling upstairs.

"Hey, what's up, man?" Rob said, shaking my hand.

"I'm good, man," I said, fixing my tie.

"Look at him, Rob, he looks nervous," Tonita joked.

"Do something about your wife, man," I said to Rob.

While we were talking, Brimone walked down the stairs in a beautiful long dress. She looked so mature my mouth dropped to the floor.

"Hi, Daddy," Brimone said.

"Hi, baby," I said, knowing that after tonight our relationship would never be the same, "ready to go?"

"Yes, sir, I'm ready."

"Hey, have her home by ten, young man," Rob said.

"Yes, sir," I replied.

"Y'all have fun," Tonita said.

Brimone and I had a wonderful dinner and I explained to her what she should and should not expect on a date. She asked numerous questions and I answered each one. When the date was over and I took her back to her mother's house, I kissed my baby on the cheek and she kissed me back. I think in both of our minds we knew that that was the last kiss as daddy's little girl.

chapter 18

A few weeks later on an unseasonably late warm spring Friday, the office girls were about to face the inevitable, and the unbelievable at once.

7:15 a.m. Tazzy walked into the office and cut on the lights. She walked through as she normally does and adjusted the thermostat, cleaned around Tina's desk, and prepared for the morning meeting. *I am sleeping with Cynthia in my arms.*

7:30 a.m. Susan walked into the office, retrieved the notes for the morning meeting from Tazzy, and sat at her desk. *Cynthia wakes up, and jumps on my back. "Let's do something special today."*

8:30 a.m. The entire office is in attendance and enjoying the day as usual. *Cynthia gets sick while eating breakfast and decides to see the doctor.*

10:00 a.m. Susan holds the morning meeting and they resume working as usual. *I take Cynthia to doctor's office.*

10:30 a.m. The office girls have their monthly diet contest weigh-in, and then resume their daily work schedule. *Cynthia finally gets to see the doctor.*

11:00 a.m. The office girls are listening to the morning radio show and adding their own comments. *The doctor completes Cynthia's examination, and informs us that we are with child.*

12:00 p.m. The office girls are preparing to go to lunch. *Cynthia calls Ms. Virginia and Tina and asks them to join us on their lunch break. They both say yes, but they have to run a couple of errands first. So we agree to meet at one o'clock.*

12:20 p.m. "Listen, ladies, you all can have an extended thirty-minute lunch break this afternoon. Just don't leave at the same time. We are almost out of claims so we all may be getting out of here early today, anyway," Tazzy said, walking through the office and heading back to her office.

"Tazzy, you know I'm not coming back after lunch, don't you?" Ms. Virginia asked.

"I know," Tazzy answered, going into her office.

"Tina, are we still meeting the Forresters for lunch? They said they had some big news for us," Ms. Virginia said.

"Uh-huhn, oh, that reminds me! Don't forget everybody; Mike and Cynthia's belated surprise wedding party is tonight at my house," Tina said.

"We know! We know! Party at your house, Tina," Darsha said. "Boy, you know when niggahs get some new shit, they got to show it off."

"You damn skippy!" Tina said.

"They been married for damn near a year now, Tina," Wanda said.

"It's only been a couple of months, girl," Tina said.

"Tina, I'm about to leave so give me your debit card so that I can deposit the money in your account."

"Okay, everything is already ordered. I just have to pay for it and pick it up on the way home." Tina reached in her purse and pulled out her debit card.

"Damn, Tina, Ms. Virginia is like your husband."

"Bye, ladies!" Ms. Virginia said, laughing at Wanda's joke. "I don't even want to hear this."

"Me neither," Tina said.

Tina and Ms. Virginia left the office at the same time.

"I am so glad for Michael and Cynthia," Alicia said.

"You know what, me too," Pam said.

"Yeah, y'all let Mike come in here and turned y'all asses out!" Wanda said.

"Mike didn't turn out anything over here!" Lisa said.

"I wasn't even talking about you, Lisa. Everybody know Val turned you out."

"Don't start that shit, Wanda," Lisa said.

"We all family up in here. Let's end the charade! It's time to bring that shit out of the closet, L. Kelly. What the hell is up with you and Val, Lisa?"

"There's nothing up with me and Val, that's just my girl."

"Bullshit!" Wanda shouted. "Bring that shit out!"

"Wanda, stop instigating." Pam laughed.

"And there you go, you get a promotion and now you can't talk about nobody no mo'!"

"I ain't mad at you!" Lisa said.

"Yup, that's how I got the promotion!" Pam said, giving Lisa a high-five.

"Before you go any further, ain't nothin' goin' on between me and Lisa," Valerie said. "We just cool."

"But y'all got to admit it's some strange shit done went on with you two."

"Strange, like how?" Lisa asked.

"Like the way y'all always hanging around each other," Wanda said. "And the way Lisa's daughter call you, Daddy."

"Shut the hell up, Wanda!" Valerie said.

"Wanda, you better back off before Val kick yo' ass," Darsha said.

"Kick my ass? Val can kiss my ass!" Wanda said.

"Y'all are the most foul-mouthed women I have ever met," Pam said.

"Ain't you the pot calling the kettle black?" Wanda said. "Get yo' stuck-up ass on outta here, Pam, and let me finish my talk show."

Pam laughed, and balled her fist at Wanda.

"Back to y'all," Wanda said, pointing at Lisa and Valerie, "are y'all lesbos or what?"

"Let's get this straight right now, Wanda! I am not a lesbian, I have never been a lesbian, nor will I ever be a lesbian! My best friend is a lesbian, and I don't care what anyone thinks!" Lisa responded.

"Calm down, Ellen DeGeneres! I don't want no trouble!" Wanda said, throwing her hands in the air.

"You're going to get more trouble than you can handle if you don't shut that big mouth of yours," Lisa said, playfully covering Wanda's mouth.

"Seriously though," Valerie said, "Lisa and I have been through some hard shit these last six or seven months and we've just been there for each other. I don't want her labeled as being a lesbian because I know how that can be, but as far as I'm concerned, I am a proud lesbian. I'm queer! I'm here! And I ain't goin' no damn where!"

"Dammit, Val, stand up for your people!" Wanda shouted. "Pam, let's get out of here before we have a rebellion up in Upskon."

"Okay, girl, let's go, let me finish this report," Pam said.

The office cleared out and only Tazzy and Susan remained.

"Are you coming to the party tonight?" Susan asked.

"Yeah, I guess I'll make it."

"You guess?"

"Yeah, I feel kind of awkward hanging with them now."

"Tazzy, please don't turn into Jaline."

"I won't, but sometime I feel like they don't want me around."

"Tazzy, that's all a figment of your imagination. If they accept me, the only white girl in the office, plus I'm the supervisor, they will accept you, too. But you have to want to accept them as much as you want them to accept you."

"I guess you're right, Susan."

"So pep it up, so that you can be more enthusiastic tonight, okay?"

"I will," Tazzy said, "by tonight, I'll be rejuvenated."

"Good," Susan said, "well, I'm off to lunch."

"Okay."

As Susan was closing the claims department security door, a man passed her with a bouquet of flowers trying to seek entrance into the building.

"Excuse me, may I help you?" Susan asked.

"Yes, I'm trying to find the claims department."

"You have to have a security badge to get inside, sir."

"Oh, I just wanna drop off these flowers, Ma'am."

"It's not a problem for me to take them inside and drop them off for you."

"Uh, that won't be necessary."

"Who are they for?"

"Uh, Tina. Do you have somebody named Tina in your office?"

"Yes, we do. You sure you don't want me to take those flowers for you?"

"I'm positive."

"Okay." Susan said, leaving the man standing outside of the door.

Cynthia and I arrive at the restaurant early to get us a table. We wait and wait, but neither Ms. Virginia nor Tina show.

2:00 p.m. "Now, I gave these ladies an extended lunch and they are still taking their time getting back to this office," Tazzy said out loud, pacing the office floor.

The telephone rang and Tazzy picked up.

"Good afternoon…this is the supervisor, may I help you…yes, you've reached the correct department, how may I help you…Oh, my God! Okay, I'll get a head count as soon as everyone gets back…thanks for giving us a call…okay, bye-bye!"

As Tazzy hung up the telephone, Susan walked in.

"It's crazy out there, what's going on?"

"I'm not sure. I just received a phone call from security and they want us to give a head count of everyone in our office."

"Why?" Susan asked.

"I don't know, somebody must have gotten robbed."

"I hope not, but if they did Wanda is walking me to my car tonight."

"Me too, Susan!" Tazzy joked.

"What's going on outside? The police are everywhere?" Lisa asked, walking into the office with Valerie and Darsha.

"I don't know, I'm waiting for security to call me back with some information," Tazzy said.

"Something horrible must have happened," Lisa said.

"Yeah, they have the police tape blocking off that side street," Darsha said, pointing outside.

"Let me go call these people and see if I can get some information." Tazzy said, walking back into her office.

"What in the world is going on out there?" Alicia said, entering the office.

"We're still trying to find out," Susan responded.

Tazzy walked out of her office. "At this point, ladies, we still don't know exactly what has happened. But we do know that we are not allowed to leave our office until security notifies us."

Wanda rushed into the office breathing heavily and very excited.

"Guess what? Two people got shot up here at Upskon and they dead!"

"How do you know, Wanda?" Darsha asked.

"The police told me!"

"Wanda, why would the police tell you anything, and not security?"

"'Cause I'm inquisitive, that's why!"

"Wanda is just runnin' her mouth, Tazzy, don't pay no attention to her," Valerie said.

"I'm just runnin' my mouth, huh," Wanda said to Valerie, then taking a deep breath to talk as fast as she possibly could. "Two women were spied walking at approximately twelve forty-five this afternoon. They noticed a conspicuous vehicle parked in the middle of the street at the rear entrance of the Upskon building. They investigated the aforementioned vehicle and noticed two bodies lying in the car. The first body was discovered on the first seat, while the second body was discovered moments later in the rear of the vehicle, perched on the floor." Wanda took another deep breath.

Tazzy's telephone rang again and she ran into her office to pick it up. Wanda continued to let the other women know the information she had ascertained.

"The medics arrived at the scene at approximately twelve fifty-three p.m., while the police arrived at twelve fifty-eight. The medics tried gallantly to save their lives but both victims were pronounced dead at the scene. The police are withholding the names of the victims until the family has been first been notified." Wanda took a deep sigh, and then asked, "What else you wanna know?"

"I hope it wasn't anybody who worked at Upskon," Alicia said.

"Well, at least everybody in our department is here except for Ms. Virginia and Tina," Pam said.

"Tina." Susan covered her mouth. "Oh, my God! Oh, no!"

"What's the matter, Susan?" Pam asked.

"On my way to lunch, I saw a strange man at the door and he wanted to get in. He had flowers and said he was looking for the claims department. At the time I thought he looked familiar but I was in a hurry and so I just let him in…I…I…I didn't know!"

"Didn't know what, Susan?" Pam said, quickly interrupting.

"That it was him, Pam!"

"Him who, Susan? What are you talking about?"

"It was Curtis! I'm sorry, I didn't realize at the time! I didn't know it was…"

"Somebody call Tina and see if she's all right! Now!"

Susan covered her mouth and sat in a chair.

"Oh naw, Pam!" Wanda said.

Alicia picked up the telephone and tried to dial.

"I can't think!" Alicia said, trying to dial.

"I got it!" Pam said, snatching the telephone out of Alicia's hand and dialing. "She's not answering!"

"Somethin's wrong! That girl always answer that phone!" Wanda said.

"Let's try to remain calm until security lets us know what happened," Pam said.

"I can't stay calm!" Wanda said.

"I'm going to talk to Tazzy!" Pam said, but before she reached Tazzy's office, Tazzy was on her way out.

"I need everybody to come over here for a second, please." Tazzy cleared her throat, and fighting back tears, said, "I, uh, I just received some bad news. The police have identified one of the bodies found in the car by a credit card, located on the floor of the car…and it was Tina's."

"Oh no, Tazzy!" Alicia said.

"Lord, have mercy!" Wanda shouted.

Pam started to cry and hugged Susan. Lisa hugged Alicia, then Darsha. Wanda and Valerie surrounded them and they huddled in a group.

"What happened, Tazzy?" Alicia asked.

"The security officer said they believe it was a murder-suicide. They believe the man's body is Curtis'. He didn't have any identification on him so they have to wait for positive identification."

"So he killed Tina, and then killed himself?" Alicia asked, lifting her head from Lisa's shoulder.

"I'm afraid so," Tazzy said.

"Death ain't good enough for that no-good bastard! They need to cut his di…," Wanda said.

"Wanda, that's not going to help anything!" Tazzy interrupted.

"I'll feel better! They need to cut his shit off and burn it up!" Darsha said.

"We need to compose ourselves. No other department knows of Tina's death, so upper management wants us to keep this within our department until they send out a memo. So please, as hard as it may be, let's try to get through this day, and get home to our families safely," Tazzy said.

"Don't you wanna cry, too, Tazzy? Don't you wanna stop being management just one time, and be one of the office girls?"

"Right now, my job is to be the manager! And whether you all like it or not, I will always be an office girl!"

"Look at us!" Pam said. "We come to work every day fussing and complaining about the same ol' bullshit! And with all that Tina had to deal with she came with a smile on her face. Now it's time for us to stop this and grow the hell up, and start acting like we care about each other! If Tazzy doesn't want to cry, leave her alone, and let her deal with it her way! And if y'all want to cry, cry your eyes out! Tina is dead! Don't y'all understand that? She's dead! Just stop this arguing before I lose it for real!" Pam grabbed her head and slammed herself into a chair.

"I'm sorry, Pam!" Wanda pulled her out of the chair and hugged her. "I'm sorry, baby."

"I'm tired of this shit, Wanda!" Pam said hysterically. "I'm tired of it!"

"Come here, Pam," Tazzy said, pulling her away from Wanda, then hugging her closely. "No more arguing, Pam. It's okay! It's okay!"

"No more," Wanda said, wrapping her arms around Pam and Tazzy, "no more."

"Oh, my God," Lisa said, wiping her eyes, "Ms. Virginia is going to be devastated."

"Tina was her heart!" Alicia said.

"Hold on," Darsha said. "Tazzy, didn't you say they identified the body by a credit card?"

"Yeah, why?" Tazzy asked.

"You sure it wasn't a debit card?"

"What difference does it make?" Tazzy asked.

"Didn't Ms. Virginia have Tina's debit card?" Pam asked.

"Come to think of it, she sure did," Wanda said.

At that moment Tina burst into the office running to her desk.

"Tazzy, I'm sorry I'm late but the police wouldn't let me in. I think someone may have been robbed or something, 'cause the police all over the place. Did Ms. Virginia call? I was supposed to meet her, Cynthia and Mike for lunch, but I was too busy getting ready for tonight."

The office girls stood in silence and stared at Tina.

"What's going on? Why y'all staring at me, like that?" Tina asked.

"It's two-thirty; I can't believe Tina nor Ms. Virginia didn't show up," I say.

"Something must have happened," Cynthia says, "Tina may be rude enough to stand us up for lunch, but not Ms. Virginia. Something's wrong."

"Call them and see what happened," I say.

Cynthia calls several times, but gets no one.

"Yeah, something's up," Cynthia says. "They're not answering their cell phones and nobody at the office is answering their phones, either."

"Come on, Cynt, you know they're planning a surprise party for us. Why do you keep pretending like you don't."

"Well, I don't know the day," Cynthia says, "do you think it's today?"

2:27 p.m. "NOOOOOOOOOO!" Tina screamed, and then fell to her knees, "NO! NO! NO! NO!"

"Tina! Tina!" Alicia shouted, kneeling beside her, and trying to lift her. "It's going to be all right!"

"NOOOOOOOOOO! NO! Please, God, no!" Tina said.

Wanda and Tazzy kneeled down beside Tina as well, and tried to pick her up.

"Tina! Tina, she's gone!" Wanda shouted. "She's gone!"

"Let her cry!" Pam said. "Please, if she wants to cry, let her cry!"

"Pam's right, y'all," Valerie said. "Just leave her alone!"

Tina sat on the floor and cried until she couldn't cry anymore. The other office girls kneeled over and watched her until she had no more tears. Once she finished crying she stayed on the floor in the fetal position, motionless.

4:00 p.m. Tazzy sent everyone home but she remained in the office to finish cleaning out Ms. Virginia's personal items from her desk. As she closed the box, and taped it, she collapsed in Ms. Virginia's chair, putting her head down on the desk, then cried.

"I know if you were here you'd tell me to stop crying, pick myself up, and stand tall. So, I'm going to get up from here and do what you expect me to do. I love you!"

Tazzy stood up, and carrying Ms. Virginia's box in her arms, cut off the lights, and sadly left the office.

"*I've been calling Ms. Virginia and Tina all day, at work, on their cell phones, and neither one of them are answering,*" Cynthia says.

"*Stop being so impatient, woman. You'll get your chance to tell them about the baby at their surprise party tonight that we don't know about.*"

"*But I can't wait!*"

"*Well, you're going to have to wait.*"

"*Aw, but I don't wanna!*" Cynthia says, poking her bottom lip out.

"*But you gotta!*" I say, mimicking her.

7:30 p.m. Cynthia and I were sitting in our den, when office girls pulled up in separate vehicles. As they piled out, we knew it had to be a special occasion. It had been a while since they had come over as a group. Cynthia could barely contain herself.

"Baby, they brought the party to us!" Cynthia said, peeking through the window.

I had to literally hold Cynthia back from running to the door and opening it before they knocked.

"What are all y'all doing over here?" Cynthia asked, as she hugged them individually.

"We came over to give you some news," Alicia said, "bad news."

"What?" Cynthia asked, very surprised. "What happened?"

Tina walked in the door last, and immediately hugged Cynthia, then me. When she hugged me, she started to cry and squeeze my neck.

"Mike," Tina said. "Mike, she's dead."

"Who's dead?" I looked around at everyone for answers.

"You guys need to sit down," Pam said.

"Sit down for what? What's going on?" Cynthia asked.

Alicia reached out for Cynthia's hand and led her into the den and sat her down. The rest of us followed behind them. I walked with Tina, who was still crying, back into the den and sat her down next to Cynthia. She let go of me, and embraced Cynthia. At that point I thought something must have happened to one of Tina's children. But that didn't explain why they would have to prepare us so delicately.

"Listen, stop trying to pamper me and tell me what's going on!" Cynthia said, becoming a little annoyed.

"Ms. Virginia was shot and killed at work today, Cynt," Pam said.

"What?" Cynthia asked, looking around at everyone.

"Someone shot Ms. Virginia at work today," Alicia said.

"What in the world are you talking about, Alicia?" I asked.

"Wait a minute," Cynthia said, standing up and walking away, "are y'all trying to tell me that Ms. Virginia was killed?"

"Yes," Pam said, "she died this afternoon."

"No," Cynthia said, walking over to the telephone, "no, Ms. Virginia is not dead. I talked to her this afternoon. Let's call her and get this straightened out."

Cynthia scrambled through her purse and found her cell phone.

"Cynthia, we can't call her, sweetheart," Pam said, walking over to her and taking the telephone out of her hands.

"Yes, we can, Pam!" Cynthia said, holding the telephone tightly.

"Cynthia!" Alicia said. "Cynthia, sit down, baby! You have to sit down!"

"No," Cynthia said, "let me call her, Alicia?"

I pulled Cynthia into my arms and held her as she started to cry.

"Mike, let me go so I can call her."

"Cynt, baby, they wouldn't tell us this unless they were sure."

"No, Mike, why her?" Cynthia raised her head and started to cry.

"What happened?" I was still confused.

"We don't know for sure," Pam said. "All that we know is that a man came to the job today with flowers looking for Tina. A little while later a man and Ms. Virginia's body was found in a car on the side street at Upskon. We think it was Curtis."

"Are you sure it was Ms. Virginia?" I said, still trying to hold on to the slim optimism.

"We just came from the morgue to identify the body," Pam said. "It was Ms. Virginia's body they found."

"Oh, my God!" I said.

"Oh no," Cynthia said, burying her face in my chest and crying.

"It's my fault!" Tina said, covering her face with her hands. "It's all my fault!"

"Tina, baby!" Alicia said, sitting beside her, and rubbing her back. "This is not your fault."

"Yes it is!" Tina shouted.

"Tina," I said, patting Cynthia on the back as she released her tears on my chest, "you can't do this to yourself."

"Why not, Mike?" Tina asked.

"Tina, stop it!" Pam said. "Stop blaming yourself, and stop pitying yourself. This is not your fault! Nobody blames you, but you! Ms. Virginia is gone, and the time now is for us to show our love for her."

"You know what, Pam?" Tina said. "You're right. I have to stop feeling sorry for myself. Let's try to think about Ms. Virginia."

"The first thing is to make sure her funeral arrangements are in order," Pam said. "Ms. Virginia doesn't have any close family, does she?"

"I remember her saying that Susan's husband is her nephew," Wanda said, wiping her eyes. "You think he should make the funeral arrangements?"

"I don't know," Pam responded. "I don't know how close they were."

"I don't care how close they were!" Wanda said. "Ms. Virginia was our family and we are going to make her funeral arrangements."

"What if her family wants to be involved?" Lisa asked.

"They can be involved all they want, but we're going to take care of Ms. Virginia!" Wanda said.

"I agree with Wanda!" Tina said. "We got this!"

"Me too!" Darsha said.

"And dammit, me three!" Valerie shouted.

"Who's going to give the eulogy?" Cynthia said.

"Let's ask Tazzy," Pam said quietly.

"I think Tazzy should do the eulogy," Tina said.

"I think Ms. Virginia would like that," Pam said.

"Aw, look at Pam getting all sensitive," Wanda said.

"Shut up, Wanda," Pam said jokingly, and wiping a tear, "you're always trying to crack a joke."

"You know me," Wanda said in a very serious tone, "even when the tears fall, I try to bring a little joy."

"You couldn't have picked a better time," Pam said. "That's why you're my girl."

"And that's why you my niggah!"

"I will pick up Ms. Virginia's death certificate on Monday, speaking of which, I may as well dig through my crap and find my birth certificate to have my visa validated."

"Yo' visa? Where the hell you going?" Wanda asked.

"To hell if I don't pray!" Pam joked.

Cynthia stood up and cleared her throat.

"Hey, you guys, Mike and I have some joy to share as well," Cynthia said, "although right now it doesn't seem like the appropriate time."

"Any good news is appropriate at this time," Tina said.

"Well, we are going to have a baby," Cynthia said modestly.

"You've got to be kidding me!" Alicia said excitedly.

"Are you for real?" Pam said, covering her mouth.

"Yes! We are going to have a baby!" Cynthia said again, rubbing her stomach.

"Come here, girl!" Wanda shouted, hugging her.

The office girls join in the hug.

"When did you find out?" Tina asked.

"This afternoon,."

"This is truly amazing," Tina said. "On the day that Ms. Virginia dies, you find out you're going to have a baby."

"That just goes to prove that old adage," Alicia said.

"What old adage?" Cynthia asked.

"First of all, what the hell is an adage?" Darsha asked.

"The one that says, life hasn't changed since the beginning of time. Whenever a baby is born, you know somebody else is dying," Tina said.

"Yeah, that's true," I said, trying hard to fight back the tears, "but rarely do both happen to you on the same day."

We sat around for the remainder of the evening talking about Ms. Virginia and trying to notify as many of her relatives as possible of her death. Susan and her husband had already begun reaching family members, and we contacted her church.

As the news spread, the calls started to come in volumes. We had no idea Ms. Virginia knew as many people as she did. We always thought of her as being a reclusive private woman with no immediate family. But as it turned out, she had many friends and acquaintances across the country.

chapter 19

The Office Girls was released a week earlier than scheduled, and it was already in bookstores. I received my twenty author's copies at my doorstep the following Saturday morning after Ms. Virginia's death.
Cynthia answered the door, and quickly brought them to me. She was wearing a big grin as she stood in front of the television holding the heavy box.

"Lookie what I got, baby!" Cynthia said, holding the box in her hand.

"What's that?" I asked.

"These are your copies of your books, silly!"

"What?" I said, walking over to her and taking the box out of her hands. "The book is not supposed to be released until next week."

"Well, I'm sorry to tell you, Mr. Johnny Come Lately, they've arrived."

I pulled one of them out of the box and held it in my hand. "I never thought I'd ever get to this point again, Cynt."

"Well, Mr. Writer, how does it feel?"

"It feels..." I paused for a moment. "It feels like I need some rest."

"Oh, I'm curious to know what name you used for an alias," Cynthia said, digging in the box and pulling out another book. "Why'd you pick that name? It's so old and plain."

"You don't know whose name that is, do you?"

"No, I do not, please inform me. Is it your grandma's?"

"No, Cynt. It's Ms. Virginia's real name. Her real name was Cora."

"Cora? Ms. Virginia's name was Cora?"

"Yes, it was."

"I didn't know that."

"I'm quite sure she told you."

"Now that's eerie."

"What's eerie?"

"That you chose her name for your pseudonym and the day before you receive your books, she dies. Oh, that's eerie. It's like you had a premonition."

"Well, I wish the true story was as exciting as your version, but I asked Ms. Virginia to use her name because that big engagement ring I gave you was a gift from her. She said she wanted you to have it because our relationship reminded her so much of her relationship with her fiancé who was murdered."

"Oh my," Cynthia said, starting to cry, "that's so sad."

"Cynt, please! Stop with the waterworks, will you?"

"Okay! Okay! Okay! I'll save them for my office girls."

I put the books back in the box and sat in my recliner.

"What time are we supposed to meet the rest of the girls?" I asked.

"About one o' clock."

"We need to start getting ready then, Cynt."

"Mike, we have plenty of time," Cynthia said, hitting me on the head with one of the books, "you're not excited about your book."

"There'll be time for that. We have to take care of Ms. Virginia first."

"We're going to pick out a casket, Mike, not a prom dress."

"Ah, shut up, and let's get ready."

A little later we met with some of the office girls to pick out Ms. Virginia's casket. Afterward, we went to her house and started packing her things. Instead of being sad, we laughed and told stories of our experience with Ms. Virginia. It is sad that misery loves company, had it not been for each other that Saturday, many of our tears would not have come from laughter, but pain.

As they started to leave, Tina, Cynthia and I stayed behind to finish packing. I went into her basement, which we had failed to cover throughout our clean-up sweep of the house, to see if there was anything of value.

To my surprise, there were old, or should I say, antique items scattered from wall to wall, old paintings that looked like they came over on the Mayflower. I knew, however, that these antiques were of great value, if not financially, then certainly sentimentally.

I carefully looked over everything, inhaling the aging dust into my lungs. I happened upon an old black-and-white painting of a young woman. The lady was strikingly beautiful. Although the painting was in black and white, the face was so detailed and clear. Her eyes were almost hypnotic, as I couldn't stop staring at them. I felt a sense of warmth and love.

As I picked up the picture and looked at it closely, I heard a soft voice call out to me from across the room. I was startled because I knew that I was blocking the only entrance to the basement. Which meant, that somebody was already in the basement when I came down, or I was being visited an apparition. Neither of those scenarios was good.

"She's beautiful isn't she, Michael?" the voice spoke.

"Whoa! Who said that?"

"It's been a long time, Michael. How have you been?"

"Bernice," I said, as the image of the woman became clearer, "is that you?"

"Yes, Michael," Bernice said. "It's me."

"What are you doing here?"

"I thought you might need someone to talk to."

"Boy, is that an understatement."

"Well, here I am," Bernice said, "shoot."

Bernice no longer wore the ponytails, nor the tomboy clothes. Her sweatpants were replaced with fitted jeans, her sweatshirt with a fitted shirt. Her hair was well groomed, and not worn in a ponytail. I guess as I had matured, so had she.

"Well, I finally have an opportunity to get that bestselling book we always talked about, but the thing is, the world will never know."

"Does that really matter, Michael?"

"No," I said, "I guess not."

"Then don't worry about the world."

"I know you're right, but that's hard to do."

"Do you remember what I used to tell you about karma, Michael?"

"How could I forget?"

"Like I've always said, karma has a way of introducing herself, even when we are not prepared to welcome her presence."

"You know, Bernice, I never quite understood what that meant."

"It means that, sometime in life we ask for things that we don't quite realize the totality of what it brings. And when you send out your spirit for unselfish reasons, it often returns to you unselfishly. But when you send out your spirit for selfish reasons, it returns to you selfishly...karma."

"So I shouldn't worry about the book? Just let time run its course and time will take care of itself."

"Couldn't have said it better myself."

"What do you think about Cynthia?" I said, changing the subject.

"I like her."

"You liked the other two as well."

"You're right, I did. Tonita and Cecelia had their purposes and I love them for that. They taught you how to love, and how to be loved. They created a perfect husband for Cynthia."

"So that means you won't be coming back to talk about divorce number three."

"No," Bernice said, "I won't be coming back at all."

"Why not?"

"Look at me, Michael, don't I remind you of someone?"

"Not right off, no," I said looking closer.

"Look a little closer," Bernice said, "look into my eyes, Michael."

"OH SHIT!" I screamed, falling backward onto some boxes. "It's you!"

"I have to go, Mike!" Bernice said. "I love you."

"Wait a minute!" I shouted. "Wait! Bernice!"

"Mike! Mike!" Cynthia said, shaking me vigorously.

"Bernice! Bernice!" I shouted again.

"Wake up, Mike!" Cynthia said. "Who's Bernice?"

"Um, nobody," I said, looking around. "I must have been dreaming."

"Oh," Cynthia said, beginning to start another sentence but stopped when she saw the antiques. "Look at all this stuff!"

"Beautiful, isn't it?"

"Oh, my God, this stuff is incredible!"

"Whoever gets this stuff is inheriting some great history."

"Tina, come down here!" Cynthia shouted.

Tina rushed down the stairs shouting, "What's up?"

"Look at all this stuff?" Cynthia said.

"Ooh, we don't have to clean up all this shit, do we?"

"Tina," I said, "this is not shit, it's antique."

"Antique! Boutique! Unique! I don't care! All I wanna know is do we have to clean it up?"

"No, girl, I just wanted you to see how beautiful it is," Cynthia said.

"Oh, it's beautiful all right," Tina said, "but we don't have to clean it up, right?"

"No, Tina," Cynthia said, "but I bet whoever ends up with this stuff is going to be more than happy to clean it up."

"Goody for them!" Tina said. "Can we go now? It's getting creepy in this basement."

"Yeah, let's go, Mike," Cynthia said, "I'm feeling a little creepy down here myself, especially with you yelling out people's names."

"I heard that fool screaming from the kitchen!" Tina asked. "Mike, who in the hell is Bernice?"

"Nobody! Now let's go!"

"That's all I need to hear!" Tina said, running upstairs. "I'm in the car!"

"How in the world did you find that out, Michael Forrester?"

"Find out what?"

"My middle name, negro!"

"What?" I said. "What are you talking about?"

"Who told you my middle name was Bernice?" Cynthia asked with a big grin spread across her face.

"Your middle name is Bernice? That's what the 'B' stands for?

"I don't know how you found out but somebody is in trouble."

"Bernice!" I said, staring at Cynthia. "You're Bernice?"

"In the flesh!"

"Wow!"

"All right, Mike," Cynthia said, reaching for my hand. Once she saw the picture of Ms. Virginia sitting to the side she screamed, "We got to take that picture!"

"It doesn't belong to us, Cynthia."

"It does now!" Cynthia said, picking up the picture and running up the stairs.

"Cynthia! I totally disassociate myself from this act of thievery!"

I began to understand that after all these years, Bernice was no longer a figment of my imagination. She was my reality. After looking into Bernice's eyes moments earlier, I realized that she was Cynthia, and Cynthia was she. Cynthia's unexplainable resemblance suddenly became crystal clear!

❖❖❖

The following Monday, Pam picked up Ms. Virginia's death certificate from the funeral home. On her way into the office she stopped by the post office to have her visa validated, not that she had any immediate plans to leave the country, but just in case someone wanted to invite her on an impromptu vacation, she would be prepared.

While she was waiting, she opened the envelope which contained Ms. Virginia's death certificate. She noticed that she and Ms. Virginia were actually born in the same city. She was aware that they were both from Alabama, but had no idea the locations were so close. Curiosity got the best of her and she pulled out her birth certificate to see if they were born in the same hospital.

As she scrolled to the hospital information she found that they were not born in the same hospital. But when she glanced at the portion of her birth certificate that divulged her mother's name it read, *Cora Cooper*. And when she glanced at the name of the deceased on Ms. Virginia's death certificate it read, *Cora Cooper*. Pam stood up and stared back and forth at the certificates and then sat back down and covered her mouth.

"Oh, my God," she said, shocked with disbelief.

She jumped out of her seat and drove maniacally to the office. She walked in hastily and went straight to Tazzy's office.

"Tazzy, can I please speak with you for a second?"

"Sure, what's going on?"

"Look!" Pam handed Tazzy the certificates and she was visibly shaken.

Tazzy scanned over both of the certificates but did not understand the relevance.

"Who is Cora Cooper?"

"Ms. Virginia," Pam said, sitting down and putting her hands on her forehead, "look at the name on my birth certificate as my mother."

"Oh, my God, Pam," Tazzy said, sitting down, "this can't be for real. Do you think Ms. Virginia was your mother?"

"I don't know what to think anymore, Tazzy. Right now, I'm in shock!"

"So am I, and it's not even happening to me."

"Well, if you don't mind I would like to go home. I need to get to the bottom of this today."

"No problem, only a few people are showing up today, anyway."

"Okay, thanks a lot, Tazzy," Pam said, standing up.

"Take care, Pam, and give me a call if you need me."

"I will, thanks."

Pam went home and called every government office in the Jacksonville and Anniston areas. She confirmed that Ms. Virginia was her mother and the existing circumstances surrounding her birth. At the end of the day she went back to the office to talk to Tazzy.

"Hey, girl," Pam said, walking into Tazzy's office.

"You okay?"

"I'm doing better."

"We found out the identification of the man in the car and it was not Curtis."

"I know," Pam said, staring at Tazzy, "that low-down son-of-a-bitch was my father."

"Your father?" Tazzy was confused and bewildered. "What is going on?"

"Let me explain." Pam sighed. "Ms. Virginia was my biological mother and no, she didn't know that she was. As far as she knew I died from complications from a beating my father gave her. My father took me from the nursery and gave me to his family. I was going to be his bargaining tool for making Ms.

Virginia stay with him once she was out of the hospital. But her family ran interference with that by taking her to their house and he was stuck with me."

"But how could Ms. Virginia not know that she had a child? Wouldn't the hospital or her family tell her?"

"Seems like since she stayed so long in the hospital after I was born, and that she was unable to speak, no one questioned what happened to me after my father took me away. Her family didn't know I survived, and the doctors didn't know of the issues between Ms. Virginia and my father so they weren't suspicious of anything. My father's stupidity and desperation was assisted by everyone else's negligence and ignorance."

"Wow! So are you going to be okay?"

"In time, but for right now I don't know if I'm coming or going."

"If there's anything I can do, let me know."

"Well, there is one thing you can do for me."

"Sure, what is it?"

❖❖❖

Ms. Virginia's funeral was on Tuesday of the next week. Early that morning we received a call from Wanda asking us to meet her and the other office girls at the funeral home. We had to rush, but we were able to get there in time.

The funeral home was a big brown house, with old briquette siding. The family that owned the funeral parlor had turned their family home into a funeral home generations ago. It smelled of medicine and sadness. I felt uncomfortable as I walked in through the corridor, then down a long hall where the ladies were waiting.

Everyone from the office was there, including Tazzy and Susan. I didn't know why we were asked to meet them there, but Wanda put my curiosity to rest as soon as she saw me.

"Hey, who picked out the pallbearers for Ms. Virginia?" Wanda asked.

"We left that up to her family," Cynthia said.

"My husband and some of their family members said that if she needed pallbearers, they would do it," Susan said.

"Susan, no disrespect, baby, but Ms. Virginia don't need no welfare pall-bearers. She didn't need them to carry her through her life and she don't need them to carry her to her grave," Wanda said. "Tell them that won't be necessary."

"And what is our back-up plan, Wanda?" Susan asked.

"Us! We need to be carrying Ms. Virginia, not them!" Wanda said.

"Wanda, we can't carry Ms. Virginia's body," Cynthia said. "She's too heavy."

"The hell we can't! She's been carrying all of us ever since we met her. Now are you trying to tell me that she's too heavy for us to carry her now?"

"You know that's not what I'm saying, Wanda," Cynthia said.

"You don't need to be in this, anyway, mama," Wanda said, with a smile, "just make sure we don't trip on anything and make ourselves look like some fools."

"I got that covered," Cynthia said, giving her the two thumbs-up sign.

"Well," Wanda said, grabbing the first handle on the right side of the coffin, "is anybody going to help me get Ms. Virginia to the church on time, or what?"

"Let's go!" Pam said, grabbing the other first handle on the left side. "So what y'all gon' do?"

"Let's go," Alicia said, standing behind Wanda.

"Now if this little prissy thang can grab a hold, the rest of y'all need to be shamed."

"Let's go!" Tina said, grabbing a handle, and standing behind Pam.

"Let's go!" Lisa said, standing behind Tina.

"Let's go!" Valerie said, standing behind Alicia.

They struggled momentarily, then lifted the casket into the air.

"Wait a minute. Where do I lift?" I asked. "I am one of the office girls, too, right?"

"For life!" Wanda said. "Mike, you get the rear to keep us steady. The rest of y'all can get in, where you fit in."

Darsha, Susan and Tazzy grabbed the bottom of the coffin on both sides, and I lifted from the very end, and we carried Ms. Virginia to the hearse. We climbed into our own personal limousine. Wanda's cousin had a hookup on Tuesday morning funeral rentals.

As we rode slowly, I noticed how traffic paused for the dead, just as we do with our lives. And just as we do with our lives, once the funeral procession passed, traffic continued with its normal hustle and bustle.

When we got to the church, the office girls and I carried the coffin from the hearse into the church. There was standing room only; it seemed as if the whole city was trying to get their last glimpse of this glorious woman.

The congregation stared in amazement when they saw the pallbearers for Ms. Virginia were all women and one man. There was a gasp, maybe because some thought we would drop the coffin. But none of the office girls would let something horrible like that happen to Ms. Virginia in her final hour, and at her finest moment.

"What the hell they starin' at?" Wanda whispered.

"We're carrying a coffin, Wanda," Alicia answered. "What do you think they're going to do?"

"Naw, they lookin' at us 'cause we women!" Wanda said a little louder.

"Wanda, would you shut your big-ass mouth before somebody hear you!" Valerie said.

"I ain't shuttin' shit!" Wanda said.

"Do y'all realize that you're in a church?" Lisa asked.

"I know where we at!" Wanda said.

"I know where we at, too!" Valerie said.

"Show Ms. Virginia some respect!" Tina said. "And shut the hell up!"

"Ms. Virginia know how we are," Wanda said, "ain't no use actin' funny now."

"Will y'all shut up before we mess up!" Pam said.

"We ain't gon' mess up nothin', stop actin' so damn nervous," Valerie said.

"Tell 'em, Val!" Wanda added.

"SHUT UP!" Tina whispered sternly.

"Tazzy, would you tell them to shut up? People lookin' at us like we crazy!" Darsha said.

"We ain't at work, Tazzy can't give no orders up in here! This God's office up in here!" Wanda responded.

"I don't care where we are, y'all need to be quiet!" Tazzy said.

"Okay, Tazzy." Wanda laughed under her breath.

"But I guess Ms. Virginia would appreciate one last laugh from you heffas!" Tazzy said, smiling at Wanda.

chapter 20

We carefully carried the coffin to the front of the church and took our places on the front pew. We held hands as the minister spoke passionately about Ms. Virginia. Saying wonderful things, but nothing we had not thought ourselves. When the moment came to give her eulogy, Pam stood up, instead of Tazzy. Pam squeezed Tazzy's hand tightly and walked to the pulpit. She stood for a moment and stared at the congregation. In my mind I could feel Ms. Virginia's presence. Her warmth and nurturing spirit was ever present. After a moment of silence, Pam began to speak.

❖❖❖

"Good morning, everybody. Most of you don't know who I am, or why I am even delivering the eulogy. My name is Pam Bettis, and this woman before you is my mother."

"What the hell she just say?" Wanda asked. "Pam done lost her mind!"

"Did she say that Ms. Virginia was her mother?" Alicia asked.

"Shh!" Tazzy said. "Listen."

The office girls whispered amongst themselves, but I kept my focus on Pam. I could not believe what I was hearing. In hindsight, it made sense.

"When most people pass on, we are taught to respect them, and say good things about them, no matter how they lived their lives," Pam continued. "But with Ms. Virginia, my mother, when you speak of the goodness of her spirit, you run no risk of lying. I loved and admired this woman so much I became angry with her when she directed her attention to someone else. But throughout it all, she never reciprocated those negative feelings. She loved me, protected me, guided me and counseled me, and all that she asked in return was that I just be honest with myself. Recently, I've realized just how selfish and silly I've been acting and I wanted to apologize to her. I told myself that I would tell her the next time I saw her. But I didn't. Then I told myself I would tell her when the moment was right. But I didn't. So finally, last Friday morning, I told her that we needed to talk. And just like Ms. Virginia, she stopped what she was doing and gave me her full attention.

"I really wanted to let her know how much I loved her and missed having her in my life, and I didn't want to do it in the office so I told her that I would speak with her later. We were planning a celebration for our friends and I thought we could slip away and have some private time. But as you know, we never got that opportunity. So of course I felt guilty and stupid for letting those opportunities slip through my fingers. But that's not the end of my story.

"On my way to work yesterday morning, I discovered that this woman that I loved so much was not just my friend, but my mother. It's a long story that I don't have time to explain, but a story that brings me complete and utter jubilation.

"When I arrived at work yesterday, I planned to only be there for a few minutes but I wanted to check my emails. I looked over at Ms. Virginia's desk and it was strange seeing it bare with none of her flowers, or the many, many ornaments that covered her desk. Once again the guilt filled my conscience, and I sat and cried quietly. But that's not the end of my story, either.

"When I logged on to my computer and opened my email, there was a message that Ms. Virginia had left on Friday. At first I was too hurt to read anything that may remind me of her. Then I remembered how waiting for the right moment cost me the opportunity to tell her how much I loved her in the first place. So I opened up the email and it read…"

Pam unfolded the printed-out email to read it: "*I love you, and I always will. Nothing more needs to be said.*

"Those few simple words brought me such contentment, such happiness, such relief. That is the spirit of Ms Virginia. Even in death, she still has the ability to bring happiness to other people.

"Though Ms. Virginia is not here with us in body, she is definitely here in spirit. I have learned that nothing lasts forever. Nothing! No matter how beautiful. No matter how ugly. No matter how great. No matter how small. No matter what it is, nothing on this earth is going to last forever. In time, everything will fade away. Everything," Pam said, wiping her eyes, "everything, but love. Love is the only thing that withstands the test of time. And this woman who lies before us is just that, love.

"I know I'm probably making a sad occasion an even sadder occasion. But even if we all stood up right now, jumped up and down, and screamed to the top of our lungs in sorrow, it still wouldn't be enough to show God just how much we're hurting over the loss of this woman.

"I often wonder what she was thinking before she closed her eyes to death. I wonder if she really knew how much we really loved her. We will never know what truly happened in that car that day. But what we do know is that Ms. Virginia finally found peace. In life and in death…"

Ms. Virginia's Story Ends...

On the previous Friday afternoon, as Ms. Virginia was getting into her car, another car pulled alongside her.

"What are you doing here?" Ms. Virginia said.

"Good to see ya again, Cora."

"Look, I have to meet somebody somewhere so do whatever you're going to do, or leave me alone."

"I just wanna talk to you for a minute, Cora. Somewhere private."

"You know I'm not going anywhere with you, Willie."

"You gon' go, or maybe I will go up in that little office of yours and blow away everybody up in there!"

"You're not that crazy!"

"You wanna try me and see?"

"No," Ms. Virginia said, getting into Willie's car, "you wanna talk Willie, talk."

"You ready to start actin' like my wife?"

"Willie, I will never be your wife," Ms. Virginia said, "never!"

"I've been tryin' to prove my love for you for all these years, and you still treat me like a dog on the streets."

"You have done nothing but terrorized me and anybody close to me for almost forty

years," Ms. Virginia said, "forty years, Willie! You have cost me a family. Happiness. All because you can't let me go."

"I ain't cost you shit!" Willie screamed. "If you woulda just acted like my wife instead of runnin' from me all these years we coulda had our own family! We over sixty years old, and we have nothin' to show for our marriage."

"Marriage? What marriage? We were never in a marriage! I was your prisoner!"

"I wanted us to be happy, Cora," Willie said. "I wanted to have the things that any other family has, but you always thought you were too good for me. But like I always told you, if I can't have you, can't nobody have you!"

"You've managed to do that for the last forty years, Willie, but today, I will be set free!"

"I ain't settin' you free today, or nan' 'nother day! You gon' always be my wife!"

"It ends today, Willie!" Ms. Virginia said. "One way or the other, it ends today."

"Naw, it ain't gon' never end! I'll kill you and everybody you know before I let you go!"

"Willie, I don't understand, why do you still want me? I'm an old woman."

"'Cause I still love you, goddammit!"

"No, you don't," Ms. Virginia said, "you can't after all this time."

"So are we gon' try to live as man and wife, or what, Cora?"

"No, Willie," Ms. Virgina said, pulling a loaded gun from her purse, "it's time for this to end."

"Now what you gon' do wit' that gun?" Willie said, not even flinching with the gun pointed in his face. "I ain't afraid to die, is you?"

"I'm not afraid of death, Willie," Ms. Virgina said, cocking the trigger, "nor you."

"So shoot me then!" Willie shouted. "Shoot me if you done got that bad, Cora!"

"Willie, I will have no problem putting a bullet in you for all the pain you've caused me."

"Well then, do it!" Willie shouted again. "I ain't got nothin' to live fa', anyway! Don't you know that? I been dead for a long time! It ain't nothin' that gun can do to me that you ain't already done!"

"I'm going to give you a chance to walk away from me, and never try to find me again."

"Listen to me, Cora! I don't care if I die! I don't care if you die! All I care about is bein' with you, why can't you see that? I love you!"

"Willie, I'm about to get out of this car, and I'm going my way and I want you to go your way!"

"I can't do that, Cora," Willie said, shaking his head, *"all I know how to do is love you!"*

"Willie, this is crazy! It's got to end!"

"I can't," Willie said, *"you gon' have to kill me."*

"I don't want to do that, but I will."

"Please, Cora, please," Willie said, wrapping his hands around the gun and putting it to his chest, *"if you don't kill me, I will certainly kill you!"*

"It doesn't have to be this way, Willie."

"It's like you say, it's gotta end, and it's gotta end today!"

"I don't want to do this, Willie."

"You ain't got no choice, Cora! I can't live without you!"

"And I can't live with you!" Ms. Virginia said, realizing Willie's obsession was beyond reasoning; something she should have realized the first time he tried to kill her.

"Then do what you got to do. Kill me!"

"I can't!" Ms. Virginia pulled the gun down to her lap.

"SHOOT MEEEEE!" Willie screamed.

"No, I can't."

"Then I'll kill you!"

"Like you said, Willie, do what you got to do."

Willie snatched the gun out of Ms. Virginia's hand and pointed it at her head.

"Now what you gotta say, Cora?"

"Our Father, which art in Heaven, hallowed be thy name..."

"Don't make me do this, baby!"

"Thy kingdom come, thy will be done, in earth, as it is in Heaven..."

"Stop that prayin'!"

"Give us this day our daily bread, and forgive us our debts as we forgive our debtors..."

"I said, stop that prayin'!" Willie shouted.

"And lead us not into temptation, but deliver us from evil..."

"Shut up!" Willie said, cocking the trigger.

"For thine is the kingdom, and the power, and the glory, forever and ever..."

Ms. Virginia braced for the impact of the bullet, looking Willie in the eyes the entire time. "Amen!"

POW!

Ms. Virginia's body went backward into the door, then slumped forward onto the seat.

"See, baby," Willie said, lifting her into his arms, "see what you made me do?

Crying and shaking, Willie rocked her back and forth in his arms. Willie put the gun to his head and pulled the trigger.

POW!

He climbed into the backseat mumbling incoherently, "Oh my head hurts, Cora. I gotta get outta here before I burn up. I gotta get outta here!"

Willie collapsed on the floor of the backseat, and panted repeatedly. Willie opened his mouth wide to try to suck in air to help him breathe, but it did not help. He closed his eyes, mouth still wide open, and took his last gasp of life.

❖❖❖

"…We will never know what truly happened in that car that day. But what we do know is that Ms. Virginia finally found peace, in life, and in death. And may God take her soul into his arms, and love her the way she has loved so many. May she rest in everlasting peace, AMEN."

After the service, the congregation stood, and aisle by aisle, waited for us to pass. One by one, we took hold of the casket, realizing the finality of the day. I managed to maintain my composure throughout the funeral, and the long drive on the way to the cemetery. But as they began to lower her casket into the ground I could no longer hold back the tears. I had tried to console and comfort everyone throughout this tragedy, and now it was my turn to release my pain. I bent my head down and cried. At one point, I wanted to stop, but couldn't. My heart needed to release the pain it was holding, and it needed to be released at that very moment. Cynthia wrapped her arms around me and patted me on the back as I cried tears that had been held beneath my eyelids from childhood.

"Baby, it's going to be all right."

"I know," I said, covering my eyes with my hands. "I know."

We were the last to leave Ms. Virginia's gravesite. On our way up the hill, we saw a man walking in our direction. He had a bouquet of flowers. The office girls blended together to form a wall. They obliviously knew who the man was, but I didn't.

"That fool is crazy!" Wanda said.

"What do I do?" Tina asked nervously.

"Keep walking!" Pam said. "You walk with us, and show no fear!"

As we approached the man, I finally recognized him. I let go of Cynthia's hand and stood in the front of our group.

"May I help you?" I asked.

"I don't want any trouble, man. I wanna talk to my wife."

"I don't think that's a good idea, bro."

"Get on away from here, Curtis!" Wanda shouted.

"I know what y'all thinking," Curtis said. "I must be a fool to come to Ms. Virginia's grave and try to cause a big scene. I would never do that. I didn't even know y'all were gonna be here. I know I can never make up for the way I behaved. And Tina, God knows that I should never be forgiven for all the things I've done to you. But I've been waiting for the day to ask for your forgiveness."

"Niggah, you got some nerves!" Valerie shouted.

Valerie's outburst triggered a domino effect with the other women and they started to scream and yell at Curtis. Amidst the chaos, I noticed something. I noticed that Curtis and Tina weren't saying a word. They were staring at each other as if they were trying to read each other's feelings. I finally stepped in and calmed the girls down long enough to get Tina to speak.

"Tina, I think Curtis is here to speak to you, so do you want to talk to him or what?" I asked.

"Yeah, Mike," Tina said, "I'll talk to him, as long as y'all are around."

"Oh, we ain't goin' nowhere!" Wanda said.

"That's fine with me," Curtis said. "I don't care who hears."

"All right, Curtis, what do you want?"

"I want to let you know that I have changed, Tina."

"Do you know how many times you told me that?"

"Listen to me, Tina. That's all I ask is for you to listen, please."

"Don't listen to that shit, Tina," Wanda snapped.

"Wanda! Please!" Tina said, then turning back to Curtis. "Why should I believe you?"

"Well, after I caused that big scene at your job I sat in jail for a few days. Then out of the blue, I got a visitor. It was Ms. Virginia. She told me that she would pay my bail if I enrolled in a program to help me with my anger. I was desperate so I said yes. I didn't really think she would hold me to it but the day they released me, she was standing outside the jailhouse door to pick me up. She took me to a nice restaurant and bought me a good meal. We had a long talk that day, and she convinced me to enroll in the program, for real. We went directly from the restaurant to the hospital.

"They taught me a lot about myself. Things like, why I am so angry. And why I drink so much. And even though I love you as much as I do, I still chased other women. It was because I didn't see love as something good. I saw it as something bad. I thought that everybody was out to take advantage of everybody else. I thought that nobody truly loved anybody because every-body who ever loved me has hurt me, Tina. That's how I saw the world. But now I know, baby. I know how to give love, and I know how to receive it. It's not going to be easy, and it's not going to be quick. But if you just give me the chance to show you who I am, it can be fixed."

"Curtis, that sounds good and all, but we've been through this so many times."

"No, Tina, we haven't been through this. I have never felt like this before in my life. My heart has never felt like this before! We've gone through changes, but we've never made changes. We've just been hanging on by a thread of hope, and not the will of love. But this time *you* have to know that it can work, and not hope that it can work. And when I say *you*, by no means am I saying that you are responsible for anything because I assume full responsibility for what has happened in our relationship. I say '*you*' because I don't need any more convincing. I know it can work!"

"Curtis, I've finally gotten on my feet, and…," Tina said.

"Me too," Curtis interrupted. "I've finally gotten on my feet, too! I don't drink! I don't do drugs! I don't go to clubs! I got my job back and I handle my business, Tina!"

"Are you trying to tell me you don't drink anymore?"

"I have not taken a drink since that day I went to jail. Ms. Virginia made sure of that."

"I don't understand why Ms. Virginia would help you that way."

"Yes, you do, Tina. She loved you. And the only reason I made it this far is because she made me believe that she loved me, too. In my whole life I always thought that I was a burden to anybody who loved me, but when Ms. Virginia showed me love, without asking for anything in return, it made me understand what love is all about."

"So where have you been all this time, Curtis?"

"At first I was in a rehabilitation clinic. Then I was in a shelter. After that, I moved in with Ms. Virginia. My first Sunday after being released from jail, I spent all day at church. I saw all of you there." Curtis said, pointing at the group.

"You were there that day?"

"Yes, I was. You don't know how difficult it was seeing you and my pretty little girls in that church and not saying anything to you."

"Why didn't you say anything, Curtis?"

"At that time I would have given you my desperation speech just to get you to come back to me. And once you did, I would have gone back to doing the same thing. I wasn't ready for a family then."

"And now you think you are?"

"Think, no," Curtis said, "I know I am."

"I need to think, Curtis."

"Take your time. Right now, I am just happy to be in your life in any way I can."

"It's good to see you're doing well, Curtis," Cynthia said.

"Thank you, I appreciate your concern, Ma'am."

"I ain't buying it, Curtis!" Wanda shouted. "What kind of man would kidnap his own kids from his wife?"

"I had nothing to do with that, Wanda!" Curtis said. "That was my crazy family. I didn't even know what happened till Ms. Virginia told me. I wanted to come to you and tell you everything but once again, she wouldn't let me, Tina."

"Maybe he's telling the truth, Tina," Cynthia said.

"Maybe my ass!" Wanda said. "That niggah is lyin'!"

"Curtis, after what just happened to Ms. Virginia, I'm scared," Tina said. "That could be me."

"No, Tina, that doesn't have to be our ending, that doesn't have to be our story, Tina! I love you!"

"I need time, Curtis."

"Take all the time you need. Just don't shut me out. Please," Curtis said, "I want to start off by going to church together this Sunday. I will pick up you and the kids, and maybe afterward, we can have some dinner. Is that, okay?"

"All right, Curtis, we'll go to church and have dinner."

"Awwww, shit!" Wanda said, stomping her feet. "No, Tina!"

"Thank you. I have to give these flowers to Ms. Virginia," Curtis said, holding a bouquet of flowers. "I brought you a bouquet of flowers on Friday but you weren't there. I thought that if I would have left them with no explanation, it would have sent the wrong message."

"Curtis, do you realize that at first, we thought it was you who killed Ms. Virginia?" Tina asked.

"Me?" Curtis asked, pointing at himself.

"Yeah, you!" Wanda said.

"What? In the short time she was in my life, I fell in love with that woman. She put food in my mouth, and put clothes on my back. She was the one who introduced me to Christ, and through Christ, I have made a turnaround in my life. I often wonder that maybe if I would have stayed at your job that day a little longer on Friday, if I could have prevented that man from hurting her."

"No one could have prevented that, Curtis," Cynthia said.

"Well, I'll put these flowers down, and let you good people go on. I appreciate your kindness, everybody. You didn't have to stand here and listen to my sob and sad story, but you did. Thank y'all for that!" Curtis kissed Tina on the cheek and walked down the hill to Ms. Virginia's grave.

"Tina, be careful. But be honest with yourself. If you think he's changed, give him another chance. If not, don't waste your time," Pam said.

When we got to the top of the hill, Tina stopped and looked back at Curtis.

"Are you all right, Tina?" Pam asked.

"Yes," Tina said, "y'all go 'head. I'll ride with Curtis."

"Are you sure that's a good idea?" Alicia asked.

"Tina, now you know I know Curtis. I knew him before you did," Wanda said, "and I been that boy's hardest critic. But for some reason I think he was telling the truth about how he felt about Ms. Virginia."

"You know what, Wanda, for some reason, I do too," Tina said.

"Tina, one way or the other, make sure you're sure," Pam added.

"For once in my life I am definitely sure about something. That man has never acted this way before. Normally he would never walk away from me until he had his way. Y'all go 'head, I'll be fine."

Tina walked down the hill to Curtis, and he wrapped his arms around her waist. She put his head on his shoulder for a second and then they sat down on the ground beside Ms. Virginia.

❖❖❖

The Office Girls became an international bestseller and later was adapted into a movie. Despite the popularity, despite the similarity, none of the office girls ever realized it was their story they were reading and watching. And none of the office girls ever realized the author, Cora, was actually, me.

I went on to become a very successful author and playwright, writing bestseller after bestseller, producing play after play. And although my next follow-up novel, *The Nature of a Woman* was a smash, nothing, however, would ever come close to equaling the success of *The Office Girls*.

❖❖❖

After Ms. Virginia's funeral, Cynthia and I maintained a pretty close relation-ship with Tina and Curtis, who became a minister, and Alicia, who became my sister-in-law. Pam invested in Cynthia's firm and became a co-partner. They have built their business into a reputable marketing force. Tina and Alicia joined the staff and they have operated like a well-oiled machine. Go figure, Pam, Alicia, and my wife, Cynthia, best friends.

From time to time we received a call from the rest of the office girls. But other than that, contact became far and few between.

Years later, we organized a reunion. We caught up with one another's lives and relived our days at Upskon. Pam explained in detail the circumstances surrounding Ms. Virginia being her mother.

By that time, every single one of us had moved on to different professions, different relationships and different friendships. We decided to meet once a year for a reunion to make sure we never forgot our time spent as the office girls. Even though we had moved on, our love for one another remained the same. For as Pam said, nothing can last forever. Nothing. No matter how beautiful. No matter how ugly. No matter how great. No matter how small. No matter what it is, nothing on this earth is going to last forever. In time, everything will fade away, everything, but love.

acknowledgments

I'd like to acknowledge my Heavenly father, God, the Almighty!

I would also like to acknowledge my mother and father, Henry and Ora Stephens, Bria, Isaiah, Simone and Alex Stephens, Patsy Porter, Glenn Moore, Ricky Stephens, Rita Parker, Ora Kirkland, Howard Stephens, Gloria Martin, Wesley Porter, Terry Staples, Teri Mathis, Kimberly Bailey, Mike Hankins, Nic Starr, Kevin Thompson, William Carroll, Cassandra Horton, Dana Mitchell, Denise Roberts, Glen Upshaw, Derek Strickland, David Hurst and my sisters and brothers of the Prince Hall Free & Accepted Masonic Lodges.

To the real-life office girls, I'd like to thank you for your contribution to the content of this book. The character of Ms. Virginia was based on the death of my dear friend Lisa (whose last name will remain anonymous), who was tragically murdered at my former place of employment by her husband, who then killed himself.

Cathren Andersen, Vicki Andrews, Arelys Arias, Tonya Bettis, Brenda Bolden, Judy Brandon, NaShonda Brooks, Cathy Chisolm, Mia Cofield, Connie Conner, Priscilla Cooper, Pauline Enahora, Kimberly Prince, Lisa Head, Amy Lyons, Wanda McGilberry, Darshan Merrick, Marcella Stewart, Kizzy Dawson, Lisa Hartfield, Felicia Toliver, Sally Terry, April Redmond, Ida Johnson, Della Harvey, Yvette White, Janelle D'Hereaux, Maureen Mwangi, Pamela Jones, Ellen McCaffrey, Susan Crump-Miller, Dana Jackson, Annie Payton, Andrea Simpson, Rosalind Jones, Maria Aceto, Dawn Rohde, Rhonda Mills, Marsha Lewis, Barbara Beardsley, Regina Junior, Jonna Phillips, Tonita Griffin-Taylor, Tina Summerour and Kelly Roberts.

Thanks for your support!

about the author

Born in Saginaw, Michigan as the seventeenth of eighteen children to Henry and Orabell Stephens, Sylvester Stephens was introduced to the arts by his elder siblings. His desire for writing was developed not by the literature of Shakespeare, or the poetry of Robert Frost, but the ever melodic soulful voices of the sound of Motown. The lyrics that emanated from the phonograph or record player, as it was called, created images of stories in his mind.

Sylvester later attended Jackson State University in Jackson, Mississippi where he honed his craft for literature. While attending college, Sylvester became a member of the largest international fraternity in the world, the Free and Accepted Masons, Prince Hall Affiliated.

Sylvester has taught creative writing courses for the Young Voices United Youth Program and has raised literacy awareness with poetry contests and book fairs in inner city schools.

Sylvester's first novel, *Our Time Has Come* was released October, 2004. *The Office Girls* is his second novel. His third novel, *The Nature of a Woman*, is sure to be equally as entertaining.

Sylvester has also written the screenplays to *The Office Girls, The Road to Redemption* and *Our Time Has Come!*

Sylvester's sensational stage plays include *Our Time Has Come, The Nature of a Woman, Max, The Office Girls, My Little Secret*, and *Every Knee Shall Bow*.

The Nature of a Woman

By Sylvester Stephens
Coming Soon From Strebor Books

"Has the first appointment arrived already?"

"Yup, she's in there," Donna said, reading a book and handing me the file without once looking up. "It's showtime!"

Donna is the receptionist, a white woman, late-fifties, sassy, with a delightfully slow southern Southern drawl. She has extremely white hair that is always pinned up. Her skin is very pale. She has extremely long eyelashes, and wears conservative long skirts and sweaters practically every day. But to her credit she also wears a big warm smile.

I never quite understood why Johnny hired her when he moved his practice here to Atlanta. Women were in abundance; surely he could have found someone younger, or prettier. But I guess when he married Alicia, she wasn't going to take any chances.

Anyway, my name is Michael Forrester and I am a writer. I am beginning my next novel, *The Nature of a Woman*. I decided to write it after the dilemma I faced while writing my previous novel, *The Office Girls*.

My initial purpose in writing *The Office Girls* was to expose women in corporate America as being just as ruthless and conniving as men, if given the same authority. After working incognito in an office where I was the only male, one by one I befriended the ladies and then, one by one, they confided in me their most intimate secrets. Although *The Office Girls* was a smashing success, I didn't feel that I had captured the complete essence of a woman. The new book, *The Nature of a Woman*, will convey the innermost thoughts and emotions of different women from different points in life. Hopefully, this will begin my road back to redemption for manipulating and deceiving my dear friends.

A funny thing happened on the way to the publisher—I began to feel terrible about the deception I had perpetrated. I had a change of heart, and I mean that literally. I fell in love with those women, whom I affectionately called 'the office girls,'—especially Cynthia, who became my wife.

To protect their identity from the world, and my life from them, I was forced to use a pseudonym upon the release of the book. Ironically, some of the office girls referred the book to their respective book clubs because of the similarities of the women in the book and themselves. But to this day, not one of them has the slightest notion that they are reading their own diaries.

This brings us to today. My brother Johnny, a psychologist, asked a few of his female patients to interview for my research. They signed a release form, and I have signed a confidentiality agreement. I will be interviewing in Johnny's office while he is away on vacation for the month of November.

He suggested I use his office to make the interviewees feel comfortable. So there I was, about to interview the first patient and I was probably more nervous than she. But I had Donna for back-up in the event one of those whackos went berserk. Luckily for me, she was kind enough to stay and make sure the office remained intact.

I had analyzed the files of each of the ten women Johnny had selected. He had managed to find three white women, Shelly Hartfield, Laura Oppenheimer, and Beth Miller; three Hispanic women, Gloria Gutierrez, Flora Arias and Xiomara Velez; and three black women, Anisa Anise Lawrence, Renee Bolden and Teri Horton. He also had managed to eke in one Asian, May Ling.

My first interview would be with Ms. Anise Lawrence. Donna handed me her file and I quickly reviewed it. Once I scanned the information, I took a deep breath and prepared for my entrance.

"So, what is she like, Donna?" I asked nervously.

"Let's just say she's special. But she's not dangerous. So don't be nervous."

"You're right, I'm conducting the interview. I'm in charge!" I said.

"Well, I'm out here if you need me, Mr. Forrester."

"Thanks," I said, walking into Johnny's office.

As I walked into the office I could see the back of Ms. Lawrence's head. She had very light-brown hair and every strand seemed to be in place. As I walked closer I paused to get a better look at her before she could get an eyeful of me. She was wearing a black business suit with a white butterfly collar. Her figure was noticeable even sitting in the chair. When I finally stepped within her peripheral view, I noticed her skin tone matched the color of her hair perfectly. Her hands were folded neatly on her lap and her legs were crossed comfortably right over left. Despite the position of Ms. Lawrence's lower body she maintained a perfect upright upper torso.

"How are you today, Ms. Lawrence? I'm Michael Forrester. You can call, me Michael," I said, shaking her hand.

"How are you, Michael? You can call me, Anise."

"It's good to finally meet you face to face. I'm glad you decided to do the interview."

"Me too," Anise said, with a very warm smile, "seems like it could be interesting."

"Well, for starters, I want you to know that we can discuss whatever you want, but on the other hand, we don't have to discuss anything you feel uncomfortable discussing. I also want to assure you that everything said in this office is completely confidential. Sound good?"

"So far, so good," Anise said.

"Tell me a little about yourself, Anise."

"Well, I'm not here because I'm crazy," Anise said, laughing lightly. "I'm not crazy and I don't need any medication. I just need to talk to someone who won't judge me."

"Crazy is a term that I'd rather not use, Anise, and it's not for me to judge anyone."

"Thank you, that makes me feel a lot more comfortable."

"Good. I feel comfortable knowing you feel comfortable."

I pushed the record button on the tape recorder and began the session. *"CLICK!"*

"Anise Lawrence, this process is an interview for character development for one of the characters in my novel, *The Nature of a Woman*. The questions in this interview are general questions created to relate to most women, and are not intended for any specific person or persons. This interview will be divided into three sections. The first section will have three segments. The second section will have two segments. The third section will be a question-and-answer exit interview. In the exit interview feel free to ask any questions you wish.

Today's topics in section one are romance, friendship and family. Some of the questions will be very personal, but please try to remember that the purpose of the interview is to capture the true element of *The Nature of a Woman*.

Though the novel will be fictional, the stories of each character will be based on true-life experiences from you and other women who will allow their stories to be told anonymously. After the completion of the interview, you will have an opportunity to review exactly what will be printed in the novel prior to signing a consent/release form. We will complete section one today, which consists of the first three segments. Are you ready for your first question?"

"Sure," Anise said.

"Have you ever had your heart broken? If so, briefly explain the scenario."

Anise paused momentarily, as if she was thinking of the correct thing to say.

"Well, of course, I've had my heart broken. But I was young, and he was my first love, so it took me a while to get over him. It wasn't anything traumatic, we were freshmen in college and he wrote me a dear "Dear Jane" letter saying that he had met someone else. I was interested in other guys as well, so although it hurt, I managed to deal with it."

"Okay, was your reaction rage, pain or denial?"

"Definitely pain. I respected him for telling me, so I couldn't feel rage. And there was no way to for me to deny it, because I never heard from him again."

"Are you skeptical of romance now?"

"I would have to say yes. Not from my first experience of love, but from later experiences in my life."

"Do you become anxious and excited at the beginning of a relationship?"

"Um, excited and anxious? I would say no. I'm too cautious and too careful. I try to enjoy the moment. I don't ask for promises, nor do I give them."

"Do you look for romance with men who may fit the bill that you have in your mind? Or do you look for compatibility in friendship first?"

"As I said, I try not to place expectations too high in the romance department to avoid major disappointment. I date, and right now, it's only in the name of friendship. So I guess the answers to your questions are, no, I don't have a bill and yes, friendship is a prerequisite for dating."

"Okay, Anise, that completed segment one. Feel okay?"

"Oh yes, I'm fine."

"Ready for segment two?"

"Sure," Anise said, still sitting in the same position as she was when I first entered the office. "Did I pass?"

"Well, this is not a pass or fail interview, Anise. All answers are passing answers," I said, laughing lightly, "ready for segment two?"

"Sure."

"This segment deals with friendship," I said, clearinged my throat. "Do you measure your friends on the amount of time, money and interest spent on you?"

"Oh, of course not. And I'm sure all of my friends would agree with me."

"Okay, is it possible for you to be physically attracted to a man and maintain a platonic relationship?"

"Platonic?" Anise said, shifting her body for the first time. "Well, I guess that depended on how attracted I was to him."

"Do you confide in your male friends as deeply as your female friends?"

"Probably. I don't have a lot of female friends. Most of my friends are males, so I probably confide more in my male friends than my female friends. Does that make sense?"

"Sure it does." I said, then moved to the next question. "Describe your closest friend."

"My closest friend," Anise said, pondering the question, "does it have to be male or female?"

"Let's go with female."

"Well, she's very attractive, outgoing, very generous, and very, very ambitious."

"If you could change anything about your closest friend, what would it be?"

"I would change the way she views herself. She is very beautiful, but she has such low self-esteem."

"Why is that?" I asked, curiously.

"I don't know, maybe she needs to see your brother, too," Anise chuckled.

"Maybe she does." I pretended to laugh, knowing that ninety-eight per cent of the time when questions about the best friend are asked, the person answering is indirectly referring to themselves. Not in the *'let me tell you about my friend'* way, but most people select their friends because they are similar to themselves. Anyway, I continued on to the final segment.

"Okay, Anise, the final segment is about your family, you ready?"

Throughout the interview, Anise had flashed her captivating smile, but as soon as I mentioned her family her smile faded. Her posture, which had been so erect and confident, was now slouched and seemed uncomfortable.

"Okay." Anise sighed.

"Are you close to both of your parents? Or are you closer to one more than the other?"

"I have a close relationship with both of my parents. My mother and I are so close we're more like sisters than mother and daughter."

"All right, if more than one sibling, do you favor one more than the other?"

"I have only one brother from my mother and father, but I have a half-brother and half-sisters from my father's later endeavors."

"Do you find that your family is reliable and trustworthy?"

"No!" Anise answered quickly.

"When you think of your family as a whole, do you think of heaven or calamity?"

"Calamity!" Anise answered. Once again responding before I could get the complete sentence out of my mouth.

"Are there family secrets that you would rather keep secret?"

"Family secrets?" Anise asked, looking very uncomfortable. She stood up and walked toward the window. She stared outside without answering the question.

"Is everything okay, Anise?" I asked.

"If you don't mind, Michael, can we discuss something else?"

"Oh sure," I said, "I would like to go back to our first segment, anyway. Is that okay with you?"

"Yes, that's fine," Anise said, walking back to the chair and then sitting down.

"So are you currently seeing anyone?"

"Well, I have a friend that I see quite regularly. We get along great but we have this one major issue and we can't seem to work our way through it."

"What is it?"

"We both think the other is unfaithful."

Smiling, I asked, "Are you?"

"Yes," Anise said, "even though we have no monogamous commitment to one another, I'm not seeing anyone else. But he, on the other hand, has confessed to sleeping with some bimbo named Monica. I have forgiven him, but he can't seem to understand that I am one hundred per cent faithful."

"What is his reasoning for thinking you're unfaithful?"

"He thinks I'm too friendly. That's just my nature. I'm friendly to men and women."

"How long have you been dating your friend, Anise?"

"About a year and a half."

"Has he always exhibited this type of behavior?"

"No, he used to trust me. Or at least I thought he did."

"At what point in your relationship did he start to act in this manner?"

"I suppose it was about six months ago."

"Did anything significant happen?"

"No, not at all."

"Do you think it centers on your outgoing personality?"

"That could be it."

"Have you asked him?"

"Yes, he told me that he thinks I still have feelings for my ex."

"Yeah," I said, "I see how that could be a problem."

"It's not a problem because I'm not in love with Sean anymore. I am in love with my friend."

"Are you sure?"

"Um," Anise said, "of course."

"Are you sure you're sure? You seem a little hesitant on your response."

"Is one ever really over someone one they truly loved?"

"I don't know. You tell me."

"Well, I guess I still have feelings for Sean, but that's it."

"Feelings? What kind of feelings?"

"I care about him."

"You sound as if you're talking about your pet, not an ex-lover," I said, "can you define, care?"

"I…I mean," Anise said, stumbling over her words, "what do you want me to say?"

"I want you to say how you truly feel. Are you over Sean, or not?"

"In my opinion, yes, I am over him."

Smiling, I asked, "Is one ever really over someone they truly love?"

Smiling back, Anise said, "In my case, yes."

"You seem to have gone from uncertainty to absolute in a matter of moments."

"I had to consider the question."

"I've read your file, Anise, and you appear to have your life in complete order. Is there anything that makes you uncertain?"

"Love," Anise whispered.

"Is it that you're uncertain of how much you love yourself? Or uncertain of how much others love you?"

"Both, I guess. I know I'm loved by my family and friends. And the guy I date practically spoils me. But somehow it's still not enough."

"Is it that he does not love you enough or perhaps you do not love yourself enough?"

"I don't know," Anise said, staring down at her pants and then brushing off invisible fuzz with her hands. "I think that's what I'm trying to figure out."

"Do your friends and family know that you feel this way?"

"No. Not to my knowledge. As far as they're concerned, I have everything together."

"Do you think you have everything together?"

"On the surface, yes."

"What about internally?"

"That I'm not certain of."

"Finally, something you're not certain of."

"You sound happy about that."

"Not happy, relieved," I said. "Now, maybe you can learn to trust me and talk more candidly."

"Trust?" Anise said. "Trust is something that has to be earned. My mother told me never to give three things away when you initially meet a person. One, my body. Two, my heart. And three, my secrets."

"So, to which do I pose a threat?"

"All and none."

"Well, what did your mother say about honesty?"

"Honesty is always a gift to everyone, a stranger or a friend."

"Then why haven't you been honest with me today?"

"I've been totally honest with you."

"Were you honest when you said you weren't in love with Sean?"

"Of course I was."

"Then why do I know Sean's name and not the man you claim to love?"

"What do you mean?" Anise asked with concern.

"Through out this session, you have referred to the man you claim to love as your friend only and I was simply wondering why?"

"I have mentioned his name."

"Trust me when I say you have not. That's why I'm still looking for the reason why you are in love with your, um, friend," I said, using the quotation symbol.

"I've told you. I love him and he loves me!" Anise shouted.

"So do you feel passion for this man?"

"Of course I feel passion for him! I love him! Passionately! Affectionately!"

"How about sincerely, Anise?"

"Of course, sincerely!" Anise said, folding her arms and twirling her feet.

I could tell she was very frustrated so I switched gears and tried another angle.

"Okay, Anise, how about your ex, do you still love him passionately as well?"

"We are spinning our wheels here. I told you, no, I do not love Sean."

"Were you in love with him?"

"Yes."

"Why did you break up with him?"

"Our passion, I think, extended beyond affection."

"What do you mean by that?"

"I mean, we sometimes argued and there were times when I was afraid that it was going to get physical."

"Who would initiate the arguments?"

"Both of us." Anise said. "If we had a problem with the other, we could never just talk things out rationally. We would start off softly and trying to understand but then we would end up yelling and screaming at each other."

"Did you seek counseling?"

"We never really considered it. I loved him and he loved me but I guess we both knew our relationship was based on a wild and passionate sexual affair, so much that we were afraid of pursuing anything deeper than that. So counseling seemed irrelevant."

"Who decided to end it?"

"I suppose I did indirectly by moving away."

"Did you ever formally break up?"

"Not really, but then we never formally confessed to being committed, either."

"You mentioned your arguments would almost get physical. Who initiated the potential violence?"

"Looking back, I think we both did, but at the time, I thought it was him."

"Why do you say, looking back?"

"Because at the time when we were both arguing with each other I knew I was not going to hit him him, no matter how angry I got. But he would threaten to hit me and there were times when I felt that he was on the verge of doing just that."

"Hindsight is often twenty-twenty. What do you wish you would have done differently to save the relationship?"

"As I look back, there was nothing I could have done to save that relationship because it never should have been."

"So there is nothing you regret about your break-up with Sean?"

"Sure. I've come to realize that pain affects people differently. I was hurting his masculinity. To me, it was silly for him to always be so egotistical. Everything was about his manhood. But now I see that it wasn't for me to decide what hurt him, it was for me to try to understand."

"Did he ever hit you?"

"No, not really."

"No, not really? That's like being almost pregnant. Either he did or he didn't."

"Well, he never punched me. He pushed me once and I thought he was going to hit me but he didn't hit me."

"Did you continue to see him afterward?"

"Yes."

"Why? Weren't you afraid that the next time he might not stop at pushing you?"

"Of course I was," Anise said, "but I had pushed him, too."

"So you initiated potential violence as well."

"No, I wasn't initiating violence, I was just so mad at him; it was all I could do to stop from hitting him."

"Like he did you?"

"No, see, I saw him chatting in front of a bar with a woman."

"How do you know he wasn't just being friendly?"

"Because he didn't want me to go out with him that night."

"Still, do you think he deserved to be pushed around?"

"Now I don't, but then I thought he deserved anything I could give him!" Anise said, with a smile on her face.

"Well, what happened the night he pushed you? What happened for him to become so angry?"

"He thought I was seeing another man."

"Why would he think that?"

"He saw me talking with a guy, a guy that I didn't even know. The guy came up to me trying to start a conversation and I was just speaking to get him away from me. Sean saw him and went ballistic."

"On the guy?"

"No, on me!"

"Did you explain what happened?"

"I tried but he didn't believe me."

"Like you didn't believe him?"

"I knew that you were going to say that but at no point was I ever going to hit him."

"Describe Sean."

"Oh my God! He was a good- looking man."

"No, describe him in detail."

"He was kind of tall, dark-brown. Muscular, very muscular!"

"Muscular, you say? Then that would probably explain why you wouldn't initiate a physical altercation as well."

"That's not it, I wasn't afraid of him."

"But you just said you were."

"Well, I mean I was afraid when he was extremely angry, but that's not why I didn't try to physically fight him. I'm just not violent."

"Do you think that in your and Sean's case, he wanted to threaten you with physical pain because he was bigger, and you wanted to hurt him emotionally because you were not?"

"I disagree."

"That's fine."

"I disagree," Anise repeated.

"Do you love him?"

"William?" Anise asked.

"Who's William?"

"William is my friend."

"Finally, he gets a name," I said sarcastically. "I would like to know about William, if you don't mind."

"Sure, what do you want know about William?" Anise asked.

"I don't know," I said, twirling a pencil in my hand, "what would you like for me to know?"

"Um, well, he's nice, very sweet. Everything I always wanted in a man, but I'm still taking my time."

"Oh, he seems like a good guy, so do you think you two have a future?"

"Well, I think so, but as I said, I don't try to put expectations on my relationships. Would you like to see a picture of him?" Anise asked.

"Well, sure," I said, feeling slightly uncomfortable, "if you have one."

"Well, of course," Anise said, going into her purse and pulling out a photo, "here he is."

My mouth dropped and I couldn't believe what I was seeing.

"Uh, is this William?" I asked.

"Yes, that's William."

"You mean, your William? The friend you've been talking to me about?"

"Yes, this is my William," Anise said, holding the picture proudly and staring at it.

"Um, Anise, you're serious, aren't you?"

"Yes, why do you ask?"

"Does my brother know you're dating this guy?"

"Yes, he thinks the world of him," Anise said, smiling broadly and putting the photograph back in her purse.

"Well, I don't know what to say, Anise," I said, standing up. "Can you excuse me for one second, please?"

"Sure, go right ahead."

I walked casually to the door and quickly opened it and ran to Donna's desk. She started to smile before I even opened my mouth.

"What the hell is wrong with that woman?" I said, trying to talk quietly.

"What do you mean, Mr. Forrester?"

"You know what I mean, Donna! You and my sick brother are in cahoots!"

"I have no idea what you're talking about, Mr. Forrester," Donna said, trying not to laugh.

"That bitch in there is crazy as hell!"

"We don't like to use that word around here, Mr. Forrester."

"Well, what did she do to have you so spooked?" Donna said, pouring a cup of coffee and then handing it to me.

"You wanna know what she did? Huh?" I asked again.

"I'm waiting," Donna said, sitting back down and folding her arms.

"She went on and on about her boyfriend William," I said, "about how great he is. And then she asked me if I wanted to see a picture of him. So I'm trying to be nice and told her, 'sure.'"

"So what's wrong with that, Mr. Forrester?"

"You wanna know who boyfriend William is? Huh?"

"I'm waiting," Donna repeated.

"William Jefferson Clinton!" I shouted. "That nut thinks she is dating an ex-president of the United States of America!"

"Calm down, Mr. Forrester, she may hear you," Donna said.

"I don't give a damn if she hears me or not! I'm getting the hell out of here!" I grabbed my jacket and slammed the door behind me.

❖❖❖

I would return to complete my research, which would reveal tragedy and triumph. So if you think that was interesting, you ain't seen nothing!

—*Michael Forrester*